Christmas Fling

Lindsey Kelk is a *Sunday Times* bestselling author, podcaster and internet oversharer. Born and brought up in Doncaster, South Yorkshire, she worked in London as a children's editor before writing her first book, *I Heart New York*, and moving to Brooklyn. Lindsey's novels include the I Heart series, *The Christmas Wish* and *Love Story,* as well as her YA fantasy debut, *The Bell Witches*. She lives in Los Angeles with her husband.

You can follow Lindsey on Facebook, X or Instagram @LindseyKelk, and sign up for her newsletter at www.LindseyKelk.com.

Also by Lindsey Kelk

I Heart Series
I Heart New York
I Heart Hollywood
I Heart Paris
I Heart Vegas
I Heart London
I Heart Christmas
I Heart Forever
I Heart Hawaii

About a Girl Series
About a Girl
What a Girl Wants
A Girl's Best Friend

Standalones
The Single Girl's To-Do List
Always the Bridesmaid
We Were on a Break
One in a Million
In Case You Missed It
On a Night Like This
The Christmas Wish
Love Me Do
Love Story

Savannah Red Series
The Bell Witches

LINDSEY KELK

Christmas Fling

HarperCollinsPublishers

HarperCollins*Publishers* Ltd
1 London Bridge Street,
London SE1 9GF

www.harpercollins.co.uk

HarperCollins*Publishers*
Macken House, 39/40 Mayor Street Upper
Dublin 1, D01 C9W8, Ireland

Published by HarperCollins*Publishers* 2025

1

A catalogue record for this book is available from the British Library

ISBN: 978-0-00-868772-4 (PBO)
ISBN: 978-0-00-875874-5 (US, CAN Only)

Typeset in Melior by HarperCollins*Publishers* India

Printed and bound in the UK using 100%
Renewable Electricity at CPI Group (UK) Ltd

For The School Plimsolls – may the odds be ever in your favour

CHAPTER ONE

'Laura Pearce, you're officially on the naughty list.'

Throwing an awkward smile at the bus driver, I fumbled with my earbuds as I dropped into the first available seat, my best friend Desi's voice echoing through my skull. It was one of my most deeply held beliefs no one should ever be allowed to talk on the phone in public without headphones and anyone who did ought to be sent directly to the centre of the earth, along with Cybertruck owners, people who post movie spoilers on social media and any man who has thought about starting a podcast, ever.

'What are you talking about?' I said as the bus took off, hurtling down the high street. 'I'm not on the naughty list, you're on the naughty list.'

'Naturally, I'd be gutted if I wasn't,' Desi replied. 'But you're the one who used all the milk then skedaddled out the flat. What am I supposed to do, make tea *without* milk? Drink it neat like some kind of animal?'

'Neat? You consider milk a mixer?'

'Where are you?' she asked. 'And the answer better

be either at the supermarket or gone to the farm to buy a cow.'

'That's right. I'm negotiating with Old Macdonald right now. Do you think you can pick me and Buttercup up in your Honda Jazz or should we call an Uber?'

The man in the seat beside me let out a pitch-perfect, passive-aggressive huff and I pulled my scarf up over my mouth to muffle my voice. If I could tolerate the amount of aftershave he was wearing, he could tolerate my chat for another three minutes.

'I'm on the way to the flat,' I said as quietly as I could. 'Remember? I asked if you wanted to come with me to help measure up and you said you didn't believe in unpaid labour.'

'Manual or emotional,' she replied. 'How long will you be? I thought we could do something festive later, maybe have a mooch around Liberty and touch all the ornaments without actually buying anything.'

'The weekend before Christmas?' I frowned so hard my face almost collapsed in on itself. 'I would rather eat my own foot.'

'You mean you don't want to cram into a packed tube, fight with last-minute shoppers on Oxford Street then have your phone stolen out your hand by some git on an electric scooter? 'Tis the season, Lau, 'tis!'

I sighed and massaged my right temple. 'Is this a good time to remind you that you're Jewish? You don't even celebrate Christmas.'

'I celebrate the true meaning of the season.'

'You like drinking Baileys and getting presents.'

'And your point is?' Desi yawned and changed topics, bored of her own argument already. 'Are you almost there yet? I thought you said it was close.'

As if on cue, the bus came to a halt and the back doors wheezed open to spit me out on the side of the street. Yesterday had been crisp and sunny but the weather had turned overnight, Jack Frost no longer nipping at my nose so much as slapping the shit out of it. I pulled my bobble hat down over my ears, dragging the chunky pink wool all the way down to my eyebrows and tucking my red hair underneath.

'Almost,' I said. 'According to Maps, it's an even fifteen minutes door-to-door.'

'And you're sure you don't want to look for a flat a bit further away?'

'Nice try,' I said, swiping at my wind-stung face with the sleeve of my coat. 'You know you're thrilled to have me so close by.'

'I'm thrilled to have you out my place,' she countered. 'I love you very much but you're a right ballache to live with, babe.'

For the last six weeks, I'd been living with Desi and Joel, the third side of our eternal friendship triangle, after my landlord decided it would be fun to sell my lovely little flat out from under me with very little notice. The three of us hadn't lived under one roof since the second year of uni and even though Desi and Joel had managed to survive together in imperfect harmony, adding a third adult to a two-bedroom, one-bathroom flat was, it turned out, a step too far. After discovering mine and Desi's cycles were perfectly in sync, we'd agreed it would be best for everyone's physical and emotional wellbeing if I was out by the New Year; otherwise, as Joel had so sweetly put it, he was going to kill the pair of us in a way that was so inhumane, no one would be able to identify the bodies.

'Don't take this the wrong way,' Desi said, 'but I still think you're an idiot.'

As usual, there really was only one way to take it.

'In general or specifically about the flat?'

'Both but this time I am talking mostly about the flat.'

Inside my bag, her face glowered up at me from the screen of my phone. It was my favourite photo ever, taken on her last birthday, me hanging around her neck, Desi scowling straight to camera, and Joel gurning wildly, half obscured by his own arm as he took the selfie. Our truest forms, captured forever.

'It's dangerous to rent privately,' she went on, a lecture I'd heard at least ten times already. 'Especially for a woman on her own. You should've gone through a management company, the whole thing could be a scam. Anyone could be waiting for you in that flat.'

'Lestat de Lioncourt?' I replied hopefully.

'I'd laugh if you weren't serious,' she said with a sigh. 'How many times do I have to tell you, if you become one of the undead, we can't be friends any more. I like my beach holidays too much.'

'Desi, let me move into my haunted vampire sanctuary in peace.' I turned off the main road and on to a pleasant-looking side street, all the noise of the high street fading away. 'It's not as though I'm renting from a complete stranger, he's friends with Stella, and I don't think your sister would set me up with a dangerous situation.'

It was quiet for Clapham. Rows of privet hedges, lots of neatly kept front yards, no overturned wheelie bins or rats the size of small dogs. A tiny thrill ran through me at the sight of number 42, the shiny red door, the triple-glazed windows with white trim. My new home. I pulled the keys out from my pocket, excited.

'He's not Stella's friend,' Desi said. 'He's Dave's friend, and you know I've never liked Dave.'

'Your own brother-in-law.'

'Just because dickhead Dave says a man is all right does not mean you should be living in his flat without running any background checks,' she replied hotly. 'Why did you get the keys so early? Why is the rent so cheap? It's very sketchy, Laura, it's very, very sketchy. He could be a serial killer for all we know.'

'A serial killer chef?' I replied.

'Perfect cover. Late nights, knife skills, weird stains on his clothes. He might bake his victims into pies. This entire set-up has been far too easy.'

My keys slid straight into the lock and the front door swung open on silent hinges.

'I know you won't believe this but sometimes easy is good,' I said, marvelling at the white painted entrance hall, the little wooden shoe rack, the frosted overhead light. 'Dave gave me the keys early because his friend has already moved out, the rent is cheap because he wanted someone in right away rather than leave the flat empty, and if he wants to chop me up and bake me into a pie, I hope he makes his own pastry because I can't think of anything more mortifying than being baked into shop-bought. Now sod off so I can measure my new flat in peace. I'll be back in an hour or so and if you're very good, I'll bring back treats.'

There was a brief pause on the line.

'From the little bakery?'

'From the little bakery,' I confirmed as I walked into the closed-curtained living room and waited for my eyes to adjust. 'I'm going, I'll text you when I'm on my way back.'

'On your way back with pastries. Love you!'

Ending the call, I put my phone back in my pocket and took my first proper look at my new home. It was perfect. Big windows, high ceilings, hardwood floors . . . and an enormous naked man walking straight towards me.

It was very hard to say who was screaming louder, me or the enormous naked man, but I was definitely winning in the high-pitch stakes, alerting dolphins all over the North Atlantic to my current predicament.

'Oh my God!' I yelled, my earbuds popping out of my ears and falling to the floor. 'Help! Help!'

'Help you?' he shouted back while attempting to cover a most sensitive part of his anatomy with his hands. It was too late for that. Even in a panic, it was hard to miss a free-range penis when it was flying around in front of you. 'You're the one breaking and entering!'

'Am not!'

Because arguing with a wet, naked potential murderer seemed like such a good idea.

'Don't you move,' I said, hunched over in a defensive crouch, ready to spring. 'I'm armed.'

'With what?'

I clutched my bag to my body and tried to work out how much damage I could do with my Kindle, a half-eaten packet of Skittles and an infinite number of lip balms.

'My body is a deadly weapon,' I replied. 'One more move and I'll be forced to defend myself.'

We stared at each other for a moment, eye-to-eye, until I simply could not help myself and felt my gaze slipping lower.

'For fuck's sake,' the man muttered, rearranging everything he wasn't hiding underneath his cupped hands. He really was very large. Tall, broad. Strapping, my grandmother might've said but then again, if my grandmother were in my shoes, she'd have died of fright ten seconds earlier. It was a miracle I was still standing and I didn't have her heart trouble.

'OK, just be calm,' I instructed, even though I wasn't anywhere near calm myself. 'This is what's going to happen. You're going to turn around, get dressed and leave before I call the police.'

'And tell them what?' he asked. 'Why are you laughing? What's so bloody funny?'

'Well,' I waved a hand around the living room, unbidden hysterical laughter bursting out of me. 'There's a massive, stark bollock naked man in my flat so I can either laugh or start screaming again, which would you prefer?'

His shoulders stiffened.

'Your flat?'

'That's right,' I said with confidence. 'My flat, so will you please leave before I am forced to do kung fu.'

He raised a dark eyebrow.

'Not that I wouldn't love to see that,' he replied, a Scottish accent roughing up his words at the edges, 'but are you sure it's not Callum McClay's flat?'

'Callum McClay?' I repeated faintly. 'That's my landlord's name.'

The man nodded.

I blanched.

Oh no.

CHAPTER TWO

In theory, I'd met Callum McClay twice. In reality, it was more complicated.

According to Desi's sister, Stella, we'd both been at her wedding to Dave, where I'd spent the majority of the day convincing a very drunk, Speak Now-era-obsessed Desi that she really should rethink her maid of honour speech and not use it as an opportunity to list every perceived infraction Dave had ever committed. I failed, spectacularly, and after she went on to make a woman cry in the toilets by passing judgement on her shoes, I'd made the executive decision to take Desi home and we missed almost the entire night do.

The supposed second time was two years later at the Brit Bat ceremony of Stella and Dave's firstborn, a child inexplicably named Lemon Marge Kaplan O'Brien. It was a much smaller affair than the wedding, and even though Stella had checked the guestlist and insisted Callum was there, I couldn't remember anything about him at all.

But as I stood in the middle of the living room, staring

into a pair of unamused blue eyes, there was a certain similarity between this man, with a shadow of stubble covering the lower half of his face, and the clean-shaven person whose erratic social media I'd been casually stalking ever since I heard Dave had a friend who was moving to Paris and needed a tenant for his Clapham flat. Instagram Callum hadn't seemed quite so tall and Instagram Callum was facial-hair-free with close-cropped hair, but when the man in front of me took a cautious side-step toward the wall to turn on the overhead light, I realized he was absolutely, positively my new landlord.

'Callum,' I said, the red rash of rage that had been slowly creeping up my face flourishing into a scarlet stain of humiliation. 'You're Callum McClay.'

He inclined his head politely.

'Pleasure to meet you. Laura Pearce, I'm guessing?'

About five minutes too late, I spun on my heel, facing the bare, beige wall behind a navy-blue IKEA sofa, covering my eyes with my hands for good measure.

'I am *so* sorry,' I said, babbling all the words at once. 'I didn't know you were here. Dave gave me the keys and said you'd already moved out so I came round to measure up so I could order some bits in the New Year sales, not that I need many bits, I know the flat comes furnished and it's very nice, you know I've always liked a Klippan, very underrated, I'd say, design classic in fact—'

'OK, I think I've got it,' Callum interrupted before I could talk myself into a hole in the ground. 'Dave doesn't pay attention, I'm not leaving until the twenty-seventh. Didn't you hear the shower running?'

More sheepish than a rack of lamb, I turned back around, keeping my eyes trained on the ground. There was still so much of him on display, including a not insignificant rug of dark, curling chest hair and a surprising amount of muscle for someone I'd been reliably informed was moving to Paris to train as a pastry chef. Were pastry chefs usually this solid? Was there any call for this degree of burliness in the kitchen?

'Earbuds,' I explained, pointing to the little white balls of plastic peeping out of the rich brown rug underneath his coffee table. 'Noise cancelling. They're very good. Most noise cancelling headphones don't really cancel out everything but these ones go right in the ear and—'

'Do feel free to stop talking,' he cut in.

'Do feel free to put some clothes on,' I replied.

For the first time since I'd walked into the flat, he smiled. Just a little, head ducked, lips crooked up at one side like he didn't want to commit to it, but his blue eyes lit up and crinkled at the corners, and I found myself wondering how devastating a full-on grin would be.

But there wasn't time to find out.

Two seconds later, a commotion sounded outside the flat and Callum's expression flatlined. Keys in the door, voices in the hallway, shoes scuffing on the mat.

'Shit,' he said, looking around in a panic, still clutching his privates in his hands.

'Shit,' I echoed as the living room door swung open towards us.

'Hello, hello, hello, don't mind us, we're only burglars!' someone called and for the want of a better option, I yanked my bobble hat off my head and tossed it to Callum, who caught it in one hand and placed it over his crotch with the other.

Two smiling faces burst into the room, a man and a woman, both of them turning into statues the moment they laid eyes on the scene inside.

'Good God!'

The woman covered her face, cheeks the same shade of scarlet as her tailored wool coat.

'Cal,' she said in a high-pitched voice. 'You've got company.'

The man at her side didn't seem nearly as distressed, his smile broadening at exactly the same rate his companion's disappeared

'Are we interrupting?' he asked. 'Sorry, son, I told your mother we should've called first.'

Son. Mother. He had the same shade of reddish brown hair as Callum, she had a similarly shaped mouth, and they all shared the same shortened vowels and soft Scottish burr that warmed up their accents. These were Callum's parents.

'You're not interrupting, I was just leaving,' I said, turning towards the door to make a hasty exit but neither of them moved, blocking off my escape route.

'Oh no, you mustn't go on our account.'

Taking advantage of my stunned state, Callum's dad stepped towards me with open arms and before I could duck underneath them to make a break for it, he wrapped me up in a bear hug and squeezed every ounce of air out of my lungs. Desi was right, this flat was going to be the death of me but not in any way she might have predicted.

'Aye, she's a bonny one, Cal,' the older Mr McClay exclaimed. 'Not exactly how I'd imagined it but we've all been dying to meet you.'

'You have?' I replied, face smushed against his itchy jumper.

'Dad, don't,' Callum started as his father released me from his vice-like grip.

'I really do need to get going,' I squeaked, stumbling out of his arms and gasping for breath. Adrenaline coursed through my veins. Fight, flight or jump head first through a triple-glazed window? Whatever it took to get out of that flat.

'Nonsense, you're not going anywhere. You're going to sit down and tell me all about yourself while Cal finds his trousers.' His dad took a seat on the sofa and patted the open spot next to him. 'No need to run off on our account, hen, we can't stop long, only popping by on our way back from the airport. We're just back from our holidays. I'm sure he told you we've been away.'

'You'd be amazed at what he hasn't told me,' I replied with a Care Bear stare at Callum.

When I didn't join him on the sofa, Callum's dad grabbed my wrist and gave it an encouraging tug. I crumpled down at his side and he threw his arm around my shoulders, pinning me in place.

'I know she'd love to stay,' Callum said when I crumpled down at his father's side, 'But she really was on her way out, weren't you?'

'I'm *trying*,' I replied through gritted teeth, held fast by his father.

'Try *harder*.'

'Callum George James McClay.'

Everyone in the room snapped to attention. His mother's voice flicked a switch in me I didn't know was still operational after all these years, the very specific tone of a parent who was not angry but disappointed. She wasn't even talking to me and I still felt guilty.

'You were raised better,' she said. 'That's no way to talk to your girlfriend.'

I stared at his mother, she stared at her son, he stared back at me. Only his dad sat back, relaxed, perfectly happy with the situation.

'Me?' I said, pointing at myself. 'I'm not his girlfriend?'

All of a sudden, Callum let out a loud laugh, too big, too forced to be real.

'She's joking!' he said between guffaws. 'Loves to joke, this one, has me in stitches. Classic.'

They all turned in my direction, his mum and dad examining me with open curiosity as though they'd just been introduced to an entirely alien concept, like Pepsi Max Wild Cherry or Morman wife TikTok, and Callum, his beseeching blue eyes open wide and staring at me with an intensity that could've set fire to a wet paper bag. I opened my mouth to correct him but something in those eyes stopped me. They were so dark, the sapphire depths contrasting sharply against his pale skin, and suddenly my intended words of protest dissolved on my tongue.

'Classic,' I croaked instead. 'Always the joker, me.'

'Hilarious, I'm sure.' His mother sniffed, reappraising me in a way I did not care for in the slightest. 'So. You're the girlfriend.'

'Apparently,' I replied. 'But most people call me Laura.'

His father looked to Callum, arm firmly wrapped around my shoulders.

'I thought you said her name was Caroline?'

Callum bit his lip.

'I did. It is Caroline.'

'Then why would she say it's Laura?'

There was so much to not enjoy about the situation. His father's fingers digging into my non-existent bicep, the way his mother kept raising a hand to her chest as though she was one snide comment from fainting clean away, the fact Callum was *still* naked, but when he winced and mouthed the word 'please' in my direction, I found myself backing him up again.

'My name *is* Caroline,' I said. 'I was just having a laugh.'

His father let out an accepting chuckle but his mother held my gaze as I took stock of her, the same way she'd analysed me moments before. Neatly coiffed hair, little silk scarf knotted around her neck, the unmistakable look of a woman who knew beyond a shadow of a doubt there was something fishy going on. But my brand new boyfriend's shoulders sagged with relief and I shot him a tight smile. At least the people pleaser in me was satisfied, even if his mother wasn't.

'She's trouble, this one,' his dad said loudly, slapping me on the back so hard I felt the sting through my coat and woolly jumper. 'Derek McClay, at your service, and this is my good lady wife, Lizzie, although I'm sure you've already worked that out for yourself. Pleased to finally meet you, Caroline.'

'Not nearly as pleased as me,' I said as I attempted to rise. 'But I really do have to dash off.'

'Off to work?' Derek asked, pulling me right back down.

'Work? No. I'm not on rotation today.'

From the way Lizzie's eyebrows snatched together, I could tell it was the wrong answer.

'The spa she works at rotates massage therapists,'

Callum said, filling in some very confusing blanks with even more confusing answers. 'She's got training today, in a new kind of massage. Haven't you . . . babe?'

I fixed him with a fervent glare.

'Yes, that's right. Babe.'

'Fascinating.' Lizzie was still hovering near the door, upright and tightly wound, the opposite of her husband's overly comfortable slouch on the sofa. 'What kind of new massage is that?'

Every word in my supposedly clever brain dissolved into a mess of incomprehensible shapes and sounds, none of which would pass for English. A new kind of massage. What were the old kinds of massage? Across the room, I spotted a tube of tennis balls tucked down the side of an empty umbrella stand.

'The Slazenger method,' I announced with confidence. 'It's deep tissue, you do it with . . . balls.'

His mother spluttered into her hands while Callum closed his eyes and slowly shook his head.

'Shame you've got to work all over Christmas,' Derek declared. 'Won't be much fun for our Cal if you're at work, playing with your balls.'

'I'm not working over Christmas.'

As soon as the words were out my mouth, it was obvious I'd said the wrong thing again.

'You're not working?' he replied, more than a touch of confusion and annoyance in his voice. 'Then what's the problem? You can both come home after all.'

'Home?' I enquired politely, watching as all the blood drained from Callum's face.

'Home,' Derek said. 'To Braewick. Cal told us you couldn't come because you had work and he didn't want to leave you in London on your own.'

Callum's grip on my pink bobble hat tightened until his knuckles turned white.

'Right, because I did think I was going to have to work,' I said quickly. 'Then the rota changed. But we still can't come. Sorry.'

'Why not?' Lizzie asked.

'Because,' I said, 'we're spending it with my . . .'

'Sister,' Callum supplied. 'Otherwise, obviously—'

'We'd love to,' I finished up. 'Maybe next year.'

'Ah, you can't be serious?' Derek gave me another whack on the back and I had to do a quick check to make sure all my teeth were still in the right place. 'If you're spending Christmas with your sister, there's no reason Cal can't come up to Scotland.'

'Dad, leave it, would you?'

There was a clear warning in Callum's voice but Derek McClay didn't strike me as the kind of man who had taken a hint even once in his life.

'You're coming home,' he insisted, not leaving anything at all. 'You said the only reason you couldn't come was because Caroline had to work and you couldn't leave her in London on her own. She's not on her own, is she?'

'That doesn't mean I don't want to be with her,' Callum replied and without warning the atmosphere in the room shifted. A dark look passed over Derek's face and his tone switched to something more irritable.

'Enough's enough, you're coming home,' he said, leaning forward. 'Get your act together, son, you're breaking your mother's heart.'

'What's breaking my heart is the fact he's still starkers,' Lizzie said, looking away as though she'd only just noticed. 'For the love of God, Callum, at least go and put on a pair of pants.'

With a despairing look in my direction, my fake boyfriend backed away down a dark corridor before slamming a door behind him and rattling what sounded like every window frame in the flat. I gulped, sweating bullets inside my duffle coat.

Alone with the enemy.

'So,' I said, trying to fill the uncomfortable silence. 'Braewick? Sounds . . . nice?'

'It's the most magnificent place on God's green earth,' Derek replied. 'Which you'd already know if you'd been up to visit.'

Fiddling with one of the toggles on my coat, I clucked my tongue against the roof of my mouth. 'Well, it's a big step, isn't it, meeting the parents. We haven't been going out that long.'

'Has it not been almost a year?'

I looked up to see Lizzie watching me like a hawk.

'I'm not holding him hostage,' I said, a cold tremor running down my spine. 'He can go home without me.'

'Can he? That boy won't cross the street without you, it feels like.'

'I don't know about that,' I replied. 'But either way, I really can't leave London. I can't leave my sister on her own at Christmas.'

Ten minutes earlier, I'd been a single, only child and now I had a boyfriend *and* a sister. Quite an impressive morning, all things considered. Both of Callum's parents were quiet for a moment, until Derek sat up straight, a glowing lightbulb practically appearing over his head.

'Why don't you bring your sister with you,' he suggested. 'We've more than enough room.' He drew closer until I could see the wiry grey outliers peeking through his dark eyebrows. 'Hen, I'm not going to take no for an answer. All we've heard all year is Caroline this, Caroline that. Cal cancelled every trip home to spend more time with you. This is the perfect opportunity to make it up to us, isn't it?'

'As inviting as you made that sound, I don't think she'd be able to come,' I said, desperately trying to come up with an excuse. 'It's her husband. He can't go to Scotland, he's, well, he's banned.'

'Banned?'

'Yes.'

'From entering Scotland?'

'That's right.'

'Why?'

Why? Why was my non-existent sister's equally non-existent husband banned from entering Scotland?

'For impersonating Sean Connery,' I said. 'And a criminal misuse of bagpipes.'

A wall of silence came down between us. Then, with one very heavy hand, Derek slapped me on the leg and hooted with laughter.

'Just like Cal said, she's a joker,' he said, wiping away invisible tears. 'But if your sister's married, she doesn't need you to keep her company, does she?'

Without a ready response, I stared daggers down the dark corridor. What was going on? How had I ended up in this situation? And how long did it take someone to find a pair of pants?

'Tell her, Elizabeth,' Derek went on. 'Tell Caroline what it would mean to us to have our boy back home for Christmas.'

'It would be nice to have all the kids under the same roof for once,' she said, a quiet admission. 'Especially after he missed his dad's birthday to take you on that trip to Paris.'

I sucked in my bottom lip as I met her gaze. Were those tears in her eyes? Was I about to make a complete stranger cry? At *Christmas*?

Taking my hand in his, Derek blinked at me, an earnest look on his big, open face.

'Caroline, don't make a man beg.'

Sod this. I hated confrontation at the best of times, and I really hated being put in such a stupid situation. What did it matter if I agreed now then cancelled later? This was Callum's mess to clean up, not mine.

'OK,' I muttered. 'I'll come to Braewick for Christmas.'

The gleeful howl that erupted from Derek was so loud, I was sure it scattered the ravens at the Tower of London.

'Champion! It's sorted then, you're both coming home.'

Down the corridor, I heard a door bang against a wall and Callum came crashing back into the living room, still barefoot but wearing a pair of black jeans and holding a grey sweatshirt. For how long he'd been in there, I was half expecting him to be in full Scottish regalia. Not that I would've minded seeing him in a kilt, I already knew he had great legs.

'What?' he said, tugging the sweatshirt over his head. 'What did I miss?'

'All good, we'd better be off,' Derek declared, rising to his feet and patting down all the pockets of his wax jacket. 'Lots to do, long drive ahead of us.'

'You're leaving?' Callum said, fighting to get his arms into his sweatshirt like a temperamental T-rex.

His dad nodded, finally finding the item he was

looking for in the first pocket he'd checked, his phone, and tapping at the screen with big, decisive gestures.

'Aye. We're stopping over in Penrith but that's still a five-hour drive from here and you know your mother doesn't like to be on the motorway after dark. We've lots to get organised before the two of you arrive, and don't start your excuses, I know you won't want to drive, I'm sorting out the travel right now before Caroline changes her mind. The train, mind, there'll be no last-minute flights, I'm not made of money.'

'What travel, travel where?' Callum asked me and his mother as his father continued to poke at his phone. 'What's he talking about?'

Lizzie pursed her lips before she spoke. 'Your father has convinced Caroline here the two of you need to come home for Christmas.'

Without saying a word, he reached out for the door-frame to steady himself.

'You're very welcome,' his father said, putting his phone away. 'Mal's booking your tickets, he says they'll come through on the email so no need to pick them up at the ticket office. I shall see you both the day after tomorrow, have fun on the train and don't do anything I wouldn't do.'

'Or anything he would do,' Lizzie added, kissing her son on the cheek then pulling back to observe me from across the room. 'Lovely to meet you, Caroline. I'm looking forward to getting to know you better.'

'Same,' I replied, the best I could manage as I held up a hand in farewell, unable to rouse myself from the sofa.

In fact, neither of us moved when his parents let themselves out. Instead, we stayed right where we were until the front door closed and the car outside revved into life. Only then did Callum sink down to the ground, holding his head in his hands.

'OK, first question,' I said, as the sound of the engine faded away, leaving the two of us completely alone. 'Where the fuck is my bobble hat?'

CHAPTER THREE

'Your hat's in the bedroom,' Callum said, his hands rubbing at his damp hair as though he was try to massage some sense into himself. 'I'll wash it. Or you can burn it and I'll buy you a new one, up to you.'

Now he was fully dressed and it felt less like a convictable offence, I took a moment to study him more closely. Even sitting down, he was a force to be reckoned with, easily over six feet tall and broad across the shoulders. You wouldn't want to get stuck behind him at a gig, but he did seem the sort who could easily hoist you up on his shoulders for a better view, should the need occur.

'And second question,' I said, softening slightly. 'What on earth was that all about?'

He replied without looking up. 'Which part?'

'Dealer's choice.'

The sigh that passed through his lips was so heavy, it blew a stack of receipts off the coffee table and onto the floor, the wafer-thin slips of paper swirling in the shafts of morning light as they danced down to the grey tufted rug. I slid to the ground from the sofa, both of us reaching for a long receipt hiding by the leg of the coffee table. His fingers brushed against mine and a flicker of electricity ran through me. Only static, I told myself as I snatched my hand back but if Callum felt anything, he didn't show it.

'I don't really know where to start if I'm honest,' he said. 'It's a long story.'

'How about the beginning?' I suggested.

He shuffled his pile of receipts then placed them on the coffee table. I added my handful on the table, crumpled and creased, next to his, smooth and even.

'You know what? It's not that interesting and you're probably wanting to get on.' He slapped his hands against his thick thighs, the sound cracking through the silence of the room, and reset his face to a bland neutral. 'No need to worry about any of that, I'll sort it out.'

'I wasn't worried,' I said.

'Good,' he said.

Hmm. OK. If he didn't want to talk about it, I didn't want to talk about it. I rose to my feet, digging my hands deep into my coat pockets.

'Is there anything you need to know about the flat before you go?' Callum asked and I shrugged.

'You tell me. It's your flat.'

'I could give you the tour,' he offered, a little less brusque this time. 'Since you're here.'

'Why not?' I replied. 'Since I'm here.'

'The shower can be a bit difficult but you'll get the hang of it.'

He held open the door to a comically small bathroom, leaving it up to me to decide whether I would straddle the toilet or wedge myself between the wall and the sink when he decided to join me inside.

'Difficult how?' I asked, the sink digging into the small of my back. No one wanted to straddle a toilet with company present.

'When you turn it on, it'll either be really hot or freezing cold. You have to work out the right balance.'

He mimed twisting the two taps, cheeks turning red when he looked back to me and realised his hands were at exactly the same level as my chest. Slapping his arms down by his sides, he stepped swiftly out of the tiny room.

'You'll work it out,' he said, visibly flustered. 'It's only a shower, doesn't take a brain surgeon.'

'Good to know,' I replied, tempering a smile. 'So, what's taking you to Paris? Dave said you're a chef?'

'Hoping to be.' He closed the bathroom door, sealing his embarrassment inside. 'Right now I'm only a cook but I've been accepted into a culinary school in Paris to study French pastry. Six-month course with a six-month internship at the end if I qualify. After that, who knows?'

'Which explains the need for a flatsitter,' I said and he nodded. 'A six-foot pastry chef moving to Paris. You might be my roommate's dream man.'

'Six-four,' he amended before adding, 'I don't suppose she's a massage therapist called Caroline?'

'An interior designer called Desi. And she gives massages like Vulcan death grips.'

'Then I'll pass.' Holding out an arm, he directed me down a short hallway. 'What is it you do? Dave said something about the hospital.'

'I'm a brain surgeon,' I said, holding back a laugh

when he tripped over his own feet, blinking at me in disbelief.

'You're joking?'

'Generally speaking, we're not a profession noted for our sense of humour. Brains are fascinating but not all that funny.'

Callum hadn't taken his eyes off me since the words left my mouth but in place of the usual look of confusion, there was something else. He looked . . . impressed?

But he didn't say anything. Instead, he shook off his awestruck expression and guided me into the small but perfectly formed bedroom. The sheets were mussed up from what looked like a tempestuous night's sleep, the curtains were still drawn and two very expensive-looking suitcases sat in front of an empty built-in wardrobe, both of them open, clothes spilling out from each. He really *hadn't* been expecting company. Barging past me, he slammed the open drawer of his bedside table shut before hastily pulling up the duvet to cover the bedsheets.

'All the stuff I'm leaving will be locked in the closet in the hallway,' he stated, cocking his head back towards the door. 'Obviously, you'll have all your own bedding and . . . stuff.'

'Obviously,' I agreed, trying to pretend I had not seen the bottle of bedside lube he'd tried so hard to hide. 'Thank you.'

On behalf of all women, I wanted to add but did not.

The living room was a little brighter when we returned, the sun deciding to show its face for the first time all day, and Callum looked at me again, the muscles around his eyes contracting very slightly, as if bringing me into sharper focus.

'You're really a brain surgeon?' he asked.

'Technically a neurosurgeon,' I said, hugging my coat closer. 'Or I will be when I finish my training. We treat the whole nervous system – not only the brain – but that is part of it.'

'How long is the training?'

He sounded curious but not wary. There was no sign of The Fear in him, at least not yet. Most men, straight men at least, were weird about a female surgeon. Much like female pilots and truck drivers and presidents of the United States of America, it was one of those jobs that just didn't sit right with them and we all suffered because of it.

'Five-year medical degree, two-year foundation programme then at least eight years of training. I'm about halfway through but there's a long way to go yet.'

'Wow.'

His eyebrows climbed up his forehead as the facts registered.

'I know, don't worry, I've heard it all,' I said, preparing my standard spiel. 'You don't look like a neurosurgeon, you don't hear about woman surgeons very often, I wouldn't want someone who wears days of the week underwear digging around in my brain, et cetera, et cetera.'

'You don't look like a neurosurgeon,' Callum agreed. 'Not that I've given it a lot of thought but if you'd asked, I'd have assumed they were all old white men. That's terrible, isn't it?'

'Terrible but nine times out of ten, correct.' I gave him an exaggerated once over. 'What about you? Wouldn't exactly have you pegged for a pastry chef.'

'Goes to show, you really can't judge a book by its

cover,' he said with a sly smile. 'And for the record, if you hadn't mentioned it, I would never have guessed you were wearing days of the week underwear.'

'Really? What kind of underwear did you think I was wearing?'

The surprise that registered on his face was nothing compared to the shock on mine. Ducking my head, I spotted my earbuds still tucked into the rug, and bent over to retrieve them. Where did *that* come from?

'Well, I'm honoured to have you renting the flat,' Callum said, blessedly changing the subject. 'If a bit surprised you aren't in the market for something nicer.'

'Still a trainee,' I reminded him, pocketing the earbuds and recovering my composure. Just. 'Working for the NHS. In London. Things could be worse, admittedly, but I'm still paying off my student loans. It's too easy to get into a lot of debt as a student in this city, especially when you didn't have any money to start with.'

'And I can't imagine days of the week underwear are cheap.'

At last, he unleashed the full force of his grin. It was glorious. His teeth were straight and white, his lips full and soft looking, and he lit up, all the warmth of his expression pouring into me like a no-contact hug. His wavy hair was almost dry now, a dark, russet colour, and just long enough to curl up around his cheekbones, framing those incredible eyes, and when he stepped into a shaft of sunlight, I could've sworn I heard a choir of angels singing. Which was when I noticed a car parked outside the window, blaring Christmas carols at full blast.

'That's everything, I think.' Callum waved his arms around the small space as I leaned against the wall, attempting to recover myself. Someone had spent altogether too much time in the hospital lately and that someone was me. 'You've got my number, give me a shout if you come across any problems and I'll send someone round. Or you can always ask Dave, I'm sure he'll help. Even if he is a bit of a dickhead.'

'You really might be my roommate's dream man,' I said. 'Thanks for the tour and yep, I'll let dickhead Dave know if I've got any more questions. Since you'll be in Paris.'

'Since I'll be in Paris,' he echoed, eyes locked on mine.

'Have a nice Christmas in Scotland,' I added, reaching for the door but not letting myself out just yet. 'Say ho, ho, ho to your mum and dad for me.'

Half a laugh huffed out of him.

'No can do. I'm not going. I'd rather stay here on my own.'

'You're not serious?' I said, letting go of the door handle.

'I'd say you wouldn't understand but I reckon you got a good measure of my family in your five minutes.'

'A bit overwhelming,' I admitted. 'But ultimately well-meaning?'

Callum didn't look convinced. His smile disappeared, replaced by a frown that stole all the light from his eyes, the easy vibes in the room vanishing with it.

'A neurosurgeon,' he said in a rapidly thickening voice. 'Your mum and dad must be really proud of you.'

'I suppose so. We don't really talk about it,' I replied quietly. 'Why, you don't think yours are proud of you?'

A pause.

'I know they aren't.'

'They seemed awfully keen to have you home for Christmas.'

'Aye, where they can keep an eye on me,' he replied. 'My parents won't be happy until I get married, knock out a couple of grandkids and move back to Braewick.'

'The most magnificent place on God's green earth,' I snapped my fingers and shot him with a finger gun and a wry smile. 'I totally remember, babe.'

He almost smiled back. 'Aye, Dad was right about one thing, it is beautiful. Scottish Highlands, about an hour north of Inverness. It's also the arse end of nowhere. More sheep than people.'

'Not many opportunities for a pastry chef,' I guessed. 'So, what happened exactly? You invented a girlfriend to get them off your back?'

'That's the short version.'

'And the long version?' When he gave me an uncertain look, I shrugged and leaned against the wall. 'Go on, I've got nowhere better to be.'

'Fine.' Callum took a deep breath in and settled onto his sofa. 'I suppose I owe you an explanation.'

'At least as to how you chose her job. Massage therapist? Really?'

Pulling at a loose thread on the cuff of his sweatshirt, he leaned forward, resting his forearms on his thighs, looking as though he couldn't believe he'd got himself into such a mess.

'I was on my way for a massage, on the phone with Mum when she asked what Caroline did for a living.' He held up his hands to acknowledge the lack of creativity. 'There was no nefarious plan or anything, mostly I didn't want to hurt their feelings. They never understand why I can't cancel work stuff to go back and visit at the drop of a hat, but when I said I was seeing someone, they seemed more understanding.'

'Your job keeps you away from Braewick but a girlfriend gets them one step closer to grandkids,' I reasoned. 'Emotional mathematics, the equations don't always make sense but there's usually a pattern.'

'And that's why you're the brain surgeon and I'm not. You're a genius.'

I waved a hand to reject the notion but I wasn't exactly mad about it. The pieces of a very confusing puzzle started to slot into place. Annoying parents, fake girlfriend, easy answer.

'But why tell them I'm Caroline instead of explaining I'm renting the flat from you?' I asked.

'Because I'm an idiot?'

It was hard to argue against it.

'They assumed, I panicked,' he said with an apologetic glance in my direction. 'Sorry I dragged you into it.'

'Don't be, it's not your fault. Like you said, you're an idiot.'

We smiled at each other, Callum wringing his hands while I squeezed the earbuds in my pocket.

'What are you going to do now?' I asked. 'They're expecting both of us.'

His reply was a long, low groan that sent an unexpected shiver running all the way down my spine and I had to bite my lip to stop it from ricocheting all the way back up again.

'I don't know,' he admitted, combing a hand through his hair, breaking up the waves from the back to the front. 'I'm not desperate to be alone on Christmas but if I show up in Braewick without you after they've bought both our train tickets? Nightmare material.'

'Then call them right now!' I ordered, pointing at the phone he produced from the pocket of his jeans. 'Tell them not to buy me a ticket!'

His eyes scanned the screen from left and right until he landed on something and turned it around for me to see.

'Too late.'

A receipt. A QR code. Two tickets booked on the Caledonian Sleeper.

Two incredibly expensive, non-refundable tickets booked on the Caledonian Sleeper. As someone who grew up without any money, who was mired in student debt, the number on the screen made me feel sick to my stomach.

'Don't worry about it, this isn't your problem,' Callum said when he saw the look on my face. 'I made my bed, I'll hide underneath it until my parents stop shouting at me. I'll call them, explain we're not coming, stick it out here on my own.'

On his own. Even a self-professed Grinch like me couldn't stand the thought of him skulking around alone all Christmas, it was too depressing.

'What if you tell them I dumped you after they left?' I suggested. 'Then they'd have to be nice to you?'

'If I break up with Caroline, I lose my get-out-of-going-home card and I'm not ready to part with that just yet and if I show up at home without you, they'll probably lock me up in the tower to keep me there, and I really wish I was joking.'

'OK, Rapunzel,' I muttered. 'Your hair isn't *that* nice.'

'It's not your problem,' he said again. 'Worry about the hot water tap in the bathroom, don't stress yourself out about me.'

He was right, it wasn't my problem, but I hated the thought of him hanging around this empty, tree-less flat all Christmas and I really hated the thought of his parents wasting so much money. It all seemed so unnecessary, especially when there was an alternative. Even if it was a deeply, deeply stupid alternative . . .

'What if I did come with you?' I said. 'I don't have any big plans and, you never know, it might be fun. I could be Caroline.'

Callum stared right through me, two lines bracketing his mouth as he pursed his lips. I squeezed the tape measure in my pocket until the edges bit into my palm and stared right back. For some reason, whenever he looked at me, I couldn't quite work out what to do with my hands.

'You're joking,' he said. 'Of course you're joking.'

Was I? Of course I was. Unless I wasn't.

'It's only an idea,' I replied. 'I mean, how difficult could it be? Nice train ride, couple of days in Scotland, smile and nod at your family. Would it be so ridiculous?'

'Yes,' Callum answered without hesitation.

'Right,' I agreed. 'Completely.'

'And it wouldn't really solve the problem in the long term,' he added. 'What are you going to do, come with me every time I have to visit my parents for the next ten years?'

'Or,' I said, a concept of a plan forming in my mind, 'we make Caroline so unbelievably awful they beg you to never bring her back to Braewick ever again.'

The creases between Callum's eyebrows smoothed out slowly as his eyebrows crept up his forehead.

'Really and truly heinous,' I added. 'I'm talking tracks mud all over the house, talks on her phone at the dinner table, puts empty After Eight wrappers back in the box horrible. We could really make them hate her.'

'I may have led my parents to believe Caroline isn't especially social,' he muttered, more to himself than to me. 'All you'd have to do is show up then avoid them for the rest of the trip.'

'For how long?'

'The train leaves tomorrow night, gets into Inverness on the twenty-second and we'd travel back to London on the twenty-sixth.'

'Show up, be rude, hide in my bedroom for four days,' I surmised. 'Yes, that sounds like a proper family Christmas.'

'It's such a lot to ask.' Callum glanced at me from underneath his very long eyelashes and I could tell he was tempted. 'We don't even know each other, I can't expect you to give up your Christmas to help me out of my own stupid mess.'

'There's really nothing to give up,' I assured him. 'It's just me and my two friends eating an entire Chocolate Orange each and watching *A Muppet Christmas Carol* on a loop.'

'That sounds like more fun than hanging out with my family . . . What about work? Surely you don't get much time off?'

'I've been saving up my holidays, I don't go back until the twenty-ninth.'

The not-quite-a-lie sailed smoothly through my lips. No need to tell him I'd been politely forced to take the whole week off because I hadn't used any of my holiday allowance for the last two years. I was always happier when I was busy, when I had a project to keep me occupied, like researching the roles of pericytes and neighbouring cells in ischaemia and dementia patients, catching up on the latest developments in remyelination, or pretending to be a masseuse named Caroline.

'OK, don't take this the wrong way,' Callum said, almost guaranteeing there was only one way to take it. 'But what's in it for you? Why would you even want to help me?'

I had a hundred ready answers. Because his family Christmas in Scotland sounded more appealing than another non-Christmas on Desi's sofa. Because I'd never been to the Highlands and I had a pair of Grenson Nanette boots still in their box that I impulse purchased more than three years ago. Because I was tired and burned out and felt like doing something stupid. Because nothing about the entire season had felt the same since I lost my mum and I didn't want to spend another December twenty-fifth steeped in sad memories.

'It's Christmas, isn't it? You're supposed to help the needy,' I said instead, tossing away the words as though they meant nothing. 'You're doing me a massive favour letting me rent the flat. Pretending to be someone else for a few days really isn't that big a deal in the greater scheme of things.'

He looked at me, chin lowered, cheeks sucked in while he considered the proposal.

'You're serious?'

I swallowed and nodded. I was serious. Seriously certifiable. But now I had a vision of myself wandering through fields of heather in my box-fresh hiking boots, wind blowing through my hair, deep-fried Mars bar in my mouth, I was more invested than ever.

'I'm not twisting your arm, you can say no,' I said.

'You can stay here on your tod and eat a microwave dinner on Christmas Day—'

'Laura, I literally cook for a living.'

'—or you can say yes and get a life-long pass from parental hassle. It's entirely up to you.'

Callum wrapped his hands around the back of his neck, eyes closed as if he couldn't believe what he was about to say. 'If you're serious, I could give you a month's free rent. As a thank you.'

And just like the Grinch before me, my heart grew three sizes at the thought of going into the New Year with a non-negative bank balance for once.

'So we have a deal?' I asked.

'We have a deal,' he replied.

I held out my hand and he took it, his handshake firm and professional, but the way his thumb trailed over my skin when I pulled away made my breath hitch in my chest.

'To Caroline, the antisocial masseuse,' he said with a smile.

'To Caroline,' I repeated. 'And a very merry McClay Christmas to all.'

CHAPTER FOUR

'You're completely out of your mind and I've never been so angry with you in my life.'

Desi wasn't taking take the news about my trip as well as I'd hoped.

'You're telling me you've agreed to nick off to the Scottish Highlands with a complete stranger *on Christmas* so his weird family can lure you into some ritual sacrifice and skin you alive?' She stared at me, eyes popped wide, mouth hanging open. 'I should lock you in this room and board it up from the outside.'

'Probably,' I agreed as I rummaged through the pile of clean washing on the bed, randomly tossing T-shirts and socks at my open suitcase. 'Sounds fun, doesn't it?'

'No,' she replied. 'It doesn't.'

'I think it sounds fun,' Joel commented from his spot on the floor where he was currently curating my festive wardrobe.

Since my work clothes were all horribly dull and neutral, I had a tendency to go the other way with my downtime outfits. Not that I was ever out of sweatpants or pyjamas but if I did decide I wanted to venture out into the world, my civilian wardrobe was made up of random brightly coloured bits and pieces bought on a whim. Desi had more than once accused me of having the style of a hyperactive toddler. I preferred eccentric rainbow fan. Her description was more accurate.

'Fun *and* sexy,' Joel added. 'I love a Scotsman. Does he have an accent? Tell me the bit about him covering his peen with your bobble hat again. Did it all fit?'

'It's only a few days,' I said to Desi, ignoring Joel to the best of my ability. 'Think of it as a minibreak, a wee jaunt up to bonny Scotland with Dave's friend to get some fresh air and . . . well, I'm not sure what else. Whatever people do in Scotland.'

'Drink whisky, toss cabers and wear kilts?' Joel offered.

'That sounds a tad stereotypical.' I frowned. 'I'm sure there's a lot more to it than that.'

'No, I'm saying that's what I did last time I was there.' He closed his eyes and smiled at a memory. 'My cousin Naima's wedding, it was brilliant. Right up until Uncle Bikram fell arse over tit and showed everyone what a real Scotsman wears under his kilt. Nearly turned me straight on the spot.'

'Thank you for that very insightful input,' Desi scowled at Joel while he held out two different dresses for my approval. I nodded towards the more conservative red velvet maxi offering. He tossed a neon-pink mini alternative into my case instead. 'Best-case scenario, you fall in love with him and get your heart broken. Worst-case scenario, they're going to roast you over an open fire and eat you for Christmas dinner.'

'She does love a scenario, this one,' Joel muttered,

contemplating a pair of skinny jeans over a pair of wide leg leopard-print trousers. 'How are they the only two options? There have to be a thousand more. What if the train breaks down on the way and they get trapped in a frozen wasteland and the passengers resort to cannibalism? What if his mother is a witch and there's a curse on the family that turns them all into Loch Ness monsters? What if they drive through a fairy circle and find themselves stuck in *Braveheart* times, or whatever the fuck happens in *Outlander*?'

'You really have got to start actually watching the telly rather than reading the Wikipedia articles while it's on,' I told him. 'And who's to say *he* won't fall in love with *me* and get *his* heart broken?'

Desi marched across the room to her bookcase and began pulling out a selection of brightly coloured paperbacks, hurling them at my cowering form. 'What's this? Oh look, a book about two people who fake date then fall in love. And what happens in this one? A fake engagement that ends in the couple catching feelings. This is the formula, Laura, you make a deal, you swear you won't catch feelings then he sweeps you off your feet and bangs you senseless in your just one bed. But guess what? The bit where you end up together is *not* guaranteed.'

'I never said I wasn't going to have sex with him, I said I'm not going to fall in love with him,' I replied casually. 'He is pretty fit, I wouldn't kick him out of bed for eating biscuits.'

Desi said nothing, only blinked.

'Sorry,' I fluttered my eyelashes in her direction. 'I meant I wouldn't kick him out of bed for eating shortbread.'

'You're an idiot,' she said with a sigh. 'An absolute fool.'

'Calm down, Des,' I said. 'It's not going to be holding hands and moonlit strolls, more like dirty looks and temper tantrums, no PDA involved whatsoever. It's all been agreed. I don't have to convince his family we're in love, only persuade them to hate my guts.'

'And how exactly are you going to pull that off?'

'Easy. I'm going to pretend I'm you.'

She wasn't even a little bit offended.

'You've lost your mind.'

'And you're overthinking it,' I replied, turning back to my packing. How many pairs of knickers would I need for five days away? Ten? Twelve? Twelve seemed safe. 'It's going to be a breeze. Pretty sure his mum already hates me so half the job is done but they're not going to hurt me. She was wearing a silk scarf. Fastened with a *brooch*. Whoever heard of someone who owns a brooch skinning people alive?'

Joel launched himself onto the bed, right in the middle of my pile of clean clothes.

'Question. If you do shag him and you get free rent, does that technically count as sex work?'

'You tell me, you're my accountant.'

'Hmm.' He rubbed his chin and frowned. 'I think he'd have more of a problem than you, since you've got a written agreement and everything. As long as he's not making a profit or you don't pay more than seven thousand five hundred pounds in a single tax year, he doesn't have to report it. If you're just subletting for cash under the table, there wouldn't be an issue.'

Desi dumped herself on the bed beside Joel and took my hand in hers, her long black hair snapped back in a claw clip, a genuine expression of concern on her pretty face.

'You're too nice, that's your problem,' she said, almost gently but not quite. 'What sort of psycho suggests something like this in the first place?'

'I suggested it,' I replied and she covered her face with a pair of red tartan shirt-and-shorts pyjamas and groaned. 'What? He gets a fake girlfriend for five days and I get a month's free rent and a holiday in Scotland. I've got nothing to lose.'

'Unless his family does skin you alive,' Joel commented. 'Some things are better with the skin on, Lau, like a nice little potato wedge.'

Rational thought was a mystery to the pair of them.

'Look, I'll be careful,' I promised. 'Obviously I'm not actually going to have sex with him, that was a joke, and I'm definitely, definitely not going to fall in love with him. You know I'm a feelings-free zone—'

'Until you're fully qualified, we know,' Desi completed my sentence for me, parroting the reasoning I'd used time and time again whenever conversation turned to my barren love life. 'You don't need any distractions, we know, we've heard it, we've rolled our eyes at it.'

'We've talked about it behind your back,' Joel added. 'Extensively.'

'He's not my type anyway,' I said airily. 'He's too tall and healthy looking. Seems the type to go outside voluntarily and enjoy it.'

Joel gave a scandalised gasp.

'Not . . . *outdoorsy*?'

'Exactly, like he'd suggest going on a long walk wearing shorts in the winter,' I confirmed. 'You know I prefer an indoor pet.'

'Rat-boy is your usual preference,' Desi admitted. 'But types can change.'

'Trust me, if you'd met his parents, you wouldn't be so concerned.' I let out a little laugh, mentally pasting his dad's eyebrows onto Callum's face. Instant ick. 'I can see how this might look like a reckless decision from the outside but aren't you the one always saying I need to be more spontaneous?'

'No, I've literally never said that.'

'I have but I was talking about maybe getting the train to the seaside or something instead of spending your day off on the sofa with all the Real Housewives again,' Joel said. 'Not agreeing to trek up to the other end of the country and spend all of Christmas with a random hot Scot you barely know.'

I snorted out another laugh as I pulled a pair of tights out from under Desi. 'It's all going to be fine, you're both overreacting. I'm a doctor, I'm good at staying detached. From here on out, I'll think of Callum as a patient instead of a human being.'

'Surgeons don't think of patients as human beings?' Joel's question pitched up with panic.

'Forget I said that,' I muttered. 'The point is, you can't get hurt if there aren't any feelings involved and surgeons are very good at compartmentalising feelings.'

Joel looked at Desi. Desi looked at Joel.

'But if by some bizarre, inexplicable chain of events I *did* get attached,' I continued loudly, 'I swear I will never mention it to either of you, not once. Even if he metaphorically rips my guts out and I spend the rest of my days wandering the world in a Miss Havisham-esque nightmare, the name Callum McClay will never again pass my lips, unless I'm referring to him as my landlord or that bloke I went to Scotland with that one time at Christmas.'

'Which brings me to my second complaint. I can't believe you're ditching us.' Desi grabbed my wrist as I reached for a pair of black leggings and yanked me down onto the bed, creating a three-friend-cuddle-puddle with me as the littlest spoon. 'Leaving me and Joel all on our own? How will we survive?'

'By getting rat-arsed on Baileys and passing out before the King's speech same as you do every year.' I tried to twist around to look at them but a shooting pain in my neck spun me right back. Ten years of yoga and I was as flexible as a slab of cement. 'If you can't bear the thought of Christmas without me, you could always come to Scotland, you were invited.'

'We were?' Joel said, perking up.

'Technically, they invited my sister,' I clarified. 'You could be my brother-in-law if you like?'

His forehead creased with confusion.

'But you haven't got a sister.'

'I'm not a massage therapist called Caroline either,' I replied. 'I don't think an imaginary sister is going to be the straw that breaks the camel's back on this one.'

'The situations you get yourself into.' Desi sighed as she stroked my hair, the comforting scent of her woodsy perfume settling around me. 'I don't know, Lau, I still think you're going to regret this.'

'Then you have full permission to say I told you so if it goes tits up,' I said with a loving smile. 'Until then, can we all agree it's a fun, silly adventure that we'll all laugh about a week from now when we're moving me into my lovely rent-free flat?'

'Delulu is the solulu,' Joel announced. 'You might be a silly goose but you're our silly goose. Here, take these.'

Breaking ranks from our three-way cuddle, he sat up and reached into the pocket of his jeans to produce the same black leather wallet he'd been carrying since Desi gave it to him for his twenty-first birthday. Opening it up, he pulled out a seemingly endless strip of condoms.

'What is that thing, the TARDIS?' I asked as he crammed the golden concertina into my hands. 'How many condoms do you carry around on an average day?'

'Better safe than sorry and better sorry than knocked up. Take them.'

'There's another box in my drawer, better pack them as well.' Desi jerked her chin towards the bedside table. 'I'll humour your nonsense but I am not raising your Scottish love child.'

'And you say I'm the ridiculous one.' I clucked my tongue as I dropped the eight-condom strip into my suitcase. Just in case. Be prepared, prevention better than cure and all that jazz. 'It's a good job I love you two.'

'You wouldn't survive without us,' Joel said. 'At least not for long.'

'Doesn't bear thinking about,' I replied with a grin, pulling myself out of the cuddle puddle to grab my trilling phone from the bedside table. A text from Dad, a picture of him waving from the bow of the ship. 'I don't even know how I'll cope for five days.'

Desi reached over to open the drawer where I stood, revealing, as promised, a jumbo-sized box of condoms. 'By filling your suitcase with these. Read my lips, no love child.'

'Message received and understood,' I said with a

salute. 'All I'm bringing back is myself, my suitcase and hopefully some shortbread if there's time to stop at the shop.'

'Laura,' Joel said gravely. 'If life has only taught me one thing, it's that there is always time to stop for shortbread.'

Truly, they were words to live by.

CHAPTER FIVE

By the time I arrived at Euston at nearly nine on Monday evening, I'd talked myself in and out of my festive fake relationship a thousand times over, but when I saw Callum standing by the entrance to platform one, there was no turning back.

'That's him?' Joel gasped on my left when he spotted the three of us and raised a hand in greeting.

'Why's he wearing all black?' Desi asked on my other side. 'Who does he think he is, James Bond?'

'Black hides the blood stains better,' I replied, waving back to my new boyfriend. 'Can the two of you behave for one minute? I knew I shouldn't have let you come.'

'I wanted to look him in the eye before he takes you off for the ritual sacrifice,' she said, her steely eyes locked on Callum. 'He needs to know who he's dealing with.'

'A twenty-seven-year-old graphic designer from Kent?'

'Who can't even watch *The Vampires Diaries* on her own because it's too scary,' added Joel.

'I don't like it when their faces go all veiny,' she muttered right before I dug an elbow into her ribs. 'OK, ow?'

'Hi!'

I broke ranks from my friends, taking a large step forward as Callum strode towards us. He was exactly as handsome and as tall as I remembered, but his hair was more red than brown now it was completely dry, falling around his freshly shaven face. And when he saw me, I could've sworn I saw his eyes light up, a vibrant blue, shining like sapphires against the dull, dark shades of grey that made up London's most depressing train station.

'Right on time.' He glanced at my escorts. 'And you brought friends?'

'Desi and Joel,' I replied by way of introduction. 'They've come to make sure you're not a murderer.'

'How would you know?' Callum asked, eyes definitely sparkling. 'Is there a test?'

'Desi has a sixth sense.' Joel extended an arm to shake his hand while Desi glowered at my side. 'She always knows who's going to get voted off on *Bake Off*, as well. Seriously, I've made so much money off her predictions, she's never wrong.'

Callum squinted at my friends. 'You can bet on *Bake Off*?'

'You can bet on anything,' Desi answered when he turned to shake her hand. '*Bake Off*, *Strictly*, how long it would take me to hunt you down and tear you to pieces if you hurt my friend.'

'I'm not a murderer,' he said, his smile tightening by a fraction.

'Sounds like the kind of thing a murderer would say.'

'Well, thanks for seeing me to the station,' I said, clapping my hands together loudly. 'You can both fuck off now.'

'I've hidden AirTags in all her things,' she went on, still gripping Callum's hand like she was ready to tear it off. 'And you don't have to submit to a DNA test now but—'

'That's enough, Olivia Benson,' I interrupted, pulling my backpack off her shoulder and hoisting it onto my own back. 'I'll be back on the twenty-sixth.'

'With all her limbs intact,' Callum promised. 'Scout's honour.'

'Were you a scout?' Desi asked.

He gave her a dazzling smile. 'I don't know, was I?'

'He's so hot,' Joel whispered into my ear as I leaned in to hug him goodbye. 'I take it all back, poke holes in those condoms, please have his baby. We need that DNA in our bloodline.'

'Text us when you get there,' Desi instructed loudly, still eyeing Callum over my shoulder. 'And call me. A lot.'

'I'll make sure she sends you a daily selfie holding the morning newspaper,' he promised, taking my suitcase from Joel. 'Unless the two of you want to come with us? I'm sure my parents will make room.'

'Enough,' I declared, before they could take him up on the offer. 'We have to go, don't want to miss the train.'

After one more group hug, Desi reluctantly let me go, Callum inclining his head to my friends as he rolled my suitcase ahead of us.

'Nice of your mum and dad to bring you to the train,' he quipped. 'If you don't want to come, there's still time to back out.'

'Same to you,' I replied, pulling my backpack all the way up on my shoulders and fastening the straps tight against my body. 'If I'm honest, I half thought you might not be here when I arrived.'

He gave a nervous laugh that suggested that had at the very least been a possibility.

'Then what would you've done?'

'Gone to Scotland without you. Had a lovely Christmas with Derek and Lizzie, convinced them to disinherit you and adopt me instead.'

'They'd love that,' he said, almost smiling. 'A neurosurgeon would be more of a welcome addition to the family than a pastry chef.'

'If that's true, they've got their priorities all wrong,' I told him. 'Most people will never need a neurosurgeon. *Everyone* needs a pastry chef.'

His smile grew broader as we reached the long line of sleek teal carriages rumbling gently on the platform.

'Hold on, that's too big to go in the carriage.' A man wearing a green suit and a stern expression stepped out of the train to block my suitcase. 'It'll have to go in the luggage car.'

'We've got a cabin,' Callum offered when I blanched at the thought of being separated from my precious things. 'Is there not room in there?'

He gave my backpack and Callum's black leather holdall a pointed look.

'Not with the two of you and your other bags.'

'It's fine,' I said quickly, trying to remember exactly what I'd stashed in my backpack. After all my years in medicine, I was a professional overnighter. I never went anywhere without deodorant, a toothbrush and a spare pair of knickers upon my person. I'd be fine. 'It's totally OK, it can go in the luggage car, I don't need it for tonight.'

'You're sure?'

'Sure I'm sure,' I nodded. 'Unless there's a formal dress code for dinner?'

'I think you might be overestimating the train,' Callum warned as the conductor passed my suitcase over to another man in another green suit and ushered us aboard. 'The Orient Express, this is not.'

But I didn't want to hear it. I loved the romance of trains, the soothing sway of the carriages, the reliable rumble of the tracks. All my life, I'd wanted to take an overnight journey. So what if we were on our way to Inverness instead of Venice? Visions of polished oak, tartan blankets, heavy-bottomed crystal tumblers full of amber-coloured scotch and whatever other wonders awaited us danced through my head as the conductor tapped a key card against an unassuming electronic lock. I held my breath, ready to behold the beauty inside.

'I call the top bunk,' I exclaimed as the door slid open.

Only there was no top or bottom bunk.

Inside the cabin, was just one bed.

One not-quite-as-big-as-a-double bed, set in a distinctly beige, distinctly plastic cabin with hardly enough room to carry a kitten, let alone swing a cat.

'Is this it?' I asked in a defeated whisper.

'Aye, this is the Caledonian Double En-Suite,' the conductor confirmed. 'She's our finest cabin.'

'But we're supposed to have two beds,' Callum replied as I tried to reset my disappointed face.

'Afraid not, sir. As I said, you're booked in the

Caledonian Double En-Suite. Double meaning double bed.'

If he wasn't careful, I was fairly sure I could get around to hating this man.

'But we need two beds,' Callum stressed as I began to sweat. 'Can't you move us?'

The conductor sucked the air in through his teeth like he was about to tell us our carburettor was buggered and I knew before he spoke what the answer would be. 'I'd like to help but the whole train is fully booked. It's very close to Christmas.'

'Is it really?' I replied, earning a tiny jab to the ribs from Callum's elbow. 'Oh, I know!' My eyes popped open, ever the optimist. 'Do you have any of those little rollaway beds?'

Both Callum and the conductor gave me a look and I briefly considered throwing myself under the train. Eyeballing the sliver of space between the bed and the bathroom door, I sucked in my bottom lip.

'That'll be a no then,' I muttered.

'Grand, glad we got that sorted.' The conductor clapped his hands together even though we had in fact got nothing at all sorted. 'If you don't mind, I'll leave you be. We've a full house tonight, as I said, but I'll be back once we've left the station to make sure you've got everything you need.'

'Everything except two beds,' I muttered as he sailed off down the corridor, leaving us alone.

Turning back, I poked my head into the room once again. It was tiny. It was so tiny and so beige, and there wasn't so much as a trace of tartan to be found.

'It's giving ferry,' I said, reluctantly stepping inside the plastic pod. 'It's giving institutional.'

'Utilitarian,' Callum agreed, still in the corridor. 'Do you think they hose it down between every journey?'

I turned to give him a horrified look. 'I *hope* they hose it down between every journey. It's all very wipe clean, isn't it?'

With a half-hearted scowl of acceptance, he entered the room and closed the door behind him. It was like being locked inside a Zara changing room with Big Bird's hot Scottish cousin.

'Pretty snug,' I commented, backing in until I hit the window. 'Pretty, pretty, pretty snug.'

Suddenly silent, my oversized roommate picked a laminated card up from the bed, scanning it quickly then turning it over to read the back while I eyed the rest of the cabin. Bed, window, little sink, tiny towel, mirrored door that should've made the space feel larger than it was but instead reflected an anxious-looking redhead and her equally unnerved giant companion, trapped in an impossibly claustrophobic space. I couldn't work out how to take off my coat without elbowing Callum in the ribs but it was too hot to keep it on and even the tiny amount of extra space it took up around my person was too much. We needed every inch we could get.

'Right,' Callum said eventually, dropping the card back down on the bed beside what looked like a couple of amenity kits that I was shamefully desperate to claw open. 'Well.'

'Well indeed.'

The train pulled away from the platform and we were off. No time to back out now. I undid the toggles on my coat and shimmied my arms out of the sleeves, allowing it to fall to the floor behind me before bending over to pick it up, my forehead grazing his crotch as I went. He took a step backwards and collided directly with the closed door of the cabin.

'I'll sleep on the floor,' he offered, rubbing the back of his head and bashing his elbow into the wall at the same time.

'You'd have more hope of sleeping on the roof. You're taller than the room is long.'

I turned in three tight circles, searching in vain for somewhere, anywhere, to hang my coat. Wordlessly, Callum took it and hung it on a hook hiding on the back of the door.

'It's only for tonight and I've definitely done worse,' I said, arms flapping uselessly at my sides. 'If I can share a blow-up bed with Desi in Joel's nan's caravan in North Wales for a week, I can manage this. It won't be that bad.'

I offered a hopeful smile and the tight set of his granite jaw softened very slightly.

'Just so you know, I told Mum and Dad we needed separate rooms at the house.'

'And how did you explain that?'

'I told them you have night terrors,' he replied. 'Very violent night terrors.'

Ignoring the slight sense of disappointment that tugged at my sleeve, I threw up my hands. 'Then we'll manage. We're grown-ups, we can share a bed for one night.'

'You're right,' Callum concurred and the tense atmosphere of our beige cell settled. 'We should start as we mean to go on. How about a toast?'

Wedging his weekend bag between the wall and his body, I watched as he unfastened the zip and rooted around inside with one giant hand. With a snort of success, he let the bag fall onto the bed and held up a bell-shaped bottle of dark amber liquid, a silver stag's head emblazoned on the front.

'Whisky?' My mouth went dry at the sight of it.

'The Dalmore 15. It was supposed to be my dad's Christmas present but he can make do with a box of chocolates from the shop at the station. If he's lucky. Here.'

He opened the bottle then held it out to me.

Generally speaking, the darker the drink, the worse my hangover, but I'd always wanted to be a whisky girl and this felt like as good a time as any to commit. Caroline, I'd decided, was a whisky girl. She was also a woman who smoked cigars, knew how to change a tyre, and could rock a rollneck jumper without looking like she was wearing a cervical collar. Bracing slightly at the unexpected weight of the bottle, I tipped it back and let the liquid run into my mouth, scorching the back of my throat. It stung my nose, eliciting a full-body shiver. An involuntary reaction, I told myself as I resisted the urge to gag. An automatic reflex, the contraction of the bilateral pharyngeal muscles and elevation of the soft palate, millennia of evolution designed to stop human beings from choking on foreign objects and stop Laura Pearce from knocking back a shot of whisky without humiliating herself in front of an attractive man.

Passing the bottle back, I pinched my eyes shut and rubbed at my nose, willing my body to keep it down, but Callum was already too busy taking a deep gulp to notice my struggles. I watched him drink, head tilted back, his lips wrapped around the opening of the bottle, his huge hand clasping the weighted glass as if it were no bigger than a teacup. His hair fell back away from his face and his long eyelashes grazed his cheeks, eyes closed in a moment of rapture. My own face heated instantly, burning with the twin flame force of the alcohol and an unexpected flicker of desire as I noticed how his throat bobbed when he swallowed.

'Bloody hell, that's good,' he gasped, coming back up for air and offering me the bottle again. Against my better judgement, I took it. 'You can really taste the orange and the ginger notes in there.'

'Totally,' I lied.

It tasted like embalming fluid and nightmares. Two sips in and I was already entertaining visions of myself embracing the toilet bowl within the next twenty minutes. Caroline might be a whisky girl but Laura was not. Fail number one. While Callum capped the bottle and stashed it back in his bag, I rested my hands against the window, watching the outskirts of London pass by. Cramped streets full of tall buildings gave way to terraced houses with small gardens gave way to bigger homes and green spaces and, finally, fields and fields and fields. Five quiet minutes in and my mind was starting to fog, senses softened by the two unnecessarily large chugs of a drink I never touched, and when the train shifted unexpectedly, I stumbled forward, straight into Callum's arms.

'Hello,' I said, resting my hands on his waist and leaning my head back to look up at him. He was so tall, so solid. He took up so much space without even a whisper of apology and I wondered what it must be like, to move through the world feeling that way.

'Hello yourself.'

He placed his palms on my shoulders, a safe, neutral

body part. 'Perhaps we jumped the gun with the whisky. Have you eaten yet?'

'I had a Pret Christmas sandwich for lunch.' I lowered my voice so no one else would hear me. 'And I've got another one in my backpack.'

'Two mouthfuls of whisky and she's pished,' he said with a grin. 'Don't worry, that can stay our little secret but we ought to get some proper scran in you. Dining car?'

'Dining car.' I opened the door to the cabin and waved him through, ignoring his chuckles. 'And I'm not pissed, I'm pleasantly tipsy.'

'Famous last words,' he groaned as I followed him down the corridor. 'Famous last words.'

CHAPTER SIX

'I'm officially declaring the neeps and tatties a success,' I declared, shovelling a giant forkful of vegetables into my mouth. 'Remind me what it is again?'

'It's supposed to be mashed potatoes and mashed swede.' Callum's face was a picture of disgust. 'Whatever that is on your plate is neither neeps nor tatties.'

Taking another bite, I chewed thoughtfully.

'Tastes like potatoes and swede to me.'

'It looks unwell,' he said with sniff. 'Have they even used any butter? Has it so much as seen a salt shaker? Wait until we get home, I'll show you how it's done.'

'I'm assuming you don't want to try my haggis then?' I prodded the mound of brown stuff at the side of the plate. 'And don't bother telling me what's in it until I'm done because I won't eat it if you do.'

Sitting back against the teal booth, Callum poked at his own beige pasta dinner. He might have liked the look of mine but you couldn't have paid me to taste his. Unwell veg beat soggy pasta every time.

'At least the wine is passable,' he said, unscrewing a second mini bottle of red and moving to top up my glass.

'God no,' I yelped, covering it with my hand before he could pour. 'I'm a complete lightweight. You saw what two sips of your dad's whisky did to me. One glass is more than enough.'

'Suit yourself,' he said as he filled his own up to the brim. 'Aren't you glad you didn't go with formalwear for dinner now?'

'Might've been a bit overdressed,' I admitted with a furtive look around the carriage. Plush garlands of tinsel had been strung up along the walls and Mariah played softly through the speakers but, other than that, there was a distinct lack of sense of occasion in the club car. All the other passengers were resplendent in their comfiest clothing: sweatshirts, jogging bottoms, the odd Christmas jumper, and distressingly, more than one pair of pyjamas. People had no shame.

'You can't blame me for being excited, I don't get many opportunities to dress up,' I told him, digging back into my dinner.

'Not many black tie occasions in neurosurgery?'

'The white coat tends to clash with a ballgown,' I confirmed. 'I think the last time I got properly dressed up was Stella and Dave's wedding.'

Callum leaned against the window, his washed-out mirror image staring back at him in the dark glass. It was pitch black outside. Wherever we were, an hour into our journey, there was barely a light to be seen.

'Funny how I don't remember seeing you there,' I said before braving a forkful of haggis. Hmm, grainier than I'd expected.

'Maybe you did and I didn't make much of an impression.'

'I don't know about that. You're an eighteen-foot-tall Scotsman with red hair.'

'Six-four and it's more auburn,' he replied, looking back to me and waving a hand in front of his face. 'I had a full beard back then, hair was shorter. Shiv didn't like it long.'

'Shiv?' I repeated then left a pause, waiting him to fill in the gaps.

His eyes closed for a brief moment, mouth pulling into a grimace.

'My ex,' he said, blowing out a noisy breath. 'Shiv is my ex. Siobhan Hamilton.'

'Girlfriend?'

'Fiancée. Sort of.'

One thing I'd learned as a doctor was when to talk and when to listen. Not that I always managed to put it into practice outside work, no one loved a good ramble as much as me, but I could tell from the pained look on his face this was definitely a listening moment.

'I never actually proposed,' he explained. 'We *were* talking about it but she jumped the gun and told everyone we were getting married, my parents, her parents, fuck even the milkman sent his congratulations. When I told her I wanted to decide for myself when I would propose, she said it was now or never.'

'And you chose never?'

'I don't like being backed into a corner,' he confirmed. 'She didn't take the break-up very well and neither did anyone else. It was messy, we've known each other since we were kids, she's practically family. My girlfriend, my sister's best friend, her dad and my dad play golf together. Everyone loves Shiv.'

'How did the milkman take it?'

'Tried to run me over with his milk float.'

I snorted into my napkin.

'Oh yeah, it's hilarious until there's three hundred pints of semi-skimmed coming straight at you down a narrow country road,' Callum replied, a smile dancing in his eyes even though he was doing his best to look annoyed. 'Not my best Christmas ever.'

'This all happened at Christmas?' I asked, rubbing at my nose with the back of my hand.

'Last year. Another good reason why I've been avoiding a trip up home.'

Another thought occurred to me. 'She lives in your town. Will she be around this week?'

'I can't say a definite no but I wouldn't think so. We haven't talked much since she moved back up to Braewick. Or at all.'

Was it my imagination or did he look disappointed?

'If I were your real girlfriend and not your fake one, this town-wide ex-girlfriend worship might concern me,' I said lightly. 'Next you'll be telling me she's a world-famous supermodel who works at an animal rescue in her spare time.'

Callum's gaze shifted down to the table, his mouth twisting awkwardly.

'Oh my God, she's a world-famous supermodel,' I breathed.

'No, she isn't,' he said hurriedly. 'She does volunteer with animals, there's a donkey sanctuary half an hour or so from her parents' house, that's all.'

'But she's not a model?'

He took a quick drink from his glass of wine.

'Not in any professional sense.'

Without a word, I picked up my glass of wine and necked the whole thing.

'What about you?' Callum asked. 'Any homicidal delivery men in your past?'

'If anyone is taking out a delivery driver, it's me,' I assured him. 'If they don't stop hiding my ASOS packages behind the bins, I'll take out every single one of them. As far as I'm aware, I'm not on anyone's shit list.'

'No heartbroken exes I should know about?'

I looked up to find our server opening another mini bottle of red wine and dumping it directly into my glass. I did not stop her.

'No one who's likely to chase us up the country and demand to know your intentions. My job doesn't really lend itself to dating. "Sorry darling, I won't be home in time for dinner, I'm assisting Dr Nakhil with an EC-IC bypass and I'm covered in bits of brain" doesn't tend to go over very well.'

His face turned grim. 'Really glad I didn't order the haggis now.'

'See?' I pushed my plate away, no longer curious to know what it was made of. 'Not exactly the most romantic of professions.'

'Fine, tell me about something outside your job then. What's going on in your life?' Callum clarified, leaning forward, elbows on the table, his broad shoulders swelling under his shirt. 'I ought to know something about your life if we're going to pull this off.'

Cupping my hands around my stubby, stemless wine glass, I crossed my ankles under the table and tapped my toes inside my trainers.

'Nothing to know,' I told him. 'I work, I sleep and, if I'm lucky, I eat. If my eyes are open and I'm not in the hospital, I'm either reading, watching reality TV or staring at a blank wall.'

But he wasn't about to let me off that easily.

'What kind of books? I'm a big reader myself.'

'Anything, everything,' I replied. 'People leave all sorts in the hospital, we've got a very good library going. Fantasy, romance, thrillers, you name it, I've read it but please don't ask me to name the last thing I read because I literally cannot tell you.'

'If only we knew someone who understood how brains work who could explain such a phenomenon.'

'It's called the Yerkes-Dodson Law and it states that low arousal causes things not to be remembered in the first place and high arousal causes too much stress for them to be remembered, meaning we only retain things in circumstances of optimum arousal – and don't you dare start giggling because I just said arousal three times.'

'Four times,' Callum said, fighting a smile. 'And I'm sorry.'

'As you should be,' I sniffed, looking away so he couldn't see the corners of my mouth quirking upwards. 'You child.'

As the train raced along, Callum traced a finger around the rim of his glass, his broad shoulders moving with his breath, the blue, green and black checked pattern of his flannel shirt contrasting sharply against the aggressively bright lighting of the train carriage.

'Shouldn't we be worrying more about Caroline than me?' I suggested. 'All I know about her so far is she's an introvert with a passport who is passionate about furthering her professional education. Aside from nicking off to Paris to avoid your dad's birthday, what else have you told your family about her?'

'Nothing much.' He looked up as though there might be a more detailed answer printed on the ceiling. 'Nothing major that I can recall. Only that you're not on social media and you don't like having your picture taken.'

'Ahh, an intellectual,' I said with a sage nod. 'Note to self, stay off TikTok.'

'Other than that, just be yourself,' Callum said. 'I don't want to make it difficult for you.'

'Absolutely not!' I exclaimed. 'I'm going full method. The goal is to convince your parents they never want to see Caroline again and I am nothing if not goal-orientated. I am going to be the most passive-aggressive, antisocial, self-absorbed weirdo they could ever hope to meet.'

'Is that right?'

I nodded proudly. 'Caroline is monstrous. No eye contact, new toilet installed before my arrival, all the brown M&Ms removed from the bowl and twenty white kittens in the dressing room monstrous.'

Leaning back against his seat, Callum grinned. 'You're making me wonder what I see in her.'

'She's amazing in bed.'

My eyes popped open wide as I heard the words that had fallen out my mouth.

'Pretend I didn't say that,' I told him, my heart soaring when I saw our server coming out of the kitchen with dessert. Sugar. I needed sugar. And no more wine. 'Moving on, what do I need to know about wannabe pastry chef, Clapham resident and haggis connoisseur Callum McClay?'

'He's amazing in bed as well.'

The laugh that snorted out of me echoed around the carriage, attracting every pair of eyes within hearing distance. But more importantly, it drew a smile from Callum so big, I could see every single one of his straight, white teeth.

'Sticky toffee pudding,' the server said, sliding a plate down in front of me as I smothered my laughter with my napkin. 'And a cheese plate. Anything else I can get you?'

'More wine,' Callum answered immediately. 'Please. For the love of God.'

He picked up a chunk of what looked like cheddar and broke it in two, the pale cheese crumbling between his thumb and forefinger as he examined it before placing it in his mouth. It was indecent for a man to have such soft-looking lips but I couldn't stop myself from wishing I was that piece of cheese. As the thought passed through my mind, I pushed my glass of wine away. Clearly, I'd had more than enough.

'What else?' he mused, covering his mouth with his hand as he chewed then swallowed. 'I'm the same as you, work, sleep and eat. I like to play football when I've got time but I had to quit my Sunday League team because of work.'

'What about your friends?' I prompted. 'Family?'

He cocked his head to one side as he munched his cheese. 'You already know Dave.'

'And the less said about him the better. Family?'

'You've met Mum and Dad, both retired now. Mum worked at a charity shop in town, Dad was a farmer.'

'A farmer, really?'

A farmer meant a farm. A farm meant adorable

animals and freshly laid eggs and probably not baby goats at this time of year but a woman could dream. Callum, on the other hand, didn't look nearly as thrilled.

'Fourth-generation dairy farmer. Prepare yourself to hear what a disappointment I am because I don't want to live in the middle of nowhere up to my eyes in manure for the rest of my life.'

'Well, when you put it like that,' I replied, my fantasies fading away. 'You mentioned a sister?'

'Elsie, yes, two years younger, she works with Dad on the farm, lives in a cottage next door,' he said as he speared a second piece of cheese. 'And I've a younger brother, Rory. He's at university in Glasgow.'

'Studying what?'

'Alcohol poisoning, mostly. He's twenty-bloody-four but every year he changes his mind about what he wants to do and starts a new degree.'

'Sounds fun,' I said, picking up my spoon and digging into my dessert. It was so much better than the neeps and tatties. If there was such a thing as a shit sticky toffee pudding, I had yet to meet it.

'You don't need to worry about any of that.' Callum grabbed a grape and popped it in his mouth. 'Or at least heartless, callow Caroline doesn't. The less you know the better, I think. What about you? You said your mum and dad are away for Christmas?'

I took one more bite of my dessert, savouring the sweet sponge and custard. No point putting it off any longer, time to get the uncomfortable conversation out of the way.

'Dad is. With his wife. My mum died when I was thirteen.'

'Laura, I'm sorry.'

A momentary look of embarrassment I recognised very well coloured Callum's expression.

'Don't apologise, really.'

I set down at my spoon and tucked my hair back behind my ears, all at once thirteen again. 'It's been fifteen years, I'm OK. The worst part is having to tell people, you never know how they're going to react. You'd think we'd be better at talking about death as a species by now – spoiler alert, we're all going to have to deal with it at some point.'

Callum didn't answer right away. Instead he studied me with that same intent look I'd seen when I told him about my job.

'Is that why you're a doctor?' he asked.

Wannabe pastry chef, Clapham resident, haggis connoisseur and more insightful than I'd given him credit for.

'She died of an aneurysm,' I said, nodding. 'It was such a shock, I found it really hard to accept at the time. One of my teachers suggested reading up on the causes to help me make sense of everything. Learning how brains work, what causes neurological events . . . Losing my mum will never make sense but understanding the medical reasoning of *how* it happened did help.'

'And now you're helping other people.'

The look of quiet awe that widened his eyes and softened his smile only made me look away again.

'Do you want to try this?' I offered, thrusting the bowl across the table. 'It's very good.'

'No, thanks,' he held up a declining hand. 'I'm a self-confessed snob when it comes to pudding, can't help it, one of the perils of the job.'

'All the more for me,' I shrugged, scooping up another delicious mouthful. 'What did you do before you were accepted into culinary school?'

'Working in different kitchens, mostly,' he replied as I inhaled my dessert. 'Few bar jobs here and there, a couple of bakeries. I went wherever they would pay me to cook, ridiculous hours, worked for pennies.'

'You must really love it,' I said as I scraped my spoon along the bowl to secure the last precious bit of toffee-laced custard.

Callum beamed, genuine happiness shining through him.

'I do. I used to bake with my granny when I was a kid. There's nothing like putting something you made yourself in front of someone and watching them enjoy it. Take that pudding, for example, it's good, yeah?'

'There is no more pudding to take.' I presented my clean bowl. 'And yes, it was good. I will not hear a word against it.'

'But I could make you a sticky toffee pudding that would make you scream,' he said, leaning forward and lowering his voice in a way that made my toes curl inside my shoes. 'And don't get me started on proper custard. Double cream and egg yolks from the farm, my own personal stash of vanilla. One taste and you'd never go back.'

All of a sudden, my mouth was very dry.

'We should go over our plan,' I said, abruptly changing the subject as I abandoned my empty bowl and reached for my wine. 'We'll be there before you know it and I really should have the full lie of the land before we arrive.'

'Aye, right you are.' His smile fell away and his sensible, serious expression returned.

'We get into Inverness station tomorrow morning,' I started, waiting for his confirmatory nod. 'What's the drill after that?'

'Someone's picking us up at the station. Braewick's about an hour's drive from there.'

'Is it near Loch Ness?'

'Near enough.'

'Will we have time to visit?'

'No.'

'Have you ever seen the—'

'Don't,' he interrupted. 'Do not ask that question.'

I leaned all the way forward with bright eyes.

'Because you think it's a stupid question or because you have seen it?'

'Because it's a stupid question and I've been asked it more times than you've had hot dinners.'

'I think Caroline believes in the Loch Ness monster,' I said archly, attempting to toss my hair but only managing to get it snarled up in my chair's headrest. 'I think she'd probably really like to go and see the loch.'

'I thought we'd agreed Caroline would mostly be staying in her room and reading when we weren't showing my family what a terror she is?'

'Can't stay locked in a room for five whole days, now can I?' I bounced back. 'Surely there's time for a quick visit? So I can take a photo?'

The sigh that issued from Callum's lips was so weighted, you'd have thought I'd just asked him to slice open his abdomen and show me a kidney.

'I'll see what I can do,' he relented, elbows on the table, face in his hands.

'So, we arrive tomorrow,' I went on brightly, saving my questions about kilts and Highland cows for later.

'We're being picked up at the station, we get to the farm, then what?'

'Food, knowing my mother, then hopefully nothing. I've told them we'll be wanting to take it easy for the first day.'

'I probably didn't sleep well on the train,' I reasoned. 'On account of the night terrors.'

He pointed my way and dipped his chin in agreement. 'So, an easy afternoon then I'm taking you to the pub for dinner. After that, we'll work it out as we go.'

The train tilted slightly to the left, one of the grapes on his plate rolling away across the table. I cupped my hands to catch it as it made a break for freedom.

'Is this insane?' he asked as I dropped it back on the plate next to his barely touched pile of cheese. 'Can we really get away with this?'

'We can,' I replied with confidence. 'Trust me, I'm a doctor.'

He picked up his glass and tilted it from side to side, letting the deep ruby colour whirl up and coat the insides.

'Laura?'

'Callum?'

'Have I said thank you,' he asked, 'for doing this?'

'You don't have to,' I told him, reminding myself of all the reasons I'd suggested it in the first place: to go on a spontaneous adventure, to visit somewhere I'd never been before, to escape another miserable Christmas, to finally get some wear out of those over-priced Grenson boots. Nothing to do with the way my hair rose on the back of my neck as his gruff baritone scuffed the edges of every word that spilled over his lips.

'Tis the season,' I added before raising my glass. 'I do have one more question though.'

'What's that?'

'Are you going to eat the rest of that cheese?'

Callum laughed and I grinned, the sound warming me through like a crackling wood fire.

'Go for your life.' He pushed the plate across to me. 'The cheddar isn't half bad but the stilton leaves a lot to be desired.'

'I've got a feeling this is the beginning of a beautiful friendship,' I said as I tossed a sizeable chunk of acceptable cheddar into my mouth. 'Especially if you keep giving me your food.'

'Play your cards right and I'll make you that sticky toffee pudding,' he promised with a wink. 'Your life will never be the same.'

'Looking forward to it,' I replied, meeting his toast then taking a drink.

It was very much not a lie.

CHAPTER SEVEN

Whatever concerns I might've had about sharing a double bed on a moving train with a man I'd only met the day before were completely alleviated by two swigs of whisky, three glasses of red wine and the way Callum's eyes twinkled when the conductor came to tell us he was shutting down the club car for the night.

'Be quiet,' Callum ordered, shushing me dramatically. 'Everyone else is asleep.'

'No one is asleep,' I argued, pinballing down the carriage and bouncing off every door. 'This train is bouncing more than a guinea pig on a trampoline.'

'Have you ever seen a guinea pig on a trampoline?'

'Yes. Once. God rest its soul.'

'I have no further questions.'

He stopped outside our cabin and patted himself down for the key, exactly the same way his father had.

'Train gets in at eight forty-five,' he said, finally locating the key in the chest pocket of his corduroy trucker jacket, the sheepskin collar nestling against his jaw. 'They bring breakfast to the room at half seven so if we want to be up and awake by then, that gives us . . .'

'Seven whole hours to sleep,' I replied. 'That's *Sleeping Beauty* numbers for a doctor.'

'And a baker. I was at work by three a.m. for three years.'

'Poor you,' I said in a coddling voice. 'Did you have to hold surgical instruments still while your boss poked around inside someone's brain for five hours, blasting Coldplay over the stereo the entire time as well?'

He blanched, his pale skin turning somehow paler.

'Five hours of Coldplay?'

'Whoever is operating is in charge of the music,' I nodded. 'I've timed it: if you start the Eras Tour when you scrub in, you're wrapping up a cranioplasty right before they shoot the confetti at the end of "Karma".'

The miniscule scale of our cabin struck me all over again, the space shrinking in size when Callum joined me on what felt like the only open square foot of floor.

'I'll use the bathroom first, if that's OK?' he said, edging around the room to grab his bag from the bed. 'Brush my teeth, change into my PJs.'

A sudden vision of myself snipping the tags off my brand new red tartan pyjamas and very cleverly packing them on the very top of my suitcase popped into my head. Only it wasn't very clever because my suitcase was somewhere in the luggage carriage and I would not see it again until 8.45 in the morning.

'My PJs . . .' I groaned, slapping a hand against my face. 'I left them in my suitcase.'

'No worries, that's all right, not a problem,' Callum muttered, pawing through his bag, his face screwed up in concentration. 'You can borrow mine.'

'What will you sleep in?'

He pulled at his shirt then let the fabric spring back, tight around his chest.

'I've got a T-shirt under this I can sleep in.'

'Just a T-shirt? Like Winnie the Pooh?'

'I was planning to keep my boxers on but since you've painted such a beautiful image . . .' he replied with an eyeroll, handing me a wad of navy-coloured cotton. 'Mum buys me a pair every year. They are clean, I washed them especially.'

I held up the blue drawstring trousers and matching button-up shirt, measuring each item up against my five-foot-three frame. The bottoms were bigger than I was.

'Might be a bit on the roomy side,' he said with a frown.

'They're perfect, thank you,' I said, clutching them to me. Was I supposed to change in front of him or . . . ?

'I'm going to clean my teeth,' he announced, holding a toothbrush aloft like a tiny sceptre and backing into the bathroom. 'Back in a tick.'

The moment the door locked, I dove across the bed to my backpack and rooted out my phone. I hadn't seen this many unread text notifications since the time Joel sat next to Harry Styles in Polpo in Soho and there was nobody there to witness it. Making sense of his and Desi's messages as I scrolled back was like trying to read *War and Peace* backwards but the general gist seemed to be that Desi didn't like the look of Callum one little bit while Joel liked the look of him very much. It was hardly a surprise: he was very much Joel's type, six-foot-something, dark russet hair, pale white skin and prone to the occasional smouldering, the perfect man for anyone who had grown up on a daily dose of Edward Cullen.

Abandoning hope of making sense of their back and forth, I scrolled down to the most recent message, an all-caps plea from Desi to confirm I was still alive.

'Still wearing my own skin for now,' I muttered the words aloud as I typed, the added clarity needed for my wine-fogged mind. 'Going to bed, will text in the morning if alive.'

The phone bounced on the thin but firm mattress when I dropped it before hastily peeling off my jumper, the whirr of a tiny motor and a tap running buzzing through the bathroom door. Truly there would be no privacy in this cabin. Shucking off my jeans, T-shirt and jumper, I yanked the pyjama top over my head. I hadn't changed clothes so fast since year eight swimming lessons. The hem fell halfway down my thighs, the sleeves dangling way past the tips of my fingers. Swathed in soft, navy-coloured cotton, I inhaled deeply. Whatever Callum used to wash his clothes smelled divine, clean and fresh and cosy. I was still inhaling the fabric of the bottoms when the bathroom door clicked open.

'Are you sniffing my pyjamas?'

Callum stood in the open doorway like a backlit auburn-haired angel.

'Yes.' I hopped into the bottoms, pulling the drawstring tight around my waist then shuffling across the cabin, inches of excess fabric pooling over my feet. 'Are you done in there?'

'I am.'

He pressed himself back against the window to let me scoot past. 'You're sure you don't mind sharing the bed? I'm very happy to sleep on the floor.'

'No one is very happy to sleep on the floor,' I replied, gesturing at the very small space between us. 'Honestly, it's fine. Believe me when I tell you I've slept in worse situations than this. Junior doctors will sleep ten to a wheelie bin if it's the only option.'

'As long as you're sure.'

Perching on the edge of the bed, still in his trousers and T-shirt, he tested the mattress with one flat hand. 'Would you rather have the inside or the outside?'

'Outside. I've had wine and whisky and will almost certainly need to get up for a wee and I don't know why I said that out loud.'

Callum laughed as I shut myself in the bathroom. I furiously scrubbed at my teeth with the toothbrush I kept in my backpack, reminding myself of the other reason I wanted the outside of the bed. Just because I was sworn off romance until I was fully qualified didn't mean I'd signed up to celibacy. At least, I wasn't against the idea of sleeping with someone, as long as there was no prospect of mess or feelings, and even if feelings weren't a problem here, I couldn't think of anything messier than hooking up with my new landlord. The idea of being caught between his enormous body and the wall of the train, surging along the tracks, the constant rhythmic rocking . . . No, thank you. It wouldn't take much, the accidental brush of a hand, a catch of breath, red wine, one bad decision. I was trained to consider all outcomes in advance and the odds on this weren't worth the risk.

Callum was already under the covers when I came out of the bathroom, waiting until I slid under the thin sheets to turn out the light.

'I had fun tonight,' he said into the semi-darkness.

'You sound surprised.'

Even without the lights on, I could feel the smile in his voice. 'I didn't know what to expect. You're very easy to talk to.'

I punched my anaemic pillow and curled my arm underneath my head, keeping as much distance as I was able. His body ran hot, I could tell that from here. 'Good bedside nature is part of the job.'

'That must be it,' Callum replied. 'Does that mean our conversations are covered by the Hippocratic oath?'

'No, so don't tell me anything you don't want plastered all over the Fuck Callum McClay Facebook group.'

'You're joking but I'd be shocked if it doesn't exist.'

It wasn't quite dark enough in the cabin, the beige plastic recast in shades of grey as light leaked in from underneath the cabin door and all around the edges of the blind that covered the window.

'It's probably because I'm your fake girlfriend and you fake love me very much,' I reasoned. 'Caroline might be a lot of terrible things but she's also a pretty good listener.'

A low chuckle rumbled out of his chest, vibrating across the meagre mattress and into me.

'That must be it.'

'Or because you know it's not real,' I suggested, gripping the edge of the bed, my back to Callum. 'And this time next week, Caroline will be back in London, you'll be off to Paris and who knows when we'll even see each other again?'

'Who knows?' he said, the mattress shifting underneath me as he rolled over to face the wall. 'But at least this week will be a laugh.'

'Yes,' I agreed weakly. 'A real laugh.'

CHAPTER EIGHT

Like a true idiot, I'd always thought travelling overnight on a train would be romantic. Who wouldn't love being gently rocked back and forth, lulled to sleep by the chug of the engine, the rush of the rails?

Me. That's who.

For what felt like forever, I had tossed and turned on my six inches of mattress at the edge of the bed, too hot, then too cold, almost rolling across the cabin every time the train swept around a bend, which it did roughly eighteen thousand times between London and Scotland. According to my watch, time ticked by but I was almost positive it was moving more slowly than usual. That or I was trapped in some sort of too-tired purgatory, dehydrated from the whisky and wine and, whether I liked it or not, horny as hell. For all my talk about being able to sleep any*where*, I'd forgotten how difficult it was to sleep next to any*one*. Naturally, Callum passed out the moment he turned out the light. Eyes closed, arms above his head, dead to the world, and every time he moved, I was hyper aware of him, the heat that emanated from his body, the soft sighs issuing from his lips, the gentle nudges against my back each time he rolled over.

Eventually, right as it was almost time to wake up anyway, overwhelming exhaustion loosened my tight muscles and pulled me towards a fitful sleep, the room slipping away and dragging me down into relaxation. Until an arm slung itself over my torso, drawing my stiff body in towards a warm, supple one. Suddenly wide awake, I froze as Callum stirred, pressing against my back and curling in closer, one huge hand passively wrapping itself around my waist and making my skin tingle from head to toe. His breath was soft on my neck, making my hair dance with every exhale. Unfortunately, his breath was the only thing about him that was soft.

A low groan rumbled out of his body, sending shockwaves all the way through me and straight between my legs. Ripping my phone and its charger from out the wall, I shot out of bed and into the bathroom, where I slammed the door shut and locked it behind me. I was practically panting when I closed the toilet lid with a noisy clatter and crouched on the top like the floor was on fire. The tingling was an automatic physiological response, nothing but frisson. Blood vessels dilating, blood rushing to the surface of my skin, a perfectly understandable reaction to one body's physical closeness to another. My heavy breathing, dilated pupils and unexpectedly clenched thighs on the other hand . . .

My phone buzzed to life in my hand. Startled, I almost dropped it but managed to catch the tail end of the charging cable before it could clatter to the floor.

Banged him yet?

Of course it was Joel, an annoyingly chipper early

riser. Desi wouldn't see anything other than the insides of her eyelids for another two hours at least.

Don't ask why but we had to share bed . . . I typed furiously, still crouched on top of the toilet.

Just woke up, I added, **he's got a . . .**

Before I could complete the sentence, Joel replied with a barrage of GIFs: a rocket taking off, Pinocchio's nose growing and a skeleton shooting up straight to attention.

Not helpful but yes, I replied. **What should I do?**

Grind on him and see what happens, came Joel's helpful reply.

When I sent him a thumbs down, another three bubbles appeared.

Can you shuffle around and pop it in?

You have never had sex with a woman and it shows, I tapped out, listening for movement beyond the bathroom door. Was that Callum climbing out of bed or just another creak of the train? My phone vibrated in my hand again, this time signalling a phone call.

'Are you bouncing on it?' Joel asked, unnecessarily perky for 6.45 in the morning. 'Am I technically part of a threesome right now?'

'Yes, with me and the toilet,' I hissed. 'I'm hiding in the bathroom.'

'Sexy. Wait, no, opposite.'

'What am I supposed to do?' I asked in a panic. 'He's going to know, isn't he?'

'That he's got a hard-on? Yes, I expect so.'

'That *I* know he's got a hard-on!' I exploded as quietly as I could. 'He'll be mortified. I'm mortified. We haven't even got to Scotland yet and I'm already mortified. How am I going to get through the next five days?'

'Are you OK?' he asked. 'Is this bad?'

I considered the question before I answered.

'No, not bad,' I confessed. 'Just surprising.'

'Then as much as I hate to damage your fragile ego, it's not a big deal,' Joel drawled. 'He probably wakes up with a boner every day. The only difference between today and any other day is that you could've given him a hand with it and instead you're hiding in the bog like a mutant.'

I sat up straight, banging my head on something sharp behind me. The taps for the shower. The shower that hung directly over the toilet. This really was *not* the Orient Express.

'What's the problem? Why are you so bothered?'

I curled my toes around the toilet lid, phone hot against my ear.

'Because . . .' I began, struggling to finish the sentence, even though I didn't know why. 'Because I don't usually wake up with a penis sticking in my lower back?'

'Which is half your problem. You're being so weird. You've seen him naked, he's fit as fuck, and you're all right—'

'Oi.'

'You're supposed to be his girlfriend, aren't you? You should have a quick go on it just in case anyone asks you about his attributes.'

'We're spending Christmas with his parents, not going through a green card interview,' I reminded him. 'I can't imagine our sex life is going to come up that often. Can you at least try to be helpful?'

'Straight people are so boring,' Joel replied with a tut of disgust. 'Fine, this is what you want to hear. He's probably dying of shame right now and, odds are, he's going to pretend nothing ever happened. Is that better?'

Leaning my head to one side to avoid the tap, I closed my eyes and nodded.

'Much. Thank you.'

'At least that's what I'd do if I woke up in bed with a weirdo who went to hide in the toilets because I had a hard-on.'

'Stop helping now.'

'Your biggest problem is going to be explaining why you bolted into the lav and stayed locked in there so long. There's really only one reason I can think of.'

'Thanks, Joel, appreciate it, good chat.'

I ended the call with a particularly violent jab at the screen and all my embarrassment turned inwards. Joel had a point. Callum's erection didn't mean anything. The average healthy male could get a hard-on from walking into a doorknob at the right angle. I was a warm body in a soft bed and I'd completely overreacted. It was not like me at all.

Accepting the fact I couldn't hide in the loo forever, I held the phone back up to my ear and opened the door to see a slightly sheepish Callum sitting on the edge of the bed.

'OK, yeah, no, that's OK, I was awake anyway,' I said into my phone, rolling my eyes and pulling a face at my bunkmate. 'It's in the kitchen cupboard, top shelf. Call me back if you can't find it.'

'Anything wrong?' Callum asked when I ended the non-existent phone call and blew out a loud, braying sigh.

'Just Desi.'

I stretched my arms overhead in a show of relaxation until my too-big pyjama bottoms began to fall down and I had to grab them to avoid an inadvertent flashing disaster.

'Couldn't find the toaster.'

His eyebrows drew together, a quizzical look on his face.

'Didn't you tell me you were living with her?'

'Yes?'

'And she doesn't know where the toaster is in her own flat?'

I ran my tongue over my top teeth, eyes sliding over to the window as if an answer might pop out of the fields and hills as we whizzed by.

'Wouldn't know where her head was if it wasn't screwed on,' I offered. 'Useless is Desi.'

'Should I bother asking why she keeps the toaster on the top shelf of the kitchen cupboard?'

'Desi has a gluten intolerance. We try to keep the crumbs out of her way. Because of the intolerance.'

'So she needs the toaster because?'

There was no way he believed me. I didn't even sound as though I believed me. But at least neither of us were thinking about his penis any more. Or at least we weren't until I looked directly at his crotch and coloured up at once.

'Train's running on time,' Callum said brusquely, standing up and turning his back to me as he pulled his plaid flannel back on over his T-shirt. 'Breakfast should be here in half an hour unless you'd rather eat in the club car again.'

'Club car sounds good to me. Change of scenery and all that,' I replied, still clutching my phone in one hand and pyjama bottoms in the other. 'Why don't I meet you in there? Say in five minutes?'

He didn't need telling twice.

'Sounds like a plan.'

He opened the door, gave me a nod and then he was gone, door clattering closed behind him.

'Oh, Laura,' I muttered to myself as I dropped to my knees to recover my backpack from under the bed. 'So much for staying detached.'

Underneath the bed, right next to my bag, was a small square of worn, brown leather. A wallet. I opened it up to find the usual: credit cards, loyalty cards, a driving licence and, in a clear patched pocket on the other side, a photograph. It was Callum's wallet but he wasn't alone in the photo. His hair was much shorter than he wore it today, cropped almost to his skull, but his eyes were shining and he grinned at the camera in a way I really hadn't seen yet, carefree and unburdened. Pressed up against him, cheek to cheek, was a woman. Long blonde hair, crystal-clear green eyes, a flawless complexion. It had to be non-world-famous supermodel and donkey saviour, Shiv, supposedly out of his life but still in his wallet. They looked perfect together, utterly gorgeous, made for each other.

Clearing my throat, I tossed the wallet on the bed and went back to my bag, pulling out clothes and dressing quickly, a new and unexpected sense of frustration blossoming. If Callum didn't want to marry Shiv, if he was the one who broke up with her a whole year ago, why did he still have her photo in his wallet?

When searching for a diagnosis, I'd been taught to make a hypothesis then look at all the available evidence to prove or disprove it until I was left with the most likely result. Right now, all the information available to me pointed towards one incontrovertible truth. The photograph. His careful wording. The fact this stupidly hot man had remained single for an entire year and made up a fake girlfriend rather than find a real one.

'He never said he didn't *want* to marry her,' I whispered to myself, glancing down at the open wallet, a slender crease in the plastic pocket slicing the happy couple in two. 'Only that he wanted to decide when to propose.'

If I had to make an educated guess, I'd say there was at least a ninety percent chance Callum McClay was still in love with his ex-girlfriend.

And I didn't like that at all.

CHAPTER NINE

Scotland was cold.

It shouldn't have been a shock, the country didn't exactly advertise itself as a balmy, tropical destination, but I was not prepared for the bitter blast of frigid air that greeted me when I stepped off the train at Inverness. A gust of wind so strong it almost knocked me off my unprepared feet blew down the platform, and I cursed myself for choosing my adorable pink duffle coat rather than the practical puffer Desi tried to foist on me. A mental run-through of my packing confirmed I was going to be cold for the following five days unless I wore all my clothes at once.

I would be wearing all my clothes at once.

'All right?' Callum asked as he took custody of my suitcase from the porter.

'I'm freezing to death,' I replied, rubbing my hands together. 'I mean it, my blood is freezing in my veins.'

'For a doctor, you're very prone to hyperbole.'

'For a pastry chef, you're very prone to . . .'

He smirked as I watched my breath fog in the air in front of me.

'Prone to what?'

'I don't know,' I admitted. 'It's too cold for witty comebacks.'

'It's only going to get colder so get used to it.'

'Amazing, frostbite for Christmas,' I sulked, blowing on my hands. 'It's not like I need my fingers for my job or anything.'

'And it's not like you could've predicted it would be a wee bit chilly up here or anything.'

Pulling the collar of my coat up around my exposed neck, I gave him the filthiest look my frozen face could muster. With a tut and a sigh, he drew the scarf from around his neck, reaching over to wrap it around mine. But I jerked away as though he'd been planning to throttle me with it, leaving his arms outstretched, a look of confusion on his face. Slinging the scarf back around his neck, Callum produced our tickets from his pocket as I stalked off up the platform. Cool, calm, detached. Whatever that photo in his wallet meant to him, to me it was an explicit reminder to stay NFI. No feelings involved. I wasn't upset, I was annoyed. He should've told me he was still in love with his ex, or still had feelings for her or whatever it was that made him want her picture with him at all times.

'Who's picking us up?' I asked civilly. 'Your dad?'

'No, uh, it'll be Mal.'

He inserted my ticket into the barrier first, waited for me to pass through then did his own, pushing my case ahead of him.

'And Mal is?'

'He works for us. For my dad.'

'On the farm?'

'Sort of.'

Before I could dig any deeper, a short, stout, older man wearing a tweed three-piece suit appeared in front of us. No coat. No top layer whatsoever. I'd never felt like such a weakling in my life.

'Hullo, Cal, you wee shite!' he cheered, punching Callum hard in the arm. 'How are ye?'

'Ah, away wi ye, ye aul bampot, nae bad, yersen?'

I stared at the two of them, lost in the cloud of their rolling burrs.

'This must be the lovely Caroline.'

Mal held out his hand for my suitcase and Callum surrendered it without question.

'Caroline,' I confirmed with an enthusiastic nod. His eyebrows were spectacular. 'That's me.'

'Och, you're a bonnie one,' he beamed. 'Ye reet hen?'

'I'm a right hen?' I translated out loud, looking to Callum for confirmation who covered his mouth to stifle a laugh. 'Are you calling me a chicken? Because I'm wearing a coat? Because I know you live here and you're used to it but I can assure you it is objectively *very* cold and—'

'Cal, ye total bawbag. Ye havnae educated your wifey in the local dialect?' he replied, pairing what I assumed was an insult with a look even filthier than mine when Callum shrugged in response. 'Sorry, darlin', I'll go slow. I was only asking how you are. Is this your first time up to the Highlands?'

'It is,' I confirmed gratefully as he put his arm around my shoulders and steered me through the growing crowd of travellers.

'First time to Scotland?'

I shook my head. 'I've been to Edinburgh before.'

'Aye, then it is your first time to Scotland,' he replied,

still wearing a cheerful smile even as we exited the station and the arctic blast almost killed me on the spot.

He cackled as the boot popped open then rose slowly towards the still dark sky. It hadn't occurred to me that the sun wouldn't come up until later this far north. It was almost nine a.m. and still practically pitch black.

'Nice car,' I said to Callum, taking in the new car smell as I slid into the backseat.

'Impractical car,' he replied. 'Dad's retirement present to himself. Mal drives it more than he does.'

'Too right he does,' Mal confirmed. 'Homeward bound, hen, make yersen comfy.'

'Will do,' I replied, closing my eyes and sighing happily when he shut the driver's side door and turned on the seat warmers. At least if I was going to feel like an idiot, I wouldn't freeze to death at the same time. It was better than nothing.

Following our drive on my Maps app, I couldn't help but feel apprehensive when Mal turned north and kept on going. The further we went, the colder it got, the temperature dropping into minus figures, but I was soon distracted from the sub zero numbers by some of the most beautiful scenery I'd ever laid eyes on. Rolling hills that ebbed and flowed like the tides, towering trees and endless stretches of perfectly still water that began to peel away the protective layer that life in the city had wrapped around me.

I hadn't travelled much, Dad preferred to stay close to home after Mum died, at least until he remarried, and I'd gone straight from school to university to work, which hadn't left time for exploring the world. And as the hospital's lovely HR director pointed out when she informed me I was taking an extended leave of absence over Christmas whether I liked it or not, I really hadn't taken any holiday at all since I started the neurosurgery programme. My rare days off were spent asleep in bed or practically comatose on the sofa, and even if I'd known how stunningly beautiful the Scottish countryside was, only a few hours away, I still wouldn't have been moved to investigate it on my own, not when I could be studying for my upcoming exams or catching up on research papers.

As we crested another hill, crossing over a broad river, the sun began to rise, the sky shifting shades from deep and murky grey to a more promising wispy white, hints of blue appearing from time to time but never fully committing. But it wasn't only the natural beauty outside the car that caught my attention. Callum's entire demeanour had changed since we got off the train. He was looser, more relaxed, his broad shoulders heaving laughter that came readily, almost every time Mal opened his mouth. As the sun climbed up the horizon, keeping low but brightening the day as best it could, his profile sharpened against the sky and I couldn't stop stealing glances, following the straight line of his nose, the angular cut of his jaw, the swell of his bottom lip. He glanced over his shoulder, smiling when he caught my eye, and I jumped as though he could read my mind, knocking the back of my head against the padded leather headrest.

'All right?' he asked. 'Caroline?'

'Fine,' I replied. 'Babe.'

With a smile and a wink, he looked away and I pressed a burning cheek against the freezing glass of the window. NFI. NFI. NFI.

'Your mother has every minute of every day planned,' Mal said, running through our itinerary as he floored it up the A9. 'Hope you came with an empty stomach because I've seen Lizzie's menus and you'll no' go hungry while you're here.'

'Your mum has planned menus?' I repeated, meeting Callum's eyes in the rearview mirror. 'Is that not all a bit much?'

'You did meet his mother, did you not?' Mal replied. 'No such thing as too much for the lady of the manor.'

'He's exaggerating,' Callum said as the older man laughed. 'Take every word out of his mouth with a grain of salt.'

Lady of the manor? Only a figure of speech, surely. I took out my phone to text Desi and Joel for support but there was no service, not even one bar. Even the map had gone blank, nothing left but a tiny blue dot moving up a featureless landscape.

'It's just her way, don't bother about aul' Lizzie,' Mal went on. 'She likes things done a certain way but she always warms up once she's got a drink or two in her.'

'Have you seen Elsie?' Callum asked as I leaned all the way across the backseat, futilely waving my phone around.

'Speaking of people who need to warm up . . .' he replied with a grimace. 'I see Elsie every bloody day, thanks to you. Best be warned before you get home, she's not your biggest fan right now.'

Callum's mouth curved into a bitter smile. 'Was she ever?'

'Aye, fair point. At least I always know where your sister is, unlike your brother. Your ma says he should be arriving tonight so I wouldn't expect to see him before Christmas Day. That boy wouldn't know how to get anywhere on time even if his life depended on it. It'll be a miracle if he arrives before the New Year if you ask me.'

'*Did* anyone ask you?'

'Never stopped me sharing my opinion before.'

Mal's laughter filled the car, the rough-hewn sound smoothing the edges off my nerves.

'What I do know is, we're all very excited to meet Miss Caroline here,' he said, his crinkly eyes meeting mine in the rearview mirror. 'The way Derek was carrying on when they got home yesterday, and your poor ma, set to sorting out the house as though we're expecting another royal visit.'

'Because that went so well the first time?'

'You're joking,' I said when Mal only chuckled in response. 'Tell me you're joking.'

'It was one day, twenty years ago, and they only stayed for a minute,' Callum replied.

'What do the two of you talk about?' Mal asked as I blanched whiter than a sheet of A4. 'Has he told you nothing about the family at all?'

Callum opened the glove box and pulled out an open bag of wine gums he seemed to have been expecting, rooting through for a red one before holding the bag out for me.

'I told her all the important things. That's why I never mentioned you.'

For a brief second, one tiny black bar appeared in the corner of the screen and a little red circle appeared over the text icon, fifteen messages awaiting my attention. But by the time my thumb flew across the screen to open it, the bar was gone and the messages had not downloaded. I was on my own.

'You're a brave girl, venturing into the lair of the beast without knowing what you're in for,' Mal intoned as we pulled off the wider road and onto a narrow one, the railings disappearing, replaced by bushes and bracken. 'And at Christmas of all times of year.'

'If you're trying to scare me, you're doing a good job,' I replied, slipping my useless phone back in my bag while Mal dug into the bag of sweets and stuffed his cheeks full, padding out his smiling face like a particularly chuffed hamster.

'Ignore him,' Callum instructed. 'Everything is going to be fine.'

'Famous last words,' I replied, echoing his own line from the night before. 'Famous last words.'

A little over an hour after we left Inverness, Mal interrupted his own running commentary to announce that we were almost home.

'It's so pretty!' I said as we turned onto a side road, passing through a green farm gate that opened automatically as we approached. 'Are those your sheep?'

'Yes.' Callum's voice was a flat monotone. 'They're our sheep. Just like the others and the ones before that.'

'I don't know, do I?' I said, pouting and indignant. 'You said your dad was a dairy farmer, not a sheep farmer. I've never been on a farm before, how am I supposed to know you can have both?'

Mal said nothing but the lines that bracketed his mouth ticked with amusement. Callum looked less entertained, twisting against his seatbelt to look at me.

'What?' I said, tossing my hair over my shoulder as

best I could while tethered to the backseat. 'Caroline isn't a mind reader.'

'But she does like to refer to herself in the third person?' he commented as we crawled up the road so as not to disturb his woolly neighbours. 'Yes, we've got sheep and cows and chickens and a couple of horses and do we still have the goats, Mal?'

'Aye, there's a handful of goats,' the older man nodded. 'And your sister took in two rabbits from a kiddie who was moving away so now we've about five hundred of the wee sods hopping around the place. Puts me in the mood for rabbit stew.'

In front of us, a quaint farmhouse came into view. A limestone cottage with a pitched roof and two chimney stacks, both of them smoking. The white window frames matched the neatly painted pipes and guttering, and each of the four panes of glass at every window glinted in the sun. It was like something out of a storybook, with old chimney pots on either side of the door full of deep purple winter pansies.

'It's exactly how I imagined it,' I breathed, forgetting my role for a moment. 'So beautiful.'

'Thank you,' Mal dipped his chin as he continued driving, leaving the farmhouse behind. 'I do my best to keep her in good shape.'

Turning around, I watched the cottage disappear out the back window and the car began to climb up a steep hill.

'I can't help but notice we're not stopping,' I said, one hand grasping each of their seats. 'Why aren't we stopping?'

'That's Sleagh Cottage, where Mal lives.' Callum folded the top of the bag of wine gums over and over until there was nothing left to fold. 'Mum and Dad are at the top of the hill.'

'Right,' I nodded, sitting back. 'I did think it was a bit small for five of you.'

'Then how does this suit?' Mal asked as we crested the hill, another larger, grander building coming into view. It was beyond stunning. A sprawling estate, etched majestically against the morning sky, the ancient stone walls, their lines softened by time and the elements, arched wooden doors marked with iron struts and studs, and an honest to goodness tower stretching up until it almost touched the low clouds.

'Dear old Balmaclay, home to the McClay family since 1786 with plenty of room for five or more.'

'Oh my God, it's a castle,' I gasped as Callum's childhood home loomed ahead. 'How did you not tell me you grew up in an actual castle?'

'It's not a castle,' he argued as Mal smothered yet another laugh. 'It's a house.'

'No, it's five houses joined together,' I corrected. 'With a *tower* and, bloody hell, is that a moat?'

'It's a pond.'

'A pond that just so happens to go around your house and has a bridge we have to drive over to get to the front door?'

'We didn't dig it ourselves and it doesn't go all the way around,' Callum replied stiffly. 'It's a naturally occurring pond.'

'I think if you wanted to call it a moat, you could,' Mal offered helpfully.

'You live in a castle,' I whispered, digging my hands deep into my pockets and, not for the first time that day, wondering exactly what I'd got myself into.

CHAPTER TEN

'Here we are, everybody out,' Mal cheered when he brought the car to a halt on the gravel in front of Balmaclay's front door. Its huge double front door and the stone staircase that led up to it.

Unclipping my seatbelt, I let myself out, the sheer scale of the building in front of me knocking the air from my lungs. My childhood home was a 1960s semi, three-up, three-down, with a garage and a greenhouse and just enough of a back garden for my dad to send me out to play every day in the summer holidays. As far as I was concerned, this was a castle – whatever Callum claimed. A sprawling stone structure, rooftops rising and falling, peaking in a four-storey tower, complete with a fairytale turret. The walls of Balmaclay were almost the exact same shade of grey as the mid-winter sky and veins of deep red ivy wrapped their way all around the building, breathing life into the centuries-old home. Beyond the house were tall trees, a far-reaching loch and endless mountains, cast in romantic shadows and stretching up to meet the clouds themselves. I couldn't speak, I could barely breathe. It was all too beautiful for words. Shiv's dedication to becoming Mrs Callum McClay made even more sense now. Who wouldn't want to live in a place like this? Other than Callum, supposedly.

'On a scale of one to Jeff Bezos, how rich are you?' I asked as Mal and the car rolled away.

'Not me, my family.'

'Exactly what a rich person would say.'

I took a step back to better take in the view, only remembering about the alleged pond when I turned and saw it right behind me. If I fell in I would freeze to death in an instant.

'I don't take money from my parents,' Callum said. 'My grandfather left me an inheritance I used to buy the flat, that's it.'

'Sounds like a you problem,' I told him, still shaking my head in awe. 'You need to lower my rent.'

'The rent you're not even paying for the first month?'

Tearing my eyes away from the house, I looked over to see him smiling.

'We're not struggling to rub two coppers together but there's no Scrooge McDuck room full of gold coins or anything like that,' he explained, picking up my suitcase and starting for the front door. 'The farm doesn't bring in half of what it used to and keeping a place like this going? Total money pit. If it's not the windows, it's the roof, if it's not the roof, it's the heating, if it's not the heating it's structural damage and the only person qualified to fix it costs five grand a day.' He gestured to the fairytale in front of me as though he saw nothing but a burden. 'The entire Campbell wing was closed for the best part of fifty years until Mum scraped the money together to restore it. Every penny we ever had, every penny they ever made, goes back into Balmaclay.'

'We'll come back to the fact your childhood home has wings in a minute,' I promised, holding back as he mounted the steps. 'But before we go in is there anything else I should know?'

His eyes slid over to the left, pouting mouth pulled to the right as he wracked his brains.

'Nothing I can think of.'

If I hadn't found a photo of his ex in his wallet and literally just discovered he'd grown up in a castle on the banks of a loch, I might've had more faith in his answer, but there wasn't enough time to press for more details. A woman's voice echoed from inside the house and his spine stiffened.

'Ready, Caroline?' Callum asked, glancing my way.

'Ready, babe,' I replied with a saccharine smile. 'They're going to hate my guts.'

'That's my girl.'

A mixture of anticipation, excitement and dread churned in the pit of my stomach as I replayed my mantra for the week. WWDKD? What would Desi Kaplan do?

The doors flew open with theatrical flair.

'Callum, Caroline, right on time!'

Mal had not been wrong. Lizzie McClay was every inch the lady of the manor, even more put together than she had been two days before, when she was, to be fair, standing in her son's living room, trying to pretend he wasn't stark bollock naked. Another silk scarf was fastened around her graceful neck, pinned with an antique-looking gold brooch, her short greying blonde hair swept back from her face to display high patrician cheekbones. A lifetime in the Highlands had worn away her hardest edges, softening the sharpest angles and etching the fine lines around her eyes and mouth that disappeared when she stopped smiling.

And she stopped smiling the moment she laid eyes on me.

'Here you are, the two of you.' She ushered us inside and I followed gratefully, chilled through to the bone. 'I half thought you would change your mind, Caroline, given such short notice.'

'Couldn't let Callum down, Mrs McClay,' I said, wrinkling my nose. 'Even if it did cock up all my plans.'

'Quite,' she replied without emotion. 'How was your journey?'

'Terrible. Felt like I was going to throw up the whole way. Might still if I'm honest.'

'Caroline gets travel sick,' Callum said when his mother paled. 'That's one of the reasons we haven't been up to visit yet.'

'But not too sick to go to Paris in the summer?'

'Well, no, but that was *Paris*,' I said. 'Not . . . whatever this is.'

The tiny squeak that emitted from her throat confirmed I'd nailed my thinly veiled insult but, the truth was, her home was incredible. 'Foyer' was not nearly a grand enough word for the room I found myself in. Twice as high as the ceilings in a normal house, the stone floors were covered by richly coloured rugs, the walls painted a warm ochre and dotted with paintings that could not possibly have been created in this century or the last, and behind Mrs McClay was a grand staircase, wooden banister polished to a high shine and curving upwards to a balcony that led off in opposite directions. But most impressive of all was the centrepiece. Right between the two staircases stood the most magnificent Christmas tree I had ever laid eyes on. It was so tall, I had to crane my head backwards to see the star on the top, and decorated with soft white lights and tasteful silver-toned ornaments. Even a certified Grinch like me couldn't help but be impressed.

'Look at your tree,' I breathed, trying to recall how long it took to cause permanent nerve damage through compressed cervical vertebrae since it appeared I would be spending the entire week gawking up at enormous, gorgeous things.

'Do you like it?' Callum's mother asked, warming up a fraction. 'I love to decorate at Christmas but the boys never cared much and Elsie always says I've gone over the top.'

'Not at all, Mrs McClay. It's perfect.'

'Thank you,' she replied, touching my wrist. 'And, please, call me Lizzie.'

Callum draped a solid arm over my shoulders and squeezed my upper arm, bringing me back to the moment. Shit. One look at a shiny tree and I'd already forgotten I was supposed to be an arsehole.

'I mean, it's not how I would decorate but you've done what you can,' I said, reappraising the beautiful tree through Caroline's eyes. '*Lizzie*.'

'You know what? I'd love to jump in the shower before we do anything else,' Callum said before his mother could reply. 'The one on the train wasn't up to much and I could do with changing my clothes.'

'Aye, you look like you've been dragged through a hedge backwards,' Lizzie replied before adding, 'Cal that is. Not you, Caroline, dear.'

And we were back on track. I knew a passive aggressive woman when I heard one and, clearly, I was dealing with a pro.

'Right-o,' she said to Callum with a smile. 'You're in your room and Caroline has the one next door. On account of her night terrors.'

I wrinkled up my nose in a condescending smirk and Lizzie looked away. Another point to me.

'Where's Dad?' Callum asked, looking around the empty foyer.

'You know your dad, always busy,' she replied vaguely. 'I'd better go and check on the food, Fi's cooking up a storm. I know you said you wanted an easy day so it's an early lunch then we'll leave you to your own devices. You go and get settled in, I'll call when it's ready.'

'Better not be too long,' I said a shade too loudly as Callum guided me up the staircase, leaving his mother fuming in the foyer. 'The food on the train was inedible. I'm bloody starving.'

'And the Oscar goes to,' he whispered in my ear. 'Well done, very impressive.'

'Probably because I'm not acting,' I muttered back over the sound of my rumbling stomach. 'If we're not fed inside fifteen minutes I'm going to eat you.'

The sound of his laughter bounced off the stone walls of the foyer, echoing behind us all the way upstairs.

No matter how much Callum insisted otherwise, I simply could not accept that normal people, everyday human beings who blew their noses and sometimes put their pyjamas on the wrong way round on the first try, lived in a home like this.

'There are tons of places like Balmaclay in Scotland,' he said, two steps ahead of me as I dawdled behind, taking everything in. 'It's not that big of a deal.'

The portraits of his ancestors glowering down at me with reproachful glares.

'No,' I said. 'I'm afraid it is quite a big deal.'

'If you've changed your mind, there's still time to back out. I can get Mal to drive you back to the station, put you on the next train back to London.'

'No one said anything about changing their mind,' I replied after a quick glance registered his panic. 'Look, I'm not going to lie, the castle – sorry – the house was a bit of a surprise but I said I'd help you and I will. Obscenely rich people have problems too, right?'

'We're not obscenely—'

'But this is your last chance to tell me,' I said as he ran an exasperated hand over his face. 'Is there anything else at all I should know? Like, is someone suddenly going to announce a traditional Christmas Eve hunting party? Is Claudia going to pop up and announce I'm actually starring in a new series of *The Traitors*?'

'As I said before, nothing I can think of.'

'And there's nothing else I need to know about your personal situation?'

Boring holes into his soul, I willed him to bring up his ex. I just needed to know. I just needed to hear him say it.

Callum stopped in front of a dark wood door and turned the brass doorknob.

'This is your room,' he said, opening the door and changing the subject. 'After you.'

'I'm not leaving,' I replied, changing it right back as I sailed blindly into the bedroom. 'If there's anything else you want to tell me, you can. Professionally speaking, it's always better to disclose all information, get everything out on the table up front so we can address everything head on and oh my God look at this place.'

It was a haven. Soft cream rugs on top of dark floorboards, delicate floral wallpaper and exquisite pieces of antique furniture, all arranged around the four-poster canopy bed and a tiled fireplace that was already lit. The flames danced, crackling happily, and filling the room with the most welcoming glow.

'I'm definitely not leaving,' I declared as I took off my coat and hung it carefully on the coat rack by the door. 'I mean I'm not leaving ever. Tell your mum I'm moving in, I'll have Desi send on my things.'

Outside the enormous bay windows, I had an unobstructed view of the garden, a neatly kept lawn, dotted with trees and lined with flowerbeds, and beyond that, as breathtaking a sight as you could ever hope to see. A still and steady body of water, reflecting the December sky as it wended its way out of sight to the north and the south. I felt as though I'd wandered into a fantasy novel. Balmaclay was the last home at the end of the world and I was a lost girl in an unknown realm, trapped with a mysterious stranger.

'Have you ever read a book called *A Court of Thorns and Roses*?' I asked Callum, glimpsing his dark hair, brooding eyes and broad shoulders out of the corner of my eye.

'No?'

'Then never mind,' I replied, putting unhelpful thoughts out of my mind. 'This is all so beautiful.'

'I suppose. I imagine you'd feel different if you'd

spent nineteen years here, dying to get away. To me it feels like a trap.'

'A trap with snacks,' I said, pointing at a tray on the bedside table stacked with Tunnock's Teacakes. Anything I'd ever thought about Lizzie McClay before this moment was completely reversed, she was my favourite person in the entire world.

'I wouldn't fill up if I were you, they don't know the meaning of a light lunch here.'

'Fill up? What is this completely foreign concept?'

The corners of Callum's eyes crinkled with a smile.

'I'm glad you like Balmaclay. The whole place has me feeling claustrophobic.'

'Then you must be out of your mind,' I said. 'because it's literally massive.'

'Is that your professional opinion?'

'I'm training to be a neurosurgeon, not a psychiatrist,' I reminded him as I tore into a teacake. 'And I'm officially off the clock this week. Please only come to me with massage-related enquiries and don't go out of your way to bother with those because I've never given a massage in my life.'

'Never?' He looked surprised.

Through a mouthful of chocolatey goodness, I scrunched up my face and shrugged.

'Doesn't come up much during brain surgery.'

'I'd hope not. But not even . . . in your personal life?'

The subtext slowly became text.

'I'm not really a personal massage kind of girl,' I said, my words stilted. 'That seems like more of a relationship thing.'

'And that's bad because?'

'Because I don't have time for relationships,' I replied,

very ready to end the conversation. 'Sorry, what time do you think food will be ready?'

Tearing curious eyes from my scarlet face, Callum checked the time on his phone.

'Knowing Mum, I'm sure it was ready the minute we walked through the door. How long do you need?'

The only thing I needed was some alone time.

'Long enough to shower and change,' I told him, giving myself a desultory sniff. 'I can't go down in this state.'

'Why not?' he asked. 'You're not trying to impress anyone, remember?'

'New plan. I charm your mum and dad, they disinherit you and adopt me.'

'How about we get through the family feed first then see how you feel,' Callum suggested, tickling my ears with a low chuckle. He pointed to a white-painted door on the other side of the room. 'You've got the en suite, through there, and I'm next door if you need anything. Otherwise I'll knock for you at . . .' He looked down at a particularly lovely leather-strapped watch I hadn't noticed before. 'Half-Eleven?'

After a sleepless night, not nearly enough coffee and a distinct lack of sunlight, I had no idea what time it was but I was fairly used to operating in high-pressure situations under those exact circumstances, and so I agreed with a disorientated nod. Callum cocked his head to one side, a concerned half-smile on his face.

'You sure you're good?'

'Never been better,' I lied, holding my breath until he looked away. 'Look at this place, it's heaven.'

'Then I'll be back in a bit,' he relented, heading for the door. 'And we'll get this show on the road.'

CHAPTER ELEVEN

Forty-five minutes would normally be more than enough time for me to get ready for anything. Years spent on call at the hospital meant I could function on very little sleep and had my ready-to-go routine down to a five-minute art but, somehow, I'd lost more than half an hour in the hot, steamy shower, luxuriating in the fancy shampoos and shower gels in a way I never allowed myself at home. When Callum knocked on my bedroom door, I was still running around in my underwear, trying to choose between two of my more reliable outfits: jeans and a jumper or a skirt and a shirt. One of the benefits of wearing scrubs was not having to care too much about your day-to-day clothes. Without my professional camouflage, I felt exposed.

'I can't believe I'm going down with wet hair,' I seethed, furious with myself as I followed Callum down the corridor in my mismatched skirt and jumper combo 'Your mother is going to think I'm a monster.'

'Good. They're not supposed to like you, remember?'

'Not going to be a problem,' I replied. 'I thought you

might be wearing a kilt. Jeans and T-shirt doesn't feel very Scotsman.'

He looked back at me over his shoulder. 'Say more things like that and you'll have no problem offending them.'

'Don't worry, I'm fully armed with offensive stereotypes,' I assured him. 'Worst comes to the worst, I'll pull out my *Braveheart* impression and we'll have this whole plot wrapped up and put to bed before Christmas Eve.'

'I was thinking,' Callum began as we passed through the grand foyer, the tree still sparkling beautifully. 'We should have a code word. In case you need an out.'

I raised an eyebrow. 'Such as?'

'It needs to be something specific,' he went on as we walked down a long hallway lined with windows, 'that you wouldn't normally use in everyday conversation so I'll know what you mean when you use it.'

Not a code word, a safe word. He was suggesting we needed a safe word.

'OK, you pick one,' I told him, absolutely not flashing back to every single spicy novel I'd ever read. Callum bobbed his head in time with his steps.

'Mackerel?' he offered.

'Mackerel?' I was outraged. 'What about me makes you think about mackerel?'

'Nothing! It was the first thing that came into my head! You choose one.'

'How about anastomosis?' I said. 'That's a fun word.'

'For you maybe,' he replied. 'What does it even mean?'

'In layman's terms, joining together two previously unconnected structures. Like, nerves or blood vessels.'

Callum considered then shook his head. 'Thank you

for breaking it down to a layman. Oddly sweet but no. If you can't say it after two drinks, it's too complicated.'

The end of the corridor was only a few steps away, a grand pair of double doors concealing what sounded like an awful lot of activity.

'Tamagotchi,' I suggested.

'Claymore,' Callum returned.

'Bombadil.'

'Épassir.'

'Justin Bieber.'

'Bungalow.'

'Smorgasbord.'

'Batholith.'

'Ooh, that's a good one,' I replied. 'What does it mean?'

'I can't remember,' Callum admitted. 'But I learned it for my Geography A level.'

'Did you pass?'

'Not well.'

'Then let's go with something else,' I said. 'Narwhal.'

'Narwhal?' Callum repeated.

'Narwhal,' I confirmed. 'Unicorn of the sea. Who doesn't love a narwhal?'

'Narwhal it is,' he agreed. 'If you feel like you want to get out of a situation, a conversation, whatever, just narwhal me.'

'Possibly should've suggested a word that worked itself into conversation more easily,' I said with a frown.

'Hey, it's your safe word, not mine.'

Callum opened the door to the dining room before I could reply, took my hand and pulled me inside, two pink spots high on my cheeks.

The dining room was formal and elegant, fancy wallpaper on the walls, more antique furniture, and another Christmas tree, a little bit smaller than the one in the foyer but still impressive, tucked away in a corner. Sitting at the head of the kind of dining table you'd expect to be covered in piles of fruit and an entire roasted pig, was a beaming Derek McClay, and beside him, Lizzie stared at me in a rather pinched way.

'I thought you'd got lost,' Derek declared without moving to stand. 'Can you bloody sit down so your mother will let me eat? I'm dying of starvation over here.'

Judging by the neat little pot belly that tested the strength of his shirt buttons, this was factually untrue.

'Did you not find the hairdryer, Caroline?' Lizzie asked, half-rising out of her chair. 'I'm sure there's one in the wardrobe.'

'There is, I saw it, please don't get up,' I insisted, immediately anxious to have caused distress. The only thing stopping me from running back to my room was Callum pulling out my chair and gently pressing on my shoulder until I sat. I was not Laura. I was Caroline. Caroline didn't give two shits about Lizzie's concerns.

'Because, um, I don't use a hairdryer. I hate them.'

I glanced at Callum who inclined his chin in approval as he took the seat across from me.

'They're bad for the environment?' I added. 'And climate change? And sea levels?'

'Is that so?' Derek stood as his wife sat and reached over to pour me a glass of water. 'See, there Elizabeth, you learn something new every day.'

'I'll make sure it's gone before you get back to your room,' Callum said, giving my hand a pat. 'Don't give it another thought.'

'If you'd told me ahead of time I would've taken care of it,' a humbled Lizzie admonished her son. 'Is there anything else you need?'

Nodding, I shook a starched linen napkin onto my lap. 'If I could get the WiFi password, that would be amazing. There's literally no reception up here, I don't know how you survive. My phone must think I've had my hands chopped off.'

Both of his parents stared at me, bewildered.

'Your phone?' Lizzie gave a terse smile. 'But Callum said you didn't have one.'

'I'm sure he didn't,' I replied, staring daggers across the table. 'Because that would be completely insane. Everybody has a phone.'

'She has a flip phone for emergencies,' Callum explained to his mother, barely missing a beat. 'She doesn't have a smartphone. Caroline doesn't believe in social media.'

I nodded slowly. He had told me that, the social media bit at least. I quietly praised past me for leaving my iPhone back in the room.

'It's destroying society,' I confirmed, trying to recall exactly what Joel had said the last time he deleted TikTok from his phone before putting it back three minutes later when he couldn't find his crush on Instagram. 'Turns people into mindless zombies with no opinions of their own.'

'Lizzie loves a good dig around Facebook, don't you? Likes to keep an eye on what everyone else is up to.' Derek reached across the table for a bottle of wine, corkscrew in the other hand. At eleven forty-five in the morning. A man after my own Christmas holiday heart.

'He says it like he hasn't got his phone attached to his hand around the clock,' she tutted. 'I'm in full agreement with Caroline. We should have a phone-free Christmas starting now, how about that?'

Derek looked horrified.

'But what about Nimbus?! They're taking him up to his grandmum's for the holidays, they've made him a wee Christmas jumper and everything. You know he's never been on a plane before.'

'You'll survive one week without watching a stranger halfway around the world torture their cat for views,' Lizzie said in a clipped voice. 'What do you think, Callum? No phones while you're home, concentrate on some quality family time. Especially since we've seen so little of you this year.'

The corner of his left eye twitched. 'Sounds good to me, Mum.'

My eyes slid from Derek to Lizzie to Callum. It was impossible to say which of them looked the most annoyed. Five minutes in and Mission: Cock Up Christmas was going pretty well.

A door at the far end of the dining room opened and a bright-eyed older woman in a well-loved white apron backed in, an enormous platter of food in her arms.

'Would you look at that, ye havenae starved,' she trilled, placing it in the centre of the table with a flourish. Roast beef, roast potatoes, carrots, parsnips and Yorkshire puddings. I'd been expecting a sandwich and a cup of tea. My mouth began to water to the point I wondered whether it would be out of order to ask for a bib.

'Callum, son, good to see you at bloody last.' She squished his head against her body, muffling his response and roughing up his hair into the bargain. 'Mal got you back in one piece?'

'Just about.' He grinned up at her when she released him, his hair fluffed up in a staticky halo. 'Fi, this is Caroline. Caroline, this is Fiona, Mal's wife.'

'If that's the only thing I've got going for me after all these years, I should ask you to take me out the back and shoot me like a lame horse.' She wiped her hand on her apron then thrust it in my direction. 'Pleased to meet you, hen. Glad to see someone has taken up with this numpty despite his being such an ugly wee shite.'

I replied with the saddest, slipperiest handshake known to man.

'Technically, Fi's the housekeeper,' Lizzie said as Fiona pulled her hand away in horror. 'But she's really part of the family.'

'But they still have to pay me so, really, I'm doing better than the rest of them,' she replied. 'If you need anything while you're here, you can always come to me. Derek and Cal are about as much use as a one-legged man in an arse-kicking contest. Excuse me while I go and get your lunch.'

'Mine?' I leaned across to Callum when she scuttled back into the kitchen. 'Is this supposed to be all yours?'

'We've done our best to accommodate your dietary restrictions.' Lizzie's mouth twisted into an uncertain line. 'Maybe now the family chef is home, he'll be able to help Fiona with some recipes.'

Something flashed between the mother and son, a dark look from Callum, a sniff from Lizzie. Even Derek paused in his mission to open the bottle of wine.

'Here you go,' Fiona sang as she returned carrying a

single, smaller plate. 'Now, I'm no expert in vegan cookery but there's no meat, no dairy, no eggs.'

As she put the plate down in front of me, Derek stared in my direction as though they'd just unveiled a new fifth horseman of the apocalypse: war, death, famine, pestilence and veganism.

'No meat, no dairy, no eggs, no taste.' He punctuated the sentence with the pop of a cork. 'No offence, Caroline, love, but I never thought I'd see the day my son brought a vegan into this house.'

A vegan.

I glared at Callum. This was definitely new information.

'So thoughtful of you to let your family know,' I said, trying not to gag at the plant-pot-shaped pile of brown mush in front of me.

'I forgot I'd mentioned it,' he replied through gritted teeth. 'Remember when you couldn't meet Mum and Dad for dinner last time they were in London? Because you were boycotting the steak restaurant?'

'Was that because they were serving *narwhal*?' I asked pointedly.

'Nae, hen, just regular cow,' Derek answered. 'Tuck in.'

Fiona waited at my side, hands clasped, breath held as I picked up my fork. Vegan food didn't bother me. I stuck to a relatively strict Veganuary every year, as long as I wasn't hungover, and tried to do meatless Mondays, but the meals I made for myself never looked or smelled quite like this.

'What is it?' I asked as politely as possible. It was one thing to turn the family off Caroline in general, it was another to outright insult another woman's hard work. I simply couldn't do it.

'A vegan roast,' Fi replied proudly. 'It's all the veggies from lunch mixed together with a dash of vegetable oil and baked. Took a hoon's age to find the blender. And no complex carbs either, whatever that means.'

'It looks . . .' I glanced over to Callum, who at least had the decency to look apologetic. 'It looks so . . .'

'It looks fantastic, Fiona,' he supplied. 'Stunning. Couldn't have done better myself.'

'Oh get away with you,' she cackled. 'High praise from the master chef. I want to see four clean plates or there'll be no pudding.'

'What's for pudding?' I asked hopefully.

'Steamed chocolate pudding with custard for them and you're having sliced apple surprise.'

'What's the surprise?'

'That it's a sliced apple because I couldn't pull a vegan dessert out of my backside with only twenty-four hours' notice.'

The heartbroken sob was out my mouth before I could stop it.

'Thank you, Fi,' Callum said quickly. 'You're amazing.'

'Yes, amazing,' I echoed. 'Thank you, Fi.'

The kitchen door rattled shut, leaving the four of us alone in an uncomfortable silence.

'I don't know about you but my stomach thinks my throat's been cut, everybody dig in,' Derek declared, standing to pour wine for Callum. Even though I'd had far too much the night before, I eagerly held out my glass. Anything to help the vegan roast go down more easily.

'No need to be polite,' he said, shaking his head and passing me over to pour for Lizzie. 'You don't believe in phones, you don't eat meat, you don't drink. I'm starting to wonder what it is you do do. Besides massage with balls.'

'Sorry, what?' My head flicked back to Callum. 'I don't what?'

'You don't drink.'

I watched Callum wince, presumably remembering something he'd forgotten.

'That's why we couldn't come on the distillery tour back in July. We hadn't been seeing each other that long, I didn't think it was the best way for you to meet the family.'

'Narwhal,' I whispered, defeated. 'Narwhal narwhal narwhal.'

'Each to their own, that's what I say,' Derek cheered. 'But I hope you're not planning to preach the evils of alcohol while you're here.' Callum chewed on the inside of his cheek but didn't offer to help me escape. Why bother establishing a safe word if I was not in any way, shape or form, safe?

'No,' I assured his dad. 'I wasn't planning on it.'

While the three of them tucked into their delicious-looking food, I poked at my lovingly prepared vegan roast. It held together with more conviction than it should, and I was sure I could see Fiona's handprints moulded into each side when I squinted.

'I have to admit,' Derek's voice boomed as though I were sitting three rooms over and not across the table. 'You're not at all how I imagined you.'

'Am I not?' I poked at an unidentifiable beige chunk that separated itself from the mass, offering itself up as tribute. 'What were you expecting?'

'I could've sworn you said she was a blonde,' Lizzie said first. 'Did he not, Derek?'

Her husband agreed. 'Aye, I'd have said the same thing. Wasn't expecting you to be a redhead. And I cannae hear the Swedish accent at all.'

Beside me, Callum choked into his napkin and I struggled to swallow my first regrettable mouthful.

'Are you all right?' Lizzie asked in alarm.

'He's fine,' I replied without even checking. 'No Swedish accent, right, well, that's because I've been in England so long.'

'Probably stronger when you're in Sweden,' Derek reasoned.

'Probably,' I agreed. 'Like Callum. His accent is much stronger up here than it is in London.'

'That's because he forgets where he's from,' Lizzie said. 'Or he tries to.'

Callum's fork froze halfway to his mouth and I recoiled from the tension between mother and son.

'A redhead from Sweden, I bet you don't get many of those to the pound,' Derek guffawed, either oblivious or ignoring it. 'The daftie refused to send us a photo, said you hate having your picture taken. It's like getting blood out of a stone, getting him to tell us anything about you.'

'Except that I'm a vegan Swedish masseuse who doesn't drink,' I said, sucking my teeth when Callum coughed.

'A blonde, vegan Swedish masseuse who doesn't drink.'

Everyone looked up at once.

Standing in the doorway was a tall woman, auburn hair pulled back in a ponytail, the exact same sapphire blue eyes as Callum set in her offensively pretty, make-up-less face.

'Brother,' she said.

'Elsie,' Callum replied. 'This is Caroline.'

'Is it.'

Elsie. His sister. She glared at me and it didn't take the mind of a neurosurgeon to work out she wasn't especially pleased to see either of us.

'Didn't know you were here,' Callum said. 'Aren't you sitting down?'

Her heavy-looking work jacket rustled as she crossed her arms.

'I'm always here, I live here. I'm also working, farms don't take days off.'

'Och, sit down, Else, have something to eat.' Derek shunted his seat backwards, the wooden legs creaking loudly. 'You take my plate, I've barely touched it. I'll get another from Fiona.'

Still eyeing me with more suspicion than I was comfortable with, she shook her head. 'No time, Dad. I need to move the sheep out of the high field, there's a flood warning.'

'Is there? Let me help you.'

He started to stand but Lizzie grabbed his wrist.

'You'll sit down and eat your lunch,' she instructed. 'Elsie knows what she's doing. If she wanted help, she'd ask for it.'

'I'm here if you need an extra pair of hands?' Callum offered, pushing up his sleeves, looking ready to wrangle a dozen lambs there and then.

'She meant if I needed help on the farm, not someone to bake a souffle,' his sister returned coolly and beside me I saw Callum swallow hard, sinking down into himself. 'Couldn't have you getting your precious hands dirty, Cal. Unless you need to impress the delicate little princess here.'

Oh. *Oh*. My eyes popped open. She was talking about *me*. I didn't care what Elsie McClay had heard about Caroline, that was fighting talk.

'Callum doesn't need to prove himself to me by chasing livestock around a field,' I assured her, sweet enough to rot teeth. 'He doesn't need to do anything to impress me.'

'Just as well because he's fucking useless.'

Elsie looked at me and smiled. It was venomous, the smile of someone who had just engaged a worthy opponent. Around the table, all three of her family members reached for their wine glasses at the same time.

'Well, don't let us keep you, sounds like you've got a lot of important things to do,' I said, returning her vile expression. 'We can chitchat later when you don't smell like you've been up to your elbows in cow shit all morning.'

'Better to be up to the elbows than listen to it coming out of Callum's mouth.' Her eyes flashed as her dad snorted wine out of his nose. 'Mum, please tell Fiona I won't be here for supper, I've got important things to do.'

With that, she turned on her heel and left the room, the door swinging back and forth in her wake.

'And now you've met Elsie,' Callum said before taking another, much deeper drink as his mother dabbed at his father's face with her napkin.

'Only Rory to go and you've got the whole set,' Derek said with a half-hearted attempt at a laugh. 'How are you enjoying your roast? It doesn't look half as bad as the first one. Fiona was experimenting all day yesterday. I'm sure she'll have it perfected by Christmas Day.'

'Can't wait,' I replied as I forced down another regrettable mouthful. 'Cannot bloody wait.'

CHAPTER TWELVE

The moment I'd finished my sliced apple surprise, I feigned a migraine, excused myself from the table and locked my bedroom door on the McClay clan. Stationed in the comfy chair by the window, I tried to forget lunch and concentrate on my book, but instead of losing myself in the cosy ghost of Christmas past romance, my mind kept straying back to the events of the day so far and after every couple of pages, I found myself staring out at the mountains, wondering exactly what I'd done to offend Elsie McClay.

There were plenty of women out there who weren't walking rays of sunshine, me included, so I never bought into the concept of a woman being a stone-cold bitch without grounds. I was sure Elsie had her reasons for behaving like we were in the middle of a *Real Housewives* reunion rather than a friendly family meal but I'd have been much happier if someone had bothered to let me in on them before we met.

The fatal flaw in my ingenious plan to stay out of the way was revealed exactly one hour after I slammed my door shut. I was gasping for a cup of tea and there was no resisting the siren song once the thought had taken root.

After two wrong turns, I made it to the kitchen without encountering another living soul and after opening a million different cupboards, drawers and cabinets, managed to locate mugs, find the teabags and finally, the milk. Everything in this house was an ordeal, I wasn't surprised Callum preferred his tidy little flat. Balmaclay was beautiful, no doubt, but this was altogether too much faffing around for a cup of tea. Before my landlord so rudely evicted me, I had a travel kettle in the bedroom for emergency cuppas. Between late nights and long shifts, sometimes it was too hard to roll all the way from my bed to the kitchen. I'd even considered putting one in the bathroom so I could freshen up my drink while I took a bath but I settled for a giant insulated travel mug instead.

'What are you doing?'

Lizzie McClay stood in the kitchen doorway, jumper, gilet, ever-present silk scarf, lips brought together as though she'd walked in on me masturbating with her rolling pin.

'You could help me by wearing a bell,' I gasped, pressing my hands to my chest to hold my thudding heart in place. 'You scared the life out of me.'

'You're making tea?'

She set a basket down on the huge table, a solid block of wood that dominated the farmhouse-style kitchen. Only it wasn't farmhouse-style, it was literally a farmhouse kitchen. Weird.

'Is that all right?' I asked before catching myself. Caroline wouldn't ask permission. 'Because, yes, that is what I am doing. Making tea. For myself.'

It took every ounce of strength in my body to prevent me from offering to make Lizzie a cup. Asking a Brit not to offer another Brit tea was like expecting Desi not to make snide comments during an episode of *Love Island*, denying a psychological imperative, and almost completely beyond our control.

'I wouldn't have thought it was good for migraines,' she said, breezing past me to take out her own mug and her own teabag. I tried not to stop breathing at the shame of it.

'To the best of my knowledge, there hasn't been a study that confirms a causal relationship between average tea consumption and migraines,' I said, reacting as I always did, distracting myself with facts and stats. 'Excess caffeine intake can cause them in some people, caffeine withdrawal can bring migraines on too. Some people think tea could actually help prevent them but there's even less evidence to support that theory. Unfortunately.'

'Sounds like you've done plenty of research.'

More research than the average massage therapist.

'If you were a migraine sufferer, you would understand.' I held the back of my hand against my migraine-less forehead and let my head loll back dramatically. 'It's a debilitating and often misunderstood illness. Nausea, vomiting, fatigue, numbness, visual disturbances, it goes on.'

'I see.' Lizzie loosened her scarf as she stared me down. 'But you're well enough to make tea.'

'I suffer through it,' I replied in a hero's whisper.

This was my first real test. One on one with my fake boyfriend's real mother, caught in her kitchen, hand in the proverbial cookie jar, and if she'd been three minutes earlier, it would've been the literal biscuit tin but thankfully I'd managed to stuff two non-vegan chocolate digestives into my mouth and three into the pocket of my hoodie before she appeared.

Other people's mothers always made me anxious. My personal experience was so minimal, I didn't know what to expect. Desi's parents moved to New York with her dad's job right after she started university, so she almost always went to them rather than the other way around, and Joel had almost as little to do with his family as I had with mine. Attitudes towards queer kids might be changing by and large but not quickly enough when it came to his parents. The thought of anyone rejecting my kind, generous, beloved best friend made me so mad. But I'd heard other people's mothers were their greatest champions. Lionesses ready to fuck you up for looking at their cub the wrong way, mama bears just waiting for an excuse to claw you to death for mistreating their precious little baby. I glanced down at Lizzie's neat but sharp nails. That wasn't a farm manicure. She could do some damage there if she wanted to.

'Where's Callum?' I asked, mashing my teabag against the side of the cup then dumping it in the sink.

The corner of Lizzie's mouth twitched. The spent teabag had barely struck the stainless steel before she swept in, scooped it out and transferred it to the bin.

'Down in the shed with his dad.'

'The shed?'

'Cattle shed,' she clarified. 'Elsie had it completely rebuilt over the summer, Cal hasn't seen it yet since the two of you weren't able to make it up for a visit. We're planning on a new parlour next, milking parlour that is. Derek will be wanting Cal's opinion, I'm sure.'

'Does he have an opinion on milking parlours?'

'Callum might not be working on the farm right now but he's very familiar with it all. Yes, I imagine he'll have opinions.'

She poured boiling water from the kettle into her cup and did not flinch when a few drops splashed out and hit the back of her hand. The woman was stone cold.

'Did he tell you our family has been farming this land—'

'He did,' I cut in with a yawn. 'I won't lie, I'm not *super* into it. Isn't dairy farming super cruel?'

'Some people think that,' Lizzie said as she poured milk into her tea with a pointed look. 'But some people think massage parlours are knocking shops so it only goes to show people aren't always correctly educated.'

Shots officially fired.

'I'll get out of your way,' I said, clutching the scorching hot cup, not worrying about potential third-degree burns. 'Thanks.'

'Since you're feeling better why don't you stay?'

I froze.

'Callum always loves my mince pies, I'd be more than happy to share the recipe with you,' she said. 'You can knead the pastry, show off some of your skills.'

'They're not necessarily transferrable,' I demurred, eyes on the hallway. So close but so far. 'And I think I can feel my migraine getting worse . . .'

'If you feel any *visual disturbances* coming on, say the word and I'll carry you back upstairs myself,' Lizzie shot back. 'You have my word.'

I turned to face her, eyes narrow slits. WWDKD? What would Desi Kaplan do?

'I can't touch the pastry. It's not vegan.'

'You can spoon in the mincemeat.'

'Mincemeat isn't vegan either.'

She pulled a glass jar from her basket and held it up for me to see.

'Says it right here, suitable for vegetarians, vegans, people with gluten intolerances and nut allergy sufferers.'

'Well, you've thought of everything, haven't you?' I said with a very bright and very fake smile. 'Let's make some mince pies.'

Baking was not my forte. The kitchen was not my favourite place to spend time. Get in, open the fridge, get out, that was my game plan. And if I ordered take-away or brought food home with me, the kitchen could usually be avoided altogether. Coffee on the way to work, lunch in the canteen, dinner from the twenty-four-hour Sainsbury's by the bus stop. Why dirty plates when you didn't have to?

Lizzie McClay clearly did not share my sentiment. Her kitchen looked like something from a fancy cooking show. She had everything, matching mixing bowls, appliances, baking trays, pastry cutters passed down through four generations. Her kitchen scales were older than both of us combined but they were still accurate to the ounce. Her well-practised pastry came together with ease, flour, water, a dash of salt, some cubes of butter, and even though she'd claimed to need my kneading expertise, the second she started baking, it became very clear I was there to look but not touch. Not once did she have to search for a recipe on her phone, smearing the screen with greasy fingers, screeching at me to run out and buy bicarbonate of soda because all we had was baking powder and apparently they are not the same thing. Desi and I had agreed never to speak of our attempt to bake Joel a birthday cake again. Turned out it was essential to know the difference between tablespoons and teaspoons when it came to adding salt to a Victoria sponge.

'And into the oven they go,' Lizzie said, dusting off her hands with the same satisfaction as any surgeon who had perfectly executed a surgical procedure. And even though I had not tasted the goods (and never would), I felt confident saying she'd nailed it.

'Callum said he used to bake with his grandmother,' I said as she moved all the dirty dishes over to the sink. 'Was that your mother?'

'No, that was Derek's mum,' she replied with shake of her head. 'Callum never knew his grandmother on my side. We lost her just before he was born.'

On the opposite side of the kitchen table, I felt a twinge. Lizzie had lost her mum, just like me. But I couldn't say anything. Both of Caroline's parents were alive and well and enjoying a Caribbean Christmas cruise, it had been established.

'Does Elsie like to cook as well?' I asked, leaving the grandparent situation well alone. There was no comfortable way to broach it.

'Elsie likes to do what Elsie likes to do and you'll be hard pressed to guess what that is even while it's happening.' She turned on the tap and blasted hot water into her mixing bowl. 'I'd say you'll get used to Elsie's ways but I can't guarantee it.'

While Lizzie still had her back turned, I swiped at the open jar of mincemeat and licked the sweet sticky stuff from my finger.

'Because she's unpredictable?'

'Because it takes her a long time to warm up to people and who knows when we'll see you again.' She filled the bowl with soapy water, turned off the tap then came back to the table. '*If* we'll see you again.'

'What's that supposed to mean?' I asked.

'Only that Callum's been so intent on hiding you away,' she replied, all innocence. 'If I were a more suspicious woman, I might think he was ashamed of you.'

'If I were a more suspicious woman, I might think he was ashamed of you.'

It was a stand-off. Lizzie McClay, lady of Balmaclay, baker of pies and queen of backhanded burns, versus me, the rookie bullshitter, who could hardly keep her lies straight, let alone rise to meet such a master of passive-aggressive insults.

'Och, would you look at the time,' Lizzie said without looking at the clock on the wall or the watch on her wrist. 'Here I am talking your ear off when I've so much to do, the fun never stops around here.'

'Don't mind me,' I replied, still sorting through the implications of her possible insults. 'I'm sure Balmaclay is a demanding mistress.'

'And I'm sure you'd know all about that. The mince pies need to come out of the oven in ten minutes. Do you think you could manage that, Caroline?'

My reply came through gritted teeth. 'I should think so.'

'Not as daeless as she looks,' she said sweetly. 'If you need any help, Fiona should be back in half an hour or so.'

'But the mince pies will be done in ten minutes?' I said as she removed her apron and hung it from the hook on the wall.

'Better not need any help then, eh?' she replied, vanishing out the back door and out of sight.

Alone in the kitchen, I pulled one of the slightly broken biscuits out from the pocket of my hoodie and munched angrily. So much for our plan to convince his parents they wanted nothing to do with Caroline.

It seemed to me that decision had already been made.

CHAPTER THIRTEEN

'Come in?'

Some hours later, the door to my room opened to reveal Callum's imposing frame. He was so at odds with the antique elegance of the house, all awkward angles, with his head ducked, one hand in his coat pocket and the other wrapped around the back of his head, a sharp elbow pointing up to the ceiling.

'How are you feeling?' he asked as he stepped into my room, a quick glance in either direction to make sure no one was watching as though we were still teenagers and might get told off.

'As well as anyone else with a pretend migraine,' I said, closing my book. 'Callum, what does daeless mean?'

'Helpless,' he replied. 'Feeble. Why?'

'Never mind.'

I made a face at the empty doorway behind him.

'Mince pie?' he offered, holding out a small plate. 'Mum made them herself.'

'I think you'll find I was also involved,' I said. 'But

no thanks, I'll pass. Exciting afternoon down on the farm?'

'It would take a very generous definition of the word exciting for me to say yes.' He peered around the room, his eyes briefly resting on my rumpled bed covers before skirting quickly away. 'But I've got good news, we've been given permission to decamp to the pub for the rest of the evening. Dad lobbied hard for a family Scrabble tournament but I told him you needed some fresh air.'

'The fresh air of the pub.'

'You can stay here if you'd rather, I'll get Fi to send something up.'

I had one foot in a boot before he even finished speaking. 'Give me three seconds to get ready. No offence to Fiona.'

'You could've chucked it in the fireplace and there'd have been none taken,' he said with a laugh. 'She's tough as nails. Has to be after forty years of being married to Mal.'

'Forty years?' I whistled, impressed. 'She doesn't look old enough.'

'Tell her that,' Callum advised. 'She'll be thrilled.'

With one hand on the wooden post of my canopy bed to steady myself, I rammed my other foot into the other boot. 'You do realise it's another weird thing, though? Having a housekeeper. And a driver. And staff in general.'

His great shoulders hunched together, expression guarded. 'They're not staff. Fiona and Mal are part of the family, Balmaclay is as much their home as mine. Mal isn't the driver, he's the ghillie.'

'Which means?'

'It's difficult to explain,' he said as I wound a scarf

around my neck until only my eyes were visible. 'In layman's terms a ghillie is someone who stewards a specific area of land in the Highlands, in Mal's case, our twenty thousand acres. But it's more than a job. Mal was born into the role, he's the fifth generation of his family to work alongside my family.'

'Thank you for breaking it down to a layman,' I said waiting for his wry smile. 'So he's, like, an indentured park ranger?'

'Not quite. Mal is and always was free to go and do whatever he wants with his life but if you were to ask him, he'd tell you there was never a question of him doing anything else.'

'And after him?'

'He's two boys, both at university, both fighting over the job. I expect they'll share the duties to be honest.'

'What about Fiona?' I asked, pulling on my mittens. 'Also destined to be the world's finest vegan chef?'

At that, he laughed.

'Fi was born to keep Mal in line and she'll tell you that herself. She moved into Sleagh Cottage with his family after they got married and started helping his mum around Balmaclay. When Eileen passed on, she took on the job full time.'

'She must really love that man. Imagine living with your in-laws.'

Callum grabbed my coat from the rack beside the door and held it out for me. I slipped my arms through the sleeves, privately enjoying the gesture.

'Derek and Lizzie would treat you like a queen.'

'Except they'll never be my in-laws,' I pointed out, 'because I'm not really your girlfriend.'

Fully clad in my winter gear, I turned to face him.

He was so close, my breath hitched in my chest and a tiny gasp escaped. Callum's eyes held mine as though he were searching for something and I blinked, suddenly afraid of what he might find.

'Sorry about earlier,' he said softly, pulling my hat down over the tops of my ears.

Inside my mittens, my fingers scrunched into tight little fists.

'Which part?'

'Dealer's choice.'

He took a small step back and I stumbled forward, the space he left between us too much for gravity to bear.

'Mum must have been keeping notes after every phone call,' he added apologetically. 'I'd forgotten half the stuff I told her about you.'

After taking a moment to collect myself, I crossed the room to retrieve my phone and put some necessary distance between us.

'About Caroline,' I corrected. 'Not me.'

Eyes down, he patted his pockets in traditional McClay-man fashion.

'I thought we could walk to The Clach if you're game?'

Slipping my phone, a hair tie, two lip balms and a packet of Polos into my pocket, I gave him a questioning look. 'The Clach?'

'The Clachnaharry,' he explained. 'My local, back in the day. It's not so far.'

My questioning look transformed into a suspicious squint.

'How far is not so far?'

'Down the lane and along a bit. What Mal would call a wee bimble.'

'Then I'm game,' I agreed, glancing proudly down at my virgin hiking boots. Now was their time to shine. 'As long as it's not too cold.'

Tucking his gloveless hands into his pockets, Callum smiled as I passed through door, avoiding bodily contact at all costs.

'Practically summer out tonight,' he assured me. 'You'll be fine.'

'I literally hate you,' I declared as Callum opened the door to the pub, trying not to laugh. 'No hyperbole, no exaggeration. If you were drowning and I had a length of rope, I would use it to make a scratching post for my neighbour's cat before I tossed it to you.'

It turned out Callum's interpretation of distance and temperature was wildly different to my own. Walking three miles in sub-zero temperatures was bad enough but I'd also been forced to learn the hard way about the perils of breaking in brand new hiking boots. Hobbling over to a wooden chair by the fire, I almost wept with joy as I collapsed into a chair, taking the weight off my poor, burning feet.

'Will you forgive me if I get you a drink?' Callum asked, standing over me.

'No,' I replied. 'But get me one anyway.'

'Anything in particular?'

Grasping the tops of my woollen mittens with my teeth, I peeled them away from my hands, eight fingers and two thumbs cramping inside.

'Cup of tea and some crisps and some nuts and anything else they've got that's edible.'

'I'm not asking for tea in the pub.'

Callum balked and I fixed him with a hard stare.

'If I don't get a hot drink, I'm going to tell your dad we both want to watch his holiday videos every single night until we leave,' I replied. 'And I'm going to pause it to a question every fourteen seconds.'

Shaking his head but smiling again, Callum left me at the table, heading to the bar with his orders. As the roaring fire burned the chill from my bones, I watched him cross the room, long legs and easy grace. It was a stark contrast to the way he'd moved around his family home, so tightly wound, like he was afraid to make a sound. Here, he seemed so much more relaxed, drawn up to his full height, a ready smile on his face for anyone who crossed his path on the short walk to the bar. Callum might've grown up in Balmaclay but he stuck out like a sore thumb. No, more like a sore middle finger, taller and more pissed off. Even when the uneven ceiling sloped so low he had to stoop, Callum fit right in at The Clach. Dark wood and wine-red leather, cardboard coasters bearing the logos of brands and breweries. Warm, familiar and easy.

I loved a good pub. It was the one thing I'd shared with my dad, Thursday nights down at the Three Legged Stool for the weekly quiz. Whether or not a thirteen-year-old should be at the pub every Thursday was neither here nor there but the Christmas decorations at The Clach reminded me of home, antiques in their own right. A silver tinsel tree that had seen better days sat in the window, angels made from the cardboard inner tubes of toilet rolls and dated doilies lined the fireplace and someone had tied repurposed string between two mounted stag heads to display their Christmas cards like clean washing. The thought of the white-haired man behind the bar going into a cupboard or an attic to bring them out year after year made me smile. Everything about this place was welcoming, everything was a comfort. Even to a southern jessie like me.

Once I had defrosted well enough to manipulate my fingers again, I picked up the small handwritten menu that lay on our little table. Beer-battered haddock and chips, mussels in a cream and garlic sauce, Scottish sirloin steak, langoustines with homemade bread, haggis bhajis and cullen skink. My stomach growled with hunger and I knew I'd gratefully take whatever could be ready the fastest, even cullen skink, whatever it was. My only Cullen frame of reference was vampiric and this didn't look much like a *Twilight*-fan pub.

'This is the best I could do.'

Callum reappeared carrying a steaming glass mug and two tumblers full of what looked like whisky.

'James behind the bar says this'll warm you up. Coffee first then a glass of Old Pulteney.'

I took a cautious sip from the mug, fumes igniting inside my nose. The coffee had been spiked with whisky. Or someone had diluted a mugful of whisky with coffee, it was hard to tell.

'And I'm drunk,' I announced, eyes watering. 'Irish coffee?'

'Scottish coffee.' He folded himself into the chair next to mine, eyes twinkling. 'Because it's made with Scottish whisky, and because James said so. Don't think he won't turn you back out in the cold if he hears you talking like that.'

I wanted to argue but as the feeling came back into my defrosted feet, they began to throb in the very specific way only women who had stubbornly tried to walk in ill-fitting shoes could ever understand. I would say whatever anyone wanted as long as it meant I didn't have to walk anywhere again for the foreseeable.

'So.' I rested back in my chair, gloves off but still bundled up in my hat, coat and scarf. Callum peeled off his thin woollen coat, nothing but a long-sleeved T-shirt and jeans underneath. 'This is your local?'

'Used to be,' he nodded, smacking his lips after taking a sip of the whisky, holding his glass up to the light like Indiana Jones beholding a rare artefact. 'The Clach is about the only place you can get to without a car from Balmaclay and I was never allowed to borrow the car.'

'Because your parents were worried about drunk driving?'

'Because the day after I passed my driving test, I borrowed it to go to the cinema and instead drove all the way down to Glastonbury festival, lost my phone, and they didn't know where I was for five days.'

'I wouldn't lend you the car either,' I replied, wondering what my dad would've done in that situation. He mostly took the bus to work so there was a good chance he wouldn't notice I was gone as long as the car was back before he needed it to drive to football on Sundays. 'You were a terror as a kid, then?'

'Terror isn't the word for it. Couldn't wait to get away, could you, fannybaws?'

A man around our age slapped Callum around the back of the head with a well-used tea towel, a blue apron tied around his waist over a white T-shirt and black shorts, and a huge, friendly grin on his face.

'That means cool genius, by the way,' Callum replied before standing to clap his arms around the other man in an aggressive hug.

I stared at him in awe. Bare legs? In this weather? He had to be the toughest human being on the planet. That or he should be studied for science. Whipping away the tea towel, Callum used it to snap the backs of his legs, earning a litany of curses. Or at least I assumed they were curses, I only understood about three words out of every ten.

'Laura, you might as well meet Graham since it's too late to pretend I don't know him,' Callum said eventually.

'Caroline,' I corrected quickly as I rose from my chair to shake his hand. 'I don't know who this Laura is.'

Graham laughed, ignoring my hand and pulling me in for a hug.

'Och, Cal, you've done it now, rolling in that much fud down south you can't keep their names straight?'

'Aye, that's right,' Callum replied, throwing me an appreciative glance for the save. 'I'd like to keep it to one wifey, London's too far for your ma to travel.'

Graham beamed at me, legs splayed in a confident stance, hands planted at his waist. 'As much as I'd love to listen to your mannie blether on all night, we're too busy for his shite right now. Are you wanting to eat?'

'Yes,' I replied before Callum could even open his mouth. 'Yes, please.'

I read the menu over again and my stomach howled. Remembering my fake name was easy, remaining vegan outside Balmaclay was another thing altogether.

'Does the steak come with chips?' I asked, pressing my hands against my belly.

'No, love, it comes with hamshank sauce and a hand shandy.'

'Yes, it comes with chips,' Callum said, arm flicking

out lightning fast to slap his friend in a sensitive area with the back of his hand. 'I'll have the same, thank you, Gray.'

'Hope I don't forget which one's been marinating in the cludgie. Welcome home, you wee shite.'

And with that, he gave me a wink, punched Callum in the arm and took his leave.

'He seems nice,' I said as Graham staggered away, openly rubbing at his crotch as he went. Callum, still adjusting his too long limbs to the too small chair, smiled and nodded.

'Gray? He's harmless. We grew up together.'

'Funny that you both ended up as cooks.'

My question only earned a dismissive shrug.

'Only one of us by choice,' he replied. 'I don't think he'll be able to mess up steak and chips but it's not exactly Gray's calling. His dad, James, owns the pub. He's been working here since he was old enough to pick up empty glasses. He used to be the barman but he kept giving away free drinks to all the girls.'

I cast an eye around the room. Old men as far as the eye could see.

'Can't imagine that made much of a dent in the profits.'

'He didn't mind sampling the wares himself while he was at it,' Callum admitted with a laugh. 'And it would be fair to say I didn't put my hand in my pocket for a few years. Probably owe James half my life savings. Gray is safer in the kitchen than he is with his dad's collection of rare single malts.'

'Correct me if I'm wrong but I think I'm picking up on a theme,' I said as I sipped my boozy coffee, the good kind of burn scorching down my throat and into my stomach. 'Mal, Graham, your dad. Lots of men around here following in their fathers' footsteps.'

He was still smiling as he brought his drink to his lips but the light was gone from his eyes. 'Yeah, well, there aren't that many jobs around here. If there's a family business to fall into, most are grateful to get on with it.'

'But not you.'

It was a question, a statement and a show of admiration all in one, but I couldn't be sure how Callum interpreted my words. He sniffed, rubbed the back of his hand against his chin then waved my words away.

'I wanted to say sorry about Elsie earlier.' He pushed up the long sleeves of his shirt and the muscles on his forearms contracted when he leaned them on the wooden table. 'I didn't think she'd be around until later or I'd have given you more warning. Don't take anything she says personally, it's not about you. It's me she's upset with.'

'Any particular reason why?' I asked, finally feeling brave enough to remove my bobble hat and open my coat. I wasn't quite ready to take it off but I could at least unfasten the toggles. 'I don't have any brothers or sisters but that felt a bit more intense than your average sibling rivalry.'

The question sat for a moment and I could tell Callum was trying to decide whether or not he wanted to answer it, pushing his glass around in circles like he was making patterns on a spirograph.

'You don't have to talk about it if you don't want to,' I added. 'It's none of my business.'

'You're here, you've borne the brunt of Elsie's temper, it's your business,' he replied. 'I'm just trying to work out how to tell the story in a way that won't make you hate me.'

I scrunched up my face, scoffing at the unlikely outcome. 'What did you do? Set fire to her Barbie dolls?'

The bittersweet smile on his face didn't budge.

'Dad wanted me to take over the farm,' he began, forcing out his words as though he resented each and every one. 'Like his father before him and his father before him and so on and so forth, all the way back as far as anyone can remember. And according to my dad, every McClay son has taken on this sacred duty with a willing heart, all of them born to it, farming in their blood. Well, something went wrong when he had me because I never wanted to stay on the farm. Not that there's anything wrong with the place, it's beautiful, you can see that.'

I nodded in agreement. He wasn't wrong.

'Every minute I wasn't at school, if I wasn't doing my homework, Dad would drag me into the fields or the sheds, trying to bring out some latent love for the farm, but it was never there.'

'Because you loved cooking?' I nudged for him to continue as he took a drink.

'Because I always wanted to get out and see what else was happening in the world. Cooking is something I fell into, you can pick up kitchen work anywhere in the world, but I came to love it. If I'd stayed here, I might never have known that about myself.'

'And how does that bring us back to Elsie?'

Callum wiped a hand over his face and groaned.

'It broke my dad's heart when I left to go travelling. Because I let everyone down, Elsie took my place. Followed Dad around everywhere, learned how to do everything. Tried to be everything he wanted me to be.'

'So you left and Elsie had to give up her dreams to take your place,' I surmised. 'I can see how that would rub her up the wrong way but I don't think you should blame yourself. She chose to take on the job the same way you chose not to.'

'That's the stupid thing,' Callum shook his head, confused. 'She didn't give up anything, she loves it. Else is better at running the estate than I ever would've been and she's already made it more profitable than it was the whole time Dad was in charge. But she's still so angry with me.'

'I wish I could offer up a theory but I've got nothing,' I admitted, feet still throbbing in my boots. 'Have you tried talking to her about it?'

'We can't even have a civil conversation without her biting my head off.' He gave me a sad smile and I felt a flutter in my stomach. 'I thought my dad might be angry at me for walking away from the farm. I didn't know it would cost me my sister.'

I closed my eyes and sighed. Most neuroscientists were in agreement that we only understood about ten percent of the brain's full capabilities, but even with that in mind, brains still made more sense to me than most people. Imagine having this incredible computer inside your head, billions of neurons all firing at once, giving you the ability to walk and talk and think and feel, and you chose to use all those unimaginable complexities to be mad at your brother for no reason.

When I opened my eyes again, Callum was staring into the fire, a melancholy look on his face. I noticed a tiny freckle under his left eye, a tiny golden fleck, and when he looked back at me and smiled, it disappeared into the crease between his eyelid and his cheek.

'Your dad must be so proud of you,' he said. 'A neurosurgeon? It's incredible.'

And now it was my turn to get uncomfortable. A fair exchange of vulnerability.

'I suppose,' I replied, shuffling in my seat. 'We never really talk about it.'

'Your job or whether or not he's proud of you?'

'Either,' I answered. 'Both.'

Someone opened the front door behind us and I wrapped my coat around myself at the sudden sharp chill.

'It was hard for him, after we lost Mum,' I went on, even though I wasn't sure why. I didn't talk to anyone about my dad, not even Desi. 'Thirty-six and stuck at home with a grieving teenage girl. He didn't really know what he was doing and we didn't have a lot of other family nearby to help. We muddled along until I left for university and met Desi and Joel. They're my family now. I see Dad when I see him.'

'And he's gone away for Christmas?'

I nodded but kept my eyes focused on my coffee.

'After Mum . . . it didn't feel the same really. We still bought presents but that was about it. When I was sixteen, he said he was too tired to put the tree up so I climbed into the loft to get it, slipped off a beam and fell through the ceiling. Broke my leg in three places. That more or less put an end to Christmas altogether in our house. Now I just do whatever, hang out with Desi and Joel, work if I can. I'd be at the hospital now but HR made me take time off because I haven't used any holiday all year.'

'Christ, Laura, I'm so sorry,' Callum said softly. 'Here I am complaining about my petty family squabbles and . . .'

'And I'm here Scrooging it up,' I said with a quiet laugh. 'Ignore me, honestly, I'm fine. It must be the whisky, I'm not used to it.'

He slapped the table with the flats of his hands, making our glasses do a little jump.

'If that's the case you know there's only one cure for that.'

'And what's that, Dr McClay?'

'More whisky.'

Picking up his glass, he tossed back what was left then eyed mine, signalling for me to do the same.

'Good girl,' he smiled as I screwed up my face, chasing the burn of the scotch with a mouthful of still-scorching hot coffee. 'I'll get another round in, doctor's orders.'

I watched him as he wove his way through the other patrons, his broad shoulders tapering down to a narrow waist, auburn hair curling at his collar, a clear head taller than everyone else milling around the bar. He really was something.

Resting my elbows on the table, the warmth of the whisky flushed through me and I bravely took off my coat. The alcohol made my blood vessels dilate, sending blood rushing to the surface of my skin, but I knew, soon enough, my core temperature would drop and I'd be even colder than before. Sometimes being a doctor was no fun. At least if nothing else came of this week, perhaps I'd learn to hold my scotch. Just as long as I could hold my own against Elsie, keep Lizzie and Derek at a distance, survive Fiona's cooking and not offend Mal.

'Last week you cauterised a man's brain while he was wide awake,' I muttered to myself. 'How was that easier?'

The front door opened again and I shivered, the sound of female laughter ringing out across the old man pub loudly enough to make me turn in my seat in search of sisterly solidarity. Instead, I found two women staring at me as though I was holding up a sign that said 'I eat puppies, ask me how'.

'Ah, bollocks,' I muttered when I realised I recognised them both.

Elsie's happy smile slipped into the same sneer I'd seen at lunch but the pretty blonde at her side was already looking away, too busy staring daggers across the bar to worry much about me. But in her defence, if I'd been all but engaged to Callum McClay and lost him to a life of Parisian pastries, I might've looked just as angry as Siobhan Hamilton.

CHAPTER FOURTEEN

As soon as our eyes met, Shiv turned to leave but Elsie grabbed her arm, shaking her head before guiding her through the chairs and tables towards me. A sharp stab of guilt cut through my guts, every instinct in me telling me to run, but there was nowhere to go unless it was through the window or into the fire.

'If it isn't my brother's beloved.'

I should've chucked myself into the fire.

Elsie loomed over me, a shark-like smile on her face, the one that said behold, my worthy adversary. I didn't want to be her adversary, I didn't want to be her anything, I wanted to drink my drink and eat my steak, be vaguely obnoxious until Boxing Day then go home and never, ever see her again.

'Caroline, you must meet my friend, Siobhan. Siobhan, this is Caroline . . .' She paused for maximum effect. 'Cal's new girlfriend.'

'Pleased to meet you.'

The blonde held out a hand that looked as though it would rather poke around in a bin full of broken glass than make physical contact but, to her credit, she met my firm handshake with one of her own before snatching her hand away and shoving it into the back pocket of her jeans. The three of us were still staring at each other in silence, three points of the world's most pass-agg triangle, when Callum sauntered back from the bar. He spotted the scene and stopped so abruptly, whisky splashed out of the glasses in his hands.

'Elsie,' he said, his face grim. 'Shiv.'

'Cal,' Siobhan replied.

'Caroline,' I added, just in case.

Callum set down both glasses then wiped his palms against his jeans.

'Just came over to say hello,' Shiv said, already looking away, swiping at a watering eye. 'We'll leave you to your evening.'

'Unless you'd like us to join you?' Elsie grabbed the back of an empty chair from an occupied table without asking if it was free and pulled it up next to me. 'Looks like there's just enough room at the inn.'

'For Jesus, Mary, Joseph and the donkey,' I muttered under my breath.

'Come on, Elsie, I'm sure they'd rather be on their own.' Shiv tugged on her friend's sleeve but it was too late, she was already down and perusing the menu.

'Everything looks so good,' she said, smacking her lips. She looked up at her brother who was still on his feet and offered a syrupy smile. 'Don't you think, Cal?'

'Sit down,' he said to Shiv, pulling out a chair for her before lowering himself into his own. 'It's nice to see you.'

'Is it?' She sounded hard, brittle even. 'I'd have thought you'd be at home.'

'Because most people who hadn't visited their parents in a year would choose to spend the evening with them,' Elsie said. 'Should've taken into account this is you we're talking about.'

The sharpest knife in the world couldn't have sliced through the tension at our table. A diamond-tipped chainsaw might've done it but there were no guarantees.

Elsie prodded the full glass of whisky that wasn't already in her brother's hand. 'Who's this for? If she doesn't drink?'

'Who's she?' I replied, cradling my Scottish coffee, warm and precious and full of secret booze. 'The cat's mother?'

'You don't strike me as a cat person. Getting more dog vibes. When I look at you, I definitely think bitch.'

'Elsie!'

It was Shiv who admonished her. Callum only sat back in his chair, his jaw clenched, granite solid.

'It's for Graham,' I replied lightly, as though no offence had been implied. 'But since you're clearly in desperate need of a drink, why don't you have it? I'll get him another.'

'I'm not desperate,' she said with a scoff.

'Really?' I batted my eyelashes sweetly. 'You mean you always behave like this?'

She grinned, showing too many teeth, her eyes gleaming.

'It has been a particularly bad day, now I think about it. I'm having trouble with a new heifer. She doesn't realise she's destined for the slaughterhouse.'

'That does sound annoying. Have you tried sitting

down and talking to her for two minutes? She'll probably run down there of her own accord.'

It was a direct hit. Elsie's expression didn't change but she flinched, very slightly.

'I'm going to the bar,' Shiv announced. 'Elsie, will you come with me?'

'No.'

What a great friend she was.

It was obvious Elsie and Callum were related – same colouring, same tall stature – but looking at them side by side, they could have almost been twins. As well as their auburn hair, they shared an identical strong, straight nose and the same almond-shaped eyes that tilted downwards at the corners. Her mouth was smaller and her lips fuller, but she had more lines and freckles, despite being the younger sibling. There was no doubt that the McClay genes ran strong, at least as far as physical appearance went.

'For fuck's sake, Elsie,' Callum hissed as soon as his ex was out of earshot. 'Go and sit somewhere else. You're torturing poor Shiv.'

'And what about Caroline?' When she glanced over at me, I wondered if she'd ever experienced a genuine, pleasant emotion in her entire life. 'Or are you not worried about hurting her feelings?'

'Caroline can hold her own,' I said. 'Don't worry about me.'

'No one is worried about you,' she assured me, a quick flick over her shoulder.

As brother and sister bickered between themselves, I leaned back in my chair, nursing what was left of my spiked coffee. With every second I spent in his family's company, Callum's rationale for not wanting to come home became clearer and clearer. Before I thought I was doing him a favour; now I realised I was performing community service.

'Here we are, two steak and chips.'

Graham presented my dinner with a deep bow, leaning in to loudly whisper in my ear. 'Don't touch his, I pished on it.'

'Funny-looking vegan steak,' Elsie said as he strolled away, the sight and smell of the succulent beef almost enough to bring me to tears.

'I'm only eating the chips.' I choked out the words, the thought of losing my precious hunk of cow making me shake with grief. 'Both steaks are for Callum. He needs the protein.'

'He needs a slap.'

She grunted into the pint of whatever it was Shiv put down in front of her when she returned from the bar, shuffling her seat as far away from Callum as she could without launching herself into the fire.

In my pocket, I felt my phone buzz.

'I'm going to the loo,' I declared, standing so quickly my chair almost tipped over. 'Does anyone want anything from the bar while I'm up? No? Good.'

Hobbling down a passageway to back of the pub, I opened my texts to find a new message in the group chat.

Have they Wicker Man-ed you yet?

I shuffled down the narrow hallway, tapping out a furious reply, and pressed send. Filled with righteous anger at Elsie's abhorrent behaviour, I forced open a heavy door, only to be spat out into the still and silent night. It was beyond cold, absolutely bitter, but the chill felt good on my rage-fired skin and I turned my face up to an endless map of stars.

'Looking for an escape?'

Off to my left, emerging from behind a row of wheelie bins, Graham appeared, packet of cigarettes in one hand, lighter in the other. He held the pack out to me but I declined, shaking my head.

'Hardly,' I said with a smile. 'Not in my line of work.'

'Didnae realise massage therapists were particularly anti-smoking,' he said, tucking both items back into the pocket of his apron. Even though it was well below freezing, he was still in his shorts and T-shirt, not so much as a goosebump visible on his skin.

'Yes, very much so.' I nodded feverishly, the tip of my nose already numb. 'Lymphatic drainage and all that.'

'Never had any trouble draining my lymphs.'

'I can imagine.'

It was almost impossible to resist his broad grin and I was quite sure he wasn't lying.

'So,' I said, trying to be tactful. 'What's the story with Callum and Shiv?'

He laughed, green eyes disappearing into full cheeks. Not so tactful after all.

'You don't mess about, do you?' he replied. 'Straight to the point, I like that. But it's not my place. I don't want to get into trouble with Cal.'

'If he's still in love with her, I want to know.'

If only to satisfy my curiosity, I added to myself.

'Ahh, Caroline.' He kicked a pebble and I watched it bounce along the uneven ground, settling at the edge of a dark puddle. 'What makes you say that?'

'Women's intuition?'

He eyed the door behind me as though he was expecting someone to burst through at any second and catch him saying something he shouldn't.

'If he wanted to be with her, he'd be with her,' he said. 'Isn't that what they say?'

'I don't know,' I replied. 'Is it?'

'All I know is, Cal and Shiv were boyfriend and girlfriend before we even knew what it meant.' He scratched the back of his neck, squinting as he spoke, as though deliberating how much of the story I needed to know. 'Everyone around here thought they'd be together forever because they'd always been together forever, and nobody was more sure than our Shiv. I'll never forget the look on Cal's face on careers day when our teacher went round the class, asked everyone what we wanted to do when we left school, and Shiv said they were going to be laird and lady of Balmaclay.'

'Wait, the McClays aren't *actually* aristocracy, are they?' I asked, suddenly feeling a little bit nauseous. What if it wasn't just a turn of phrase?

He threw his head back in a throaty guffaw. 'No, hen. A laird isn't the same thing as a lord, it means something closer to landowner. You can tell the actual nobility apart from the rest of us easy enough. I've never met a duke with a Scottish accent, they all sound like you.'

'Like they grew up outside Nottingham?'

'Like they went to school in England,' he clarified. 'Because most of them did. No, Balmaclay might be a grand house and Lizzie has her airs and graces but the McClays are farmers down to the bone. All of them except Cal, that is.'

'So, they were still together when he moved to London,' I said, pulling the conversation back on track. 'She stayed here? They did the long distance thing?'

Graham nodded.

'He travelled around a bit for a couple of years but she didn't want to leave home. When he settled in London, she went with him but Shiv was never going to last long in in a city that size. She thought it was a temporary relocation and they'd make their way back up here eventually.'

There was no disputing the fact Braewick was a long way from London, both figuratively and literally. I'd been counting the days until I could leave home, and I still found London overwhelming when I first arrived. I couldn't imagine suffering alone in a city you didn't love for someone else's sake.

'And they broke up because she gave him an ultimatum about getting married,' I said. 'Last Christmas?'

'Aye, I'd say that's accurate enough.'

His eyes broke from mine, darting around the little back yard behind the pub.

'But?' I said, rubbing my hands up and down my quickly cooling arms.

'But what?' he replied as his solid stance shifted into something less steady. 'There's no but. That's what he told you, that's the truth.'

As a doctor, you had to develop a certain sixth sense for when people weren't telling you the whole story. *Have you been taking your medication? Have you had any other symptoms? Would you like to revisit the number of units of alcohol listed here?* One third of my patients gave me the straight facts, one third underplayed things, the remaining third were total hypochondriacs. A finely tuned radar for bullshit was as essential as a stethoscope, a Starbucks loyalty card and a sense of humour, and in that moment it was pinging off the charts.

'Look, Graham, Callum's your friend.' I held out my hands, my sweet, innocent little hands to show I meant no harm. 'You want him to be happy, I want him to be happy. We both want the same thing, right?'

Tilting my head to one side, I waited patiently, watching as he pulled the lighter back out from his apron, flicking the wheel, sparks of gold at his fingertips.

'As his friend, if there's anything at all you think I should know, I won't tell him it came from you,' I added. 'Whatever it might be, goes with me to the grave.'

Which would be in about four minutes if I didn't get back inside soon.

'There's nothing to tell,' he said but the strain in his voice suggested otherwise. 'I was surprised he moved on so quickly, that's all, given how long they were together. If I had to say anything. If there was something to be said. That would be it.'

Only Callum hadn't moved on. He was still single. So single he'd felt he had to make up a fake girlfriend rather than go to the effort of finding a new one. Perhaps because he didn't really want a new one . . .

'Shiv is part of the family. Second daughter to Derek and Lizzie, big sister to Rory, Elsie's best friend.' Graham considered his last statement before adding, 'Elsie's only friend.'

'No surprises there,' I said and heard him scoff with agreeing laughter.

'I know he's got itchy feet now but if you want me to be brutally honest, I always thought he'd come home eventually, and when he did . . .'

'You thought he'd get back together with Shiv,' I finished for him.

Shrugging shoulders swallowed up Graham's nod.

'We all did.'

They weren't the only ones. A slight prickle stung the backs of my eyes which really made no sense at all. I was not Caroline. Callum was not my boyfriend. This did not affect me.

'Could be I'm wrong, it's clear he's mad about you,' Graham declared loudly. 'But if there's a less than warm welcome at Balmaclay, don't take it personally. I miss the wee bawbag as much as anyone, but Lizzie and Derek, they're getting older, they want their boy home. Anything that keeps him away is the enemy. Haven't seen them in the bakery for months, I think they're even holding a grudge against puddings.'

'And Shiv?'

The best he could manage was a rueful smile.

'I'll level with you, Caroline. It's hard to imagine Cal staying away from Braewick forever, but who knows how long she's prepared to wait?'

I sniffed in a lungful of air so cold it burned the inside of my nose and tore at my throat. At least I'd lost all feeling in my sore feet. Thank heaven for small mercies.

'Especially if he stays in Paris,' I said.

'Why would he stay in Paris?'

'Lots of people do,' I reasoned, picturing Callum swanning around the Champs-Élysées, baguette in hand. 'After they take the pastry course and do the internship, quite a few people end up getting a job and staying in France.'

At least according to the three a.m. Google search I'd done on the train.

Graham looked at me, confused, and suddenly the thought of freezing to death didn't seem so bad after all.

'Sorry, hen, you've lost me.'

'Paris,' I repeated. 'He's going to Paris to study at some fancy culinary institute?'

The shock on his face morphed into immeasurable pride. 'He got in?'

I gave the tiniest inclination of a nod.

'That sneaky wee bastard!' He whooped with joy while I winced at both the gust of wind that almost blew me off my feet and my own inability to keep my mouth shut. Callum hadn't told him. 'No, he hasn't told me. And I'd wager his parents don't know yet either, or his shrew of a sister.'

'Shit. I shouldn't have said anything,' I replied, looking back over my shoulder at the door to the pub. 'He probably wanted to tell you in person, please don't let on I ruined the surprise.'

With a huge grin, he rubbed the closely cropped hair on the top of his head with the palm of one hand.

'I can haul me wheesht if you can haul yours. Shall we get you back inside before you freeze your tits off? Your lips turned blue about three minutes ago and I think there's an icicle hanging off your left ear.'

It was the invitation I'd been waiting for.

Graham sauntered casually behind while I practically ran back inside, pressing as much of my frozen body as possible against the ancient radiator clunking away in the corridor, my teeth chattering so hard I was worried I'd break my jaw. The door to the kitchen swung open in front of us, the smell of fish and chips restoring my sense of smell and will to live.

'Since we're sharing secrets, do you think you could do me one more favour?' I asked, salivating at the sight of so much fried food.

'Anything as long as it requires nae effort on my part.'

'I can't eat my steak in front of Elsie. Do you have a box or something so I can take it away?'

'I know she's a wretched thing but she's nae so hackit you cannae eat in front of her,' Graham replied, looking deeply offended. 'That was the best steak I had and you want to let it go cold?'

'It's a very long story,' I said, just about ready to drop to my knees and beg. 'Please Graham, I need that steak more than I need to live, but for reasons best left unsaid, I can't eat it until I get home.'

'Bloody southerners,' he muttered, grumpy but amenable. 'Fine. I'll come and get your plates and make you a doggy bag. Just when I was starting to like you, as well.'

With an exasperated sigh, he hurled himself at the swinging kitchen door, disappearing back into the steam and smoke and pots and pans, yelling back and forth with a woman in a blue and white striped apron, his accent so strong, I could no longer understand a word that came out of his mouth.

Not that it mattered, he'd already said more than enough.

CHAPTER FIFTEEN

'Laura? Are you awake?'

'No,' I replied. 'I'm fast on.'

Callum slipped inside like a shadow, closing the door silently behind him.

'Couldn't sleep,' he said, keeping a safe distance from where I sat in the chair by the window. 'I thought I heard you moving around and wanted to make sure everything was all right and— are you eating a steak with your bare hands?'

'I didn't think popping downstairs and asking for a steak knife would be a good look for a vegan,' I replied, slipping what was left of my dinner back into the double-layered doggy bag Graham had begrudgingly prepared and wiping my hands on the flannel I'd been using as a napkin.

When I got back inside after my chat with Graham, Elsie looked like she was having a great time while Callum and Shiv looked ready to launch themselves directly into the sun, and the moment I mentioned the return of my migraine, the two of them raced each other to call it a night. It wasn't even eight when Shiv offered to give us all a ride back to Balmaclay, forcing me to choose between the physical pain of walking home in my too-small boots or the emotional discomfort of spending even more time in her company. As soon as we climbed into the battered old Land Rover, I knew I'd chosen badly. I could put plasters on my heels to cover my blisters but medical science had yet to come up with a reliable way to erase ten minutes of memory. Something for me to work on when I got back to the hospital.

Elsie kept up a constant stream of vaguely insulting chat but Callum could hardly keep his eyes off Shiv while she kept watch over me via the rearview mirror, radiating the kind of disdain I was only used to seeing from the woman who kept watch over the Nando's soft serve machine. They say it's bottomless but after your third visit, they really like to let you know you've had enough.

The moment we pulled up to the house, before the car had even come to a complete standstill, I was out the back and running (limping) back up to my room where I'd been, on my own, ever since.

'If you've come to apologise again, you don't have to,' I said as he settled against the windowsill, back to the glass, rather than committing to the second armchair that looked out onto the late-night loch. 'And if you want me to share this steak, you're dreaming.'

'Understood,' he replied, warm lamplight stretching his soft shadow across the room.

'How was the rest of your evening?'

'You'll be thrilled to hear Dad isn't sure if you're "hardy enough stock" to survive a Scottish winter.'

'He's right, I'm not,' I said. 'Although, you can never tell him that, obviously.'

'He didn't see you take down Elsie in The Clach. I've never been more impressed with anyone in my entire life.'

'Your sister has a gift,' I said, Callum's small smile graduating into a fully fledged grin. 'It's not nearly as easy as I thought it would be to act like a complete cow, except when it comes to your sister. I'm very anti-violence but she really is begging for someone to punch her right in the tit.'

When he laughed, smothering the sound with a hand over his mouth, I felt a shiver run through me and pulled my feet up onto the chair, tucking the blanket I'd found in the bottom of the wardrobe underneath them.

'Callum?'

'Laura.'

'Why haven't you told anyone you're moving to Paris?'

A small sound huffed from the back of his throat.

'How do you know I haven't?' he asked.

I pulled the blanket up to my chin, covering my red tartan shirt-and-short pyjamas.

'Because I accidentally let it slip to Graham but he promised he would keep it a secret. Sorry.'

Callum waved away my apology, still smiling in my general direction. 'It's fine, I was going to tell him tonight if I'd had a chance.'

'What about your mum and dad?'

'I was planning to tell them when I was safely on another continent.' His fingers curled around the windowsill and he ducked his head. 'Me getting into this programme means they have to take my career seriously and accept I'm never coming home to run the farm. Me and Shiv ruined last Christmas, I don't want to ruin this one.'

'I should think not,' I replied with a sniff. 'That's a job for Caroline.'

The lengths this man had gone to so he could avoid face-to-face confrontation with his family were absurd. But he hadn't asked for my opinion on the matter so I didn't comment. And ultimately he was trying to spare their feelings, hardly a bad thing.

He looked at odds with his surroundings again, the cosy antique aesthetic of Balmaclay clashing with his rumpled grey sweatpants and tissue-thin white T-shirt. His hair was a mess, as though he'd been tossing and turning, and even in the low light of the room, I could see shadows underneath his eyes. But he was still breathtakingly beautiful. I saw dozens of different people at work every day, hundreds a week, thousands a year, but I couldn't remember ever meeting anyone who made me stop and stare the way I was staring at Callum McClay.

'Mum and Dad still think I'm going to give up and come home,' he said, echoing Graham's theory as I tore my eyes away, concentrating on the hem of my blanket. 'They know I'm not earning much as a cook and they know the money Grandad left me is all gone. As far as my parents are concerned, it's a waiting game. When I tell them I'm not coming home and am in fact moving to another country to train to be a pastry chef, there's going to be hell to pay. You don't want to be here for it.'

'You mean *you* don't want to be here for it.'

Our eyes met and I felt as though I'd been pinned to my chair.

'Are you ever planning to tell them?' I asked.

A half-smile tugged at one side of his mouth.

'Eventually.'

'If only you had an incredibly demanding and difficult girlfriend who takes up all your time meaning you can never come home to visit.'

I looped my arms around my shins and rested my chin on my knees and his half-smile tugged higher.

'Shiv seems nice,' I added, mostly to be polite. Nice was a stretch. Shiv seemed fine, as long as you weren't me.

His smile disappeared without a trace.

'She is.' Callum turned to face the window, gazing out into the endless black. 'Shiv is about the nicest girl in the world.'

Before he'd come into the room, I'd sat in the darkness, allowing my eyes to adjust until all the shades of the night had revealed themselves, from deep blue to dove grey, the still water of the loch acting as a mirror to an icy white crescent moon. More stars than I'd ever seen in my life were scattered across the sky. In my day-to-day life, I was always too exhausted to look up at the end of a busy day and I wasn't sure how long I'd spent gazing at them in wonder. But now the window revealed nothing but flat black, loosely sketched outlines of my room and rough reflections of us, staring blindly out into nothing.

'Not to overstep the fake girlfriend line,' I said, swallowing hard before I finished my sentence. 'But do you think she might still have feelings for you?'

As if he'd read my mind, Callum reached over to the

lamp and turned it off. The reflected room disappeared in instant and, one by one, all the stars in the night sky flickered back into existence. In the heavy silence, my pulse thudded loudly in my ears, my heart rate picking up, skipping faster and faster, and I did not care for it at all.

'I don't know,' he replied honestly. 'Either way, sometimes feelings aren't enough. Doesn't mean things will work out.'

He moved from the windowsill to the second armchair. It was positioned at an angle and his legs were so long that when he stretched them out in front of him, they crossed in front of my chair, brushing against the drape of my blanket. The fabric moved against my skin and I shivered.

'Isn't it a choice?' I asked. 'Nothing is easy, you always have to make an effort if you want something to work.'

'Laura, why are you single?'

It was such an unexpected question, delivered so abruptly, I was lost for words. He didn't turn to face me when he asked it and there was just enough moonlight to sketch out his profile but not show his expression. I had no idea what he was thinking.

'I don't have time for a relationship,' I told him after a moment's deliberation. 'The career I've chosen, it's a big commitment, more than a job. It's a vocation. Doesn't leave a lot of time for going on dates, getting to know someone.'

'That's the only reason?'

'The main reason.' I squeezed my hands together, trying to control the feelings that washed over me in waves, anxiety, anticipation, intrigue. 'It's a lot to ask someone to take on, a relationship with a surgeon.

You're not dependable, always on call, always missing important occasions. Most people don't understand, and I don't think it's fair to expect them to.'

'Isn't it a choice?' Callum replied. 'Nothing is easy. You always have to make an effort if you want something to work.'

I held my breath as he leaned forward, elbows on knees, oxygen-depleted blood thundering around my body. I wasn't used to someone else's presence having this kind of effect on me. I wasn't used to anyone else's presence having any kind of effect on me.

'Another person can't complete you,' I said, no weight to my words whatsoever. 'Not everyone has to have someone.'

'No,' he agreed. 'But everyone deserves someone. You deserve someone.'

We both turned, only by a fraction, but at the exact same time. Our eyes met for a moment then Callum looked away and I felt winded, like I'd fallen from a great height, and all the air had been knocked out my body.

'How come you weren't asleep?' he asked, flexing his bare feet against the floor.

'I was hungry.'

Not a lie but it wasn't the whole truth either. I was always hungry. The thing that had me staring at the ceiling until I eventually climbed out of bed and started my midnight snack, was the thought of Callum and Shiv, childhood sweethearts, meant to be.

'What about you?'

'Same.'

In silence, he rose from his chair, and I felt a tug in my chest.

'I'll let you get back to . . .'

His gaze fell on the side table.

'Eating a piece of steak with my bare hands?'

There it was, that smile again. I felt an unexpected throb in the pit of my stomach.

No, lower. It caught me off guard and I clenched my thighs together.

'Goodnight, Laura.'

'Goodnight, Callum.'

I didn't move when he let himself out. Instead, I sat in silence and listened for him in the room next door. Nothing. He said he'd heard me moving around. Had he really? Perhaps. I couldn't hear him but I could feel him, sense his presence on the other side of the wall, imagine him sitting in the chair still, watching the night alongside me.

'This is not good,' I whispered to myself, pulling the blanket back up to my chin as I stared out at the loch, legs pressed tightly together. 'This is not good at all.'

And for the second night in a row, I failed to get even a wink of sleep, all because of Callum McClay.

CHAPTER SIXTEEN

'I'm sorry you're not feeling well again. You're sure you don't want to come with us?'

Lizzie McClay stood with her spine so rigid, I was sure if someone were to flick her in the forehead, she would shatter into a million pieces.

With my duvet wrapped around my head and clutched underneath my chin, I shuffled across the kitchen floor. Behind his mother, Callum watched on, his face a picture of concern.

'You've done enough,' I sniffed from inside my cocoon. 'I'll be all right once it's all out my system.'

'I've never heard of anyone getting food poisoning from tap water,' Lizzie said, wringing her hands. 'You're sure it's not something you ate at The Clach?'

'I didn't eat at The Clach, they didn't have anything . . .' a dramatic hand pressed against my forehead, eyes closed, 'vegan.'

'You're probably just hungry,' she replied, turning to the fridge. 'Let me make you some toast. Toast always helps when you've an upset stomach.'

'No complex carbs,' I protested weakly. 'Think of my gut microbiome.'

'Caroline needs to rest.' Callum pulled his mother away from the fridge, reassuring hands on her shoulders. 'You'll be all right, won't you, babe?'

Slumping over the kitchen counter, I closed my eyes, weakened by the effort it took to breathe.

'Eventually.'

I added a pathetic cough for extra drama.

'We won't be gone too long,' Lizzie said when Callum began to guide her towards the door. 'Only we always visit Derek's sister before she drives down south to see my nephew and—'

'Go!' I ordered, flinging an arm over my face to shield my sensitive eyes from the weak morning light. 'Leave me be!'

Fighting a smile, Callum gave her a careful shove out the door.

'Go on, Mum. I'll be out in a minute.'

Lizzie looked to her son, full of alarm, but he nodded and, with great reluctance, she left the two of us alone.

'Very well done,' he emphasised his praise with a slow clap. 'You look like a lunatic.'

'Thank you, I do my best work under pressure.' I dropped the duvet, leaning casually against the counter in my PJs. 'How long do you think you'll be out?'

'It'll be a while, Auntie Jean loves a chat and Dad will want to stop at the pub for a swift one with Uncle Jimmy. The whole family used to come here every year but my cousin, Drew, moved to England, so now we go to them on the twenty-third, they go south to him on Christmas Eve, and he comes back with his husband for Hogmanay. God forbid we break with a family tradition, you know how it is.'

'We don't have any so no, I don't actually,' I said with a bittersweet smile. 'Actually no, that's not fair. We used to have traditions.'

'Like what?'

'The usual stuff, nothing wacky. Decorating the tree, presents in stockings, me and Mum would always go to the carol service in the town hall, that sort of thing.'

Callum took a beat, his eyes watching me as I filled a glass with allegedly poisonous water.

'Your tap water is delicious,' I muttered. 'In case you didn't know.'

'I know you don't really have food poisoning but are you sure you're OK by yourself?' he asked over the sound of an engine turning over outside the window. 'Fi's out for the day and Mal's driving, you're on your own.'

'You won't believe this,' I replied, hopping up onto the kitchen counter, 'but I've been on my own in a house before.'

He smiled, running a finger along the edge of the wooden kitchen table.

'I could stay. If you wanted me to.'

I took a long drink from my glass of water to moisten my suddenly dry mouth. Callum waited for me to swallow before I replied with forced indifference.

'Why would I want you to stay?'

'Not entirely sure.' He raked a hand through his hair before resetting with a hard exhale. 'Right, I'll see you later. Oh, and I made you breakfast, it's hiding in the oven. Feel free to use a knife and fork this time.'

'Text when you're on your way back!' I called as

he departed, hopping down from the kitchen counter to peek out the window and watch him climb into the passenger seat of Mal's Mercedes like a crazed stalker.

Once the car had disappeared, I bolted across the room to the dark green AGA at the heart of the kitchen. As someone whose culinary expertise began and ended with toast, I would never even consider getting involved with anything so complicated myself, but it was stunning to behold in the same way I could appreciate other beautiful things that were of no practical use to me, like a fancy sports car or Timothée Chalamet.

'Hiding was right,' I muttered, unlatching one oven after another, different temperatures blasting me in the face. 'Where the bloody hell is my bloody food?'

Behind the bottom left-hand door, I finally found my prize. A full Scottish breakfast. Callum had outdone himself, fried eggs, bacon, black pudding, square sausage, beans, mushrooms, tomatoes and something that looked a bit like a cross between a triangular pancake and a slice of bread. When I broke off a piece, it tasted like potato.

'Why have I never been to Scotland before?' I wondered out loud, furious at myself for suffering through so many years without this bounty.

Before anything could get cold, I moved the plate to the kitchen table, rifled through the drawers for a set of cutlery and got stuck in. Out of everything on the plate, Caroline could probably just about stomach the baked beans, everything else was either meat, carbs or cooked in bacon fat, but Laura was thrilled. Every mouthful was delicious. When I was done, I washed my plate and cutlery, located their homes and put everything away. The kitchen looked as though I'd never been there in the first place.

Exactly how it would be on Boxing Day when I left and never came back.

'You're being so stupid,' I whispered as a strange sadness settled on my shoulders, smothering my post-breakfast buzz. 'It's not like you're banned from Scotland. There have to be a million places around here, probably even nicer than this.'

Was there a place nicer than this? Hard to say, I'd only seen the hall, the kitchen, the dining room and my bedroom. By my rough calculations, that left ten thousand other rooms to investigate.

'No time like the present,' I declared, scooping my duvet up from the floor and dragging it along behind me as I trotted back upstairs to get dressed.

When we'd first arrived, Derek had been itching to give me the grand tour of his ancestral family home, but his enthusiasm wavered after our first awkward meal together. It was fine by me. So far, pretending to be Caroline was not nearly as much fun as I'd hoped it would be. I'd been expecting arsey parents and an evil ex, not complicated family dynamics and a walking, talking, broken-hearted Barbie doll. As for my cosy Scottish fantasies, yes, I had the open fire and my books. But there would be no more whisky for this non-drinking vegan, and my walking boots had given me blisters so brutal, I'd let out a silent scream when I slid out of bed that morning and shoved my feet into my slippers without thinking.

I was so grateful for my ability to emotionally detach, I thought, as I wrapped myself up in a soft mohair sweater and long satin skirt, both a deep shade of red that clashed terribly with my hair but made the right sort of festive statement. Desi and Joel might accuse me of being a robot but anyone else would struggle to keep their feelings straight in this kind of situation. Anyone else might get pulled in, either by Elsie's relentless abuse or Callum's confusing relationship with Shiv. But not me. My job wasn't exactly a straightforward nine-to-five. It required a delicate balance of empathy, trust and distance. Sometimes you couldn't avoid forming relationships with patients, and there was no way around the fact things didn't always go the way we hoped they would, but that was why doctors had to learn to stay detached. And I was so good at bundling up my feelings and stashing them away so the pain couldn't touch me. Even when the worst possible thing happened, I could always reassure myself that I'd done my best, that we, as a team, had done everything we could for our patients.

So what if I'd been awake until the wee small hours, staring at the canopy hanging over my bed, and fantasised about Callum coming back into my room, taking me in his arms and absolutely blowing my back out? Fantasies didn't mean anything. Sex wasn't love. It wasn't as though anyone could pretend Callum wasn't attractive, objectively speaking, and if I were in the market for a relationship, I might have considered him. But I wasn't, so it was a moot point.

'Moot,' I said to the empty hallway when I left my room. 'Absolutely moot.'

One thing about me, I talked to myself altogether too much, but sometimes things made more sense when you heard them aloud. Not to other people, obviously, it made me look completely insane, but the habit was set now and there was no breaking it.

Fighting the urge to strip naked and dance through the house to a Sophie Ellis-Bextor song, I meandered down the hallway, trying door handles as I went and poking my head inside various rooms. Most were locked but even the corridors and hallways were enough to stun me into silence. Hospitals were drab by design, insipid institutional colour palettes and antiseptic scents, and the contrary splendour of Balmaclay was an assault on my day-job-dulled senses. I'd never seen so many different patterns of wallpaper in my life. I hadn't even known so many different patterns of wallpaper existed. Colour was everywhere, deep jewel tones and rich earthy shades, complementing thoughtfully placed pieces of furniture in mahogany and oak. A console table here, an umbrella stand there. Then there were the little touches, a milk jug filled with dried heather, a vase of preserved wildflowers, antique plates and bowls, lamps and sconces, and painting after painting after painting. The sheer amount of dusting this house must require brought me out in a rash. Every time a doorknob gave in my hand and I tiptoed inside, I heard myself gasp with wonder. A study. A sitting room. A library. Any second now, I expected an anthropomorphic candelabra to jump out at me and start singing about my next meal.

I came to the furthest end of the newly reopened Campbell wing and found a large, ancient-looking door. It wasn't locked but it was impossibly heavy, too heavy for me to open without gargantuan effort. So naturally, that's what I gave it. If it wasn't locked, it wasn't forbidden. I had to know what was behind that door. Putting my whole weight behind it, I shoved the rusted iron latch upwards, puffing out my cheeks with the strain, and when it began to give, I jostled it back and forth. I was determined to get inside. The door creaked and complained, screeching across the stone floor as I forced it open an inch at a time, a gust of cold air racing by like I'd released some malevolent force.

'Which I haven't,' I told myself sternly. 'Because there are no such thing as ghosts.'

But if there were, this was where they would be.

Sliding through the barely open door, I entered a small stone room, only a couple of metres square, and in the middle of the small stone room was a staircase. Craning my neck back, I looked up. The tower! I was in the tower. Even though I was knackered from opening the door, the thought of the view from the top spurred me onwards. Or at least it did for the first three flights of stairs, at which point I had to take a break before tackling the final two.

It was worth it. Worth the lactic acid building up in my glutes and quadriceps, worth sweating through my brand new dry-clean-only jumper, worth the fact I was so out of breath, I couldn't even stand up straight for a solid minute once I reached the top. I didn't even regret snagging my skirt on that bare nail, mostly because it wasn't mine in the first place; I'd borrowed it from Desi.

The tiny town of Braewick was celebrating Christmas Eve Eve with a bright and cloudless sky, and I felt like I could see to the ends of the earth. The mountains curved and rolled, looking like they would be soft to the touch thanks to the tall, dense pine tree that lined the slopes. Nestled below, the loch rippled with a harsh breeze, darkest blue at the banks, stretching lighter into the distance. It reminded me of Callum's eyes, all those different shades marbled together to create something unique, sapphire and aquamarine, with an almost black limbal ring encircling the iris.

'The oxygen must be thinner up here,' I mumbled, leaning as far out of a small, square, open window as I could, the wind effectively slapping me back to my senses.

Then something occurred to me. The best thing about this skirt, aside from the fact I hadn't paid for it, were the pockets, and in one of those pockets was my phone. It totally made up for the fact I'd had to wear uncomfortable seamless knickers to avoid a VPL. I gasped when I swiped the screen into life to see four full bars of reception. This was the best skirt, the best tower, and I couldn't dial Desi's number fast enough.

'About fucking time,' she barked, answering the moment my call connected. 'Joel, call the police and tell them she's alive, they can call off the search.'

His voice came across loud and clear when she put him on speakerphone.

'They never started. They looked her up and said no great loss.'

'Ha ha, very funny, I miss you too.' I rested my elbows on the ledge and let the wind ruffle my hair. 'There is literally no reception up here, it's terrifying.'

'And no WiFi?'

After harassing Callum for the password, I'd discovered there was internet at Balmaclay but it was terrible. Just about strong enough to send a text, provided you held your phone at exactly the right angle in exactly the right location, but not clear enough to make calls or, even worse, stream Netflix. When I asked how his parents managed to communicate with the outside world and he said they called them on a landline, it was all I could do not to shrink back in horror. The only place I'd had dependable internet service was inside the main bar at The Clach and, thanks to Elsie's presence, smartphone-free Caroline hadn't been able to take advantage of it.

'How goes it?' Joel asked, the sound of whatever was playing on their TV fading away into the background. 'Have you boffed him yet?'

'Don't be stupid, Joel. She's not going to boff him, remember? She's not interested in the tall, handsome pastry chef whose family live in a great big massive house next to a great big massive lake.'

'How do you know about the house?' I asked Desi, perplexed.

'Because I'm better at online sleuthing than you,' she replied. 'I also know where he went to university, where he works and what car he drives. If you can find out the name of his childhood pet, I'll have his blood type and National Insurance number by the end of the day.'

'You're genuinely frightening sometimes.'

'So you'll ask him?'

'As soon as he's back,' I promised. 'Never hurts to know someone's blood type.'

The wind kicked up a playful gust and I shivered, moving away from the glass-less windows, a loud bang sounding from somewhere down below. If I'd known I'd be exposed to the elements, I would've worn my coat. And Callum's coat. I would've worn as many coats as I could get my hands on.

'Go on then,' Joel said, his impatience simmering down the line. 'Tell us everything. How's it going?'

'It's going,' I replied. 'Turns out I'm not quite as good at being a massive cow as I thought.'

Desi scoffed. 'Then you're not trying.'

'Maybe I don't have the same motivation as I do at home,' I suggested and Joel laughed. 'The whole fake girlfriend situation is more complicated than I realised and if you even think the words "I told you so" I will teleport back to London and punch you in the boob before you have time to finish the sentence.'

'Complicated how? I thought you said you haven't shagged him?' Joel asked as Desi cackled happily in the background, taking my admission as vindication.

There was nothing Desi loved more on this earth than being proved right.

'I haven't and I'm not going to.' I scraped a stray strand of hair out of my eyes and tucked it forcibly behind my ear only for it to blow right back out. 'It's his family. They're just, well, they're a lot. Plus I met his ex and she's actually really nice. I just feel really bad for everyone.'

'Why?'

The confusion in Desi's voice reminded me she was incapable of feeling bad for anyone about anything except, for some reason, the romantic tribulations of Jennifer Lopez. She still hadn't got over the Bennifer 2.0 divorce.

'His parents want him to come home to run their farm and live in their great big massive house, as you so elegantly put it, that has passed on to the eldest son for centuries. His sister resents him because she has to run the farm instead, and his ex I haven't quite got a handle on yet but, if I had to put money on it, I'd say she's still in love with him. And,' I paused to take a breath. 'There's a chance he's still in love with her too.'

I clamped my mouth shut, eyes squeezed shut while I waited for their verdict.

'If he's still in love with her and she's still in love with him, why aren't they together?' Joel asked.

'Because she wants to live up here and he wants to learn how to make croissants in Paris.'

'If you're going to learn to make them anywhere,' he reasoned.

'Sounds like he's stitched you up.' Desi sounded annoyed, or rather, slightly more annoyed than usual. 'Assuming he knew about all these complications and didn't bother to mention any of it when he proposed this ridiculous plan in the first place.'

'When *I* proposed this ridiculous plan,' I corrected. 'He didn't beg me to do this, Des, I offered.'

'Too nice,' she admonished. 'This is where being too nice gets you.'

'Doesn't matter anyway, I'm here now.' I stamped my feet on the wooden floor as a chill started to creep into my bones. 'And I'm supposed to be making them hate me. Any suggestions on how to be a wildly dislikable human being without committing actual hate crimes?'

'Have you tried starting every sentence with "Well, actually"?' Joel offered.

'I've got a good one,' Desi said. 'How would they take a passionate speech about how much you love Meghan Markle?'

Joel sucked the air in through his teeth. 'Oh, that's a good one. That would finish my dad off.'

'Anything else?' I asked, deliberating as I pulled the sleeve of my jumper down over my left hand.

'You can always fall back on the classics,' Desi said. 'Backhanded compliments, thinly veiled insults about their son, pointing out how you've had to fix his poor upbringing, that sort of thing.'

'I always find a well-timed sigh can be pleasingly annoying,' Joel added. 'Then when they ask you what's wrong, just say nothing. It really pisses parents off, I have no idea why.'

'Triggering,' Desi confirmed. 'Very triggering.'

'And how is he, the hot chef?' Joel asked. 'Are the two of you getting on?'

'He's fine, I think.' I leaned back against the cold stone wall of the tower and blew out a heavy breath. 'He's funny, easy to talk to. Cooks an excellent breakfast. None of this is his fault, it's a shit situation.'

'Sounds rough,' he replied with great sympathy. 'Poor Callum.'

'I know,' I agreed even though I wasn't quite sure whether or not he was being sarcastic. 'You'd both really like him though. He's funny.'

'You've already said funny,' Desi replied. 'He can't be funny twice.'

'What are you two doing?' I asked, diverting the subject. I knew that tone of voice, she was about to say something I didn't want to hear.

Joel replied through a mouth full of something. 'We're watching *A Muppet Christmas Carol* and eating.'

'Eating what?'

'Everything. My patience ran out, we opened the Christmas cupboard a day early.'

I sighed loudly. The Christmas cupboard. Cadbury's Roses, Miniature Heroes, mint Matchmakers, After Eights and a never-ending supply of mini mince pies.

'That's it. Laura, I think you should come home,' Desi declared. 'This is not what you signed up for and you sound really stressed out. Call an Uber and get the next train back.'

'I can't.'

'Yes, you can.'

'No, I literally can't,' I told her, flipping through my apps. 'There are no Ubers.'

'Christ on a bike,' Joel gasped. 'Where the fuck *are* you?'

'It's not as bad as I'm making out,' I said again, more determined this time. 'The house is gorgeous, and honestly, you should see the scenery. Besides, I can't leave Callum in the lurch. He needs me.'

My statement was followed by a pause so long, I had to check my phone to make sure we hadn't been cut off.

'Hello?' I said. 'Are you still there?'

'You mean you don't want to leave,' Desi said calmly. 'There's nothing stopping you but you.'

'Maybe you should come here,' I answered with an unnecessary touch of petulance. 'It's only an eleven-hour drive to Balmaclay.'

'Don't tempt me,' Joel replied. 'You know I love a road trip.'

I laughed loudly at the thought of the two of them bickering in Desi's Mini then almost fell backwards down the stairs when a massive black bird flapped past the window.

'You OK?' Desi asked when I shrieked.

'Fine,' I replied, watching it fly away. 'Bird.'

A hint of homesickness poked at me. It would've been nice to be squished on the sofa like three sardines, eating junk and doomscrolling, while Michael Caine put in the greatest performance of his life on the TV.

The fact he didn't get an Oscar for it was a travesty. Perhaps I could convince Callum to watch it with me later.

'I'd better go,' I said as my teeth started chattering. 'It's freezing here.'

'Cold in Scotland?' Desi said with sarcastic surprise. 'You don't say?'

'If I don't call you again it's because I couldn't be arsed to climb a five-storey tower to get the reception, and no, I won't be elaborating on that statement,' I said as Joel blew kisses down the line. 'Happy Christmas Eve Eve, love you.'

'Love you too,' they chorused before the call ended with three beeps and I was alone in the tower again.

It really was stunning. Thin strands of cotton wool clouds had appeared out of nowhere, stretching across the sky as if someone were trying to wrap up the world. Down on the loch, I spotted a handful of small boats, men with fishing rods, and wondered if their catch would be on the menu at The Clach later. Gorgeous as it was, I hadn't been kidding when I told Desi and Joel I was cold. Not outside-the-pub, bitter-to-the-bone frozen, but uncomfortably chilly. After taking dozens of photos from all four sides of the tower and texting them back to my friends, I gazed out at the landscape one more time to commit it to memory, then dashed down the stairs, dreaming of the open fire I hoped was still burning in my room.

But when I reached the bottom of the staircase, the door I'd left open was closed.

Hmm.

Not panicking even a little bit, I attempted to push the latch upwards but it didn't budge an inch and, in the back of my mind, I remembered the loud bang I'd heard at the top of the tower when the wind blew in.

Double hmm.

Bearing down in a semi-squat, I heaved the latch upwards again. Still nothing.

'Hello?' I called, banging on the door from the inside. 'Hello? Is anybody there?'

No one answered.

No one was home.

And I was trapped in a freezing cold tower wearing a sweaty mohair sweater and a satin skirt and uncomfortable underwear all by myself.

CHAPTER SEVENTEEN

'Help!' I yelled, hammering on the door. 'I'm trapped in here! Can anyone hear me?'

Strangely enough, there was no response from the completely empty house. I didn't know if Elsie had gone with her parents and Callum or she was working on the farm but, even if she were around, she was just as likely to leave me here to freeze to death as help get me out.

Without too many options, I trudged back up the stairs, whimpering by the time I got to the top, practically on my hands and knees.

'Hello?!' I was screaming now, the back of my throat scratching with the effort. 'Hello!'

But the boats on the loch were too far away, any farm workers out of earshot. Even the cows in the closest fields ignored me when I shouted in their direction.

'Don't panic, no need to panic,' I chanted to myself, pulling out my phone and searching for the spot of reception. I would simply call Callum and he would come home. He'd already been gone a couple of hours, his aunt couldn't live that far away, he wouldn't mind cutting the visit short. I scrolled through my contacts, looking for 'Callum Landlord', and jabbed at the call button with shaky fingers.

The phone rang.

And rang.

And rang.

'Answer your bloody phone!' I sobbed, leaning further out the window as the connection began to cut in and out. 'For fuck's sake, Callum, I swear—'

'Hello?'

The sound of his voice soothed me instantly and I heard myself burst into tears.

'Callum,' I said, breathing a shivery sigh of relief. 'It's me.'

'I guessed that from your name on the screen,' he replied. 'What's up?'

'Oh, not much,' I laughed not at all hysterically. 'Don't panic but I'm trap— argh!'

A massive black bird, possibly the same massive black bird as before, swooped down from the sky and into the tower, brushing past my face with a nightmarish caw. I stumbled to the side, arms shooting up to protect me from its talons but as my hands covered my face, my phone slipped through my fingers, sailing through the air. I watched with horror as it landed on the solid stone ledge of the window, bounced twice, then settled, balancing right on the edge.

'Hello?' I heard Callum's tinny voice reverberating through the tiny speaker. 'Laura, are you there?'

And then my phone fell from the top of the tower, crashing all the way down to the ground.

'Well, fuck,' I said flatly.

On the opposite side of the window, the bird cocked its head to one side and stared at me with one shiny eye.

'If I die up here, you have to promise not to eat me,' I told it, my back pressed against the wall as I slid all the way down onto my arse. It cawed again, flapped its wings and launched itself out the window with considerably more grace than my phone.

And that was it.

I was done for.

Shivering in earnest, my clothes offering no respite from the weather, I wrapped my arms around myself and huddled into a ball. Even the glorious blue sky had turned on me, turning almost white with a chill wind that cut through to my bones. In the worst possible conditions, a human being could die from hypothermia in fifteen minutes. These were not those conditions but there were variables to take into account. My lack of proper outerwear for example, not to mention the fact I was a big giant baby. My final outfit was not flattering. My final Instagram post, the one all my friends would flock to and leave their heartbroken condolences, was of me sitting in a lecherous Santa's lap at the work Christmas party, three sheets to the wind and, if you zoomed in, showing my knickers. And in my final conversation, I'd instinctively chosen sarcasm over immediately asking for help. Being a smartarse was literally going to be the death of me. As far as last meals went, I couldn't complain there, but what I wouldn't give to have a Terry's Chocolate Orange to soothe me through these dark final hours, as was right and traditional on Christmas Eve Eve.

I moaned sadly as a list of all the things I would never

eat again ran through my head. Fresh French bread, a hunk of sharp cheddar and a bowl of baby tomatoes. Joel's spaghetti Bolognese. Dairylea Lunchables. I would never find out what shape was in the final window of the Galaxy advent calendar I'd squished in my suitcase rather than leave behind for Desi to plunder. Dozens of patients had told me stories about their lives flashing in front of their eyes in life-or-death circumstances but all I could think about was the Costa Coffee melted snowman gingerbread biscuit and how I'd never taste its like again.

'Unless there really is a heaven,' I sniffed.

If there was, heaven probably had a Costa. I couldn't see them going for a Starbucks.

No, I decided, wiping a tear away from under my eye before it could freeze to my face. I was not going out like this. Not when I had an unopened bag of Cadbury Snowballs in my backpack. No, they weren't as good as Mini Eggs but damn it, they were the best we could do. At least until the first of January when the shops put all the Easter sweets out. So help me God, I would live to eat another Creme Egg.

Forcing myself to my feet, I rubbed my runny nose, sniffing the razor-sharp air and letting it cut through my panic like a knife. There were people around, they just couldn't hear me. All I needed was another way to get their attention, like a flare gun or a flag. A bright red flag. With grim acceptance, I looked down at Desi's skirt. Desi's bright red skirt.

'She doesn't like it anyway,' I told myself as I wriggled out of the flimsy fabric, letting it pool around my feet on the floor. 'She never wears it. She probably hasn't even noticed I borrowed it. She'd rather have me alive than one random red skirt hanging in her wardrobe.'

I hesitated for a moment. Was that true? Hopefully. Hell hath no fury like a Desi who wasn't asked permission. If I was wrong, she'd likely drive all the way to Scotland to march me back up here and throw me over the side with my phone.

It didn't matter. All that was important now was attracting someone's attention with my holly-berry-red satin flag. I leaned out of the window as far as I dared, starting on the side of the loch, waving the skirt wildly, my half-bare backside exposed to the elements. It was a long jumper but it wasn't quite long enough. None of the boats made any attempt to move so I switched sides, angling myself sideways in the direction of the farm. Maybe one of the bulls would see and charge all the way across the fields. That would get someone's attention. Or it would crash into the side of the ancient tower and bring it down, and I would die that way instead. Either/or, at least I wouldn't be up here on my own, freezing to death.

'Hello!' I yelled again, rubbing my legs together as I jogged on the spot. 'Anyone? Can you hear me? I'm going to die in about ten minutes!'

No response.

'Oh, for fuck's sake,' I screamed. 'I'll even take help from Elsie if she's around!'

'Christ, things must be bad.'

I howled with delight at the sound of another voice, gripping the edge of the window and peering down to the ground. It was a man, not Callum, although they looked similar from all the way up here.

'Hello!' I shouted down, still waving my skirt-flag.

'I'm stuck. The door blew shut behind me and I can't get out. Can you help me?'

'And you are?'

It was a fair question.

'Lau— Caroline,' I corrected myself, lightning fast. 'Yourself?'

'Rory,' he said with a salute. 'Did Elsie lock you in there?'

'Not as far as I know but I wouldn't put it past her.'

Of course, the youngest McClay, home from university in Glasgow. He laughed to himself, muttering something I couldn't hear.

'Where is everyone?' he called up.

'Out? Visiting family?'

'What about Mal and Fi?'

'Also out,' I replied. 'Can you open the door?' I asked again. 'I'm literally freezing my arse off.'

He nodded, patting himself down for a set of keys, the same as his dad, the same as his brother. 'Aye, LaCaroline, can do. I haven't got the upper body strength to climb up your hair, so we'll have a crack at the door instead.'

I let go of my skirt with one hand to give him a confirmatory wave as he disappeared inside the house, only for the wind to snatch the slippery fabric from my frozen fingers and whisk it away out of reach.

'Perfect,' I groaned, all the colour draining from my face as I watched it settle in the top branches of a very tall silver birch, winding itself around the slender branches. 'Just perfect.'

Because nothing said nice to meet you, thanks for rescuing me and Merry Christmas to your boyfriend's brother like missing the bottom half of your outfit.

Even if it was considerably more than Callum had been wearing when we first met.

Opening the door took a lot more effort the second time around.

'It's wedged tight,' Rory shouted through the wood. 'What did you do? Solder it shut behind you?'

'*I* managed to open it,' I exclaimed, trying to jostle the latch from my side. 'And I'm weak as a kitten.'

'I'll have you know I work out five times a week with special emphasis on the vanity muscles and they're the ones I'm trying to tear off the bone right now to get you out.'

'Maybe you should go and get help,' I suggested, rubbing my palms up and down over my bare thighs, trying to chase away the goosebumps. 'Or call your brother?'

'And have everybody rip the piss out of me all Christmas? I don't think so,' he scoffed. 'Give it a shoogle from your side.'

'I'm shoogling!' I shouted, shaking the rusted iron as best I could. 'I've been shoogling! I'm all shoogled out!'

I combed my hands through my hair, palms pressed against my skull. It was completely hopeless. Rory couldn't get the door open on his own, my legs were turning a beautiful shade of corned beef mottled pink, and I couldn't feel my feet at all. Completely and utterly hopeless.

'I reckon it's going to open any minute,' Rory said. 'Give it one more good shove.'

'OK,' I said, pulling the hem of my jumper down over my arse and sinking down on the bottom step of the staircase. 'Try it now.'

'Are you pushing?'

'Yep,' I lied, examining my nails while I tried not to cry.

'It's nearly there . . .' he groaned with the effort. 'It's nearly there . . .'

To my extreme surprise, the door screeched open and a red-faced Scotsman collapsed through it, falling to the floor in front of me.

'Rory!' I jumped up, flung my arms around his neck and kissed his sweaty auburn head. 'Oh my God, I love you!'

Without waiting for a reply, I raced out of the tower and back into the house proper, hurling myself at the first radiator I came to, stretching out my arms and pressing my whole body against it. Warmth. Magical, wonderful warmth. I would never take central heating for granted again.

'Might help if you'd bothered to put on your trews this morning,' Rory said, climbing back to his feet.

I yanked the hem down again, the jumper fully stretched out of shape, and it still only just covered my backside.

'I'm not leaving my room again without a full set of thermals,' I assured him. 'But seriously, thank you. I really thought I was going to be stuck up there.'

I looked up to see him frowning down at me.

'What's wrong?' I asked, yanking my jumper lower. 'Apart from the obvious?'

'Nothing,' he replied. 'Only, I was sure Callum said you were blonde.'

'After that I did molecular biosciences for a year but all the second-year lectures were in the morning and

I'm not a morning person.' Rory poured two very strong cups of tea from his mother's stoneware teapot. 'I switched over to astronomy but I couldn't see a future in it so I'm doing history of art instead.'

'Because there's so many more careers in that field?'

'Right,' he agreed, missing my sarcasm completely. 'Immunology was probably the most interesting subject I've done but who wants to get caught up in all that if there's another pandemic?'

'Immunologists?' I suggested.

Heaping a very large teaspoon of sugar into my mug, I considered the youngest McClay sibling as he produced a jug of milk from the fridge. He was tall like everyone else in the family and had the same shade of rusted brown hair but instead of blue eyes, his were grey, like his mum's. Rory was a knockout. There was a mischievous glow about him that was missing in his siblings but I recognised it as pure undiluted Derek McClay. Third time lucky, they'd created a perfect blend of both parents.

He stuck out the tip of his tongue, concentrating as he added milk to his mug and still managing to spill it all over the table.

'Who knows what I'll do at the end of this year. Might be time to try something different.'

'A job?'

'Fuck no, I meant a different course.'

'Right.' I smiled when he went to pick up his tea, neither crying over or even bothering to clean up the spilled milk. 'If you enjoyed immunology, I really think it's worth giving it a second look. There are tons of opportunities, you'd get to travel and the field has some funding right now, compared to most others, that is. No one ever has enough funding.'

Rory squinted at me.

'How come you know so much about it? Aren't you a massage therapist?'

'A passing interest,' I blustered, wrapping my still frozen hands around the roasting hot mug. 'Sort of a hobby.'

'Could you not spend your spare time doomscrolling on TikTok like normal people?'

We both laughed, me with nerves but Rory as carefree as I assumed he always was. After ten minutes in his company, I got the feeling Rory McClay didn't worry himself too much about anything.

'You're an interesting one, aren't you?' He kicked his feet up onto the kitchen table, surveying me with a curious eye. 'How did you and Callum meet again?'

Shit. I had no idea what he'd told them, if anything.

'It's such a boring story,' I lied through a yawn. 'If I tell it again I'll put myself to sleep. Tell me about Glasgow, is it fun? I've never been.'

'It's the best, you should go.' He took the bait happily, jumping on my offer to talk about himself. 'Perfect place for the black sheep of the family.'

'You?' I grinned as he dug around in the open biscuit tin between us. 'I thought Callum was the black sheep?'

'Callum is the prodigal son,' he corrected. 'Dad's waiting for him to come home and beg forgiveness, trust me. I also did a semester of ecumenical studies, I know what I'm talking about.'

I helped myself to a chocolate digestive and gave it a dunk.

'I never did understand that saying. The black sheep can't be that bad, everyone wants his wool in the nursery rhyme.'

'That's me all right. They all want a bit of me.'

Rory gave me a sly grin and I matched his expression with a smirk of my own.

'Which only leaves one question. If Callum's the prodigal son and you're the black sheep, what does that make Elsie?'

'All work and no play, makes Elsie a dull coo,' he answered. 'There's no helping my sister. Chop off her arm and you'll find the word "martyr" running through her like "Blackpool" through rock.'

'And if I cut you open, we'd find the words "work-shy bastard".'

Elsie stormed into the kitchen with perfect and terrible timing. Hair scraped back, clad in a well-worn wax jacket, her cheeks pink from the cold, she gave the both of us a look that would strike a lesser man dead.

'Elsie, my dearest, darling sister,' Rory said, utterly unmoved. 'Merry Christmas.'

'Is it?'

I braced myself for impact when she turned her eyes to me.

'Can you explain why Callum has been screaming at me down the phone, demanding I come up to the house to check on you when you're sat here scranning biscuits with Rory?'

I shrugged.

'Just a thoughtful person, I suppose.'

'He's an idiot,' she snapped back. 'He's a selfish, inconsiderate, heedless idiot. You can call him back and tell him you're alive, I'm not his bloody servant.'

I'd met a lot of disproportionately angry people in my time – Joel when Netflix recast Henry Cavill in *The Witcher*, Desi when faced with even the most minor inconvenience and even me when they changed the recipe of Percy Pigs – but I wasn't sure I'd ever met anyone filled with quite so much irrational rage as Elsie McClay.

Before she could skewer me with another sharply worded attack, I heard a car door slam outside, footsteps dashing quickly over the gravel. A quick look out the window showed Derek letting himself out of one passenger side back door as Mal opened the other for Lizzie.

'You're OK!'

Callum burst into the kitchen, running straight past his sister and rushing towards the table as if to tackle me. Then he stopped short, slamming his hands onto the wooden surface instead.

'Why did you hang up on me?' he demanded. 'Why didn't you call me back? Why is your phone off? I thought you'd broken your neck.'

'All right, drama queen.' Rory spoke with perfectly executed side eye. 'Calm down before you have a heart attack.'

'I didn't hang up on you, I dropped my phone,' I replied, flushing from head to toe under the force of his panicked glare. 'And my phone isn't off, I couldn't call you back because it's broken. Why are you shouting at me? Shouldn't you be at your aunt's house?'

'Aye, I should,' he replied, voice still raised. 'But apparently you broke your phone and Elsie couldn't be bothered to let me know if you were dead or alive so I'm back here.'

'I'm here, aren't I?' Elsie threw out her arms to confirm her place in the kitchen but he was too angry to listen. 'I was just about to call you.'

'I rang an hour ago! I know you saw my messages.'

'I was busy,' she replied coolly. 'I didn't realise it was an emergency. I was going to text you.'

'No, she wasn't,' Rory corrected. 'She just said so.'

'What's all the bother?' Derek strolled into the kitchen, an anxious-looking Fiona behind him. Outside, I saw Mal resting against the car, face turned up to the sun with a happy smile on his face, unbothered, probably not moisturised but happy in his own lane. I was insanely jealous.

'Caroline,' Lizzie looked at me with alarm. 'You're all right?'

'She's fine,' Rory jumped in to answer before I could, waving a half-eaten Jammy Dodger in the air. 'Cal's panicking over nothing.'

Both parents considered me as I bared my teeth in a grimace of a smile. Derek looked annoyed but relieved. Lizzie, on the other hand, looked ready to swing.

'We thought something terrible had happened,' she said. 'With the food poisoning.'

'The what?'

'The food poisoning,' Callum replied with wide eyes. 'The food poisoning that kept you up all night.'

'Oh, that.' I shrank down in my seat, trying not to look at a bemused Rory. 'No, I'm fine now. All good.'

'You're fine?' she replied.

I nodded.

'Then what you're telling me,' Lizzie said, turning her ire on Callum, 'is that we left your Auntie Jean's, so you could race back for no reason whatsoever?'

'Not no reason,' he protested. 'How was I supposed to know Caroline was safe when she wasn't answering her phone and Elsie didn't bother to reply?'

'Selfish, inconsiderate idiot,' Elsie muttered under her breath. 'Classic Cal.'

I'd heard enough. Shooting to my feet, I slapped both hands on the table and five heads swivelled in my direction.

'Stop having a go at him, all of you!' I yelled, silencing everyone else in the room. 'I got stuck in the tower and dropped my phone and if Rory hadn't come home when he did, I'd probably have hypothermia by now and would have to go to hospital because Elsie certainly didn't rush to help me and I really don't think you should be angry at Callum for being justifiably concerned about someone he loves!'

I blinked, stunned by the torrent of words that rushed out my mouth, the last of them echoing through the room. Loves, loves, loves. Directly across the table, Callum stared at me as though he'd never even seen me before, his pupils dilated, his jaw hanging slack and, as my heart pounded in my ears, I thought I heard him whisper:

'Thank you.'

No one else said anything but as I recovered myself, I couldn't help but notice they were all looking me up and down.

'Caroline, what's that you're wearing, hen?' Derek asked.

I looked down at my bare legs and the jumper that just barely covered my backside. In my freezing panic and the rush for tea, I'd forgotten all about what I was or rather wasn't wearing.

'This?' I opened my mouth and hoped something believable would come out. 'It's a dress. They're all the rage in London. Everyone's wearing them.'

'No wonder she almost caught her death,' Lizzie muttered. 'God help the southerners.'

'Caroline, can you come with me, please?' Callum cocked his head towards the door. 'I've got something for you.'

'Aye, his toorie,' Rory muttered, earning a scolding slap around the back of his head from his mother.

Derek pressed one hand into his lower back. 'I need a bloody drink. And don't any of you tell me what time it is, I don't bloody care, my back is killing me.'

'What have I said about leaving the farmwork to Elsie,' his wife said as she helped him into a hard-backed chair, his eyes closed, teeth clenched together. 'He was up at the crack of dawn, chasing those bloody sheep around again. Now you're going to be in agony all Christmas.'

'Dad, I've told you, if I want help I'll ask for it,' Elsie snipped, something like embarrassment or guilt pulling at her features. Suddenly, her face smoothed out and she looked up, smiling right at me. 'But I know what'll sort you out. Caroline, why don't you give my dad a massage?'

All the blood in my body drained down to my feet, fixing me to the spot.

'Sorry?'

'Why don't you give my dad a massage?' Elsie repeated, carefully enunciating each and every word. 'The man is in pain. You're not going to stand there and watch a man suffer when you could help, surely?'

'Don't be foolish, Elsie,' Callum answered when I couldn't. 'She's not here to work.'

Derek arched his back, eyes closed in anguish before he opened one to peep at me.

'Don't worry about me, hen,' he said through a groan. 'I'll muddle through. Not that I'd complain if you twisted my arm, mind.'

'I don't have any of my things,' I replied, scrambling for a decent excuse. 'I don't have any, um, oils or those little hot stone things.'

'Little hot stone things?' Rory chuckled as he sorted through the biscuit tin for chocolate digestive. 'She's a pro.'

'Mum's got oils,' Elsie piped up. 'Remember, Mum? I bought them for you last Christmas? I know you haven't used them all, if you've even opened the bloody box.'

'There might be a wee bit left,' Lizzie hedged, eyes skirting away. 'A tiny wee bit.'

With a gratified clap, Elsie beamed in my direction.

'Perfect! It's so kind of you, Caroline, to take such good care of your boyfriend's old dad. Who knows, he might be your father-in-law one day, you want to take good care of him.'

It was impossible to say who turned white the fastest, me, Lizzie or Callum.

'You don't have to,' Callum said. 'If you don't want to.'

'Why would she not want to?' Elsie cut in. 'Stop being weird, Cal, Rory is right, she's a professional masseuse. Isn't there a masseuse code that says you have to help someone when they're in pain?'

'We prefer to be called massage therapists,' I said feebly.

'Then you'll do it?' she asked.

Sometime, the only way out was through.

I nodded my head.

'You're sure?' Callum asked as a suspiciously spritely

Derek leapt to his feet, practically sprinting out the room. I rose slowly, glaring at Elsie and her Cheshire cat grin.

'Trust me, I'm a masseuse,' I said through gritted teeth. 'By the way, if you get a chance, could you get my skirt down from the silver birch by the tower? Long red satin one, you can't miss it.'

'Should I ask why your skirt is in a tree?'

'No,' I said, yanking my jumper down one more time before following Derek out the kitchen. 'I wouldn't bother if I were you.'

CHAPTER EIGHTEEN

The bedroom was lit for romance. Candles flickered, soft music played from a portable speaker and a tall, broad, auburn-haired man lay face down on the bed, naked except for the pair of white sports socks pulled halfway up his calves and the hand towel draped over his backside. Unfortunately it was the wrong tall, broad, auburn-haired man.

'Is that you, Caroline?'

Derek's head popped up from the bed, a cheery grin on his face.

'For my sins,' I replied, inching around the edges of the room and pawing at the walls in search of a light switch. 'It's a bit dark in here, shall we put some lights on?'

'I thought you'd feel more comfortable if we recreated the spa experience,' Elsie's voice purred from the doorway.

Squinting at a small brass knob jutting out from the wall, I turned it all the way to the right, illuminating more of Derek than I cared to see. Adjusting it back down to halfway, I scowled at Callum's sister.

'The thing is, I'm more of a functional massage therapist,' I informed them both. 'I don't go in for all that airy-fairy self-care stuff. I completely understand if that's not your thing, Mr McClay, I won't be offended if you've changed your mind.'

'How many times do I have to tell you, call me Derek,' he cawed from the bed. 'Don't you worry about me, hen. I can take whatever you can dish out. I can't imagine a wee slip of a thing like you could do much damage to an old codger like me.'

I wished I could say the same. The mental anguish alone was likely to take me down.

'Mind if I stay and watch?' Elsie asked. 'I've always been curious about massage.'

'Yes, I do actually,' I replied and kicked the door shut, her look of surprise as it slammed in her face almost worth the horrors I was about to endure.

'Let's get the music off as well,' I suggested, fiddling with the speaker, failing to find the off button and shoving it into a drawer instead, Enya's dulcet tones warbling from within. 'And you're sure about this, Mr—Derek? If you're really in pain you should see a doctor. Massage is more complicated than people realise, if it's not done correctly, it can make injuries much worse.'

If done by someone who had never, ever given a massage in her entire life, for example.

He smiled at me with his big blue eyes then dropped his face into the pillow. 'Don't worry, Caroline, I trust you.'

General anatomy and physiology never had been my strong points. Neurosciences were always my goal, and like all good specialists, I forgot at least half of what I'd learned as soon as I didn't need it any more. Could

I learn it again? Absolutely. Could I have passed an exam right there in the room? Absolutely not. But no one was asking me to cut him open and repair a ruptured tendon or torn meniscus, all I had to do was give the man a rub down. A simple, straightforward, non-injury-inducing massage. I would simply treat it like a patient consult. I'd done hundreds of those, thousands even. Ask him what's wrong, listen to his symptoms, try not to make the problem worse. The first two parts of the plan would be easier than the third.

'Ready when you are,' Derek said, face down in a pillow.

Worst-case scenario, I could always smother him.

With great reluctance, I stepped forward and rolled up my sleeves.

'Narwhal,' I whispered under the haunted music that echoed from the drawer. 'Narwhal, narwhal, narwhal.'

'What's that?'

'Just centring myself with a mantra,' I replied with forced enthusiasm. 'Now, Mr— Derek. Can you tell me what seems to be the problem?'

'It's my lower back. A few years ago, I took a kick from one of the bulls, right in my bahookie.'

'Which would be?'

'Backside,' he explained helpfully. 'Got me right in the arse, it did. Put me out of action for a week and the whole left cheek was black and blue. I've a photo on my phone, if you'd like to see it?'

'No, you're all right.'

The mental picture was more than enough to keep me from sleep for weeks. 'So, it's your . . . backside that's bothering you?'

'More my lower back,' he replied and I had never been more relieved in my life. 'But also my arse, aye.'

'Well, let's start with the hip and go from there.'

I uncapped the bottle of body oil I found on the bedside table and gave it a sniff. The label said Cranberry Bliss but the scent said year seven changing rooms and I tried not to gag as I poured some out into my hands, immediately splashing it on my mohair jumper. Two items of clothing destroyed in one day, what a great day's work.

'We need to work our way down to the lower back,' I said, rubbing my hands together and closing my eyes in a silent prayer, although I could not say who or what I was praying to. The patron saint of idiots seemed most likely. Palms hovering over Derek's shoulders, I took a deep breath in and slapped them down on his skin.

'Help ma Boab, your hands are like ice!' Derek shrieked but I kept my palms flat on his back, holding him down in place. 'I wouldn't call that a healing touch.'

'It's all part of the therapy,' I told him, tapping his skin in a patty-cake motion. 'Starts cold then gets warmer.'

He shivered, goosebumps breaking out all over his body. 'And when exactly does it get warmer?'

'When you shut up and let me do my job.'

'Aye aye, captain.'

My stern instructions worked for a little while, Derek offering nothing more than the occasional squeak or grunt as I switched from a patting motion to a chop with the sides of my hands. Quickly checking my watch, I scoffed in disbelief. Less than two minutes had passed. The longest two minutes of my life.

'Is there a problem?' Derek asked in a strained voice.

'No, not at all,' I shook my head then paused, hopeful. 'Unless you're uncomfortable and want to stop?'

'No pain, no gain.' His chuckle turned into a groan when I dug a knuckle under his shoulder blade. 'You keep on. This can't be worse than listening to those three kids bickering downstairs. You'd think they were still wee bairns, not fully grown adults. It's always the same when they're under one roof.'

'I thought that was what you wanted?' I asked, recalling our conversation in Callum's flat. 'To have them all home for Christmas?'

'This is how I know you don't have children of your own,' he replied. 'Even though it drives me doolally, the sound of those three going at each other is a happier tune than that of an empty house, especially one this size. Balmaclay was never meant to be an empty nest.'

I squirted another burst of Cranberry Bliss on his back and he sucked his teeth in at the freezing cold liquid.

'When me and Lizzie got married, my parents were still with us, God rest their souls. They helped raise all three kids, the way families are supposed to. I thought we'd have the sound of wee ones running through the halls again by now, that's why Lizzie's been working so hard to get the house back on its feet, to make room for the kids' kids when they come.'

'Is that right.'

I applied a little more pressure to his rhomboids than necessary.

'I'm sure your mum and dad feel the same.'

'I'm sure.'

If there was an Olympic medal for biting your tongue, I deserved gold.

'That's the thing about being a parent,' he went on, blissfully ignorant of my situation. 'You get to a point where you're so knackered, you can't wait for a minute's peace but by the time it comes, you're counting down the days to the grandkids. Me and Lizzie wanted to have kids right away when we got married but it took a while. Better to have bairns when you're young enough to keep up with them, that's what I say. The sooner Cal moves back home and gets on with it, the better.'

'But he doesn't want to move home,' I said. 'He's already told you that.'

'He doesn't know what he wants.' Derek's voice turned gruff and he shifted under my touch. 'This time last year, he wanted to marry Shiv.'

I transferred all my weight into my elbows and pressed down until he squealed.

'No pain, no gain,' I reminded him, pulling back before I could cause any damage. 'Sorry.'

'It's fine for now,' he replied, fidgeting in place. 'Running around London, playing games in the kitchen, but he has a duty to Balmaclay and I know my son, he won't let the family down. You couldn't possibly understand, love, this house, the farm, the land, they've passed from father to son for generations. Cal isn't going to be the one who draws a line under that kind of legacy.'

He was right, I didn't understand.

'What about Elsie? She loves the farm, why can't she inherit Balmaclay?'

Derek let out a laugh so loud, he almost lost his little towel. 'Elsie will always have a home here but what if she gets married? Am I supposed to hand the keys over to whichever goon from town ends up being fool enough to take her on? She wouldn't even be a McClay any more!'

And I'd thought Lizzie was the problem. Derek McClay wasn't quite the happy-go-lucky, laugh-a-minute man he made himself out to be after all. Nope, he was nothing more than a good old-fashioned chauvinist.

'You're supposed to realise it's the twenty-first century,' I said with distaste. 'She might not get married. She might get married and not change her name.'

He was still laughing as though I'd said something hilarious.

'My point is, your children don't always see what's best for their long-term future when there's something bright and shiny right in front of them.' He turned his face towards me, pink and creased from the pillow. 'As the parent, it is your job to point them in the right direction, even if they don't thank you for it until much later.'

'Callum isn't a child.' I held his gaze without blinking. 'And he's perfectly capable of making his own decisions.'

'That's what we all think when we're your age,' he replied. 'Callum wants his freedom, he wants to roam. For now. But Scotland is in his soul. This house isn't just a home, it's part of who he is. In the end, he'll realise what's best for him and I would hate to see anyone get hurt when he does.'

'Anyone meaning me,' I guessed.

It wasn't too difficult to put together his not-even-slightly subtle clues. I might not be a very good massage therapist but I wasn't a complete idiot. I was, in fact, a brain surgeon.

'Don't take it personal, Caroline. I'm sure you're a very nice girl—'

'Then you're mistaken.'

He blanched, hesitating for a second before he carried on.

'But I don't know if you're cut out for life as a farmer's wife.'

'Is there a job description I could have a look at?' I asked. 'What's the salary? What's the holiday allowance?'

Derek shifted, his towel dangerously close to absconding altogether.

'That's the kind of attitude I'm talking about,' he said. 'You don't understand what this place means. Balmaclay isn't a job, it's a legacy. Cal will come home and when he does, he'll have Siobhan waiting for him because she does understand.'

The audacity of the man. Not to mention the brass balls on him, given the fact he was at my absolute mercy and could easily be relieved of his testicles at any second. Not that I wanted to think about Derek McClay's testicles but speaking as a surgeon, I was entirely capable of removing them, quickly, cleanly, and just in time to turn them into a pair of earrings to give to his wife for Christmas.

But I didn't. I breathed in, pulled my shit together and smiled.

'Shall we carry on with the massage?'

He eyed me carefully but gave something like a nod and lowered his head again.

'I'm telling you for your own good,' he said into the pillow. 'You see that, don't you, hen? He may run off and sow his wild oats, struggle on with this cooking thing for another year or two but, before all is said and done, he'll be back home. Where he belongs. His ties to Balmaclay are too strong.'

I was annoyed because he was arrogant, I was angry because no one had the right to tell another person how to live their life and I was furious at being referred to as nothing more than a receptacle for Callum's oats, wild or otherwise.

'What I see is you driving your son away,' I told him, pinching the trapezius muscles in his shoulders sharply. 'What Callum does is entirely up to him. I don't tell him how to live his life, I trust and respect his choices. I know you mean well but I strongly suggest you learn to do the same before you lose him altogether.'

'This is father and son stuff,' he muttered. 'You don't know what you're talking about. You barely know the boy.'

Perhaps not but I did understand how to dig my thumbs into the rock solid knots in his shoulders.

'Too much pressure?' I asked when he shrieked.

'I think that's enough for now,' he replied tightly. 'Thank you very much, Caroline, I'm sure that was a great help.'

'I hope so,' I replied, closing up the body oil and slamming it down on the bedside table. 'For your sake.'

CHAPTER NINETEEN

I was still muttering under my breath when I got back to my room, reeking of the artificially sweet fruit scent and boiling over with rage. How dare Derek talk to me like that? How dare he presume to tell Callum how to live his life? I was apoplectic, outraged on behalf of both my fake boyfriend and non-existent Caroline.

Flying through the door, I slammed it shut, gratified by the loud bang that echoed through the house. Let Derek explain that to his wife.

'Hard day at the office, dear?'

'Is everyone in this family trying to give me a heart attack?' I gasped, back pressed against the door, when Callum appeared in front of me. 'What are you doing in my— oh!'

Before I could finish my question, the six-foot fir tree wedged between the fireplace and the window answered it for him.

'Is that a Christmas tree?' I asked, drawn across the room by the evergreen beauty.

'I hope so,' he replied. 'Otherwise I don't know what we're going to do with all this stuff.'

Scattered on the floor around the tree were boxes and boxes of ornaments, brand new and unopened.

'I thought we could decorate it together,' he said, hands in his pockets. 'The way you used to with your mum.'

All of my rage melted away. I picked up one of the boxes of ornaments, a set of pretty iridescent glass spheres, and saw my surprised face reflected in the shiny plastic cover.

'Where did you get these?'

'In town. Mal ran me in while Mum and Dad were at Auntie Jean's, I didn't feel like going in for another lecture. Gray brought the tree over, it turns they had one too many at the pub.'

It wasn't just the tree. There were decorations everywhere, fairy lights wrapped around the curtain rail, a potted poinsettia on my bedside table, a stuffed reindeer sitting on the bed, and two matching red and white stockings hanging from the fireplace, one on either side.

'It's amazing,' I said, so moved I was almost afraid to look at him for fear of bursting into tears. 'Thank you.'

Callum shrugged as though it was nothing. He was wrong, it was very much something. No one had ever done anything so thoughtful for me.

'After what you've just been through, I wish I could do more,' he said. 'How was the massage? Did my dad survive?'

I opened my mouth to tell him everything his father said, to let forth a torrent of rage and frustration. Then I looked up at the anxious smile on his face and I couldn't do it. How would it help? He already knew how his dad felt, there was no point in starting another argument. Better I took it on the chin and poured all my rage-y energy into Caroline's performance as promised, even if the suspicion that Callum was destined to end up here, destined to end up with Shiv, hung around my shoulders like the world's saddest weighted blanket.

'When I became a doctor, I took an oath to do no harm,' I said instead. 'Today I fear I broke that oath.'

'I can't apologise enough.' Callum pulled a penknife from his back pocket and sliced through the tape I was struggling to peel from the box of ornaments. 'This is a start. If I can get into the kitchen without my parents having a heart attack at the sight of their son and heir in an apron, I owe you a sticky toffee pudding as well.'

'If I didn't give your dad a heart attack just now, he'll survive anything,' I replied, carefully opening the box and taking out one of the baubles. It was so delicate, something I would never buy for myself. I wouldn't trust myself with it.

'I'm surprised he didn't keel over when you stood up without any trews on. It's been a tough day for Derek, hasn't it?'

'I'm sure he's had worse,' I said as I stepped back to consider the tree, placing my ornament right in the centre with surgical precision.

'I'm going to need a ladder to get to the top,' I told Callum, admiring my handiwork.

'No, you're not.'

He bent down to pick up a sparkling silver star then reached up to place it right on top of the tree. 'That's what I'm here for.'

'Knew you had to be good for something,' I smiled,

the fire from the logs crackling in the fireplace heating my face and something else, something unfamiliar but not at all unpleasant, warming me from within.

'At the end of the night we had to clean out the fryers.' With a happy, easy smile, Callum handed me another bauble for the tree. 'You open the tap, drain out all the grease, close the tap, fill the fryer with baking soda and water then turn the fryer on. Cleans itself, simple.'

'But?'

He grinned. 'Remember, I'm exhausted. I'm working a morning shift in the bakery and the night shift in the restaurant, my head's a shed, I hardly know my own name, let alone how to clean a fryer.'

Hanging the ornament, I winced at what was to come next. 'Go on, how badly did you mess up?'

'I forgot to close the tap after emptying the grease. Baking soda, water and grease are not a good combination. I dumped the cleaning stuff in the fryer, went off to do something else and when I came back ten minutes later, it looked like the kitchen was having a foam party. There I am, up to my knees in greasy, stinking foam, it's already midnight and I'm supposed to be back at the bakery by three a.m.'

'No!' I cackled with laughter as I stood back to weigh up my placement. Hmm. Needed to go one branch to the left. 'What did you do?'

'Spent three hours hosing down the kitchen, mopping up my mess and sobbing to myself. Rolled straight into the bakery, stinking to high heaven and passed out five minutes later. My boss thought I was ill and took pity on me, I never bothered to correct him.'

'That is brutal,' I admitted. 'I would've laid down in the middle of the foam and cried.'

'Oh, I did. Around two a.m. I went delirious and started making foam angels. Still a mystery how I managed to get it all cleaned up.'

He poked around in the last box still full of ornaments, all the others strewn on the floor behind us, empty. Pulling out a small, plastic, glitter-coated cow, he held it up for my approval.

'Perfect,' I announced, holding out my hand.

'I feel like I'm in the operating room with you,' he said, passing it over. 'Scalpel, retractor, miniature Highland cow.'

I confirmed with a very serious nod. 'This is exactly the same. Only we didn't scrub in so there's every chance the tree is going to develop septic shock.'

'What's the coolest thing you've seen in your job?' Callum plucked the cow from my fingers to assist when I reached for a high branch and missed.

'Teamwork makes the dream work,' I said and immediately wished I hadn't. 'What's the coolest thing I've seen at work? Hmm. Off the top of my head—'

'No pun intended.'

I replied to his cheesy smile with an eyeroll. 'I don't know, there are so many exciting developments at the minute. There was this one patient, you might've read about it, but they started remembering childhood memories during surgery, things they had totally forgotten. Now we're conducting trials on deep brain stimulation, placing electrodes in the hypothalamus with the trajectory intentionally travelling through the fornix to see if it will help patients with Alzheimer's.'

'Wow.' He stared at me as though I'd just told him I

could travel through time. 'I understood about every fifth word of what you said but it sounds impressive.'

'It's pretty incredible,' I agreed. 'And I wasn't there in person, it was before my time, but some of my colleagues were in the room when this incredible doctor removed a tumour from a violinist while she was playing the violin.'

The curiosity in Callum's eyes shifted into something altogether more alarmed.

'They were operating on her brain while she was awake?'

'It's quite common,' I confirmed. 'They wanted to make sure they didn't cause damage to any of the tissue that controlled her ability to play so what better way than to have her thrash out a bit of Bach while she's there. Actually, I think it was Mahler. There's a video on YouTube, do you want to see?'

Callum responded with a violent shake of the head. 'Never ever, not even if I live to be five hundred years old, are you to show me that video. Imagine being awake while they – you – fiddle around inside your brain. Doesn't it hurt?'

'There are no nociceptors in the brain. You can poke around in there all day and it won't hurt the patient.' I tipped my head to one side as I considered my answer. It was nice, talking about my work with someone who was genuinely interested. 'At least, it wouldn't cause physical pain. Ideally you want to be in and out as quickly as possible, same as with any surgery. Awake craniotomies aren't new, they actually haven't changed that much at all over the last few decades, but with all the advances in imaging technology, we know a lot more than we used to prior to the surgery and the more you know the better. These days we have a much clearer map of the brain before we go in.'

He stood stock-still, a slight green tinge to his fair complexion.

'You're pure giving me the boak. Wish I hadn't asked.'

'And you wanted to know why I'm single,' I reminded him. 'It takes a strong stomach to date a neurosurgeon.'

'I still think it's amazing,' he said quickly, shaking off his sickly pallor. 'You save people's lives, Laura.'

'Not always.' The corners of my mouth flickered and the lights on the tree suddenly went out of focus. 'But that's part of the job too.'

'I don't know how you do it,' he replied. 'It must be so hard.'

'People say you get used to it but you don't,' I said. 'At least, I haven't. My job is to listen, to deliver information and not get emotionally involved. You have to sort of switch off, stop being a human for a minute.'

'And that works?'

'Well enough.'

The truth was it worked too well. Every time I flipped the switch, it became that much harder to go back. Numb was preferable to sad.

'Some people talk and some people listen,' I said when he didn't reply. 'I'm a listener, I take stuff in, always have.'

'But who listens to you?'

I looked over to see him staring at me with the sort of quiet awe that might've been too much if he hadn't been holding a pair of tiny, bedazzled bagpipes at the same time. This time, I was the one who had nothing to say.

'Anyone who isn't in total awe of you ought to have

his bollocks removed,' he added. 'With a rusty scalpel, no anaesthetic.'

'If that was the case, I'd never be out of theatre.' I said, thinking of all the times friends had tried to set me up with someone, only for that someone to cancel at the last minute or tap out after one drink. 'It's intimidating to a lot of people, I suppose. They're always cool about male surgeons but something about female surgeons still freaks a lot of people out.'

'I was about to say, try being a male pastry chef but it's not quite the same, is it?'

'You say it as though a dessert hasn't saved my life more than once,' I laughed. 'No, I hear you. Men should be cooking big hunks of meat or having a nervous breakdown over spaghetti sauce like Carmy in *The Bear*, surely?'

'Yes but you'll not hear a single straight male chef complain about Carmy,' Callum chuckled. 'More of my friends got dates after that show aired than you would believe.'

'Dates?' I raised an eyebrow.

'I'm being polite because there are ladies present,' he said, leaning in and lowering his voice. 'There were guys in my kitchen who went out and got tattoos same as his just to up their chances.'

'You can admit you're talking about yourself,' I said and he guffawed with laughter.

'Did you see any tattoos when you walked in on me the other day?'

The unexpected reminder of our first meeting brought a flush to my skin.

'Tell me.' Callum brushed past me to hang the shimmering bagpipes on the tree and I shivered from head to toe. 'What does the future look like for Dr Laura Pearce?'

'Well, I was thinking about putting the kettle on and running a bath,' I replied, digging my fingernails into my palms to chase away the residual tingling sensation. 'And I'd really like to finish my book tonight if I can.'

He looked at me as though he wasn't sure whether or not I was joking. 'I was looking for a broader picture. What's the plan for the rest of your life?'

'Callum, it's four o'clock on Christmas Eve Eve,' I said. 'I've already been trapped up a tower, broken my phone, fought with your sister and given your dad a very, very questionable massage, and now you want to hear my five-year plan?'

'If you don't mind,' he replied. 'While we're still young.'

When he tapped his watch to signal he was waiting, I sighed and looked to the ceiling as if the answer might be hiding along the crown moulding.

'Well, I've still got years of training to do before I qualify,' I started. 'Several big exams coming up. I'd like to pay off my student debts before I'm drawing my pension. And if we're really talking about dream timelines, I suppose I'd like to buy a house one day. Maybe travel a bit?'

'That's it?' Callum asked, the surprise in his voice clear as a bell. 'That's the extent of your wildest dreams?'

'I did also say I was planning to have a bath and read my book,' I sniffed. 'And I believe you have mentioned a sticky toffee pudding twice now so . . .'

'If my sticky toffee pudding is the highlight of your future hopes and dreams, I'm worried about you.'

'Then you've talked it up too much, haven't you?' I picked up a crystal-studded haggis just to have something to do with my hands. 'I don't know, I don't really think about it. My dream was to be a doctor. The only way to make that dream come true is to work hard, stay focused, no distractions. I've found the more you manage your expectations, the less likely you are to be disappointed in life.'

'What about getting married, finding a partner?' he pressed. 'You don't see yourself having kids?'

The sun had slipped away behind the hills while we'd been decorating the tree, leaving me with nothing but the cosy glow of the fire and sparkle of the fairy lights. The flames danced around, shooting up then retreating back, making it difficult for me to read Callum's expression but, if I had to describe it, I'd say it almost looked like he was disappointed. Disappointed in me? It wasn't fair. He didn't know me, didn't have any right to question the way I lived my life.

'I see myself being a doctor and that means I don't have time for relationships,' I said, flushing again but this time with frustration.

If he'd been through what I'd been through, seen the things I'd seen, maybe he'd understand. If you didn't have anyone, you couldn't lose anyone. It was that simple.

'And being a doctor means you have to live like a nun?'

'Nuns have a very nice life. Hanging out with their friends, going on trips, and they can drink, you know, I looked it up once. Besides, no one said I live like a nun, I said I don't have time for relationships. I date, I have fun.'

Or at least I could, if I wanted to. I had theoretical fun.

'What about you?' I asked, volleying his own question back. 'What grand plans does Callum McClay have for the future?'

I was ready for him to snap and call me out for my snide tone but instead he shrugged, the corners of his mouth tugging downwards.

'No idea. No fucking clue.'

'But Paris,' I said, confused by his despondence. 'Pastry cheffing?'

'I love working in a kitchen, I'm excited about Paris, but I don't know with absolute certainty this is what I want to do forever. It isn't a vocation for me the way medicine is for you.'

'Then what is?'

'I don't know.'

Callum pushed his hair back from his face as he seemed to search for a better answer to my question. 'Right up until the day I walked out the door, I thought I would be forced to spend the rest of my life running the farm and Balmaclay so I didn't waste my time considering other options. When life is mapped out for you from birth, you don't bother dreaming about all the things you can't have.'

I tried to imagine how that would feel, someone pressuring me into a life I didn't want, forcing me to be someone I wasn't. Perhaps my dad's aggressively ambivalent approach to childrearing was better than Derek's hands on approach.

'But you did leave,' I pointed out. 'You found the strength to walk away.'

'Best and worst day of my life,' he replied. 'And they

still don't believe I'm really gone. Maybe part of me thinks they're right. If all roads lead back here, why bother investing time and effort in anything else?'

It hurt to see him look so dejected. Balmaclay might be magical to me but I saw it through his eyes for the first time. A fairytale noose around his neck pulling tighter and tighter every time he came home.

'You could be anything, you know,' I told him tenderly. 'No one says you have to have it all worked out before you're thirty.'

'I'm thirty-one.'

'You know what I mean,' I said with a pointed glance. 'If you really don't want this place to be your future, you need to pull off the bandage and tell your parents once and for all. It's got to be hard to commit yourself to something else if you've always got one foot back here.'

Something else or some*one* else, I thought, an image of Shiv drifting through my mind. A half-smile cracked his face and I felt a warm shiver run through me.

'I know you're not a psychiatrist but if you ever decided you wanted to go into therapy, I've a feeling you'd be good at it.'

'Imagine it, you can do anything, be anything,' I said, glowing with his praise. 'Don't overthink it, just tell me, what do you want?'

Callum's head tilted down, rust-coloured waves falling in front of his darkening eyes.

'I can think of one thing I want very much.'

His statement hung between us like the sweet resin scent of the tree.

I couldn't move. The ridiculous sparkly haggis bauble swung from my fingertips and blood thudded in my ears. Callum's chest swelled with a deep breath in and he seemed to double in size in front of me. I looked up at him as he gazed down at me, his unruly hair glowing in the firelight that warmed his pale, pale skin. His lips parted and I felt myself mirror the movement, pulsing with anticipation.

Then I remembered something Derek had said. His ties to Balmaclay were too strong. No matter how he felt now, Callum would come home eventually. And Shiv would be waiting. *You barely know the boy.* He wasn't wrong about that. Could he be right about the rest of it as well?

'Laura—'

He took a step towards me and I instinctively took a step back, my foot landing in one of the empty ornament boxes and skidding out from underneath me. Arms windmilling wildly, I flew forward, right into Callum's open arms. He caught me easily, gathering me up around the waist and twirling me away before I could vault face first into the tree. My fingers curled around the fabric of his jumper as he held me to his strong chest, his heart thumping against my cheek. I couldn't tear my eyes away from his lips, so close to my face, slightly parted, pink and firm, and everything else blurred around me as he dragged his teeth over his bottom lip and tightened his grip around my waist.

'Sorry, low blood sugar.' I broke away and hurled myself across the room. 'Probably dehydrated.'

'Dark in here as well,' he said, the words fighting to get out of his mouth faster. 'You can't see where you're going.'

'More lights,' I agreed, practically panting. 'We could definitely use more lights.'

Pressed up against the window, I watched him bend over, rooting around behind the tree for something. Respectfully, he had a fantastic arse. It was about the only part of him I hadn't seen back in the flat and I couldn't help but regret it. But thinking about his arse and our naked meet-not-so-cute was not going to stop the ringing currently sounding in my ears or dull the throbbing in the suddenly uncomfortably tight crotch region of my jeans.

Callum made a small triumphant sound and, at once, strings and strings of fairy lights he'd wound around the tree before I saw it came to life, lighting up his whole face.

The way he looked at me made my heart stop. Callum gazed at me the same way I was gazing at the tree, like I was something beautiful. Something to be admired.

'What do you think?' he asked.

'I think it's wonderful.' My words came out weak as I concentrated on the tiny white twinkling lights instead of his rapt expression, the way they illuminated the iridescent baubles he'd chosen, the way they made the glittery ornaments sparkle. 'You made it beautiful.'

'It was already beautiful,' he replied, shaking his head as if coming out from under a spell. 'I think we can officially say this tree is decorated. First Christmas tradition officially re-established.'

'It's only a tradition if you do it more than once.'

Callum brushed a hand over the soft branches of the tree, pine needles trembling at his touch.

'Are you offering to come back and do it again next year?'

It hadn't taken long to build walls around my heart. I'd started so young, I could barely remember a time they weren't there, protecting me. But keeping them up, fortifying my defences, strengthening my resolve, that took time. Years.

I wasn't about to let them down so easily.

'If I do my job well, Caroline will not be welcome back,' I said, all the way across the room. 'That's going to make it difficult for Laura to pop up for a visit.'

His smile flickered. Something I'd said registered in a way he didn't like.

'Thank you for all this,' I added, gesturing at the tree, desperate to get back to the way things were five minutes earlier, when we were laughing so easily and I wasn't imagining how his lips would feel on mine. 'The tree and everything. It's so thoughtful.'

'It's nothing,' Callum replied. He ran his hands through his hair and I wondered if it would smell as sweet as the tree. 'If you feel like getting out the house tomorrow, there's a Christmas Eve carol service in town. They do it every year but I've never been, might be nice.'

'You've never been?' I asked and he shook his head.

'More of a Hogmanay man, myself, but I'm game to go if you are.'

A carol service. A nice, wholesome, brightly lit activity where we would be surrounded by dozens of other people. Perfect.

'If you're sure,' I nodded. 'I'd like that.'

'It's a date,' he replied before checking the time on his watch. 'Dinner will be on soon. Are you up to a family feed or is Caroline's migraine back again? Entirely up to you, I reckon we've done enough damage for one day if you'd rather not.'

He was right, we'd really outdone ourselves already,

even when we hadn't meant to. Caroline certainly wasn't winning any popularity contests in Balmaclay. I'd had every intention of skipping dinner and spending the evening alone in my room, but when his eyes drifted back to mine, the thought of sitting up here by myself when I could be downstairs with Callum seemed stupid.

'Give me a knock and we'll go down together,' I said, hoping I wouldn't live to regret it.

CHAPTER TWENTY

The atmosphere around the McLay dinner table was more tense than the time Joel came home from work and casually told me and Desi his boss was selling two face-value Taylor Swift tickets for Wembley but he'd passed.

Elsie was absent, but Derek, Lizzie and Rory were all seated at the table when Callum and I appeared, fifteen minutes later than we were requested. His father had the decency to avoid eye contact as I shuffled past, but Lizzie openly examined me with the same kind of scrutiny I applied to before and after photos of Lindsay Lohan.

'Sorry,' Callum said as he held my seat out for me. 'I lost track of time.'

'My fault, obviously,' I huffed, rubbing at my red-rimmed eyes. 'Everything's always my fault.'

Lizzie eyed her son as he took his place beside me. 'Everything OK, Caroline, dear?'

It was. My eyes were red thanks to the makeup remover I'd scrubbed over them after an aborted attempt at winged eyeliner. Lizzie McClay didn't need the facts, let her chalk it up to another Caroline nightmare.

'Everything's grand,' Callum replied for me. 'Can we just eat?'

After he'd left my room, I'd given myself a good talking to, a much needed reminder about why I was there. I wasn't in Scotland to defend Callum's life choices to his family, I didn't need to know whether or not he still had feelings for his ex or whether he'd end up returning to Balmaclay or not.

And I certainly shouldn't be entertaining ridiculous fantasies based on nothing more than proximity, fairy lights and a fantastic arse.

It went against the very fibre of my being to admit it but Desi had been right to warn me about catching feelings. I was in a big old fancy house, with a gorgeous man, at Christmas. Who wouldn't get the warm and fuzzies? All I had to do was keep a lid on myself and avoid too much one-on-one contact. Seventy-two hours from now, this nonsense would all be over, we'd be on the train back home and soon enough, the bizarre Christmas I spent in Scotland with a man I barely knew would be a hilarious brunch story and nothing more.

'It's stew for dinner,' Derek said when Fiona came in with a giant silver tureen. 'And another veggie roast for you, Caroline.'

'Been looking forward to it all day,' I replied, one single tear slipping down my cheek.

'This looks good, Fi,' Rory said as she served the youngest McClay first, the two of them sharing an affectionate look. 'Are you sure you don't want a wee taste, Caro?'

'It's Caro now, is it?' Derek looked at his son and then at me, the lines around his eyes deepening with effort as he tried to work out when we'd become such besties. 'You should've been down in the barn with me and Rory this afty, Callum, you missed a treat.'

'That's right,' Rory said. 'Dr Dickson came over and put his arm up a cow's arse, all the way up to the elbow, then it shat all over him. A true Christmas miracle.'

'You know, I'm really not that hungry tonight.' I offered Fiona a pleading smile when she placed another mound of oily, compressed vegetables in front of me. 'Maybe I could just have some toast?'

She narrowed her eyes in my direction. 'You'll eat it and like it. Bon ape-bloody-tite.'

'It's a shame your friend couldn't come with you,' Lizzie said to Rory, expertly steering the conversation in a more dinner-friendly direction. 'I was looking forward to meeting him.'

'You can say boyfriend, Mum. And it's ex-boyfriend now so don't worry yourself.'

I sneaked a sidelong glance at Derek to see how he reacted to Rory's correction but no, there was nothing. At least his attitudes towards his children weren't completely stuck in the past.

The stew Callum served himself looked delicious, so did the giant hunk of crusty bread, still warm from the oven, sitting on the plate beside it. Truly, it was everything I could do not to faceplant directly into the tureen and hoover it up like a bottom-feeding fish, and if I hadn't been distracted by a very loud bell ringing through the house, I might've cracked.

'Who would be ringing the doorbell at this time of night?' Derek wondered aloud as he stood to investigate.

'Rory, go and get my golf clubs. A four iron should do it.'

'Dad, it's not even eight,' his son replied. 'Maybe don't get on your vigilante shit until you've seen who it is.'

With a grunt and a groan, Derek left the table, chuntering under his breath as he went. I stared longingly at his plate next to my elbow, wondering if anyone would notice if I took a bite out of the bread, not really caring whether they did.

'Lizzie!' Derek yelled. 'We've got company!'

In unison, Callum, Rory and his mother all dropped their napkins and sprinted out of the dining room.

'Well, if we're all going,' I said, grabbing Derek's bread, taking a huge bite then following the family down the hallway.

I arrived in the foyer just in time to see Derek standing dumbstruck by the open door as two figures came in from the cold.

Two terrifyingly familiar figures.

Please no, please no, please no, please no.

'There she is!' Desi thundered past Derek, stomping across the entrance hall in six-inch heels to give me a very aggressive hug. 'Why didn't you tell me this place has a fucking moat?'

'It's not a moat,' I replied weakly as Joel followed her in, carrying two suitcases and throwing me a wink. 'It's a naturally occurring pond.'

'Caroline,' Derek said, reluctantly closing the door when it became clear his new guests had no intention of leaving any time soon. 'Are these friends of yours?'

'No,' I replied vehemently. 'Definitely not.'

'Correct,' Desi clucked. 'I'm Caroline's sister, Svetlana.'

I closed my eyes then opened them again, hoping the nightmare in front of me might disappear. Nope, they were still there, Desi and Joel gurning in my general direction, the entire McClay family looking horribly confused, Callum included. Ever the lady of the house, Lizzie recovered herself first.

'You didn't tell us you were expecting family,' she said to me. 'I would've invited them to dinner if I'd known they were in the area.'

'She didn't know!' Joel crowed, turning in a slow circle to take in the splendour of the house. 'We thought we'd pop in and surprise her.'

'And you're Caroline's . . . brother?' Derek guessed.

'Brother-in-law,' he said. 'Svetty here is my darling wife.'

'Are you sure about that?' I glared at the pair of them as Joel covered a laugh with a less than convincing cough.

But Desi just nodded with glee. 'Five years married and still at it like newlyweds so apologies if we get a bit handsy.'

'And what about you?' I said to Joel. 'Are you going to tell everyone your name?'

He gave me a questioning look. 'Still Joel.'

'Fantastic.' I pressed a hand to my forehead, my fake migraines quickly threatening to become a reality. 'Now, would you like to tell me what the fucking fuck you're doing here?'

'Language, Caroline!' Desi replied. 'What would your godmother say?'

She turned to mouth the words "Judi Dench" and popped her eyes wide open.

'Svetty was concerned,' Joel explained as 'Svetlana'

brushed past Lizzie with an air hug before placing extravagant kisses on Derek's cheeks. 'I couldn't have my beloved wife, who I am extremely sexually attracted to, worried all Christmas, so I said, let's get in the car and drive up there. Ten hours later, here we are!'

'Ten?' Derek blustered, trying to politely step out of Desi's clutches. 'How fast were you driving?'

'There is no speed limit on love,' my alleged best friend replied. 'And I've got a heavy foot at the best of times, haven't I, Joel?'

'All the better to step on my neck,' he swooned and, beside me, Rory didn't bother to cover his laugh this time. Callum, on the other hand, only looked alarmed.

'Come here!' I exclaimed, pulling Desi into a hug and holding her fast. 'What the fuck are you doing?' I hissed into her ear. 'You cannot be here.'

'Saving your arse. You're clearly frothing for this imbecile already, you massive simp, and someone needed to come and remind you none of this is real.' She pushed me away with tears in her eyes. 'Caroline, darling, I love you too, you sweet, simple idiot.'

'Where shall I put the bags?' Joel asked, holding up both suitcases. 'Also, where's the loo? I'm dying for a wee.'

'You . . . you want to stay here?' Lizzie looked as though she could faint clean away, which really wouldn't be a problem because I would be on the floor already to break her fall.

'Caroline said we were invited,' Desi said, turning to me. 'Isn't that right, sis?'

'No, because you said, the other day at Callum's flat,' I babbled when Lizzie redirected her glare at me. 'When I said I was spending Christmas with my sister . . .'

'So I did,' she said, stepping forward and coolly taking over the situation. 'Not a problem at all. We're delighted to have you – Svetlana. Only I don't have another room set up right now so they'll have to sleep in your room tonight, Caroline. You can bunk up with Callum.'

Desi's eyes flashed and I knew she was furious at this unanticipated flaw in her plan.

'We can share with Caroline,' she offered. 'Joel can sleep on the floor.'

Joel screwed up his face in disagreement. 'Joel has been sat in a car all day and he'll do no such thing.'

'Mum, there have to be twenty other rooms we can put them in,' Callum said, finally finding his voice.

'Yes and they're all closed up,' she replied. 'They need cleaning and heating and the beds need making and no, tonight at least, we'll have to make do. Hopefully Caroline's night terrors won't be too bad.'

'Not as bad as mine will be,' Derek squeaked as Desi's hand disappeared behind his back and dropped towards his backside.

'Fantastic, we're all settled. What's for dinner?' she asked, eyes gleaming. 'We're both starving.'

'That depends,' Lizzie replied. 'Are you vegans like Caroline?'

'Sweet Lord, no,' Joel shook his head. 'Give me all the meats.'

'Although I can't eat wheat, refined sugars or anything in the nightshade family,' Desi stated. 'And I'm not especially keen on bananas, while you're taking notes.'

'What's a nightshade?' Rory asked, eyeing them both carefully, and I answered for Desi before she could say something else insulting.

'Tomatoes, aubergines, peppers, potatoes.'

'Potatoes?' Now it was Derek's turn to look as though he might pass out. 'How do you live?'

'It's a hardship, Derek,' Desi said, her cutglass faux-posh girl accent slicing through my eardrums. 'But I soldier on. Caroline, why don't you show me and Joelly where to put our bags then we'll strap on the old feedbag. Does that sound like a plan?'

'I'll help.' Callum held out his hand for one of the suitcases but I moved to block his path.

'No need, go back and eat your dinner.' I met his eyes and silently pleaded with him to go along with me. 'We'll be back down in two minutes. It's all going to be fine.'

'Is it?' he asked in a quiet voice as the rest of the family drifted back towards the dining room.

'Seems unlikely but I'll do my best,' I muttered. 'I'll get rid of them. Is there somewhere in town they can stay?'

'Unlikely. The only rooms are at The Clach and they'll be fully booked for Christmas.'

'I'll work it out,' I promised. 'Don't worry.'

From the look he gave me as he walked away, I could tell he was definitely not reassured, but that was fair.

Neither was I.

CHAPTER TWENTY-ONE

'And then we just said fuck it, sold our shares back to Zucks, told him to shove the whole social media thing up his arse and became digital nomads,' Desi said, elbows on the table, hands cradling her heart-shaped face. 'Since then we've mostly been investing in crypto, haven't we, darling?'

'It's just as I said to Jeffy B at Davos last year,' Joel replied, wafting his glass of wine around in the air. 'You've got to keep moving forward. Stagnation is death.'

No one said anything. In fact, no one had said anything since Derek made the mistake of asking Desi if she'd like some salt about forty minutes earlier. In that time, she and my 'brother-in-law' had shared their entire life stories, from Joel's time at Swiss boarding school to Svetlana's years spent in South America, freeing elephants from cartel kingpins' private zoos.

'So then, Svetty,' Rory said, wiping his mouth with his napkin when he finished his second helping of stew. I glanced over at Callum's plate to see he had barely touched his first. 'You and Caroline don't look very alike for sisters, I can't see any resemblance at all.'

'Rubbish, we've got exactly the same breasts,' she replied and poor Derek snorted a mouthful of wine out through his nose. 'Other than that, no, we don't look that alike. Mum's weak genes, I suppose. We both look like our dads.'

'Different fathers?' Lizzie said as her husband dabbed at himself, eyes streaming. 'Your parents are divorced, Caroline?'

'They're in a polyamorous triad,' Desi said before I could confirm or deny. 'Buying sheets for the custom-made bed makes things a bit complicated but you'd be surprised how well they all get on. It's nice, really, our dads always have someone to play golf with.'

'And with two men in the house, their mum has a slightly better chance of someone taking the rubbish out without asking,' Joel added.

'They're joking,' I said loudly. 'Of course they're joking. Svetlana was adopted.'

'But I'm sensitive about it.' She waved her fork around in the air and a carrot flew off, landing right in Lizzie's lap. 'My real parents were famous actors who had an affair on set and couldn't keep me because of the scandal.'

'Who?' Rory asked as his mother placed the carrot beside her own untouched meal.

'Couldn't possibly say,' she sniffed, 'but I've never been able to watch *Titanic* all the way through if you catch my drift.'

'Always making jokes, this one,' I laughed maniacally,

having heard just about enough. 'Svetty, you must be knackered. If you're done with dinner, why don't we get you up to bed?'

'We're not going to get a tour?' she asked, awash with disappointment. 'I wanted to see the loch.'

'Tomorrow,' Callum replied. 'You can't see it in the dark.'

'I think I'm ready to turn in myself,' Lizzie said when Desi and Joel protested. 'An early night won't hurt. Lots to do tomorrow, especially now we have extra guests. Derek?'

The McClay patriarch stood to follow his wife away from the table, the red wine stain on his shirt still spreading.

'Aye, goodnight. We'll see you in the morning.' He stared at Desi with a look of restrained horror. 'All of you.'

'Who fancies a nightcap?' Rory said, clapping his hands together. 'I know where Dad hides the good stuff.'

Joel lit up. 'Count me in, I'd give my left ball for a proper drink.'

'Count him out,' I said. 'You and both of your balls are going up to bed.'

'Shame,' Rory said with a drawl before excusing himself from the table. 'I have a lot of follow-up questions about boarding school. I'll be in the living room if you change your mind.'

'Which you will not,' I said the moment he was out the door.

'Some husband you're turning out to be,' Desi added. 'Can you put your tongue back in please?'

'He was the one making eyes at me all through dinner!' Joel said defensively, pointing after the youngest

McClay. 'And I'm pretty sure he was trying to play footsie with me as well.'

'That was me,' I said, head in my hands. 'I was trying to kick her in the shins and missed.'

'Can one of you, any of you, please tell me what's going on?' Callum asked. He had the look of someone who had spent the last hour trying to walk a tightrope over the Grand Canyon and was about ready to launch himself in. 'With the two of you, I mean, not whether or not you were flirting with my little brother because you definitely were, pal.'

'We're here to check on her and help you achieve your goals,' Desi announced, keeping one eye on the door and her statements vague. 'You're welcome.'

'Also the boiler broke and the landlord couldn't get anyone to look at it until Saturday,' Joel added. 'But mostly we're here for Laura.'

'OK, get back in the car right now,' I ordered, pointing at the door. 'Don't even go back upstairs for your bags. I will bring them home, you need to leave, immediately.'

'But we're both over the limit,' Desi protested. 'We had wine with dinner.'

'A lot of wine,' Callum said. 'A truly impressive amount, honestly.'

'First thing in the morning then,' I said. 'Literally not another word to another person living under this roof before you go.'

'You'd really send us back to a freezing flat when you're swanking it up here in the Traitors' castle?' Joel said with watery eyes. 'For shame, Laura.'

I gave him a look that could've stripped paint.

'You're leaving.'

'My arse, we are. I've done enough driving today to last me a lifetime.'

Desi scoffed. 'You did two hours.'

'That's two more than I was planning on when you opened that second bottle of wine last night,' Joel volleyed back.

'Christ, maybe you can pull off cosplaying as a married couple,' I muttered, pushing my hair back from my face. 'Either way, you shouldn't have come and you can't stay.'

'Fine, whatever, we'll leave in the morning,' Desi sighed, moving on as though I didn't recognise her "I'd like this conversation to be over" voice. 'Now, I believe someone said something about whisky?'

'I believe someone said something about bed,' I corrected. 'The sooner you're asleep, the sooner you can be off.'

'Anyone would think she wasn't happy to see us,' Joel muttered as the four of us cleared the plates and took them into the kitchen. 'This is the thanks we get for trying to help.'

'They can stay.'

My head had never spun around so fast. I stared at Callum, not sure I'd heard him right.

'They can stay?'

'They can stay,' he repeated wearily. 'It'll be a nightmare drive down to London on Christmas Eve, fourteen hours at least, and I've had some experience with panicking about you when you don't answer your phone. They were worried about you.'

'I was mostly worried your family was planning to sacrifice her to the old gods but thank you,' Desi said graciously. 'You are a benevolent master.'

'Don't push your luck,' Callum said with the first thing approaching a smile since they arrived. 'I could still change my mind.'

'Please do,' I said. 'Immediately if not sooner.'

Desi wound her arm through mine, looking up at me from underneath her hair, and fluttering her fluffy false eyelashes. 'No, Lau, it's going to be fun,' she said in her most wheedling tone. 'It's Christmas, we're all together, I've even brought your Chocolate Orange up with me.'

Joel cleared his throat and sliced his finger across his throat.

'Oh, right,' she added. 'Sorry, we ate it just outside Stoke-on-Trent.'

'We'll be so well behaved,' Joel promised. 'All we have to do now is keep up the pretence that you're a vegan Swedish masseuse, Desi is the adopted love child of Kate and Leo, and I'm straight. What could possibly go wrong?'

Callum's smile froze.

'Nothing,' I said wearily. 'Now please just go to bed.'

When I heard the door to Callum's room click closed behind us, I could've happily collapsed to the ground and slept on the spot. It had been the longest day in history.

'I don't even know what to say,' I began but he was already waving away my words.

'Don't. They were worried about you, I could never fault anyone for that. They're good friends. Terrible liars but good friends.'

A reluctant laugh sounded through my closed lips as he turned on a bedside lamp. His room was a similar size to mine, the fireplace, I guessed, backing onto the one in my room, but instead of having the vibe of a cosy, boutique hotel, this room felt entirely personal.

'Welcome to the place where the magic literally never happened,' Callum said with an uncomfortable chuckle. 'And no, they haven't changed a thing since I moved out. I don't think they've changed a thing since I was sixteen, come to think of it.'

Everything was blue. The walls were painted a pale periwinkle, the carpet, cornflower, and the duvet cover on the double bed, deep navy stripes. Even the armchairs in front of the picture window were upholstered in a beautiful cerulean brocade. It was like falling into his eyes, every shade of blue I could imagine. There was a wardrobe, a chest of drawers, both made of old knotty pine, warm with age, and next to the window, two tall bookcases, both of them absolutely crammed from top to bottom with tattered paperbacks and dog-eared dust-covers.

'I was a big reader when I was a kid,' he explained when he saw me looking at his library. 'Shit internet connection and Mum wouldn't let me have a television in my room but, if anyone asks, I never wanted one in the first place.'

'Oh, totally. You were way too cool for that,' I agreed, taking a tentative step towards the bed, my backpack hanging from my hands. 'It's nice.'

'It's a head fuck,' Callum corrected. 'Every time I come in here, I feel like I'm fifteen again. Time and time again I've told them to get rid of everything and redecorate but they won't have it. Callum McClay must be reminded of where he came from. As if I could forget.'

I gave another weak impression of a laugh.

'My dad made me paint my room myself before I left for university,' I said. 'I even put my own stuff in the loft to save him a job. Thankfully I managed to do it without falling through the ceiling that time.'

'Doesn't sound like he was the most hands-on dad ever,' Callum ventured. 'I'm sorry.'

'What's worse, too hands-on or too hands-off?'

I took in a big gulp of air and exhaled hard.

'I'm happy to sleep on the floor,' I said, even though happy was something on an overstatement. 'If you can give me a pillow and a blanket, I'll be fine.'

'If anyone's sleeping on the floor, it's me,' he rolled his eyes as though I'd suggested something ridiculous. 'Or I could sleep on the sofa downstairs.'

'And have your parents think there's trouble in paradise? That would defeat the whole object of why I'm here, wouldn't it?'

Because there was a the reason, I reminded myself, and I couldn't risk forgetting it.

'It's only for tonight,' I said. 'And we've shared a bed before.'

Callum looked at the bed and frowned. 'You've seen me naked before as well but we haven't given that a second go.'

'Why, are you offering?'

Both of us blushed at once, my entire face beet red, his cheeks flaming.

'Sorry, it just came out,' I said, tightening my grip around the straps of my backpack. 'I don't know why I said it.'

'Don't worry. You make me want to do things I know I shouldn't as well.'

Face still pink, body still heated, I stayed glued to the spot. 'Anyone would think you're starting to regret this whole thing.'

'Are you?' he asked. 'Regretting it?'

Across the room, his eyes burned.

'I regret seeing your father naked,' I replied, tossing my hair over my shoulder and marching past him into the bathroom. 'Pyjama time. Excuse me.'

I'd never been so grateful to bolt a door behind me. Callum's bathroom was more modest than mine, a standard shower over a normal bath, rather than the fancy soaking tub and separate shower in the guest suite, but it was clean and tidy, even though a man had been using it for the best part of forty-eight hours. Impressive. I recognised Callum's washbag from the train and calmly, quietly, poked through it as I waited for my nerves to settle. Face wash, moisturiser, toothpaste, floss. A stick of deodorant sat on the side of the sink and an electric shaver was stashed in its own little pouch on top of a stack of towels. One used bath sheet was neatly draped over the radiator, almost dry.

Placing my backpack down on the closed toilet lid, I unclipped the top and pulled out my own toiletries and pyjamas. This was fine. Everything was fine. Except for Desi and Joel showing up. And the massage. And the fact I was going to have to explain to Desi what had happened to her skirt sooner rather than later.

I looked up into the wall-mounted mirror and sighed.

And the way I felt about Callum.

Yes, he was handsome. Yes, he was thoughtful and kind and funny and when he bit his bottom lip I wanted to do terrible things that not even the smuttiest fantasy novel had thought of yet. I was only human. Physical responses were not always tied to emotional. Unless they were. I could lie to my friends and I could lie to his face but if I was going to get through this night without losing my mind completely, I had to stop lying to myself.

You make me want to do things I know I shouldn't.

'Stop reading into it,' I instructed my reflection as I turned on the taps so he wouldn't hear me talking to myself. 'He meant this entire stupid enterprise. And inviting Desi and Joel to stay. And . . . and . . .'

And what else might I make him want to do?

It didn't matter. Nothing could ever come of this for myriad reasons. He was moving to Paris. I didn't want a relationship. Shiv. Balmaclay. Vegan Swedish masseuse. I'd successfully avoided all distractions up until now, I wasn't about to throw myself at this one and why was I sniffing his deodorant?

I caught sight of myself, stick in one hand, cap in the other, and reared back in horror, dropping them both in the sink. What was wrong with me? I pulled both pieces out and dabbed them dry. The goal was to convince Lizzie and Derek they didn't want to see Caroline again, not to reliably inform Callum that I was a total weirdo.

'Which is becoming a real problem,' I told the Laura that looked back at me from the mirror. 'Because you clearly are.'

The bedroom was quiet when I finally crept back in, freshly scrubbed and moisturised, my red tartan pyjamas buttoned all the way up to the neck, bra still on underneath. Uncomfortable, yes, but it wasn't as though I was likely to get any sleep anyway. The underwiring dug into my ribs, somewhere between armour plating and a cilice. Callum was already in bed. Callum was wearing a pair of wire-framed glasses. Callum was holding a book.

'Do you mind if I read for a bit?' He lowered the frames halfway down his nose and I almost wept. 'My body hasn't adjusted to regular hours yet, it still thinks I should be in the kitchen until midnight.'

'Starting a grease fire foam party?' I replied, refusing to look at his slutty little glasses. How dare he? 'Go for it. I'll . . .'

He raised an eyebrow waiting for me to finish my sentence.

'I was going to say check my phone but it's still in pieces on your driveway.'

Placing my backpack on the chair next to the window, I saw an old, blue Adidas shoebox sitting on a shelf. It was open, the lid long missing from the looks of the tape holding the corners together, and inside were stacks and stacks of photographs. It was impossible to mistake the pretty blonde who featured in all the ones I could see.

I turned away to look out the window. The loch was just how I'd left it and the stars had returned to season the sky with light. All was calm, all was bright. And Callum still had a box full of photographs of his ex-girlfriend, Shiv and Cal through the ages.

'How do you think it's going so far?' he asked.

Glancing over my shoulder, I saw the book lying in his lap, face down, pages splayed, his attention on me. I tried a smile and just about managed.

'I don't think your parents are going to give me access to the shared family Google calendar any time soon.'

'You should ask for it anyway, it might push my dad over the edge.' Callum sat up, curling forward. 'I've been thinking.'

'Oh dear.'

'I know,' he flashed a grin that disappeared as quickly as it arrived. 'How do you think they'd feel if they found out the truth?'

I ran a hand down the bookcase, pressed my feet into his carpet, just to make sure I was still solid, made of flesh and blood.

'About Caroline or about you moving to Paris?

'Either. Both.'

'They're your parents,' I said. 'How do you think they would feel?'

He reached for his toes, surprisingly and pleasingly flexible for a man his size.

'I think they'd be confused and upset. And hurt.'

It was a fair assumption and something I did not want to deal with firsthand.

'Do you think we can still pull it off?' he asked.

I raised an eyebrow. 'Are you suggesting the arrival of my crypto millionaire digital nomad adopted sister and her gay husband might raise some questions?'

Callum's shoulders rose with a silent laugh.

'There's nothing to worry about,' I said, trying to convince myself as much as him. 'Desi and Joel will behave themselves. If we leave first thing on the twenty-sixth, it's only two more days. Maybe we can go somewhere tomorrow, stay out the way.'

Even though the McClays were far from my favourite people, the thought of them finding out the truth made me itchy. Callum was right, they'd be furious but, worse than that, they'd be hurt, and for that, I knew he would punish himself beyond anything his parents could dream up.

I considered his bookshelves, eyeing the options. I needed a distraction.

'Sorry, they're all boys' books,' he said. 'Might not be much that interests you.'

'Unless they're written in some sort of secret code that only reveals itself to a Y chromosome, I reckon I'll be OK,' I assured him. 'How is *The Hobbit* a boys' book?'

'Just something Shiv used to say. She wasn't a big fantasy fan, said it was all male wish fulfilment and going on inefficient quests. She said there was nothing in them for women.'

'Really? I have some recommendations that could change her mind about that.'

I carefully pried the well-read paperback out from the shelf and walked back to the bed. The fire was dying out and the air was perfectly crisp, the exact right temperature to snuggle under the covers. Callum pushed his glasses back up his nose and gave me a nod, turning his book over and sitting back against the pillows. It was a classic mystery, an Agatha Christie I'd seen on lots of bedside tables at the hospital but never read myself. After puffing up the pillows on my side, I pulled back the covers and slipped into bed, making sure to avoid physical contact. We were both fully dressed, me in my pyjamas and Callum in his grey sweatpants and white T-shirt, but this close, alone, in bed? The vice around my heart squeezed harder, and when my trembling fingers managed to open the book, I had to read the first page three times over before any of the words registered.

The room was so quiet. Old, solid walls, sound didn't travel, even though Callum had said he could hear me moving around the night before. Side by side, we read in silence, occasionally turning the page at the exact same time, glancing over at each other with a shy smile. The quiet rustle of paper, his furrowed brow, the way he pushed his glasses up his nose every time they slid down. When he brought his right hand up to his tongue to moisten his index finger, I almost gasped.

'Oh!' I exclaimed when something brushed against me under the covers.

Callum's toes.

Were touching.

My toes.

'Sorry. My bad.'

He let his book fall against his chest but he didn't move his foot away from mine. 'Your feet are like ice, woman,' he said, leaning over to his bedside table, opening a little drawer and pulling out a nubby brown ball. 'I don't want to be blamed for you getting frostbite in the night.'

Before I could protest, he had scooted down the mattress, pulled back the covers and carefully rolled a pair of socks up over my feet, one at a time.

If Cinderella had lived in the Highlands.

'There,' Callum said, resuming his reading position. 'Is that better?'

'Yes,' I squeaked, breathing for the first time in thirty seconds. 'Thank you.'

It was, without a shadow of a doubt, the most erotic thing that had ever happened to me in my life.

'I might turn my light off now,' I added, my voice still too tight and high-pitched. Lying beside him fully conscious was torture. 'You carry on reading, don't worry about me. I can—'

'Sleep through anything, I remember. Goodnight, Laura, sleep tight.'

'You too.'

I rolled over to face the window, my back to Callum, replaying the shock of him touching my feet over and over and over until the memory felt more like a dream. When was the last time a man had touched me? A man who wasn't Joel or a hairdresser or that overly familiar shoe salesman at the supply store who clearly had a fetish but undercharged for Crocs so no one at the hospital complained about it? I breathed in through my nose and out through my mouth, slowing down the cycle until I reached a state of homeostasis, even and calm. The sounds of the last flickering flames in the fire conspired with the soft swish of his book to lull me to sleep and with the covers tucked up around my chin, the ebb and flow of Callum's measured breathing at my side, I let my heavy eyelids close. It was easier than I'd thought it would be. I felt so cosy.

I felt so safe.

'Laura?'

Somewhere, in a faraway world, someone said my name.

'Hnnf?' I replied without opening my mouth or my eyes.

'Nothing,' the voice said. 'We can talk in the morning.'

'Hnnf,' I replied again, drifting away from it all with a soft smile on my face.

CHAPTER TWENTY-TWO

The sound of a shower running in the next room woke me. Curled up like a dormouse under the covers, I rubbed my eyes. The first thing that came into focus was a paperback copy of *The Hobbit* that wasn't mine, next to what had to be a fifty-year-old digital alarm clock that blinked bright red numbers against a black background. It was nine thirty in the morning on Christmas Eve. I'd been asleep for almost eleven hours.

The second thing that came to me was the underwire of my bra digging into my ribs. What was I thinking?

Rolling over to push my legs out of bed, I groaned as I twisted the under band, all of my muscles protesting at being made to do any sort of work while my mind refused to come back online. I couldn't remember the last time I'd slept for so long, no wonder the neurons were struggling to fire. Callum's side of the bed was empty, the quilt pushed back and the mattress still warm when I ran a hand over the bottom sheet. He'd slept late too. But he'd been up long enough to light the fire and make two cups of tea, both of which sat steaming on his chest of drawers. Assuming one was for me, I forced my legs to carry me across the room to collect it then found my way to the armchair by the window. A frost had come in the night, covering everything outside with an icy sparkle, and I felt sure my fingers would come back covered in glitter if I reached out to touch it.

'Ahh, she lives.'

I twisted in my chair, still bleary-eyed, to see Callum emerge from the bathroom, plumes of steam billowing out behind him like dry ice on a game show. He had a towel wrapped around his waist, the hair on his head was wet and slicked back and the hair on his chest glistened, just like the first time we met. Well, except for the towel.

'Morning,' I said, forcing my eyes back up to his face as my mind treated me to an instant replay of that particular memory. 'Did you sleep OK?'

'Not as well as some people,' he replied with a grin. 'You weren't kidding about being able to sleep anywhere, were you?'

Turning back to the window, I pinched my own thigh through my shorts, very aware that I was not looking at this man respectfully and we were still under his mother's roof. I needed to put some distance between us and fast.

'What's on the agenda for today?' I asked, the sound of drawers opening and closing behind me. 'Have I got another migraine or do we need to switch it up? Sore throat? Vertigo? A sudden case of Alien Hand Syndrome?'

'Do I even want to know?'

'A neurological condition in which a person loses

control of one or both of their hands, meaning their hands frequently act against their will.'

'As tempting as that is, I was thinking of something else.'

When I looked back, he was pulling a grey T-shirt over his head, the muscles in his back flexing under the pale skin.

'We should get out for the day,' he said. 'It pains me to suggest it but—'

'Loch Ness?' I guessed. 'You're taking me to Loch Ness?'

Pulling a chunky blue jumper from a drawer he shook his head. 'I'm taking you to Inverness to get a new phone.'

My face fell.

'And I'm taking you to Loch Ness.'

I didn't care how thick the walls were, everyone in the house must've heard me cheer. And then yelp when I spilled tea on the back of my hand.

'It doesn't seem like a good idea to have your pals knocking around the house,' Callum added, laughing.

Ignoring the mild scalding, I put down my cup and leapt to my feet, jumping up and down on the spot, ecstatic at Callum's suggestion and the fact I'd decided to sleep in a bra.

'Give me ten minutes and I'm out the door,' I said, wiping my wet hand on the backside of my pyjamas. 'Although Desi and Joel might need a bit more warning. Desi especially, she's not a morning person.'

'They already know. Joel's been up for hours, we had a wee chat while I made the tea. Get yourself ready, I'll see you downstairs. I've left the poor bastard alone with my dad unchaperoned.'

I threw him a salute and marched right into the bathroom, tying up my hair, turning on the shower and only pausing when I reached down to take off my socks. Callum's socks. With great care, I rolled them back up into a ball and placed them on the chair in the corner of the bathroom. Would it be so terrible if I borrowed them as a permanent loan?

'You're talking about stealing a man's socks,' I whispered as I stepped into the shower.

I definitely needed to get out of the house.

'I think I can see it!' Desi yelled, a pair of binoculars borrowed from Mal held up to her face. 'Wait, no, it's a branch. Not a monster.'

'Give me strength.' Callum blew out a sigh as we followed a well-trodden path along the side of the loch. 'How many more times is she going to do that?'

'Twenty times an hour feels like a conservative estimate,' Joel replied. 'She's very excited.'

Even more excited than me, it turned out. Unbeknownst to any of us, Desi had been hiding a secret monster kink and was determined to find the Nessie of her dreams.

'It's your fault for giving her that book about the sexy mothman,' he muttered at me. 'Never been the same since. If it's not mothmen, it's minotaurs. If it's not minotaurs, it's orcs and if it's not orcs, it's ogres. I don't even want to tell you about the short story she sent me about the kraken.'

'Self-published?' I asked, trying not to smile at his pain.

'Self-written,' he replied, eyes bugging out of his head. 'She's the monster and you created it. I've never seen so many uses of the word "undulating" in one Word document.'

'There it is!' my best friend screeched again. 'Oh, no, log. Never mind, as you were.'

'Were you never tempted to make a Loch Ness monster suit and have a nice swim?' Joel asked Callum as we passed another group of women staring out at the water, half of them through binoculars, the others zooming in with their phones. 'If it weren't so cold my balls have gone back up inside me, I'd be tempted to do it now.'

'You wouldn't be the first,' Callum replied, the broadest version of his smile lighting up his face. 'I avoid this place like the plague. Too many tourists year round.'

'But it's gorgeous,' I protested. 'How could you not want to be here all the time?'

He rubbed his chin and considered the almost absurd natural beauty around us, the endless mountains, a forever sky and the still water reflecting it all back like a mirror.

'It is, but I prefer Loch Shin myself.'

'That's the loch behind Balmaclay?'

He nodded.

'There's something special about it. I don't know a more beautiful spot on earth.'

I couldn't help but hear the wistful note in his voice and, as we crossed off the path and onto a pebbly beach, everyone's warnings came flooding back to me. Balmaclay was more than a house to Callum, Scotland was in his soul. Whatever he said now, his ties to this place ran deep.

'Not that this isn't nice,' he added. 'All the better for the company, of course.'

'Desi aside,' Joel replied, patting him on the back when she shrieked again. 'Don't worry, you'll get used to her.'

Dores Beach, Callum's chosen visiting spot, sat almost at the most northerly tip of Loch Ness according to the map up at the little pub we'd passed on the way. From here, you could see for miles, an unbroken view of the narrow stretch of water, hills rising on either side and closing in on the loch until it disappeared in a point in the far distance. If I were a prehistoric monster who didn't mind the cold, I could imagine being quite happy there myself.

'Braw weather today,' Callum said, eyes closed, face turned towards the sun. 'Last time I was here it was pure dreich.'

'Is it me or has his accent got stronger since we left this morning?' Joel asked, not bothering to lower his voice. 'I can barely understand the bugger.'

'You're the one in my country,' Callum pointed out. 'Do you need a translator?'

'Yes,' Joel replied. 'That would be wonderful, thank you.'

'Callum, can I ask you something?'

Without warning, Desi came crashing through the three of us, sliding her arm through Callum's and drawing him a little way ahead of us.

'As long as it's not about the monster,' he confirmed. 'Ask away.'

'How come you're single?'

'Des!' I yelped. 'No!'

'Bad dog,' Joel shook his head slowly. 'Very bad dog.'

'I'm just curious,' she said, and I saw her tighten her grip around Callum's elbow. There would be no shaking her off. 'He cooks, he's fit, his family owns a castle—'

'It's not a castle.'

'How are you not fighting off the ladies?' she pressed. 'Or the gents, or both, or neither. Allies only around these parts.'

'Feel free to ignore her,' I said when words appeared to fail him. 'Or you can pretend she doesn't exist at all. That's what I do.'

Callum pulled his shoulders up to his ears as we all came to a slow standstill. 'She's going to be disappointed with my answer, that's all. I work long hours, I'm not on the apps, I don't like one-night stands.'

'Why not? Desi demanded.

'Really?'

'Really.'

'Would you ask a woman why she doesn't like one night stands?'

Desi widened her stance and intensified her gaze as though she was preparing to spear the man off his feet while I contemplated whether or not to launch myself into the loch.

'No, because I trust women,' she replied. 'In my experience, men who say they don't like one night stands are usually trying to get into a girl's pants. Ooh, I'm so sensitive, ooh, I'm not like other men, ooh, you can trust me. And it's all bollocks.'

'But you still date men?' Callum asked.

'Not if I can help it,' she answered. 'But unfortunately the heart wants what the heart wants.'

'Babe, it's not your heart that wants the D,' Joel said sadly. 'Who in their right mind would be attracted to men if they could help it? Have you *seen* women?'

'I still haven't heard an answer,' Desi said impatiently.

'Tell us, what's so special about you that you're so above one night stands? We're dying to know.'

'Unless you're horribly deformed or something,' Joel placed comforting hand on Callum's shoulder. 'Then we really don't need to know. Unless you want to whisper to me.'

'I didn't say I don't do them, I said I don't like them,' Callum replied as I knocked Joel's hand away from him. 'Me and my ex got together when we were kids, I'd never even been single until a year ago. Being that intimate with someone you don't know, well, it still feels strange.' He caught my eye then looked quickly away. 'It's like late night fast food. Seems like a good idea at the time but you usually feel worse for it the morning after.'

'You've been eating at the wrong places,' Joel told him. 'What a waste.'

'Very noble,' Desi replied. 'But it's a rare man who will turn down a shag unless it comes with a side of feelings.'

Even though it was far from a compliment, Callum still smiled at her turn of phrase. 'Is it that impossible to believe?'

'No,' I said.

'Yes,' Desi said.

'I know, Des, why don't you enlighten us as to why you don't have a boyfriend or a girlfriend?' I suggested. 'How have the heartsick masses failed to snatch you out of the jaws of singledom?'

'Not fucking interested,' she stated as though the very idea were offensive. 'Being on my own is very much an informed choice.'

'Same here,' Callum told her. 'When my relationship

ended, I applied to cooking school in Paris. Not much point investing time in dating when I'm going to be out the country for God knows how long, is there?'

No, I thought sadly, there isn't.

'So, you applied to cooking school at the end of your last relationship, interesting.'

Desi wasn't done. She clucked her tongue against the top of her mouth in time with her footsteps. 'Would you say you were running away from the heartbreak or trying to distract yourself from regret?'

'I would say it's something I'd wanted to do for a long time but my ex and I were in a long-distance relationship already and she didn't want me to push that distance even further.' Callum didn't even break his stride, taking her inquisition like a champ. 'Once I'd made my mind up to end things with her, I applied, not thinking I'd get in. I did. Now I'm going. That's it. Not a very interesting story.'

'I think it's a very interesting story. Sounds complicated. Like maybe you wouldn't have broken up if you could've come to a compromise on the long-distance thing. And who knows? Now you've both had some time to think about things, you might reconsider your situation.'

'We haven't discussed it,' he replied, stiffening slightly. 'I don't know what she's thinking.'

'And do you think you'll stay in Paris after you've finished your course? Or move back to London? Or maybe back up here to Scotland . . . ?'

I wanted to tell her to shut up, she was being so rude and so invasive, but I didn't. Because I wanted to hear his answer even more. Callum's eyes darted over to me and I mouthed a silent, fake apology.

'I'm not sure. Right now I'm focused on cooking school.'

'Leaning more towards one option or the other?'

'Des,' I said finally. 'Leave it alone.'

'No, I get it, you're committed to your career,' she said, her long dark hair whipping around her face as the wind blew in off the loch. 'Just like our Laura. She's a genius, you know. Did she tell you? Aced every exam she's ever taken, got her first choice of residency, assisting the best surgeon in the country – hey!'

'I'm not a genius,' I interrupted, skipping ahead to step on the back of her shoes and forcing her to let go of Callum's arm. 'I'm just focused, that's all.'

He gave me a thankful smile. 'I'd imagine you'd have to be, in your line of work. No one wants a brain surgeon who's thinking about what she's going to have for her tea.'

'It's not that she's short of offers.' Desi recovered herself and jumped right back in where she left off. 'If she felt like it, Laura could be drowning in cock, but no, she's dedicated to a higher purpose.'

'If anyone wants me, I'll be in the loch, looking for Nessie,' I said, pressing one hand to my forehead. 'Somewhere on the bottom. At the deep end.'

'Always drowning in something,' Joel lamented. 'Callum, tell me about the loch. Do people swim in it? Can I rent a little jet-ski and zip up and down?'

'I wouldn't bother today unless you're after freezing to death,' he replied. 'They do boat tours. You can ride a jet-ski with a permit, I think. I'm not clear on the rules for water sports.'

'And if you're going to get involved in water sports, you have to be clear on the rules,' Desi said sagely.

Joel took our friend by the arm and pulled her away. 'Desi, will you come with me please? I think I see an orc with a hard-on and it's waving at you.'

'The orc or the hard-on?' she asked as he dragged her off across the pebbles.

'I'm so sorry,' I said when Callum sat down on the beach to look out over the water. 'She's a monster. Who needs Nessie when you've got Desi?'

'She's Elsie if she had a sense of humour,' he replied. 'We have to keep the two of them apart otherwise I think the world might end.'

The wind whipped off the water as he rested his forearms on his knees, the waxy fabric of his jacket rubbing against his jeans. I pulled my coat closer around my body as I sat down next to him. Not because I was especially cold, against all odds I was getting used to the weather, but I needed the extra layer of protection against Callum. The smell of him, the warmth of him. Every time our eyes met, I was afraid I might explode if I didn't hold myself in.

I felt like I was going crazy, walking around the loch as though everything were perfectly normal, as though I was the exact same person who had walked into that flat on Sunday morning. But I couldn't be. That Laura was immune to emotions. She wouldn't have to keep stopping every ten steps or so to stare at the man beside her as though she'd discovered a new species.

Could it be that my immunity was wearing off? Love was an illness and I'd avoided it for so long but now I was showing all the symptoms and it was progressing worryingly fast.

'Thank you for bringing us out here,' I said, tucking

my hair behind my ears and continuing with the facade. 'I know you didn't want to come.'

He scrunched up his face, the tiny golden freckle under his eye disappearing. 'Don't thank me, I was being an arse. I'd forgotten how beautiful it can be here and the tourists aren't so bad. When you spend a long time in one place, you take it for granted but it's been nice. Seeing it through your eyes.'

The loch and the sky melded together in one endless stretch of blue in front of me and Callum's left thigh pressed against my right one.

'Well, still, I appreciate it,' I told him. 'I can't remember the last time I spent this much time outside.'

Leaning forward, he sifted through the pebbles between his feet, picking them up, testing their weight, running his thumb over their surface.

'What do you usually do on your days off?'

'Watch telly? Stare at my phone? The usual incredibly healthy hobbies.'

'Stop me if this is a stupid question but is it true phones can negatively impact on our brains?'

I nodded, happy to be in more comfortable territory. 'Oh yes. There have been a lot of studies on how they impact behaviour, dopamine hits, attention spans and all that stuff, but yes, there's evidence that suggests social media can impact our brain anatomy as well, not just the chemical response.'

'And you still use it?'

'Obsessively,' I said with a rueful smile. 'That's why it's an addiction.'

'Worse things to be addicted to, I guess.' He picked out a round, flat pebble and bounced it in his hand. 'At least until the Terminators arrive.'

'Just a matter of time, might as well enjoy it now,' I agreed breezily. 'I'm less worried about Chinese spies stealing all my secrets and more worried about my boss finding out how much time a day I spend watching TikToks about baby hippos. He'd sack me in a heart-beat.'

Callum pushed up off his knees and stood up. I looked up at him, blinking at the sunlight that made his russet hair glow.

'Ever skip stones?' he asked.

I shook my head.

'God no. I have terrible hand to eye coordination.'

'Aren't you a brain surgeon?'

'Neurosurgeon,' I corrected. 'What's your point?'

'Come on, I'll show you how.'

He held out a hand and I stared at it for a moment before taking it in mine, the warm, rough skin sending shockwaves down my arm and through my body. I flashed back to his flat, that static shock when we both reached for a receipt.

If Callum felt anything at all, he didn't show it. Just like before.

'You hold the stone like this then it's all in the wrist,' he said, leading me down to the water's edge before letting go of my hand. He leaned slightly to the side then flicked his wrist when he released. The pebble skipped over the water, three, four, five times before sinking through the surface. 'You want to try?'

'Why not?' I replied, bending down when he did, my fingers brushing the stones as we searched for the best skippers. 'This one?'

'Too round. You want flat and smooth.'

Not really knowing what to look for, I picked up a

random assortment while he curated a smaller selection for himself, then followed him right to the water's edge.

'Bend your knees a wee bit,' he instructed, squatting slightly, his left shoulder angled towards the loch. 'Pull your right arm back, keep it level and flick your wrist as you let go.'

He demonstrated again and I watched as the stone sailed across the water. Skip, skip, skip, sink.

'Your turn.'

'Show me again,' I said, delaying the inevitable.

I hated these kinds of things, useless feats of skill designed to make men look all clever and manly while we feeble women watched on, so impressed. A week ago, I was performing a lumbar puncture and now I was about to risk my entire self-worth cobbing a stone across some water.

'You're going to nail it.' Callum moved directly behind me and pressed his chest to my back, his arms curved around mine as though we were in a dance. 'Here, let me help you.'

I didn't protest when he rested his chin on my shoulder, the scruff of his unshaven face scratching against my neck where my hair had escaped the collar of my coat. His hand slid down my right arm to grip my wrist. Could he feel me trembling? All the sounds of the loch were lost, the rippling water, the wind in the bushes, Joel's incessant Loch Ness monster mating call. The only thing I could hear was Callum's breath in my ear.

'Left arm is your counterbalance,' he explained plainly, no reaction to me at all. 'Hold it out from your body a wee bit.'

When I didn't move, he covered my hand with his

and pulled it a few inches away from my side. The water, the sky, the rest of the world disappeared as I melted into him, covered, protected, by Callum McClay.

'Are you ready?' he asked, his words so close to my ear I felt him moisten his lips before he spoke.

'No,' I replied truthfully as I bent my knees, turned my body. 'Manage your expectations accordingly.'

With my eyes on the horizon, I tossed the pebble. To my surprise, it skipped across the loch, bouncing five times before it vanished. Callum pulled away from me and threw his arms up in celebration.

'You did it!' he cheered. 'I thought you said you'd never skipped stones before?'

'I haven't,' I replied, shocked. It was impossible to say what stunned me more, the successful skip or the way my body yearned for his the moment he moved away.

'Go on,' Callum encouraged. 'Let's see another one.'

Fuelled by beginner's luck, I tried again. Four skips.

'You should be showing me how to do it,' he grinned. 'You're a natural.'

Beaming at his encouragement, I stooped down to look for more stones, better, flatter, smoother, and we took turns tossing our pebbles one at a time, pausing to cheer each other on.

'This is much more fun than watching TikToks about Blake Lively,' I declared, frowning slightly as my first dud sank on impact, a few feet in front of me. 'So wholesome.'

'The phone reception isn't always very good,' he deadpanned. 'We have to make our own fun.'

'You really don't think you'd ever move back here?' I asked, throwing another pebble. Skip, skip, sink.

Callum's determined gaze was set on the horizon as he tossed his stone. Skip, skip, skip, sink.

'Last week I'd have said no,' he replied. 'Took me long enough to get away, why would I be thinking about coming back?'

'And now?'

'And now I'm re-evaluating lots of things I was certain about three days ago.'

With one last stone in his hand he pulled back his arm and threw. It travelled so far, I could only see the ripples on the water when it landed.

'Your friend had a lot of questions about my love life,' he said, still staring after his stone. 'Did you put her up to that?'

'No!' I exclaimed. 'No, I would never. I told you, she's a monster. Honestly, I wouldn't pry like that. You and Shiv, that's none of my business.'

Whether I liked it or not.

He turned to face me, blue eyes squinting against the wind but his expression kind.

'Because you can ask me anything, you know. I'm an open book to you, Laura.'

'As is my right as your fake girlfriend,' I replied with an uncomfortable laugh.

'As is your right as my friend.'

Friendzoned by my fake date.

I squeezed my last pebble, not noticing its sharp edge until it bit into the flesh of my palm. Silently, I pitched it across the water, my heart sinking with it as it disappeared beneath the surface.

'If we're going into Inverness to get you a phone and make it back to Braewick in time for the carol service, we should get going,' Callum said, dusting off his hands to the tune of Desi and Joel yelling, each trying to shove the other into the water. 'Do we really have to take them with us?'

'You're the one who said they could stay,' I reminded him, pushing the sting down down down, as far as it could go, and burying it alongside all the other emotions I preferred to ignore. 'They could be safely over the border, cruising past Newcastle by now.'

He stuck his hands in his pockets, one corner of his mouth quirking up.

'What can I say? I like to make my life difficult.'

'You and me both,' I muttered under my breath as I followed him off the beach and back up the path that led to the car.

CHAPTER TWENTY-THREE

As anyone alive might've predicted, Desi and Joel adored The Clach.

'It's so cool,' Desi cooed as she got stuck into her second glass of scotch. 'Like, totally authentic vintage aesthetic vibe.'

'If you mean it looks as though they haven't altered a thing since before any of us were born, you're right, they haven't,' Callum replied, expertly opening a packet of salt and vinegar crisps for everyone to share. 'It's not a vibe, it's just old.'

I followed Joel's eyes around the room, drinking in the oak beams, the low ceilings, the patinaed mirrors on the wall. 'The best thing about my job is I can do it anywhere,' he said. 'Which means I don't have to leave until I've tried every single malt behind the bar.'

'What is your job?' Callum asked.

'Accountant. I thought about running away to join the circus but I couldn't be arsed.'

'You think he's joking,' Desi chimed in when Callum laughed. 'The three of us went to Vegas after me and him graduated and he kept threatening to stay behind to join Cirque du Soleil.'

Joel pouted at the memory. 'Turns out you have to have some sort of acrobatic ability and not just wild enthusiasm.'

Huddled in the corner closest to the fire, I smiled at the three of them as they carried on, chatting as if they'd known each other all their lives. It was wild how easily Callum slotted into our misfit little trio. Many had tried and all had failed. A few had come close, a man Joel dated briefly, who was in charge of buying all the cheese for Sainsbury's and kept us in hot and cold running vintage cheddar, and a researcher at the BBC, who managed to get us all free tickets to the Eurovision Song Contest during his brief dalliance with Desi, but neither lasted more than six months. Joel liked to keep his options open and Desi claimed she bored easily. Other than that, very few people were invited into our weird, ongoing, ten-year-long conversation. Or, to be more honest, most people wanted no part of it. But here was Callum, sharing drinks and stories like we'd known each other all our lives. I couldn't decide whether to laugh or cry. My symptoms were getting worse.

'If you had to join the circus, what would your act be?' Desi asked Callum, as serious as if she'd just asked him how he'd bring about world peace. 'Joel would be an acrobat, Laura would do the flying trapeze.'

He looked at me and I inclined my head to confirm.

'I have literally no explanation,' I said. 'But I think I'd be really good at it.'

'There's nothing like baseless confidence,' he replied before turning back to Desi. 'What about you?'

'Lion tamer. Obviously.'

'Obviously.' His very old chair creaked when he leaned back against it, rubbing the top of his head as he considered her question. 'I don't know what I would do, ride an elephant?'

'Strongman?' Joel suggested. 'What about ringmaster?'

'Most likely they'd have me driving the wee little clown car,' Callum said, drawing more laughter out of my friends. 'Twenty-five numpties in the back of a Toyota Yaris.'

After leaving Loch Ness behind, Nessie-less and starving, he'd driven us into Inverness where Joel had successfully obtained his body weight in shortbread and Desi trekked from chip shop to chip shop until she finally found a deep-fried Mars bar, much to Callum's dismay. Now, we were sitting in The Clach, an early sunset painting the world outside the window with a riot of glorious colour, pink and purple and red, and as the sky dimmed, the white lights on the huge Christmas tree in front of the pub grew brighter and brighter, just like the stars.

I couldn't remember a time I'd been so happy.

'When do we have to leave for this carol service?' Joel asked, tapping his smartwatch to check the time. 'Is there time for another round?'

'Plenty,' Callum confirmed. 'Why? Will we need it with your singing?'

'None for me,' I said as the two of them rose to stand. 'Not unless you want me drunk.'

Desi poked me in the ribs and I promptly toppled off my stool, colliding face first with Joel's legs. 'You're already drunk so you might as well have another.'

I couldn't argue with her sound investigation.

'I'd better let Gray know we'll be back tomorrow to pick up the car,' Callum said, patting down his pockets for his wallet as I righted myself, the room around me very slightly off its axis. 'None of us will be driving after three drinks.'

'Can you get some more snacks while you're at the bar?' I asked, holding up a particularly well-shaped crisp, impressed by its size and thickness. God, I was drunk. 'I could go for some chips as well if the kitchen's open.'

'And to think you mocked me for eating that deep-fried Mars bar,' Desi clucked. 'Who's laughing now?'

'All of Scotland,' Callum replied. 'Every single person in the country.'

'And I could not care less,' she sniffed. 'It was bloody delicious.'

I watched him walk across the pub, fully aware I was not looking respectfully. He was so tall, so solid, so permanent. There was something about Callum that seemed rooted to the ground, like I could lean all my weight on him and he would not budge an inch. Ever since we left the loch, I hadn't been able to stop thinking about the way his body curled around mine when we were skimming stones, soaring on the high then crashing back down to earth when I remembered what he'd said.

Friends.

'You doing all right?' Desi asked, following my eyes across the bar to where Callum and Joel stood laughing with Graham.

'More than,' I said even though it was a lie. 'Please don't ask again.'

She squeezed my knee under the table.

'I really like him.'

'You don't like anyone.'

'And yet.' She rested her head on my shoulder. 'Do you think he knows how to make croissants from scratch?'

'In theory,' I replied. 'He's a pastry chef, isn't he?'

'Shame we can't keep him.'

Her words were light, a reminder, an apology, a warning.

'Don't look now but the Grinch just walked in.' Desi gave me a nudge, holding her empty glass to her mouth to hide her words. 'And she's staring straight at you.'

Without turning around, I felt the atmosphere in the pub freeze over and knew exactly who it was.

'Auburn hair, blue eyes, face like a smacked arse?'

My friend lifted her chin then lowered it all the way to her chest and I groaned at the sound of heavy footsteps that stopped right behind my stool.

'Thanks for taking the Land Rover without telling me,' Elsie said, a distinct smell of barnyard animal emanating from her ensemble. 'If I don't get the bags of feed tonight, I'm going to have to work Christmas Day.'

'I thought there were no days off on a farm anyway?' I replied, matching her gracious manners tit-for-tat. 'Besides, I didn't take it, your brother did.'

'To ferry you and your idiot family around.'

'Hi.' Desi stood, hand outstretched. 'Idiot family member number one. And judging by the state of you, you must be . . . don't tell me, ghost of Christmas past?'

'Is he here?' Elsie asked me, ignoring Desi completely. 'I need the fucking keys.'

'At the bar,' I pointed, still declining to make eye contact. There really was no point.

But Callum and Joel were already on their way back, smiling and carrying two glasses of scotch and two packets of crisps each.

'Car keys.'

Elsie held out her hand as he set down his two glasses, one in front of his empty stool, one in front of me.

'Here.' He fished them from his pocket and handed them over. 'Anything else?'

She didn't move but I was sure I could hear the cogs of her brain turning.

'You're not going to invite me to sit down?'

Against my own best interests, I twisted in my seat to look at her.

'Sorry, there's no room at the inn.'

Joel and Desi exchanged a look, Desi's mouth hanging open in delight.

'I've time for a wee dram,' she said, dropping into Callum's seat before he could. 'Nice of you to buy me a drink, brother.'

No one protested when she picked up the glass meant for me and took a sip but I heard Joel growl like an angry labradoodle.

'So, Elise,' Desi said. 'Tell us about life on the farm.'

'It's Elsie,' she corrected.

'Right, that's what I said,' Desi replied easily. 'Do you always smell this terrible or was there a particularly rancid chore on the to-do list today?'

'Caroline, why don't you remind me how you and Callum first met,' Elsie said, staring through me as though Desi didn't even exist. 'Fiona was asking but I couldn't remember the story.'

'I walked in on him naked,' I replied with a hiccup.

'In the massage room,' Callum added quickly. 'I didn't get under the sheet fast enough.'

'It's frowned upon,' I flapped my hand behind me and almost poking Joel in the eye. 'But you know how it is, if the trailer's good, you want to see the movie. He lived up to the hype.'

My tongue was furry, my mouth was dry and my head getting fuzzier by the minute, as my regrettable second whisky passed through my empty stomach and into my bloodstream, coaxing a release of dopamine and serotonin. Elsie's entire face tightened. She looked at me, looked at her despairing brother, then scanned the table, counting up all the empty glasses.

'Are you drunk?'

'No,' I declared with confidence. 'I don't drink.'

'Well, if you're not drunk, there's something else going on.'

'You got me,' I agreed. 'I am on drugs.'

'The love of a good man,' Desi said loudly, pulling me in for a side hug. 'Hell of a drug.'

'And you two.' Elsie turned to Desi and Joel. 'Imbecile family member number one, was it?'

'Idiot family member,' Desi corrected. 'Most people call me Svetty but you can call me Svetlana.'

'And he is?'

She nodded across the table and all four of us chorused the name at once.

'Joel.'

Elsie ran her tongue over her teeth, nodding slowly as though she was having a secondary, private conversation with herself.

'And what's your last name?'

'M-mine?' Joel stuttered. He never did do well under pressure. 'It's Soto.'

Elsie's most dangerous smile found its way back onto her face and I shrank down inside my coat.

'No, theirs,' she pointed at me and Desi and a tiny squeak escaped from the back of my throat.

'It's Skarsgård,' I announced with confidence. 'Our last name is Skarsgård.'

'Caroline Skarsgård,' Elsie replied flatly. 'And she's Svetlana Skarsgård.'

'Svetlana Skarsgård-Soto,' Desi said without missing a beat. 'I hyphenated when I got married.'

As if on cue, Callum, Desi and Joel all picked up their scotch at the same time and drank.

'There's something going on here,' Elsie said again, tossing back the rest of my drink and slamming the glass on the table. 'And I will find out what it is.'

'Maybe try to make time for a shower first,' Desi suggested. 'It's Christmas Eve, babes, make an effort.'

Looking around the table, we were all holding our breath when she marched away, Callum and I exhaling loudly when she passed through the door, Joel clapping his hands over his face and Desi letting out the loudest sigh I'd ever heard.

'I don't know what you did wrong in a former life to get stuck with her as a sister, but Callum, you'd better start making it up to the gods in this one,' she said, rolling her shoulders back as though we'd been through a physical ordeal. 'And you,' she turned to me, a look of disbelief on her face. 'Skarsgård? Really?'

'Name another famous Swede!' I challenged. 'And I mean last name, you can't just say ABBA.'

A gloomy cast covered Callum's handsome face. 'We

should get on to the carol service. It's a fair walk from here if we want to be on time.'

'But my chips?' I protested, still hungry, still drunk.

'We'll get some on the way,' Desi replied, hoisting me up to my reluctant feet.

'When it comes to Elsie, it's not worth getting into a fight,' Callum advised. 'Best to do as I do.'

'Invent a fake girlfriend, stop visiting your family then secretly plan to move to another country without telling her?'

All three of them stopped putting on their coats to give me a variation on a dirty look.

'What?' I said. 'Am I wrong though?'

'No but you are a lightweight,' Joel muttered, bustling me out the door.

'I know it's not easy but it's best to ignore her,' Callum said, helping with the toggles on my coat as a brisk wind slapped me wide awake. 'She's all talk. By this evening, she'll have forgotten all about it.'

I smiled, wanting to believe him, but as they strolled and I stumbled down the street towards the town hall, I couldn't fight the feeling that we hadn't escaped the wrath of Elsie McClay just yet.

CHAPTER TWENTY-FOUR

The festive vibes of the Braewick town hall were immaculate. Everywhere I turned, there was something else to delight me, the tinsel-laden tree with its multicoloured lights, trays of homemade gingerbread Santas baked by the WI, the cobbled-together nativity scene with a Teletubby standing in for one of the wise men and two T-Rexes where the donkey should be. I loved it all so much.

It looked as though the entire town was here already. Mums and dads, grandmas and grandads, what felt like hundreds of little kids running around and even a decent number of teenagers which seemed especially impressive. Everyone was dressed up, hugging, kissing and slapping each other on the back. The Christmas spirit was alive and well as the four of us inched along a row of chairs near the back of the hall, the front six or so rows already full to bursting. Five minutes more and it would be standing room only.

'Cal! Son! Over here!'

I craned my neck down the line to see Derek and Lizzie waving from across the hall.

'We've saved you seats. What are you waiting for, Christmas?'

Derek's shoulders shook with laughter at his own terrible dad joke.

'Did you know they were coming?' I asked and Callum shook his head.

'They didn't mention it,' he said with a fake smile. 'I am so sorry.'

'Don't be.' I gave them a little wave and pulled Desi and Joel behind me. 'No big deal.'

'Mum, Dad,' Callum said, kissing his mother on the cheek before taking the seat beside her. It was only when Lizzie and her husband sat back down I saw who was on Derek's other side.

Shiv.

She didn't stand, didn't move to say hello to anyone, but Callum tensed up when he noticed her, awkwardly leaning across his parents to hold up a hand in greeting.

'Hullo,' I heard him say quietly. 'Didn't expect to see you here.'

'Your dad suggested it,' she replied, eyes trained straight ahead. 'I didn't have anything else to do since . . .'

Derek leaned over the back of his seat to address the rest of us.

'Callum and Shiv used to throw a little Christmas Eve dinner party every year,' he explained, his face overly animated. 'Back when they were, you know.'

'Derek, they're starting.' Lizzie tapped her husband on the shoulder and he turned back to face the front but not before giving me a crafty wink.

'Ex-girlfriend?' Desi asked under her breath.

'Ex-girlfriend,' I confirmed, equally as stealthy.

'She's hot. Does she like girls? Because I totally would.'

'So selfless,' Joel said, clutching her hand to his heart. 'My generous, pansexual wife.'

'Do you want to swap seats, Shiv, love?' Derek asked loudly enough for us all to hear. 'Sit next to our Cal and have a wee catch-up?'

'Dad, it's starting,' Callum said, echoing his mother as his hand reached towards me. 'Caroline doesn't want to miss anything, can you shut up?'

Derek's face puckered as though he'd bitten into a mince pie and got a mouthful of cloves for his trouble. I stared down at our joined hands then looked up at Callum.

The touch receptors in my palm activated the sensory neurons, the sensory neurons shot messages along my spine and up to the thalamus, and the thalamus sent a signal to the somatosensory cortex to confirm that he was, in fact, holding my hand.

'Is this OK?' he mouthed, turning his body away from his parents.

I nodded and he squeezed gently.

'Sorry I'm late, room for a wee one?'

I heard Rory's voice, I felt the jostling of people moving on the other side of me, but I couldn't seem to tear my eyes away from the hand wrapped around mine and resting easily on my thigh.

'Welcome everyone.'

At the front of the hall, someone climbed the stairs to the small stage and, around us, everyone stood. Callum found his feet first but it took me a moment to remember how my knees worked. They could straighten as well as bend! It was a Christmas miracle! As our hands dropped to our sides, his grip loosened around mine but instinctively I held on tighter, not ready to let go. His body stayed straight but his head turned slightly in my direction. With the smallest smile, he squeezed back.

'How pleased I am to see so many faces carried over from this evening's service.' A minister dressed in a white gown over a black cassock cast a stern look across the crowd. 'And more than a few extras as well. Perhaps you'll decide to join us in the church next year, not only for the carols and mince pies.'

'And perhaps I'll chop my knob off and plant a tadger tree,' Rory muttered and Joel barked out a deeply inappropriate laugh.

'Nothing says Christmas more than a passive-aggressive telling-off from a vicar,' he murmured in agreement as the elder McClays eyeballed the pair of them.

'I can't believe they brought her,' Callum whispered right into my ear. 'I'm sorry, do you want to narwhal?'

'No,' I replied, moderating my grip on his hand. Not so loose that he'd think I wanted him to let go, not so tight that he'd consider a restraining order. 'It's fine. This is all fine.'

A pianist struck up the first chords of 'O Little Town of Bethlehem' and the whole crowd cleared their throats to sing.

'It's certainly working,' Callum added when Derek looked over at us again. 'Dad's got a face like a bulldog licking piss off a thistle.'

Sucking in my cheeks, I took a deep breath and squared my shoulders. I'd forgotten myself for the past few hours. Or rather, I'd forgotten who I was supposed to be. I was not Laura Pearce, I was Caroline Skarsgärd.

Demanding, selfish, some might even say cunty and not in the good way, and above all else, she did not stand for her boyfriend's parents interfering in her relationship.

'If he likes the hand-holding,' I whispered into Callum's ear, 'he'll love this.'

I lifted his arm and draped it over my shoulder, nuzzling into his body, wrapping my arms around his waist. Callum stiffened for a second before relaxing into the pose and gripping my upper arm possessively, pulling me in even closer. My body sang at the contact, every inch of me alive and alert.

'What happened to no touching?' Desi hissed into my other ear right as everyone launched into the carol.

'Piss off,' I replied with a blank smile. 'I know what I'm doing.'

But I didn't. I had no clue. Two drinks and a few skipped stones and all my self-imposed safety measures were out the window. I wanted to be as close to Callum as humanly possible, I wanted more of the delicious feeling that consumed me whenever he was close. The dopamine rush, the pounding heart, the prickling skin, ultra attuned to every move he made. I was addicted. When he also began to sing 'O Little Town', quietly as if embarrassed, his deep, rich baritone rumbled through his body, the vibrations passing through him and into me where our bodies touched. I softened into him, never wanting to break the connection.

It was deeply stupid, I knew that, no need for Desi to keep digging her fingers into my ribs and standing on my foot. At that moment, no amount of needling could've made me break contact by choice. When we met, I'd agreed to pretend to be Callum's girlfriend because he needed it. Now I was pretending to be his girlfriend because I needed it.

The next hour passed too quickly. Even if someone had offered me a million pounds on the spot, I could not have named a single carol or reading. I was completely consumed by Callum's physical presence. The warm scent of his hand-knitted woollen jumper cut clean by the botanical hit of deodorant every time he moved. With his arm still resting over my shoulders, his hand roamed freely. Sometimes squeezing my bicep, sometimes combing through my hair, once, only once, stroking my cheek. Every touch hit like another glass of whisky, running through my bloodstream, loosening my grip on my senses.

To anyone who dared risk a glance at the pair of us, we looked like any young couple in love, swooning, smitten and incapable of keeping our hands off each other. Only we knew the truth.

But what was the truth?

After the minister thanked everyone for coming and attempted a second hard sell on next year's church service, the tightly packed rows of people broke ranks, some milling over to the tables of mince pies and hot drinks, others sprinting straight for the door in search of hard liquor. Our unlikely group all stood but made no move in either direction.

'I don't know about you but I've got a mouth like Gandhi's flipflop,' Rory announced finally. 'Mulled wine, anyone?'

'Bloody love a mulled wine,' Joel announced. 'Svetlana dearest? Come with?'

'Just one second, my angel,' Desi cooed back. 'I'm

desperate for a slash and Caroline needs to come with me.'

Without asking, she laced her fingers through mine and yanking hard on my arm.

'What the fuck was that?' she demanded as we crossed out of the main hall and into the lobby. 'What do you think you're doing?'

'My singing wasn't that bad,' I muttered.

My best friend's eyes flashed with warning.

'Laura, I say this with nothing but love. You need to be careful. You can't be expected to go from burying yourself in work one minute to pretending to be Hottie McHotScot's fake girlfriend the next without the risk of picking up *some* residual feelings. It's like a horny contact high, you didn't inhale but you still breathed it in, only please, please, please remember, this isn't real.'

'I know that,' I said. 'You're imagining things.'

'Come off it,' she replied. 'Look at him, look at this place! You'd think this whole town had been specially designed to trick unsuspecting city dwellers to fall in love with the strapping, stoic locals. Thank God you're not a high-powered lawyer who just broke up with her financier fiancé or you'd have no chance of getting out with your pelvic bone intact. You're only supposed to be pretending to fall in love with him, Laura, *pretending*.'

'Which is exactly what I'm doing,' I said with not-so-fake frustration. 'What is so difficult—'

'I'm not done.' Desi grabbed my wrist and pulled me off to the side to allow a group of beaming, bearded, clearly tipsy men in kilts to pass by. 'Don't get me wrong, I like him, but I could start not liking him if he's using you.'

I snatched my hand away and gave her a scathing look. 'How is he using me? We have an agreement.'

'Does your agreement involve him pawing at you all evening? Does it explain why you're walking around like a heart eyes emoji? I've never seen you like this before and I don't think you're that good of an actress.'

'I'll have you know I played the caterpillar in my school production of *Alice in Wonderland*,' I replied with a sniff.

'Why is he suddenly all handsy?' she went on, not nearly as impressed as she could've been with my student acting career. 'Because his parents are here. Because his ex is here. There was no hair stroking all day long when it was just us, was there? He's acting. He's pretending. You're not.'

In that moment, under the harsh fluorescent lights of the lobby, I hated her.

'You've made your point,' I said quietly. 'Thank you.'

'I'm not trying to upset you,' Desi said, her voice tinged with regret and apology. 'I'm trying to protect you.'

'OK.'

'Really?'

'Yes.' I looked away, unable to meet her eyes. 'I'm really OK. I know you're trying to help but you're reading too much into it.'

Even though I could tell she didn't believe a word I was saying, Desi knew when to stop. She would never try to hurt me on purpose, which was why it cut so very deep.

'Good because I really do need a wee,' she said, marching on the spot. 'I'll be back in a minute.'

Slouching against the wall, I watched the residents

of Braewick cross the lobby, out into the night. Parents holding hands, half the little kids in mittens and scarves, racing ahead, the others clutching their grandparents, equally exhausted and excited, Christmas so close, they could taste it. Pulling out my shiny new phone, I opened up a photo album that rarely saw the light of day. I'd forgotten it was there until the delightful Ian in the phone shop transferred all my data from the cloud while he lectured me on the perils of not turning on two-factor authentication.

The pictures had a grainy quality compared to the rest of the snaps on my phone because most of them hadn't been taken with a digital camera. Dad always used film when I was little and my mum loved a disposable camera. There were always a couple in the cupboard at the bottom of the stairs, ready for a surprise day out or weekend away. We did a lot, I recalled as I swiped through the images with blurry eyes, spontaneous adventures. Sometimes, they'd pick me up from school and we'd drive all the way to the seaside to get fish and chips for tea. Once, she let me miss school and we spent an entire day waiting in line to meet one of the chefs from my favourite cooking show. I was, admittedly, a bit of a weird kid. I still had the signed cookbook somewhere, buried in a box. She and I made a different recipe from it every day for a week, or rather we attempted to. Neither of us were talented cooks. A month later, she was dead.

The thumbnail I was looking for waited for me, right at the end of the roll. Not a photograph but a video, someone's grainy camcorder trained on an empty stage just like the one in the Braewick town hall. I pressed play. Even without sound, the memories flooded me instantly and a huge lump rose in my throat. A row of tiny children streamed onto the stage, one by one. Second from the end of the front row, in a red tartan dress, white socks pulled all the way up to my knees and hair inexplicably crimped, was me. My eyes scanned the audience and then I waved, almost directly at the camera. The close-up pulled back to show the whole children's choir as our music teacher played the first notes of 'Silent Night' on the piano and the back of a copper-red curly head came into view, right in front of the camera.

I watched, nursing the phone in my hands, counting down the seconds until she twisted in her seat to say something to the woman sitting next to her, pointing at the stage. She must've seen the video camera out of the corner of her eye because she turned and waved, giving the camera man a big grin and a thumbs up. Two fat tears fell on the phone screen, magnifying my mum's face for one moment, until she looked back to the stage, watching me belt out Christmas carols with everything in my little lungs.

I couldn't remember who took the video. I'd found it by accident, on a Facebook group I'd forgotten I'd joined, supposedly to collect memories of our village but, every time I was bored enough to check it, the members seemed to be using it mostly to bicker about who had owned the post office first and complain about kids today. Someone uploaded this a couple of years back and I'd screen-recorded it right away, too overwhelmed to message the owner to ask for the original file. After watching myself climb the stage, pausing on Mum's happy face, over and over again, enough times to commit the entire thing to memory, I filed it away.

Seeing her like that, stumbling across her as though we'd bumped into each other in the supermarket, hurt in a way I could not have anticipated. Like someone had torn my heart open and pulled out what was inside. I was ecstatic and I was heartbroken. Thrilled to possess this precious moment and devastated by her loss, all over again. I hadn't looked at it again. Not until now, when I wanted it to hurt.

Phone back in my pocket, I sloped back into the hall, not waiting for Desi and bowed with the weight of her accusations, every word slicing at me like a papercut.

As per our agreement, Callum was pretending and I was pretending too.

Only now, I was lying to myself instead of his family.

Joel and Rory were by the mulled wine, Joel standing altogether too close to Callum's baby brother for a married man, and I saw Shiv, Callum and his parents, talking to a group of what I assumed were family friends, all of them engaged in different levels of crossing conversation. The two exes stood side by side with smiles on their faces, both laughing at something said by a woman in a velvet Santa hat, and when their eyes met, I saw – no, felt – something pass between them. A lifetime of shorthand, of stolen glances and secret code.

'Don't feel too bad,' a voice said over my shoulder. 'Everyone knows they were meant for each other.'

Elsie appeared at my side, contemplating the scene in front of us. She didn't even sound that pleased with herself, more wistful than anything.

'It was a shit move on his part to bring you up here. But that's Cal. Won't have even occurred to him how you might feel about watching him flirting with his ex right in front of your face.'

'They're just talking.' I forced the words out my mouth. 'What's wrong with that?'

'Between us, I'm no happier about this than you are. Shiv deserves better.' She moved in between me and the happy couple, blocking my view entirely. 'When she came back from London, she was devastated. We've been friends our whole lives but she refused to even talk to me about it.'

'Funny that. What with you being such a sensitive soul.'

She scoffed, sticking her hands in the pockets of her wax jacket.

'This is me trying to be nice. Whatever is going on with them, the fact remains, you're a rebound, hun. Sorry I have to be the one to tell you.'

'You don't sound very sorry,' I said, hands curling into tight little fists as my sides.

'Well, that's because I'm not,' she replied breezily. 'I don't really care about you either way, but I'm in no rush to have my arsehole brother home either.'

My fingernails pressed against the spot where I'd cut my palm on the skipping stone and I winced at the sting.

'Between you and me, why do you hate him so much?' I asked. 'Did he pull your pigtails too many times when you were kids?'

'This is how I know you don't understand my brother at all.' She pointed a finger in his direction, punctuating every word with a little jab. 'He might come off as charming but he's selfish and thoughtless, always has been. Left me here to run the family farm alone, no concern for what I want.'

'No one's making you do it,' I said, the line between Laura and Caroline blurring until I couldn't tell the difference. 'Callum left, you could leave. Stop being such a martyr.'

'If I don't, who will?' Her voice grew louder, drawing the attention of a small gaggle of nanas in their Christmas best at the side of us. 'Callum wants no part of it, Rory's spoiled rotten, indulged for twenty-four years straight and hardly knows his arse from his elbow. I'm the only one left.'

'Then that's you making your choice same as they've made theirs,' I said. 'You can't live your life for other people, even if they're your parents. If you hate the farm so much, why don't you leave?'

Her blue eyes burned. 'Did I say I hate it?'

I took in the fury on her face, the contradiction in her tone.

'You said you're only running it because Callum left.'

'Because no one ever asked me if I wanted to run the farm,' she said, seething. 'I'm better at it than he ever would've been but what does that matter? I'm still the runner-up, the last resort. No one cares what I want, they only care about Callum.'

It was too much. Callum tying himself up in knots because he didn't want the responsibility of the farm, Elsie twisting herself into something so bitter because no one had offered it to her.

'Can you even hear yourself?' I said. 'How is any of this Callum's fault? If anyone is to blame it's your dad. Be angry at him.'

'You don't understand,' she spat. 'You don't get it.'

Maybe not, but I did know what denial looked like and Elsie was a classic case.

'Look, you're right, I don't understand.' I lowered my voice, maintained eye contact, softened my expression.

'But carrying around all this anger and resentment can't be fun for you. If you wanted to talk to someone, I could recommend some people, some resources.'

Apparently this was not the right thing to say.

'How dare you?' She said with a sneer. 'You arrogant cow. You don't walk into my house and try to tell me how to feel about my family. What gives you the right? I take it back, I'm not sorry he's using you. You're as bad as him, you deserve all you get.'

My mouth opened and closed like a goldfish. So many people were watching now, Callum included.

'I was only trying to help,' I said, unexpectedly emotionally bruised. 'I'm sorry.'

'You think you know better, just like him,' she snapped. 'Well, you don't. Maybe you think it's fine to be a smug, self-obsessed vegan—'

'What is so wrong with being a vegan?' I interrupted. 'I know you're a dairy farmer but—'

But Elsie raised her voice to talk over me. 'Some of us choose to put other people's needs ahead of our own. I put my family before myself. Callum is incapable and, judging by what I've seen of you, you're the same. Either you were raised by selfish arseholes or your parents must really hate you.'

That was enough. That was more than enough.

'You're the one who doesn't know what she's talking about,' I yelled, the ability to moderate my volume completely out the window. 'You don't know me, you don't know anything about me, or my family, and if you did, you'd feel fucking dreadful about what you just said. Or maybe you wouldn't, I don't know, the basic laws of common decency seemed to have passed you by entirely. Maybe Callum is selfish, maybe he did put his own wants and needs first, and you might not like that, your parents might not like that, but he's the one who has to live his life, not you and not them.'

Panting for breath, I prepared for the final blow, Elsie practically swaying back and forth in front of me. *Finish her*, whispered a videogame voice in my head.

'Stop complaining that Callum only thinks about himself when you're just as bad. You don't really care about Shiv or your dad, you're pissed off because you think *they* don't care about *you*. You're angry because you believe they'll choose your brother over you. That's not his fault, *hun*. Take it up with them.'

Silence.

The entire town hall was utterly silent.

Joel and Rory stood still, cups of mulled wine held halfway up to their mouths. On the other side of the room, Derek, Lizzie and Shiv stared at us in various states of shock. What was happening? Why did I feel so out of control? Closing my eyes, I tracked the sensations in my body. An influx of adrenaline and cortisol left me light-headed as my amygdala shot off panic signals to the hypothalamus. I needed to breathe, I needed to calm down. I needed to apologise. I opened my eyes, not sure where to begin, but Elsie was no longer in front of me. A tall, barrel-chested body with auburn hair that fell in front of dark blue eyes stood between us, looking down at me.

'Callum,' I began, filtering through the millions of different apologies I needed to give.

But he didn't give me time to even try. Grabbing my face with both hands, Callum pressed his lips to mine with hard and bruising pressure. He was kissing me. He was kissing me like he meant it.

'Callum,' I said his name again when we broke apart, barely breathing sound into the words, trapped in his gaze, my hands gripping his wrists as my legs weakened beneath me.

'Caroline,' he replied, brushing a strand of hair away from my face, he leaned down again, tilting my head backwards before our lips met again.

Caroline.

He was kissing Caroline, not Laura.

But my heart still swelled around the knife he plunged into it and as my mouth opened to his, the rest of the world vanished without a trace.

CHAPTER TWENTY-FIVE

I came to, pulling away from Callum right as Shiv walked by. I pressed my lips together tightly, awash with shame, but she didn't even look at me. Head held high, she grabbed hold of Elsie's arm and dragged her out to the lobby.

'OK, enough of this,' Desi said loudly, punching me very hard in the arm. 'No one wants to see that amount of PDA at a Christmas carol concert.'

'Technically the carol concert is over,' I heard Joel say. 'And I'm fine with it.'

There was other chatter, people whispering, talking, but I was staring up at Callum, stunned into silence and barely able to stay upright. He looked right back at me, eyes boring into mine.

'Mal's waiting outside, everyone in the bloody car,' Derek barked, words cutting through my lust-struck haze. 'We'll not be airing our dirty laundry in public.'

'Two more minutes and they'd be airing more than their laundry,' Rory said. 'I'd say get a room but you've got one and it's awful close to mine. Maybe

I'll go down to the cottage and stay with Mal and Fi tonight.'

'Time to go,' Desi sang with a big fake smile on her face as she rounded behind me and physically pushed me forward to hiss in my ear. 'What the fucking fuck was that?'

'I don't know,' I replied with an equally enormous, fake grin pasted on my face. 'He kissed me, not the other way around.'

When we stepped out of the town hall, the ground was glittering, the beginning of a frost, the whole of Braewick white over.

'As soon as we get back, we should get in the car and drive home,' she said as Joel fell into step beside us. 'Your work is done, I feel safe in saying you've been crossed off the McClay family Christmas list.'

'It's a ten-hour drive at best,' Joel replied. 'And we're all three of us over the limit still. No one's going anywhere tonight.'

'First thing in the morning then.' Desi's glare softened when she saw the confusion on my face. 'And she's sleeping in our room with us. Where we can keep an eye on her.'

I didn't say anything. I'd said enough.

'I don't know if I've got another day of this in me,' she groaned. 'I'm exhausted.'

A silver Mercedes pulled up in front of the town hall, stopping right next to a beetroot-faced Derek. My heart stuttered in my chest when I felt a tug on the sleeve of my coat.

'Can I speak to you?' Callum asked.

'No,' Desi answered for me. 'You can't.'

She opened the back door of the car and pushed my

head down, bundling me into the back like a police suspect. As I shuffled over to make room for my two friends, Callum's eyes stayed locked on mine. And when the car pulled away, I had my fingers pressed against my mouth, still staring in his direction as he disappeared into the distance.

With Mal and Lizzie in the front of the Mercedes, me, Desi and Joel in the back, we beat the Land Rover home by less than thirty seconds. Derek pulled up right behind us, Elsie flying out of his front passenger side, Callum and Rory rolling out the backseat. Shiv had seemingly found her own way home.

I tumbled out of the car, wincing at the sound of so many doors slamming shut at the same time, the racket bouncing off the front of the house and echoing into the empty night. Desi and Joel muttered at each other while I poked at a paper-thin layer of ice on the surface of the pond with the toe of my shoe. It cracked, but the pieces stayed where they were, held in place by the rest of the frozen water, nowhere for them to go.

'Who's hungry?' Lizzie asked brightly and I followed her around to the back door of the house, leaving Callum, Elsie and their dad to share some choice words. Keys jangled in a lock, the door opened, we were inside. Rory rested a kind hand on the centre of my back before giving me a shove over the threshold.

'You don't want to be part of that,' he said. 'Trust me.'

'I might go upstairs for a bit,' I said, staring at my feet. 'I think I've got another migraine coming on.'

'Fine. You're back in your own room tonight. Svetlana.' Lizzie turned to Desi, pressing a hand to her chest as though saying the name caused her physical pain. 'I moved your things into the guest suite in the Abercorn wing. Would you like me to show you the way?'

Desi shook her head. 'I'm going with Caroline.'

'No, you aren't,' Joel corrected. 'Caroline has a migraine, give her some space.'

'And I don't think it's good for her to be alone when she's got a migraine. I'm going with her.'

She stared him down but he did not budge.

'My arse, you're coming with me.' Joel, the greatest peacemaker of our time, turned to Lizzie with the most charming smile in his repertoire. 'Mrs McClay, thank you so much. Which way to our new room?'

'Rory, can you show them?' Lizzie asked and her youngest son nodded, clicking his fingers and shooting double finger guns. Then she looked to me. 'Before you go up, could I have a word?'

Suddenly the thought of being alone with Desi didn't seem that bad. Better a best friend bollocking than a dressing-down from your fake boyfriend's mum. But I nodded. The others left us behind even as Desi tried to drag me along with them by sheer force of will.

'I want to say . . .' Lizzie tugged on the ends of the silk scarf fastened around her neck. Her eyes were red. Had she been crying in silence in the car? 'I just want to say . . .'

'I'm so sorry,' I blurted out before she could fumble for her words one second longer. It was excruciating. 'I was totally out of order and I'm mortified about the whole thing. I don't know what came over me.'

Not very Caroline of me but I couldn't help myself. The memory of my own mother at the carol service hovered at the edge of my mind, I couldn't stand knowing I'd brought Callum's mum to tears. She caught my hand in hers, delicate bones and soft skin, and shook her head.

'You might not believe it now but I had more than one run-in with Derek's family when I was young. I might have even forgotten it myself. It can consume that part of you, being a mother. Sometimes I forget who I was before.'

'It's a very difficult job,' I replied, the words stilted, still afraid she might slap the taste out of my mouth at any second. But she didn't. Instead, she unfastened her brooch and pulled off the silk scarf, shoving both of them into her pocket.

'I miss Callum,' she said simply. 'The house isn't the same without him, but we haven't been fair to him. Or to Elsie. I had no idea she felt that way. She would never have said anything if you hadn't forced it out of her so thank you.'

'Thank you?' I couldn't believe my ears. 'You're thanking me for arguing with Elsie?'

'I'm thanking you for getting her to tell us the truth,' she amended. 'I'm under no illusions about who my daughter is or the fact she's got a temper. But I didn't know how much she'd kept bottled up. It's my job, as her mother, to see to her happiness, not the other way around. That's a difficult thing to do if you don't really know what's going on inside your children's heads, and Lord knows they're never in any rush to tell you.'

'Still,' I said. 'I am sorry for causing a scene.'

'Gives busybodies in town something to talk about.' She smiled and took hold of my hand. 'You really love him, don't you?'

'I feel like I can be myself with him,' I whispered back. 'I feel like he sees me.'

She nodded then pulled me into a hug. A surprised gasp spluttered out of me but it was over almost as soon as it had begun, Lizzie breaking away and rolling her sleeves up to her elbows.

'You look peaked, Caroline. Go on up to bed and I'll send Callum up with something for your head when they're done.' She paused and I heard raised voices from all the way outside. 'Might be a wee while.'

'I'll be fine,' I replied and her face reset with grim determination. 'Thank you.'

One more nod and she spun on her heel, marching right back out the door towards her quarrelling family.

'Right!' I heard her shout. 'I have had just about enough of this! Get your arses back inside this instant and don't you dare look at me like that, Derek McClay!'

And before anyone could follow her orders, I bolted upstairs, as fast as my legs would carry me.

It was strange to be back in my room. The Christmas tree glowed, the ornaments twinkled, the stockings were hung from the chimney with care, everything perfectly prepared for me. But compared to Callum's room, the cosy luxury of this suite seemed overdone. I felt like a guest. This was Caroline's room. Laura wanted to be next door.

The rooms might be different but the view was the same from both windows. Nothing had changed outside. Unaltered from the night before and the night before that. The year before, the decade, the millennium. These mountains, this loch, stood silent sentry and observed the endless lives as they came and went. They were here before Balmaclay and they would still be there when the house was in ruins. All we had was a blink of an eye. Gone before you knew it.

I was still sitting in the armchair, staring out the window, when the door opened. The handle turned so softly I barely heard it click, ruling out Desi or Joel. Neither of my friends had ever crept into a room without making as much noise as possible in the entire time I'd known them. Derek was unlikely to be tiptoeing around my room any time soon and Lizzie had already said her piece, so there was only one other person I was expecting.

Unless it was Elsie with a shotgun.

I spun around to see Callum closing the door behind him and my shoulders sagged, thrilled to be still holding onto my head. He stayed in the far corner of the room, as far away from me as he could be while still sharing the same space. With my knees pulled up to my chin, I cocked my head to the side.

'I've come to apologise,' he said.

'What for?' I asked.

'Dealer's choice.'

There it was, that irresistible half-smile on his fascinating face. Not handsome or hot, but honestly beautiful. His massive physical presence undercut by the softness in his blue eyes, his voluptuous lips at odds with the square cut of his jaw, russet hair contrasting against pale skin. I was sure I could've studied him forever and still found new things to marvel at every single day.

If things were different.

'Let's start with an apology for what Elsie said about your family.' Callum advanced halfway across the room, stopping short by my bed. 'If she knew, she'd never forgive herself. She can be a cow, I know, but she'd never.'

'You don't have to apologise for that and neither does she,' I replied, light words carrying across the dimly lit space. 'I know she didn't mean it and I didn't help myself. She's owed an apology as much as anyone else.'

'She's not in the mood to talk to any of us right now so I wouldn't worry about it.'

He gripped one of the posts of the bed, testing its antique strength. The canopy only trembled slightly. I pulled my legs in closer, resting my chin on my knees.

'We're leaving first thing tomorrow,' I told him. 'Shouldn't be too much traffic on the roads, Christmas Day. You can tell your mum and dad I was angry about the argument and took off without telling you.'

The floorboards creaked under him as he shifted from one foot to the other, weighing up his next move. He unfastened his jacket, sliding his arms out the sleeves.

'I wish we'd met under different circumstances,' he said, laying it across the foot of my bed.

'We did meet under different circumstances,' I reminded him. 'Twice. Stella and Dave's wedding and Lemon's naming ceremony. We were both there.'

He rolled his eyes. 'Lemon Marge O'Brien. That poor kid. I only stuck my head in to say hello. Had to work.'

'You were at the wedding though?' I asked but he shook his head, his mouth a grim line.

'Not exactly the best day of my life. It was just after Shiv moved to London and she didn't really want to go. She didn't know anyone and she's never been very good with strangers. I spent the entire time trying to cheer her up until she threw a fit and insisted we leave.'

I looked out at the mountains and then back at Callum.

'Do you love Shiv?' I asked.

'Do I love Shiv?'

He seemed surprised by my straightforward question. Almost as surprised as I was by asking it.

'Yes, I love her,' he replied. 'She was my best friend in the whole world for twenty-five years and now she won't even talk to me. I miss her every day.'

Even when you prepare yourself for the worst, hearing the confirmation still hurts. I wrapped my arms closer around my shins and hugged myself tightly.

'Then why aren't you with her?'

His head rolled backwards to expose his throat, his Adam's apple bobbing up and down as he worked on his response.

'I've never been good at saying what I mean,' he muttered, a few, long, lonely seconds later. 'I love Shiv, but I'm not in love with Shiv. After we broke up, I realised I hadn't been for a long time. She deserves better than what I was offering.'

'Then why do you have her photo in your wallet?'

'How do you know I have her photo in my wallet?'

'Because I saw it when I found your wallet.'

'It's just a photo,' he said. 'I never thought to take it out, I hardly ever open my wallet these days, I pay for everything with my phone. It's been there a long time, that's all, doesn't mean anything.'

'Everyone says you're still in love with her,' I said, feeling suddenly small and timid. 'Elsie and Graham and your dad.'

'Three people renowned for their keen insight into the inner workings of my mind?' Callum leaned against the bedframe and curled his arms behind him, wrapping them around the wooden post. 'Shiv is the same as everyone else up here, she sees the version of me that she wants to see. Nothing but a selfish man who let down his family and doesn't even have a good reason for it, same as the rest of them.'

'Not wanting to stay is reason enough.'

'That depends on who you ask.'

Breaking away from the bed, he strode over to the fireplace and went down on one knee, stacking logs, adding kindling. Sparking a match, he lit a piece of newspaper tucked in between the logs, then blew it out. The tiny flame danced across the page, burning away the newsprint, flickering up and out and on. He didn't move until the flames licked at the first log and the wood began to crackle.

'They're right,' he said, still staring into the fire. 'I am selfish. I couldn't deal with the responsibility expected of me so I let her take it on instead. I don't want Dad to have to sell the farm, I don't want strangers living in my house, but I couldn't stand the pressure of having my whole life planned out for me. Where to live, what to do, who to marry. It was too much.'

'Did you tell them that?'

'There's a possibility those weren't my exact words.' He rubbed at his chin, as the flames bloomed. 'Ever since we got back, I've found myself wondering if I was wrong. What if I'd stayed? What if I'd tried? Maybe I'd be happier than I am now.

'But if I hadn't left home, hadn't taken up cooking, never got into school in Paris, I wouldn't have met you.'

My breath caught in my chest and Callum turned to face me, rising to his feet.

'You wouldn't have needed to meet me,' I returned,

my fingers winding around each other. 'No break-up, no move to London, no need for a Caroline stand-in.'

'I'm not talking about Caroline,' Callum said. 'I'm talking about you.'

The weight of his gaze was crushing, pinning me to the chair and forcing to listen to him, my arguments and witty rebuttals all choked up in my throat. With dark eyes trained on mine, he unfastened one cuff of his shirt, folding it back on itself.

'Laura Pearce, neurosurgeon, lover of Loch Ness and rare steaks and Christmas ornaments, who can't hold her whisky and has feet like blocks of ice.'

'Trainee neurosurgeon,' I corrected quietly, my legs unfurling from the chair like they were moving of their own accord. Not physically possible, I knew that, but the voice in my head was suddenly at odds with the voice in my heart and my body didn't know who to listen to. Instead it staged a coup against the both of them, ordering me to my feet, but I resisted, staying right where I was, in my chair, my safe harbour.

'Trainee neurosurgeon,' he assented and his throaty voice was rich and dark. 'Kind, generous, selfless. Too selfless to be honest. Funny. Probably the cleverest person I've ever met in my entire life. And beyond fucking beautiful.'

I lifted my chin to meet his gaze and a bolt of anticipation shot through me, lightning fast and electric.

'There's something else I should apologize for,' he said.

'There is?'

He nodded. 'That kiss.'

'You're sorry you kissed me?' I asked, more disappointed than I was ready to admit.

'No,' he replied at once. 'But I am sorry I crossed a boundary without asking.'

'Oh,' I sank back down into the depths of my desire, aching and raw, and suddenly I was too far adrift to drag myself back to shore. 'Then perhaps we should redefine our boundaries. Just so we're both clear.'

Slowly, I stood. Slowly, I walked over to where he was. It was me who positioned myself in front of him. I was the one who rested my hands against his chest. I was the one who held his heavy gaze.

'Is this OK?' I asked when his lips parted in a silent question.

'Yes.'

The word was barely a whisper but his body screamed its consent, leaning into me as my palms ran lightly over his shirt, stroking first the soft cotton fabric then pressing harder to find the solid body beneath. Callum gasped under my touch.

'Is this OK?' I asked again, my eyes still on his when I slid one hand up to his collar, my fingers toying with the open buttons at his throat.

This time, he only nodded.

With his permission, I traced his magnificent jawline, like he was a sculpture made of marble. His scruff was coming through a few shades darker than the deep russet of his hair, contrasting against his pale skin even in the low light of my room, and it scratched against my skin. We both shivered. Following the line upwards, I tiptoed my fingers along his face until I found the top of his cheekbone and rested the palm of my hand flat against it. He looked down at me, mesmerised.

'What about this?' I asked, taking a half-step into him and he spread his legs, drawing me in closer, allowing me to explore while he kept arms down by his sides. But I could feel him trembling with the effort of holding back when I slid one hand into his thick, luscious hair and tugged.

'Laura,' he said, sounding hoarse, as he tilted his chin down to meet my upturned face, our mouths less than a breath apart. 'This is more than OK with me but I need to be sure you know what you're doing.'

The sound of my name on his lips, his breath warm against my skin, made my thighs clench.

'Admittedly it's been a minute but I've got a vague idea,' I assured him, my fingers fisting the fabric of his shirt. 'I am a doctor.'

'That's not what I mean and you know it.' His teasing smile turned doubtful. 'Are we making things worse?'

'How?'

I was transfixed by his mouth, the shapes his lips made when he spoke, the fine lines that bracketed either side, invisible from a distance but clear enough close up. If he smiled more often, they'd be more prominent. I wanted to see them always.

'Because – what was it you said?' The smile and the lines disappeared, replaced by deep creases between his brows. 'You don't have time for relationships. Only fun.'

I was only half listening, struggling to process the influx of chemicals being released into my body, infusing into my bloodstream, flooding my brain. Rational thought and commonsense were drowning in dopamine and adrenaline, one chemical reaction triggering another until I'd passed the point of no return. I knew the science of what was happening to me but just like anything else in life, theory could never prepare you for practice, not really. My mouth was dry, my heart pounded and every part of me yearned for him. If Callum didn't touch me back soon, I was sure I would explode.

'We could have fun,' I told him, pushing up onto my toes to graze his ear with my teeth.

'I don't doubt it. But it wouldn't be fair.'

'Life isn't fair,' I said. 'Only short. Too short to live with regrets.'

The moan that passed through his trembling lips when I nipped at his earlobe made my body sing. Every time I touched him, he reacted, shaking or gasping, completely at my mercy. It was brand new to me, this sense of power. I thought letting my emotions take over meant losing control but I'd never felt more in control in my life.

I liked it.

Stepping away, I felt his body move with me, one magnet to another. I peeled off my jumper and let it fall to the floor then unfastened my jeans to shimmy out of the restrictive denim. My eyes passed over his body, the evidence of how badly he wanted the same thing I did, straining visibly against tight fabric at his crotch.

'Just fun,' Callum murmured to himself as I slipped back into place, my feet nestled between his feet, my whole body pressed against his.

'Just fun,' I confirmed, wrapping my arms around his neck, desperate, beyond desperate, for him to touch me.

The shadows of whatever thoughts and feelings had been holding him back passed over his face and his spine was straight and stiff. Seconds stretched out into an eternity as he screwed his eyes shut, forehead furrowed with effort, until I pressed a kiss to the exposed skin at the hollow of his throat and a long, low groan rolled out of his body and into mine.

'Fuck it.'

As the words left his mouth, before I could catch my breath, his lips were on mine, ravenous and searching. All of his restraint was gone, hands cupping my face, holding me in place as he devoured me as though he'd been starving for months and I was his first meal. Our teeth clashed as our tongues entwined and he tasted like whisky and breath mints and I wondered for a moment if he'd been planning this, before pushing the thought from my mind, all thoughts from my mind, and allowing my body to take over.

Already down to my underwear, Callum had me at a disadvantage. His hands prowled my body with intent, coasting over my shoulders, my collarbones, along the tops of my arms and down my back, blazing a trail over my skin and never once breaking contact, like I might disappear if he let go of me for even a second. There was no chance of that. I tugged at his clothes, no decorum, no respect, I wanted them off his body and his body on me. All at once, it seemed like a crime for him to be covered up and the buttons popped off his shirt, one of them hitting the top of my foot as I tore it from him. He took care of his belt, ripping it from his jeans with a vulgar snapping sound as I lavished him with kisses. Callum was an imposing man when fully dressed but somehow, stripped of his shirt's civilized restraint, he seemed even bigger. I loved his chest, running my hands over the solid musculature and the dark, curling hair that covered it, tapering away as it trailed down his stomach, disappearing into the jeans that were still annoyingly on his body.

'You don't need these,' I said, pushing the closely fitting denim down his hips, tugging extra hard in an attempt to get them past his perfectly sculpted backside. 'In fact, they're very much in the way.'

Rather than help me in my efforts, he caught my wrists in his hands, his thumb and forefinger circling them easily.

'Slow down,' he instructed, breath coming hard. 'We can slow down.'

I looked up at him and sank my teeth into my lower lip at the expression on his face. Dazed, consumed, out of control.

'You don't need to go slow for me,' I said, hazy and impatient.

'No. But I need to go slow for me.'

Carefully, he prised my hands away from his jeans and brought them up to his mouth, kissing the insides of my wrists, softly, slowly, until he reached the crook of my elbow where he sucked on the sensitive skin. When I whimpered, my nipples hardening at the sensation of his wet tongue on my warm flesh, his eyes flashed to mine and I saw the beginnings of a wicked grin on his face.

'Slower?' he asked.

I raised my chin, defiant.

'I already said no.'

Callum inhaled deeply, accepting the wordless challenge laid down before him. He resumed the trail of kisses along the inside of my upper arm, crossing over to my chest without pause. He anchored himself against the frame of the four-poster bed but I had nothing to keep me upright except my own two legs and the last remaining shreds of my composure. It was a losing battle.

'You are so soft,' he said, the cool night air chilling all the places he'd placed a kiss then moved along. 'And you taste . . .'

There was no end to the sentence. Instead he slid one finger under the strap of my bra, his eyes darting up to mine checking for a silent confirmation. When I nodded, he brought down one strap then the other, and cupped my breasts in his hands, dragging his lips across the exposed skin. When I reached behind my back to unfasten the clasp, he caught my wrist again and pinned it behind me, the merest and most pleasurable suggestion of pain shooting down my shoulder as I twisted against him. It wasn't aggressive, I could've freed my arm if I'd wanted to but I didn't want to. What I wanted was to know what he would do next.

Still holding my wrists behind my back with one hand, he brushed the thumb of his other hand over my nipple through the thin fabric of my bra. I swayed forward, sent into a full body swoon, and grabbed for the post of the bed behind Callum. How long had it been since someone had touched me like that? I couldn't remember. I didn't want to remember. Releasing my restrained arm, he held me upright and his lips replaced his thumb, tongue and teeth teasing my nipple, leaving it exposed, the cups of my bra pushed down as he turned his attention to my other breast.

'Fuck,' I whispered without meaning to.

The aching sensation that had started in my chest travelled down my body, liquifying, turning molten as it found a home between my thighs. A strong, insistent throb, accompanied by uncontrollable fluttering. I rolled my hips towards Callum, even the friction of my underwear almost unbearable.

But there was to be no relief, not yet. Callum unclasped my bra, let it fall from my body and tossed it away, aimlessly. All of his focus was on me, a glazed look overcoming his beautiful face as he gazed at my breasts and finally, finally began to unfasten the fly of his jeans, one agonizing stud at a time. He still had two to go when I reached out a hand to help.

'No,' he barked, jerking away. 'Wait.'

The house was so quiet, his words landed harsh and heavy. All I could hear was the ragged cut of breathing and the pounding of my own heartbeat in my head, all I could feel was unbearable desire. I withdrew my hand and bit my lip again, until I tasted the sharp tang of blood in my mouth. It was worth waiting for. Callum slowly rolled his jeans, then his black boxer briefs, down to his ankles before kicking them away. I'd never been the kind of person who cared about the physical attributes of my partner, particularly when it came to what was inside their trousers, but even if I were the most discerning of women, there was no way Callum would disappoint. He was a big man in every way that mattered and his cock matched him in size and stature, thick and long and hard, pressed almost all the way up against his stomach. He looked at me with those deep blue sapphire eyes and breathed in through his mouth as he stepped back towards me, hoisting me into his arms and lifting me onto the bed with one swift, smooth movement.

The mattress accepted us without protestation and the weight of Callum's body pushing me down, erasing every last thought from my head. I wrapped my legs around his waist, his mouth on my throat, his hands in my hair, the hardness of him against my soft skin, and felt out a path from his shoulders down to his hips. Grasping his backside, I pulled him closer to me, raising myself up to grind into him, knowing he could feel my underwear, soaked through. But he wasn't done torturing me yet. Insistent kisses moved from my neck to my breasts, forging a trail down my stomach until he arrived at the edge of my underwear, and I squirmed under the finger that took over from his mouth, travelling over the black cotton, slowing to a brutal pace as it arrived between my legs to find me hot and swollen and wanting.

'Oh,' I thought I heard him say and I arced up off the bed, the slender strip of fabric that remained between us edging to one side, the force of his exclamation against my most sensitive spot enough to send my eyes rolling back in my head.

When his finger parted me, slick and ready, I turned my head to the side, eyes tightly closed, fists driving into the mattress. How did anyone survive this? How was I supposed to bear his touch without screaming out his name? But I didn't dare. The house was old and the walls were thick but I was afraid if I even opened my mouth, I would bring the whole place crashing down and leave Balmaclay in ruins. The same finger slid inside me with unbearable restraint and when his tongue followed it, I had to press a pillow over my mouth as I cried out, a tiny breathless warning that I'd swam too far from shore.

The laugh of acknowledgement that left Callum's lips only sent more ripples of pleasure through me, two fingers in me now, his tongue working my clit. No matter how many times I twisted away from him, he held me in place, insistent but gentle, reading my body like it was his favourite book until my breathing calmed to a manageable degree and we found a rhythm I could tolerate. Only, he didn't stop, he didn't slow down. There was no waiting now, no prolonging the inevitable. Thighs shaking, control began to slip through my fingers, tremors threatening to overwhelm me when he spread me open to fasten his mouth on that sweet spot, fingers moving mercilessly back and forth inside me, beckoning me onwards.

'Callum,' I gasped, my hips bucking uncontrollably as he wrapped both arms around my thighs and coaxed me towards my climax.

His eyes were locked on mine as I came, blow after blow of mind-shattering pleasure dragging me down, down, down into blissful oblivion. I called his name again but it was nothing more than a whisper on the waves, and when he finally let go, wiping his mouth on his arm as he moved up the bed, my face was covered in tears, my entire body shaking. Somewhere on another planet, I heard the rustle of foil, a tearing sound, and saw Callum rolling on a condom.

'Slower?' he asked, tenderly wiping away my tears with his thumb as he settled between my thighs.

Purposefully, I pushed the hand away, pulled his thumb into my mouth and sucked, smiling when his eyes flared.

'I already said no,' I said, releasing his thumb and reaching down between our bodies to grasp his thick, heavy cock in my hand, bringing its throbbing head to my slick opening. When I squeezed, he shivered from head to toe.

'If you do that again, I'm going to come,' he said into my ear, guttural and raw.

'Good.'

I squeezed again, thrilled when he pulsed against my palm, almost there but not quite. His mouth covered mine and as Callum slid inside me, I closed my eyes, giving myself over to the sensation of him stretching me, filling me, taking me. We might be fake but nothing in my life had ever felt this real. Whatever came next, I was already in too deep. There was no point struggling now, all I could do was hope my head stayed above water.

But if I drowned in him, so be it.

CHAPTER TWENTY-SIX

When I was little, I would lie awake in bed on Christmas morning, counting backwards from one hundred over and over until I heard my mum moving in the next room, Dad reluctantly staggering downstairs in his red and blue striped towelling dressing gown to put the kettle on, turn on the tree lights, assemble the piles of present. Then I would close my eyes and pretend to be asleep, waiting for her to come and wake me, to confirm Father Christmas had in fact paid us a visit, at which point I would vault out of bed and race to the living room, Mum laughing behind me.

According to the wind-up alarm clock on my bedside table, it was almost six a.m. when I opened my eyes the next morning, those long retired feelings of excitement and anticipation fluttering in my belly. But instead of toys and games, I rolled over to see Father Christmas had been to Balmaclay and left me a gift in the shape of Callum McClay. His body curled around mine when he felt me stir, just as it had on the train, only now we were both naked and when I felt his erection pressing into my lower back, I didn't jump out of bed and run away. Instead I lifted the hand that rested so casually on my chest to my lips, kissing each finger in turn, replaying all of the places they'd been the night before. There wasn't an inch of me he hadn't possessed, claimed as his own, and there wasn't a single part of his body I hadn't explored with my hands, my mouth. We'd devoured each other, riding the tide and cresting higher and higher until we crashed to the shore, exhilarated and exhausted.

It's just the oxytocin, I told myself, practically euphoric when the fingers that had been on my lips grasped my throat as he kissed my shoulder, my back, the nape of my neck. It's nothing more than a hormone response to physical stimuli. Skin on skin, a thumb brushing the peaks of my breast, fingers splayed on my stomach, his hand between my thighs. My body was only reacting as it was programmed to, the way human bodies had been programmed to react for thousands of years, I knew that.

But still.

'Merry Christmas,' he whispered, a rough raw sound in my ear as he pushed me onto my belly, my greedy gasp affirming consent, and slid inside me with one welcome thrust.

As much as I knew I needed time to think, space to ask myself what came next, it was impossible to drag myself away from him. When we finally forced ourselves out of bed, it was only to move to the shower together and, soon enough, my back was flush against the tiles, one leg hitched over his hip, the soap dish making its disapproval known by digging into my vertebrae every time Callum drove into me.

I didn't care.

I didn't care when we brushed our teeth side by side. I didn't care when he towel-dried my hair even though I knew his vigorous rubbing would surely lead to frizz. I didn't care when I chose a nonsensical outfit of mismatched pieces from my suitcase, and I didn't care as I watched him pull on the same clothes he'd worn the day before. I was the human embodiment of bliss, boneless desire. Anything other than whatever was happening at this precise moment was a problem for future Laura. More than a decade of telling myself I didn't need this, that wanting someone, that being wanted, wasn't missing from my life, and it was all undone in a matter of hours.

I turned my phone over to see ten messages from Desi and Joel, nine texts demanding to know where I was and when we were leaving and one photo of Desi fast asleep with an eyeliner pencil moustache on her upper lip, Joel in the corner of the frame giving me a thumbs up.

'It's almost nine,' Callum said, brushing my damp hair back to cup my face in his hands. 'Everyone'll be wondering what's happened to us.'

He smiled, pupils dilated, dimples appearing in his cheeks as his goofy grin spread ever wider. I dropped my phone on the bed and my hands covered his hands. I had to be touching him at all times.

'They'll live,' I told him. 'Probably something good on the telly, *Chitty Chitty Bang Bang, Sound of Music.*'

'Mum doesn't let us watch TV on Christmas morning.

She still forces us all to go to church first then it's no telly until after lunch.'

'That's a denial of basic human rights,' I gasped. 'I'm so sorry for your suffering. But you're right, we should make an appearance. Also, I'm bloody starving.'

'Wait.' Callum rushed across the room to the fireplace. 'I've got something for you.'

He looked almost shy as he unhooked one of the stockings and held it out in front of him.

'You said your mum always filled your stocking,' he explained. 'It's not much, it's just—'

Without taking it from him, I cut him off with a kiss. Stars exploded, fireworks shot off and I didn't even care what was inside the stocking because I knew what was inside his heart. He was a good man. A kind, sweet, considerate man, and the thought that he had ever believed himself to be anything else ate me up.

'Thank you,' I said, standing on my tallest tiptoes, arms looped around his neck.

'You don't even know what it is yet,' he replied, a glassy, happy glow in his eyes. 'Could be a lump of coal.'

'I'm sure there are plenty of people downstairs who will tell you that's all I deserve.'

Releasing my grip, I took the stocking and stuck my hand inside to find three small packages. Callum took the stocking as I pulled out the slightly larger of the three and tore open the wrapping paper. Inside was a great big bag of Swedish candy.

'The food of your homeland,' he grinned. 'Don't worry, I made sure it's vegan.'

'So thoughtful,' I laughed and he held open the stocking for me to pull out the second gift.

'Ah, that's in case you decide to leave the spa and go into business for yourself. I don't know if they're the proper ones but at least there's something to get you started.'

Two palm-sized smooth, rounded rocks, so dark they were almost black, tumbled out of their loosely taped wrapping paper and into my hand and my smile stretched so wide, my cheeks ached.

'Are these for massage or for when I decide to become a world champion stone skimmer?' I asked, testing their pleasing weight in my hands. 'Because I could go either way right now if neurosurgery doesn't work out.'

'Multipurpose tools for the multitasking woman.'

He bit back a smile as I tore the wrapping paper from the final gift. Inside was a blue velvet pouch and I tipped the contents out into my palm to reveal a small silver pin. Callum took it from my hand and fastened it to my jumper, pulling the fabric away from my body to make sure he didn't scratch me.

'It's a Luckenbooth brooch,' he said, closing the fastening and sliding it into place. 'Two hearts intertwined with a crown on top and a thistle in the middle. It's a traditional Scottish symbol. To remind you of this week.'

'As if I'd ever be able to forget it,' I told him, pressing his gift to my heart. 'When did you do all this?'

'Yesterday. When Desi was trying to look up that bagpiper's kilt and I went back to the car to put money in the parking meter.'

'I assumed you were too embarrassed to be seen with us.' I was still staring at the brooch. It was beautiful. 'Thank you so much, but I feel terrible, I don't have anything for you.'

His eyes glittered. 'I'm sure you can come up with something.'

'We should go downstairs before they come looking for us,' I whispered as he pulled me close, without even the slightest desire to share him with anyone else ever.

'We should show our faces for ten minutes or so, but I think we've both got migraines coming on today.'

My entire being buzzed with happiness as we moved as one towards the door, our steps in sync. It wasn't until we walked out of my room and onto the landing I was convinced the rest of the world did in fact still exist.

'Callum,' I said, slowing down before we reached the stairs, the grim spectre of reality lurking at the bottom. 'What are we going to say?'

'What do you mean?'

He was still beaming, glowing even, not a trace of concern on his happy face.

'About this?'

I raised our joined hands between us. Callum shrugged.

'Why would we say anything? As far as anyone else is concerned, nothing's changed.'

He pulled me on and I followed, still floating, only now there was something less than appealing hovering outside my blissful bubble. Why say anything? Wouldn't we have to eventually? Unless I was about to legally change my name and retrain as a massage therapist.

'At last.' Derek slapped the sides of his armchair when we walked into the family room. 'Good of you to grace us with your presence.'

Desi shot me the filthiest look, Lizzie let out a breath

it appeared she'd been holding in since I'd last seen her, and Joel and Rory, side by side on the sofa, looked up from their phones for a second. Then looked back down.

'Coffee?' Callum asked and I nodded. He squeezed my hand before letting go, a silent promise to return while I made uncomfortable eye contact with my best friend, then quickly flicked my attention to a bowl filled with Cadbury's Roses in the middle of the coffee table. Wait, no, Roses *and* Quality Street. True decadence.

'Then we're doing presents!' Rory called when he disappeared. 'So don't take all day.'

Presents.

I tore my eyes away from the bowl of untouched sweets and peered under the tree. Mounds and mounds of beautifully wrapped presents.

'We really should wait for Elsie,' Lizzie said, worrying the hem of her knee-length tartan skirt. 'She'll be done with her rounds soon.'

But Rory was already under the tree, sorting the gifts into piles.

'She said not to,' he barked. One pile, two piles, three, four, five, six, seven, eight. 'Get real, Mother, we all know she's no intention of coming back.'

Eight piles of presents. Eight people currently in the house.

Fuck.

'Svetty,' I said sweetly, my palms suddenly damp. 'Can I have a quick word with you?'

'No.' Desi remained where she was, arms wrapped around a cushion in her lap.

'Upstairs,' I ordered. 'I need you to help me bring the presents down.'

Predictably, she sprang to life at the sound of the 'P' word.

'You brought presents with you?' she asked, bounding after me as I raced up the stairs. 'I haven't got yours. I thought we agreed we'd do gifts when you got home?'

I pushed her into my room and closed the door. 'We did and I haven't but, looking at that tree, Lizzie has gifts for all of us and I've got nothing to give her. We need to find something ASAP.'

Rather than answer, her eyes raked over the room. The messy bedsheets, my discarded underwear, the empty condom wrappers I'd promised I wouldn't need but had made excellent use of.

'I knew it!' she howled and I clapped a hand over her mouth to muffle her volume. It worked until she licked the inside of my hand and I pulled it away, deeply grossed out.

'I bloody well knew it,' she crowed. 'I said to Joel, they're shagging, and he said, no, they aren't, she's not that stupid, and I said, oh yes she is, and he said—'

'All right, Widow Twankey,' I scowled. 'Congratulations, you're right. Is that what you want to hear?'

'Better than any other present you could've given me,' she nodded happily. 'Tell me everything.'

'We haven't got time to get into it now.' I pawed through my open suitcase, raking through my colourful clothes, my meagre makeup bag. 'We need to find suitable Christmas presents for Derek, Lizzie, Elsie and Rory.'

'Elsie can have a kick in the puss and like it,' Desi sniped. 'And the rate Joel's going, Rory should be getting his Christmas present as soon as his parents' backs are turned. They're panting for each other worse than you and the other one.'

'All things we can discuss later. Do you think Lizzie would like this?'

I held up a slightly dog-eared edition of *Onyx Storm* I'd been carrying around all year and still hadn't had time to read. Desi shook her head.

'What if she hasn't read the first two?'

'Good point.'

'Even if she has, what if it gives her the mega horn and she shags Derek into a heart attack?'

'Less helpful point.'

'I don't understand why you need to give them anything,' she said, combing through the suitcase she'd watched me pack, in her flat, where I'd been living for six weeks, as though she'd never seen a single one of my possessions before. 'Isn't the entire objective of this trip to make them hate you?'

'It was,' I replied hesitantly. 'There might be a shift in direction on the horizon.'

'Oh, Laura,' she groaned, cutting herself off, hands held up in surrender. 'Nope, I'm not going to say it. I don't need to. You're a grown-up.'

'That's right, I am,' I said. 'As soon as we've come up with presents, you can call me every name under the sun if it makes you feel better. Are you going to help me or not?'

'Not?'

'Wrong answer.' I planted my hands on my hips and let my head fall back in frustration. 'This is useless. Have you got anything?'

'Nothing I'm prepared to give you. And don't look like that, you're not going to change my mind.'

'Des,' I clutched my hands together in prayer. 'Please, for me. For Christmas.'

'Nope.'

'If you help me, I'll buy you a pony.'

'No, you won't.'

'I might. We're on a farm, Derek might have one going cheap. We could tie it up outside the flat, next to the electric car charger and the bollard everyone uses as a urinal.'

'Laura, stop.'

She placed a hand on my back as I held up a packet of co-codamol, wondering how inappropriate it was to give your potential future brother-in-law prescription medication.

'You slept with Callum?'

'Yes,' I confirmed. 'And it was very good. I came twice last night and twice again this morning, he went down on me without asking and what else do you want to know?'

'You know I have a full checklist of questions but we'll get to that later,' she replied, looking relatively impressed. 'All I need to know right now is, are you OK?'

'OK?' I repeated. 'Do you mean am I sore? Because yes, a little bit, but obviously I peed afterwards. Even though did you know there's no real evidence to connect UTIs with using the toilet after sex? I looked it up. It's good practice, flush out any potentially harmful bacteria but—'

'Again, good information to have but not what I was getting at,' Desi said, pulling a face. 'I meant, are you all right? Emotionally? Like, what does this mean? Is the whole Caroline thing cancelled now? Are you going to tell his parents the truth? Are you two dating? Was it more of a one-off thing?'

A one-off thing. The idea of it stopped me in my tracks.

'We haven't really discussed it.'

Her brown eyes widened until I could see the whites all the way around her irises.

'You haven't really thought about it?' she said. 'You, Laura Pearce, had multiple orgasms with a man and didn't think to have a quick chat about whether or not you might do it again?'

'I cannot keep up with what you want from me,' I replied, lowering my voice to an undetectable hiss. 'Don't overthink things, do overthink things. Do date, don't date. I like him, he likes me, the sex was great, whatever happens next, it's not a big deal.'

It sounded hollow, even to my ears. We both knew I was lying.

'When you agreed to this, you said it was OK because you had nothing to lose,' my friend said gently. 'I don't think that's true any more.'

'What could I possibly have to lose?' I asked, clutching the co-codamol very tightly. 'I've known Callum for six days. How much impact could someone have on my life in six days?'

Neither of us said anything because neither of us wanted to admit the answer.

'Come on, let's get these presents sorted out,' Desi sighed before gesturing for me to follow her back to her room. 'And you are going to owe me. Big time.'

Looping my arms around her neck, I kissed her on the cheek.

'Thank you, thank you, thank you.'

'Saving the day as always,' she grumbled. 'Again, what would you do without me?'

It honestly didn't bear thinking about.

'Caroline, you shouldn't have.'

Derek stared at the bag of shortbread I'd just presented him with and it was very obvious he wasn't just saying it. From the look on his face, I really shouldn't have.

'It's salted caramel,' I said enthusiastically. 'Try it.'

'It's an abomination,' he muttered, scrunching the wrapping paper-slash-torn-out pages of *Grazia* magazine into the fire. Turning the box over in his hands, he squinted at the tiny print on the back then looked away in disgust. 'Made in England. Shoot me now.'

I hadn't asked Callum what they'd discussed the night before. His argument with his dad wasn't exactly top of my to-do list when he showed up in my room, but I could see now that whatever had been said hadn't gone far to resolve the tensions between them. Derek could hardly stand to look at his son and when Callum gave him his gifts, including a very nice replacement for the Dalmore we'd drank on the train, he barely murmured a word.

'Interesting wrapping solution,' Rory said as he shook a tube of Kiehl's men's moisturiser out of a red and green striped sock.

'It's environmentally friendly,' I explained, choosing to ignore the bad vibes between father and son for now. 'Most wrapping paper can't be recycled. This is what they do in Japan.'

'Why does that look like my sock?' Joel asked, wrapping the new scarf he'd received from Lizzie around his neck.

'Because it is your sock,' I replied quietly through a big fake smile. 'And your Kiehl's, please don't act out, I'll replace it.'

His eyes popped wide open.

'Too fucking right you will. Do you have any idea how much that stuff costs? I ought to strike you down where you stand.'

While Joel sulked, Lizzie tore open her own gift, wrapped in last week's horoscopes.

'Oh, lovely,' she said, examining the contents. 'What is it exactly?'

'A lip balm,' I offered. 'It's peppermint flavoured.'

'Technically candy cane flavoured,' a mournful Desi amended. 'It's a limited edition Rhode peptide lip treatment. Sold out. Worldwide. Literally impossible to get your hands on.'

'Is that right? Thank you, Caroline.'

Lizzy turned it over in her hands then placed it on the arm of the sofa where it promptly rolled off without her even noticing.

'What about you two?' she said to me and Callum, sitting side by side on the floor in front of the sofa, thighs, arms, shoulders touching. 'You're not exchanging gifts?'

'I'd say they've already exchanged enough,' Desi commented, kicking me in the back.

'Caroline doesn't believe in gifts,' Callum said quickly when I opened my mouth to tell them about my new brooch. 'She thinks exchanging material possessions cheapens an emotional bond.'

'She must not think much to us then,' Derek commented, mouth already full of filthy English shortbread. 'Although I'd say that's obvious enough.'

'I hope you won't be offended but I have something for you,' Lizzie said, fishing the last gift out from behind the tree. 'If you don't like Christmas gifts, think of it as a welcome-to-the-family token instead.'

She handed me a small quilted leather box tied with red ribbon, smiling beatifically. Callum's eyebrows pulled together in a way that made me far too nervous.

'Is it Elsie's ear?' Rory guessed and his dad threw a satsuma at his head.

The box was very light in my hand. It weighed almost nothing but with every second I sat staring at the thing, it became heavier and heavier.

'For God's sake open it!' Joel wailed. 'We haven't got all day.'

'We have though,' replied a rueful Desi. 'Literally twenty-four whole hours.'

I glanced up at Callum, whose shoulders pulled upwards in the tiniest shrug, then opened the box. Inside was a beautiful gold locket, sharp lines of intricately engraved flowers on its surface softened with age.

'It belonged to Callum's great-great-grandmother,' Lizzie explained as I stared at the necklace, the rest of the room watching in silence. 'Derek's mother gave it to me for Christmas after we got engaged.'

'But we're not engaged,' I said, still staring at the beautiful piece of jewellery.

She removed the locket from the box, a long slender chain cascading out behind it. Unfastening the clasp, she looped it around my neck where it hung low on my chest, dragging me down, down, down.

'But you are part of the family,' Lizzie said, looking back to Callum. 'I know how much you care about our Cal.'

'Elizabeth, you've gone doolally,' Derek declared. 'Completely out your tree.'

He leaned over, picked up his new bottle of whisky, opened it, poured a huge glug into his empty teacup and chugged.

Callum hadn't moved from his spot on the sofa but all the colour was gone from his face. I clutched the locket in my hand. It was heavy, substantial, in a way modern jewellery never was, at least not the jewellery I could afford. An honest-to-God family heirloom. I'd never had one before. My mum didn't wear jewellery, only her wedding ring, and my dad had kept that. When they'd got engaged, there was no money for a ring and they'd sold the few pieces she inherited from her own mum to help pay the deposit on the house I grew up in. This locket came with generations of love and, no matter what had happened between me and Callum the night before, I couldn't accept it.

After all, the name on the gift tag was Caroline, not Laura.

'It's too much,' I said, raising my arms to unfasten the necklace. 'I'm sorry, I can't keep this.'

'It is not and you will,' Lizzie insisted, pulling my hands away from the clasp. 'What good is it sat in a drawer upstairs? Better you have it now than leave it up there for another year or two.'

Desi and Joel both stared down at their feet while Callum's eyes flicked down to the necklace then up to my face, back and forth.

'Did I hear the door?' Derek's ears pricked, head shooting up like a meercat. 'I'll get it.'

As though someone had pressed play on a paused scene, everyone rolled into action at once. Derek racing for the door, Lizzie clearing up the discarded wrapping paper (and socks), and Rory diving across the room for the forbidden TV remote. Desi and Joel stood, cradling their unexpected gifts from Lizzie. Only Callum and I sat still.

'We are going to take these wonderful gifts upstairs,' Desi said in a flat voice. 'Excuse us.'

'Yes, upstairs,' added Joel as though reading lines from a script. 'We'll be back in a minute.'

'They look heavy, I'd better help you carry them,' Rory said, snatching a tiny box of chocolates off the top of Desi's pile when Joel winked in his direction, held up a miniature bottle of scotch and made a drinking motion. Lizzie manhandled her giant ball of wrapping paper out the room behind them, muttering to herself as she went.

'I can't keep this,' I said to Callum, palming the weight of the locket. 'It isn't right.'

'Don't worry about it now,' he replied, squeezing my shoulder. 'We've only today to get through. Tomorrow it's all over.'

'Well, yes but . . .'

The words died in my throat. It's all over? What did that mean?

'When do you leave for Paris again?' I asked.

'Sunday,' he replied, absently scratching his chin. 'First train out of St Pancras.'

As well as being Christmas Day, today was Friday. We would leave Balmaclay on Saturday. My face fell slack as I worked through all the variables, the potential complications. No matter which way I looked at it, nothing changed. In two days' time, he'd be gone.

'I can't believe we pulled it off.'

Callum stared at the locket, eyes gleaming with wonder. There it was, proof of our successful subterfuge. 'I won't lie, I had my doubts, but for Mum to give you her locket? They really believe we're together *and* they've accepted it?' He shook his head in disbelief. 'Feels as though we could keep it going forever, doesn't it?'

'But if they think you're with Caroline, how will we explain . . .' I waved a hand between us. 'This?'

He blinked at me, seemingly confused.

'How will we explain us?' I clarified.

'Us?'

One word. Two letters. An upward inflection.

I was torn to shreds.

'Elsie, can you at least take your bloody boots off?' I heard Lizzie say, the sound of marching feet stomping towards us as I stared at Callum.

'Fantastic, you've tracked sheep shit all through the house,' Lizzie said as Elsie strode into the living room, Derek, and for some reason, Shiv, right behind her.

'Where are the other two?' she demanded without so much as looking at me and Callum. 'Where's Svet-bloody-lana?'

'Upstairs,' I said, vacant and still cross-legged on the floor as Callum stood to meet them. 'Why?'

She grabbed Shiv by the wrist and pulled her to the fore.

'Go on,' she prompted. 'Tell them what you told me.'

Shiv pulled her rose-printed fleece around her body, shrinking inside until all I could see were her eyes, nose and hands.

'If someone would like to tell me what's going on, that'd be magic,' Derek said. 'There's a batch of mince pies coming out the oven with my name on and I'd like to enjoy them without wondering whether or not my kids are tearing each other limb from limb.'

'I knew something was up.' Elsie said when Shiv declined to offer her explanation. 'As soon as she rolled in, I knew something was off.'

Rory, Desi and Joel reappeared and the lofty living room felt very, very crowded.

'What is going on?' Desi asked. 'Did I hear my name?'

'No,' Elsie countered, inexplicably giddy. 'I asked where Svetlana was and that's not your name, is it?'

Even though I was sitting on the floor, I was sure I was about to fall over.

'What are you talking about?' Lizzie asked, stooping down to pick up a large chunk of what I hoped was mud.

'Go on,' Elsie prodded Shiv again. 'Show them.'

When the blonde didn't move quickly enough for her liking, Elsie snatched her phone out of her hand and displayed it for everyone to see, like she was showing off a prize on a game show. On the screen was a very familiar image. A screenshot from Desi's Instagram. The three of us at her birthday party last year. The same photo on my phone's lockscreen.

'Me and Callum went to a wedding in London, a couple of years ago,' Shiv said slowly, sounding like a toy with the batteries running out. 'For his friend, Dave.'

Joel reached for the doorframe to steady himself. To her credit, Desi didn't flinch.

'I didn't remember you,' she said to me, her voice almost apologetic. 'But I did meet her.' She paused to nod at Desi then sniffed. 'She was mean about my shoes.'

If I wasn't sure before, I was sure now.

'I don't know what she's talking about,' Desi fronted, not prepared to give in so easily. 'But so what if we met at a wedding? London isn't that big a place, people do bump into each other sometimes.'

'Yes, and some of those people happen to have public social media accounts with their sister-in-law tagged.' Elsie handed her phone to her father as Shiv disappeared further inside her coat. 'We found the groom's Instagram and there you are. Desi Kaplan.'

'Proves nothing,' Desi said, despite the fact it more or less proved everything.

Elsie swiped through to a picture of Joel with his tie fastened around his forehead, vanilla frosting smeared all over his face, the camera flash bouncing off the backs of his eyes, giving him the demented look of a man possessed.

'And, oh look, Joel Soto.'

'Why is she saying it like that?' he asked Desi, speaking out the side of his mouth. 'I'm not the one who gave a stupid fake name.'

Finally, Elsie turned back to me, like the cat who ate the canary, yellow feathers practically hanging out her mouth. 'Which means you must be Laura Pearce.'

I couldn't move, my limbs were lead, and mortification dragged me down into myself. I wanted to run for the hills but I couldn't. Possibly I would be able to make a small pillow fort with the sofa cushions and hide under a blanket but that was the absolute best-case scenario.

'So we lied about our names, so what?' Desi said, bravely soldiering on. 'We're weirdos, we make our own fun.'

'Is that what you're calling it?' Elsie replied. 'Because

I saw your husband making his own fun with my brother last night.'

Desi's cool exterior flickered.

'Joel was playing Cluedo with Callum?'

'Not quite. I came downstairs for a glass of water after everybody went to bed and they were all over each other in the kitchen. If I were you, I'd bleach the table, Mother.'

'A scurrilous lie!' Joel exclaimed.

'That's right,' Rory agreed. 'We were nowhere near the table.'

'Oh, Joel, no!' Desi exclaimed before pitching her last, futile attempt at maintaining the subterfuge. 'My sweet, monogamous husband. How could you?'

Her eyes darted around the room to see if anyone was buying what she was selling. They weren't.

'Couldn't even keep it in the bedroom, could you?' she said with a resigned sigh. 'Honestly, you're a disgrace.'

'Can someone please explain what's happening?' Lizzie said, raising her voice above the venomous chatter.

I met Callum's gaze and my jaw clenched itself shut so tightly, I thought I heard my teeth crack. He looked gutted. Exactly how I'd felt when he asked what I was talking about two minutes earlier.

With a triumphant grin, Elsie stepped forward pointing at each of us in turn.

'Her name isn't Caroline, hers isn't Svetlana, they're not even sisters, and those two aren't married.'

Neat, tidy, straight to the point. Worst of all, entirely accurate.

'Callum?' Derek spoke for the first time, one arm

reaching around his stricken wife. 'What is this all about, son?'

'It's about him taking the piss out of us, as usual,' Elsie snapped. 'The four of them have been laughing at us ever since they got here.'

'All right, Miss Marple, that's enough,' Desi said, pushing up the sleeves of her jumper. 'Me and you, outside, right now.'

'Gladly.'

Elsie threw off her coat, swishing it like a matador, glaring at my friend like she was a prize bull. Lizzie gasped and Shiv groaned, Derek moving to position himself between the two women and very nearly losing an eye to the zip on Elsie's wax jacket for his trouble.

'I'm moving to Paris,' Callum announced abruptly.

The tableau froze. Elsie and Desi's hands in mid-air, moments away from slapping each other silly, Shiv staring at him open-mouthed, Lizzie clutching at her throat and Derek scrunching up his face in confusion. Apparently Rory was the only McClay who still had the power of speech.

'What?' he said. 'You're moving to Paris?'

'On Sunday,' Callum nodded. 'I got into the Escoffier culinary institute and I'm moving to Paris.'

'You're going to do that cooking course?' Shiv said, her beautiful face a picture of surprise. 'You told me you weren't going to apply.'

'Well, I did,' he replied. 'I never thought I'd get in, they only take a handful of applicants and thousands of people apply every year, but yeah. I applied, they accepted me and I'm moving to Paris. So I won't be moving back home any time soon and I won't be taking over the farm, ever.'

'Paris?' Lizzie went next. 'Is Caroline going with you?'

'There is no Caroline!' Elsie yelled and everyone in the room jumped. 'Caroline does not exist!'

Their mother looked down at me and I wrapped my hand around the McClay family locket.

'In that case, would you like to tell me who she is?'

She.

From a member of the family to the cat's mother in under ten minutes. I felt my lips quiver but I couldn't find the words to defend myself.

'It doesn't matter,' Callum muttered, one hand in his hair, the other on his hip. 'Leave her out of it.'

'It matters to me!' Lizzie replied, indignant. 'I'd like to know exactly who I invited into my home. Is she even your girlfriend?'

He tipped his head back and sighed, loud and frustrated.

'Is she even a vegan?' a curious Derek asked before he could answer.

'No,' Desi and Joel replied in unison.

'Then who the bloody hell is she?!' Lizzie exploded.

I held my breath, eyes locked on Callum.

Say it, I willed silently, tell them who I am. Laura Pearce, trainee neurosurgeon. Lover of Loch Ness and rare steaks and Christmas ornaments, who can't hold her whisky and has feet like blocks of ice and you're so glad you met me.

'She's no one. Just a random girl.'

All four chambers of my heart tore apart.

'And you're just some random wanker.' Desi shoved Callum out the way and pulled me up to my feet. 'Come on, Lau, we're leaving.'

Nodding, I let her lead me through the crowd of

McClays. When we reached the door, I stopped, let go of Desi's hand and unfastened the chain around my neck.

'I'm sorry, I didn't mean to upset you,' I said to Lizzie. The hurt that dragged her fine features down was too much for me to bear. 'Well, actually, I did but not like this.'

'Your son will explain,' Desi added, wrenching my arm almost out the socket as she yanked me through the door. 'Joel, go and get our stuff, we'll be in the car.'

It felt like I was underwater. Everyone found their voices at the same time but I couldn't make out individual words, only distorted sounds and shapes. All I was sure of was Desi's hand clinging to mine, holding me down, keeping me grounded, and the knowledge I needed to put one foot in front of the other until I was out of this enormous house and this absurd situation.

'Laura, wait!' Callum followed us down the hallway, his long stride no match for Desi's quickened pace. 'Where are you going?'

'Home,' I replied with a vacant, glassy stare. It hurt too much to bring him into focus.

'Don't go.'

He reached out to catch my wrist but I pulled away before he could make contact. I didn't want to touch his hand if I couldn't touch all of him.

'We're done here, Callum,' Desi said, still marching onward. 'Go back to your super spy sister and her little friend with the ugly shoes.'

'They were not ugly, they were comfortable!'

A sudden burst of volume from Shiv stopped us all in our tracks and snapped me out my trance.

'Who wears Birkenstocks to a wedding?' Desi thundered back. 'It is a formal occasion, show some respect!'

'So you do remember her?' I asked, the two of them staring each other down in the hallway. Desi nodded.

'I do now. Honest, Lau, they were godawful. Come on.' She spoke more softly this time and wrapped a protective arm around my shoulders, a barrier between myself and the others.

'Don't go like this,' Callum begged when we turned to walk away. 'Give me a minute to straighten it all out—'

'A minute?' Desi said, hooting with laughter. 'Did Father Christmas leave you one of those *Men in Black* mind-wiper things?'

'Half an hour then, an hour, whatever. There's no need for you to leave like this. You're not going to drive all the way back to London on Christmas Day.'

'Traffic'll be a dream,' she purred. 'We'll be home by teatime.'

With an exasperated explosion of a sigh, Callum positioned himself between me, Desi and the door, blocking our exit.

'You can't run off like this,' he declared as though it were a fact, written in stone somewhere simply because he said so. 'Laura, talk to me.'

But I couldn't.

Pain, embarrassment, heartache. They all stimulated similar physical responses in the body, many of the same fight-or-flight reactions. There were studies that showed how emotional pain lit up the same areas of the brain as physical pain. The cortisol spiking in my blood told my muscles to swell as my sympathetic nervous system ramped up its efforts. My neck tightened and my chest felt like it was being crushed. But where I'd been foggy and lost only a moment ago, I suddenly felt razor-sharp and words flew out my mouth, slicing him like scalpels. I was a surgeon after all, I knew exactly where to cut to inflict the most damage. My body chose to fight.

'And say what?' I replied, colder than the icy waters of Loch Ness. 'You don't need to worry about me, worry about fixing things with your family. This was all about them, remember, not me. Either way, it was all over tomorrow anyway, isn't that what you said?'

It did hurt, saying those things, but in the same way it hurt to press on a bruise after it had already turned purple, or to poke at a loose tooth. The damage was done, at least I was in control of my own agony now.

'Forget about the flat,' I told him as Desi and I separated to walk around him across the foyer. 'I'll find somewhere else. Sorry to leave you in the lurch without a tenant at the last minute.'

Callum stopped at the foot of the stairs and we were almost at the door, almost out of the house.

'Is this about last night?'

My spine stiffened, ramrod straight, and my internal switch flipped so hard, everything went blank. It didn't hurt. I wouldn't cry. This was nothing. He was nothing.

'Are you OK?' Desi whispered, one hand on the doorknob.

'I'm OK,' I nodded before turning back to face Callum.

'Laura?'

He gave me a look, as though he was the victim.

'You're the one who said you only wanted to have fun,' he said. 'This whole thing was your idea. Last night, this week, all of it.'

'From start to finish,' I agreed, my heart a steady drum, keeping time with my measured words. 'And I take full responsibility. I'm sorry if you feel bad, I'm sorry if this week made things worse with your parents, but I don't hate myself enough to stay here a second longer than I have to. You've got a lot of explaining to do so I'm sure you won't mind if we leave, after all.' I opened the door and shot him one last agonised glance. 'I'm no one, just a random girl.'

And when I walked out the door, he didn't make a single move to stop me.

CHAPTER TWENTY-SEVEN

'I don't think I can listen to any more of this.'

In the back of the car, Joel put his hands over his ears and groaned. 'By the time we get to "Smallest Man Who Ever Lived" I'll be ready to drive us off a cliff.'

'When you're driving, you get to pick the music,' Desi shouted over the bridge of 'Down Bad'. 'This is for Laura. She needs this, it is therapy.'

'I really don't,' I assured her from the passenger seat. 'I'm really fine.'

'Oh, did you hear that, Joel? She's fine.'

'Excellent news,' he leaned forward to turn off the stereo and Desi slapped his hands away, almost steering us directly into the central reservation. 'Makes me even happier to be spending Christmas Day trapped in a Mini with you two freaks.'

There was a beat of silence in the car.

'Can we stop?' he asked. 'I need a wee.'

Desi gave him a look in the rearview mirror.

'We've been in the car for seventeen minutes.'

'I didn't have time to go before we left!' he protested. 'I was too busy packing up your stuff!'

'Too busy having another go on that bloody Rory more like,' she muttered. 'Honestly, I can't take you anywhere.'

'You'd like him if you got to know him,' Joel pouted in the back, arms and legs crossed.

'What are you basing that on exactly?' she replied. '*You* don't even know him.'

'I'll have you know it's very difficult being the only gay member of the family at Christmas,' he declared. 'You wouldn't understand the amount of pressure we're under to be incredibly hot and charming and funny.'

'What's that got to do with you sticking your tongue down his throat in the kitchen in the middle of the night?'

'Nothing,' he muttered. 'He's just really, really hot.'

'Des, turn in here,' I cut in on their bickering before I was forced to slap them both. 'There's a petrol station, they'll have a loo.'

'No.'

'And an M&S Simply Food.'

Her eyes lit up at the promise of a cheddar & onion twist.

Joel's head suddenly popped up between the passenger seats, making me jump.

'It's a mirage,' he whispered. 'It won't be open. Don't get my hopes up.'

'Let's all pray for a Christmas miracle.' Desi pulled off the road and screeched into a parking space. 'Because if I don't come out with a freshly baked chocolate chip muffin at the very least, I'm going to burn this place down to the ground.'

* * *

Luckily for all M&S shareholders, the shop *was* open, and luckily for us, it *did* have a bathroom. Joel ran through the aisles while Desi made a beeline directly for the bakery. I followed Desi, dutifully carrying the basket, my mind very much elsewhere.

'Do you want a pain au chocolat?' she asked, scanning the baked goods like she was searching for her one true love. 'You'll have to eat it before we get in the car, flaky pastry is a bastard to hoover up.'

'No, thanks,' I replied. 'I'm not hungry.'

I wasn't. The adrenaline and CRH released during my confrontation with Callum had obliterated my appetite. But knowing the scientific reasons why I couldn't stand the thought of eating, why my face looked so blank in the reflection on the glass bakery case, didn't help. Empty was the best I could hope for. Numb.

'We should get the Christmas sandwiches, since, you know, it's literally Christmas.' She dropped several paper bags into the basket before moving over to the refrigerated section of the store, me trailing along behind her. 'Do you want the turkey or the veggie? I'm assuming turkey since you don't have to pretend to be a vegan any more. Small mercies, eh?'

'Whatever.'

Desi peered at me out the corner of her eye.

'We probably don't need any crisps.'

'Probably not.'

'And I won't bother getting any biscuits or anything. One sandwich each is enough for an eleven-hour drive.'

'If you think so.'

She turned to face me, five different sandwiches balanced in her arms.

'Right, let's get in front of this before it becomes a

problem,' she said. 'You are officially you again. You eat salt and vinegar twists like they're going out of fashion and if anyone tried to take an Extremely Chocolatey biscuit out your hand, you'd surgically detach the offending appendage. I know you're pissed off and upset, and he can break your heart and ruin your Christmas, but Laura Pearce, with Marks and Spencer whoever they may be as my witnesses, I will not stand idly by and watch him take away your desire to eat carbs.'

I reached into the sandwich cabinet, pulled out the first thing my fingers touched and dropped it in the basket.

'Seriously?' She looked at me with disgust. 'Egg salad? In the car?'

I shrugged and Desi growled.

'Would it help if I slagged him off a bit?'

My eyebrow quirked with involuntary interest.

'Couldn't hurt. What have you got?'

'He's too tall, for a start.'

She removed my egg sandwich from the basket and replaced it with a Christmas club. She was right to do it.

'You'd hurt your neck, always looking up at him. He's even paler than you are so you'd be spending a fortune on SPF, and forget going anywhere sunny on holiday. What else?'

Turkey Feasts, a Pigs in Blankets sandwich and three bottles of Pepsi Max were added to the basket before she steered me towards the picky bits.

'Who wants to go out with a chef? Everyone knows they're untrustworthy. Too much opportunity to cheat, always shagging the servers in the back of the restaurant. And he wants to be a pastry chef? Not good for your health. Too much cholesterol.'

'And high cholesterol already runs in my family,' I said, reaching for a tub of picnic eggs despite the words that had just come out my mouth.

'And it's not just him, is it?' Desi went on. 'That man comes as part of a very complicated package. The mum is all right and, aside from him getting off with my fake husband, I did like the brother, but I think we all know how I feel about the sister and his dad always felt as though he was one drink away from starting a conversation with "You can't say this any more but . . ."'

'In Elsie's defence—'

'I'm going to stop you right there.' Desi brandished a package of feta-filled falafels right in my face. 'We're not defending her today. Today she is worse than Satan. Today she is getting coal in her stocking and no Christmas cards. Maybe, somewhere down the line, many, many years from now, an old lady version of me might consider acknowledging her life isn't entirely perfect but she decided to go full evil Jessica Fletcher on you at Christmas, so right now, I would happily sew prawns into her curtains and put itching powder in her unmentionables.'

'Do they still make itching powder?' I pondered as I grabbed a pack of sausage rolls. Hungry or not, Christmas wasn't Christmas without sausage rolls.

'You can get anything on TikTok shop,' she assured me. 'You're new to it but the best way to get through a situation like this is to be outrageously angry. Like, furious. Angrier than you've ever been.'

'As angry as you were when Joel finished your Crunchy Nut Cornflakes last week and put the empty box back in the cupboard?'

'Well, no, you're an amateur. You've got to work your way up to rage like that.'

I clamped my lips down on my reply, another thing to add to my buried feelings box.

Joel's head bobbed up and down behind the biscuit aisle, his bouncy stride considerably more relaxed, post-pee break.

'And don't get me started on the ex,' Desi was still ranting as she tossed bag after bag of crisps into my basket. No point in me mentioning we were driving to London not climbing Everest. 'What a wet weekend of a woman.'

'No, don't do that,' I warned her. 'We don't blame other woman when things didn't go our way. We're not those people.'

'Speak for yourself,' she clucked, tucking her hair behind her ear. 'Tomorrow can be for feminism, today is for blame.'

Joel rounded the corner, arms full of chocolate biscuits.

'Who's a feminist? I'm a feminist,' he said, unloading them in the basket. My arms sagged at the considerable weight which neither of them made a move to relieve me of. 'But just so I'm clear, why are we taking a day off?'

'Because we're slagging off Elsie and Shiv,' Desi explained.

'Oh, good,' he replied joyfully. 'That's actually an important part of being a feminist. Recognising that women can, on occasion, be totally shit, but still supporting equality in general. I read it somewhere.'

'You mean you saw it on TikTok.'

He slowly, deliberately, dropped an extremely heavy slab of Christmas cake into my basket while staring me straight in the eye. 'And your point is?'

'If anyone's a bad feminist, she's a bad feminist,' Desi went on. 'How could she take him back now? She'd have to be a masochist if she's going to convince herself this nightmare was some sort of warped romance.'

'Exactly. And what about him?' Joel added. 'If I'd known this was all some messed-up plan to get his ex back, I would've said, Laura, I would've said, do not go to Scotland with this man. Have angry sex with him on his kitchen counter by all means but do not enable his macho mind games by pretending to be his girlfriend.'

'Just in case you were wondering if what Elsie saw last night was accurate,' Desi muttered.

'If Rory was straight, you'd have been on him like a rat up a drainpipe,' he replied. 'And that's not important. What *is* important is that Callum should've been up front about the fact he's still in love with his ex before he roped you into his mad little scheme.'

'But he isn't,' I said, straining with the weight of our shopping.

'Isn't what?' Desi asked, her attention somewhat consumed by the savoury snack options in front of us.

'Callum isn't in love with his ex.'

The muscles in my back ached, my biceps and triceps groaning. God, I was going to be one of those awful people who made a New Year's resolution to join the gym, wasn't I? Rolling my shoulders, I looked up to find Desi and Joel both staring at me.

'What?' I asked, blowing a strand of hair out my face.

'What do you mean, he's not in love with his ex?' Joel asked politely.

'He's not in love with Shiv,' I said. 'That's what I mean.'

Desi pressed her lips into a white line, eyebrows drawn together. 'And you know this because?'

'Because I asked him and he said he wasn't.'

'And you believe him?'

'No reason not to,' I told her. 'He said he misses her because they were best friends but he didn't feel that way about her any more, hasn't for a long time.'

'Then why fanny about with all this fake girlfriend stuff?' she asked. 'And don't you dare say it's complicated because the last time I heard that from you I got in the car and drove for ten hours only stopping once to wee in a paper cup on the side of the road and now I'm about to drive all the way back *on Christmas Day* so I'm going to need a proper answer.'

'But it *is* complicated,' I said before clearing my throat, the very real threat of friend-on-friend violence in the air. 'Do you really want me to stand here and explain how he got in a mess by making up a girlfriend to avoid coming home because he feels guilty for failing to meet his family's expectations, hurting Shiv and Elsie, and even guiltier for not knowing exactly what he wants to do with his life, only that he doesn't want to spend it running the farm at Balmaclay?'

'Yes,' they replied in unison.

'Well, I'm not going to,' I said. 'You're just going to have to trust me that he never intended to hurt anyone.'

'Right.' Joel picked up a bag of popcorn and tossed it back and forth between his hands. 'Doesn't give him the right to use you for a one-time shag though. Wanker.'

'Well,' I started, sucking in my cheeks when they both glared at me. 'Technically, I was the one who said it was just for fun. *Technically.*'

Joel squeezed his popcorn so tightly the bag popped, sweet and salty kernels flying everywhere.

'You're going to have to help me get this straight because I'm not sure I'm following,' Desi said as Joel began to hyperventilate, huffing air in and out of the now half-empty bag. 'Callum isn't in love with Shiv any more and you know that because you asked him straight out and he gave you a proper answer.'

'Yes.'

'But he *did* use you for sex last night, right? Even if you gave him permission, that's a shitty thing to do. I mean, it's incredibly obvious that you have feelings for him and he took advantage of that.'

'Had feelings, past tense. Briefly considered a flirtation with feelings.'

Desi's eyes flashed down from my face to my chest.

'What's that?' she asked.

'What's what?'

With an almighty effort, I took the weight of the shopping basket in one hand and patted my jumper with the other.

I was still wearing his brooch.

'Oh,' I muttered, pawing at it. 'Um, Callum gave it to me. Can you take it off please? We should probably flush it down the toilet or something.'

She unpinned it from my jumper and handed it to Joel, who laid it flat in his palm, frowned, then took out his phone.

'Right, we're going to go over this one more time to make sure I've got the facts straight.' Desi pulled a hairband from her wrist and tied her long black hair back in a ponytail. Oh dear. She meant business. 'Callum isn't in love with his ex, he didn't manipulate you into a one-night stand *and* he gave you a Christmas present?'

'I'm sure you're going somewhere with this,' I replied, swallowing down an uneasy feeling. 'But yes, I suppose so.'

'Not just any Christmas present,' Joel said, looking up from his phone. 'It's a Luckenbooth brooch, a traditional Scottish love token, most often given as a token of betrothal.'

'Oh my GOD.'

'Desi Kaplan, we do not raise our voices in M&S Simply Food on the Lord's birthday,' Joel admonished. 'But we do slap our friend around the head for being an absolute mongoose when it comes to men.'

'What are you talking about?' I dropped the basket, snacks spilling all over the place when his hands shot out to clobber me around the back of the head. 'Stop it! What have I done wrong?'

'Besides walk away from a man who is very obviously obsessed with you?' Desi replied. 'Please explain to me why we even left?'

'Because you said we should!'

'Because I thought he was still in love with his ex!'

'Why would I have sex with him if I thought he was still in love with Shiv?'

'Because you're obviously as obsessed with him as he is with you!'

We were both yelling, locked in a stand-off, neither one of us about to back down.

'This is absurd,' she declared. 'What the fuck are we doing here, Laura?'

I gestured around the shop as Joel tried to kick away

his exploded popcorn and a security guard appeared at the end of the aisle, hovering ominously.

'Buying snacks?' I replied, fully aware it was not the answer she was looking for.

'I meant in general,' Desi groaned. 'What are we doing right here, right now? Why are we leaving Braewick in the first place?'

I was confused, I was frustrated, I was very angry and, somewhere underneath all that, I was starting to get a little bit hungry. All in all it was a terrible combination.

'We're leaving because I don't need his mess in my life,' I said. 'You were right, is that what you want to hear? This whole thing was a massive mistake. You said I'd get hurt and you were right, well done, now can we please get in the car and get going?'

Desi folded her arms and planted her feet on the ground. Apparently we could not.

'That's not why we're leaving,' she said. 'We're leaving because you're running away.'

'Wrong,' I replied, loud and clear. 'Completely wrong.'

'To be fair,' Joel began cautiously, 'you didn't really give him much of a chance to defend himself. We've all said the wrong thing in the heat of the moment and that moment wasn't exactly chill, was it?'

'Really? You're defending him?' I was appalled with my supposed friends. 'Whose side are you on?'

'Yours, always yours. We both are,' he paused to cast a quick look at Desi who nodded in agreement, 'that's why we're telling you the truth instead of agreeing with you and chucking you in the back of the car with a tub of Ben & Jerry's.'

'Then I'll take the ice cream option, thanks,' I said sourly. 'I've heard about enough from you two.'

'Too bad because I have one more thing to say and you're going to listen to it.' Desi stepped right up to my face, unaware she was risking life and limb. I'd never been so furious in my entire life. 'This is how you know I'm deadly serious. I was not right, you were. You're the one who said you wouldn't get hurt but he might. We should've been listening then.'

'You don't know what you're talking about,' I scoffed and turned away, not interested in her little theories.

Joel went to rest a hand on my shoulder before catching the look on my face and thinking better of it.

'You shut yourself off,' he said from a safer distance behind Desi. 'I know, it's hard to hear but you do, and it's not healthy.'

'But he's moving to Paris! And one day, he'll probably want to move back up to Braewick, regardless of what he says now. I can't work in Paris and there certainly aren't any neurology units in Braewick. Why start something that's going nowhere?'

She raised a hand to her ear, listening for something I couldn't hear. 'Oh, Joel, do you hear that?' she said. 'They're playing my favourite song, *Laura's Excuses*.'

Rage bubbled and bounced inside me, dangerously close to boiling over. I reached for the switch, the one that made the feelings disappear but it wasn't there. My safety catch was gone and I was dangerously exposed.

'They're not excuses,' I muttered. 'They're facts.'

'He might move to Paris, he might move back to Scotland, I'm hearing an awful lot of possible things Callum might do in the future and nothing about how you feel right now,' Desi said, poking me in the chest. 'You can give me every excuse until you're blue in the face but we both know it's more than that. You don't let anyone in because you're afraid that if you do, you'll lose them one way or another.'

'Is that right?'

'Lau,' she started, shaking her head sadly. 'Your mum—'

'Don't,' I warned, hovering altogether too close to the edge of my emotions. 'If you value your kneecaps, you will not say another word.'

'It's just—'

Rage charged around my body until I couldn't control it any longer and, for want of something constructive to say, I booted a Turkey Feast sandwich all the way to the fresh fruit and veg.

'Laura—'

'I said not one more word!'

Desi and Joel clutched each other's hands, stunned expressions on their faces.

'You want to share? Great, let's share,' I swiped my hair out of my face, not even flinching when it got caught in my watch strap, yanking a chunk right out my scalp. 'You were wrong, Des, but not about poor, hard-done-by Callum. You were wrong when you said I'm an amateur when it comes to being angry. I am angry all the time, every single day. I'm fucking *consumed* by it. I'm angry at my dad for not being there for me like other people's parents. I'm angry about losing my mum, angry at the doctors who didn't save her, I'm even angry *at* her for dying which is literally insane. What did I do to deserve any of it?'

'Laura.' Desi spoke my name gently, her fingertips finding my forearm, but it was no good now. The cap was off, the toothpaste was out the tube and I wasn't done.

'No!' I yelled, shaking her off. I'd started and I could not stop. 'That's not even half of it. Do you want the full list? Because I've got one. Why am I in so much debt from student loans? I'm not out there buying Chanel handbags, I'm training to be a fucking surgeon. Why do I have to deal with sexist doctors and patients who won't let me help save their lives but are perfectly happy to have one of my male colleagues on their team even though I'm miles better at my job than they are? I could go on but what's the point of losing my shit? It doesn't help, nothing changes. So I live with it. I push it down, I walk around with a smile on my face and I try to make things better for the world, knowing it will never make things better for me. And yes, I keep people at a distance because if you don't let them in, they can't let you down and give you another reason to be even angrier. Obviously I made an exception for you two and that was clearly a mistake.'

I didn't realise I was crying until Desi pulled me into her chest and I saw my tears staining the cream fabric of her shirt.

'Oh, Laura,' she said, squeezing her arms around me tightly when I tried to wriggle away. 'You're an idiot.'

'OK, not what I was expecting you to say,' I muttered through choked sobs.

'If anyone has any right to be pissed off with the world, it's you,' she replied as Joel made it a group hug. 'But you can't keep it all in because, well . . .'

'Because eventually you'll explode in the middle of a Marks & Sparks Simply Food and start bawling your eyes out on Christmas Day,' Joel finished for her. 'And walk out on the first man I've ever seen make an impression on you in the entire ten years I've known you.'

'Consider it a lesson learned,' I snuffled into my friends' bodies. 'I won't be letting my guard down again.'

Desi stroked my hair and cleared her throat.

'Are you going to hit me if I suggest that's the wrong lesson?'

'Yes.'

'OK then.'

Joel went next. 'Can I ask a question?'

'No.'

'Tough tits because I'm going to ask it anyway,' he said. 'Given how very, very good you are at keeping people out, how the bloody hell did Callum six-foot-something-Scot McClay weasel his way in so quickly?'

'She told me he made her come four times,' Desi answered. 'Does that answer your question?'

'It would if she wasn't clearly head over heels for him before he gave her the pork sword,' Joel said. 'I'm not trying to upset you, Lau, it's an honest question. What is it about Callum that broke through?'

Squished between my best friends' bodies, I closed my eyes and the first thing I saw was Callum's face. The freckle underneath his left eye, the shifting blue of his irises, that irresistible half-smile.

'He listened,' I said simply.

'Fuck me,' Joel muttered. 'The bar really is low for straight women, isn't it?'

'Yes,' said Desi, elbowing him in the ribs. 'Now shut up and let her finish.'

'I suppose,' I added, unable to shut down a horrible sinking feeling in my stomach, 'because I was playing a role, my guard was down. I wasn't worried about him getting close so I didn't bother to keep him at a distance.'

'So busy pretending to be someone else, you accidentally let him see the real you,' Desi said. 'Ironic really.'

'A little too ironic,' Joel sang, only earning himself another, sharper elbow to the guts from our friend.

My tears dried up and sobs slowed into hiccups as I recovered myself. It was true. I'd told Callum things I'd never shared with anyone else. He made me laugh. He made me feel soft and safe and strong and powerful. And to Desi's point, he had made me come four times which was, sadly, an all-time record.

'He's still moving to Paris though,' I said, carefully extricating myself from my friends' embrace. 'And I still have exams coming up. Even if I do have feelings for him and he has feelings for me, it's still terrible timing.'

'Sounds like perfectly normal timing to me,' Joel replied. 'Unless you're the sort of person who constantly looks for excuses why they shouldn't try.'

I shot him a filthy look, scrubbing at my cheeks with the backs of my hands.

'Withdrawn,' he said. 'Desi, your witness.'

'Bear with me,' she said, the three of us still standing in the middle of the snack aisle, surrounded by my overturned basket full of goods. 'What if we went back to Balmaclay and you and Callum . . . talk?'

I took a deep breath in and held it as Joel pinned the Luckenbooth brooch back on my jumper.

'Controversial,' he said. 'But it's got to be worth a go?'

'What if it turns out he's not interested?'

'Then me and Joel will beat the living shit out of him,' Desi offered with too much enthusiasm. 'An extra-special Christmas gift from us to you.'

The fluorescent overhead lights made the brooch glint and sparkle. If I didn't go back, this would all be for nothing. Desi and Joel would drive me home and I'd have something new to add to my pile of grievances with the world. But if I found Callum and said my piece, even if he didn't reciprocate, I'd still have something to hold on to. I'd still know that I was capable of something I thought was lost to me.

'For what it's worth, I'd go back.'

All three of us looked up at once to see the security guard leaning against the end of the snack aisle. '

'You meet a lot of people in this job, hear a lot of things.' He nodded sagely like the wise old man of the woods as opposed to the eavesdropping security guard of the service station. 'I'd turn around and let your man say his piece.'

'Normally I'd tell you to ignore weirdos like him, no offence,' Desi said pointing back at him – in fairness, he didn't look especially upset. 'But he agrees with me so he must be right. Lau, we should go back.'

'You're just trying to avoid the ten-hour drive,' I replied, sulking as the odds stacked up against me.

'That's true but I also think you owe it to Callum to hear him out,' she said. 'More importantly, you owe it to yourself.'

'OK, yes, let's go back,' I said, nodding, slowly at first and then so feverishly I thought my head might snap off, I swallowed and pressed cold hands to my hot face.

Desi grabbed my hand and began pulling me towards the door. 'Right this second, before you change your mind.'

'As soon as you've bought something and cleaned up your mess, you mean.' The security guard pulled himself up to his full height, one hand resting on the walkie talkie at his hip. 'I'm happy to dispense advice but I'm not your bloody cleaner. I'm already working Christmas Day for Christ's sake.'

'Oh for fuck's sake.' Joel bent down and scooped up a tub of Rocky Road mini bites. 'Go and start the car, I'll be out in a minute.'

He sprinted towards the self-checkout, followed by the security guard, while Desi picked up what she could, shoved it onto the nearest shelf and shunted the rest of it under the closest aisle with her foot.

'Good?' she asked.

'Good enough,' I confirmed, dragging her behind me and out the front door. 'Let's go.'

CHAPTER TWENTY-EIGHT

When we got to the house, no one was home.

The Land Rover and the silver Mercedes were both gone when I ran around to the back of the house to check, no one answering at any door.

'Callum said they go to church on Christmas morning,' I remembered, my adrenaline high crashing hard as I climbed back into the car, sullen faced. 'They're probably all there now.'

'No worries,' Desi said brightly. 'We'll just go to the church.'

'How festive,' Joel replied. 'I'm in.'

But I wasn't.

'We're not going to storm a church,' I said, visions of a nativity scene gone flying, Desi screaming Callum's name like she was starring in a local production of *A Streetcar Named Desire* shuddering through my mind. 'We'll wait for them to come home.'

Joel slumped against the backseat, hands tucked into his armpits.

'How long will they be? I'm freezing.'

'Literally no idea,' Desi replied. 'Lau?'

'The last time I was in a church was for my own christening so you'll forgive me for not having the faintest idea,' I said. 'I don't even know what kind of church they go to. Could be a half an hour, could be all day. Catholic goes on for a bit, I think.'

'Well, we can't sit outside in the freezing cold for an hour.' She checked the heating dials on the dash and groaned when she saw they were already at full blast.

'I have a suggestion.'

We both turned to receive Joel's wisdom.

'Pub?' he suggested.

'Pub,' Desi agreed. 'We'll come back in an hour, hopefully interrupt their bloody Christmas dinner.'

'First round on Laura,' Joel said, rubbing his hands against his arms. 'I could use a hot toddy to warm me up.'

I braced myself against the dashboard when Desi spun the car around on the driveway, barely missing the not-a-moat.

'Alcohol only warms you up temporarily,' I said. 'In the long term it actually makes you lose body heat faster.'

'Remember that first night in the student union when we couldn't find a table?' Joel said to Desi over the loud crunch of gravel. 'And you said, let's go and sit over by the redhead, she looks all right?'

'And I'll never live it down,' she muttered. 'As long as I live.'

The Clach was booked and busy. Desi went first, elbows out and practically fighting through the crowd to get the only empty table left, so far away from the roaring fire I couldn't even see it, let alone feel it.

'Two scotches and a Diet Coke?' I said, pointing at my two friends as they struggled out of their coats.

Desi pulled her sleeves down over her hands and draped her faux-fur coat over her knee for warmth.

'I thought you didn't like Diet Coke because aspartame is bad for your brain or something.'

'I don't,' I said. 'It's for you. You're driving, remember?'

'Fuck.' She blanched, wide eyes staring blankly. 'I have made a terrible mistake.'

Weaving through the packed tables, I saw happy people everywhere, smiling and laughing and hugging each other. Even as a card-carrying Christmas resistor, I had to admit I'd always liked this part. The way one day out of the year brought people together and gave them a reason to feel joy that was often so sorely missing on the other three hundred and sixty-four of them. There were couples and families and groups of friends, and a big table full of older gents who were cackling at each other like they'd sat around that same table every Christmas for the last fifty years and had no intention of changing that fact any time soon.

'Excuse me, thank you, excuse me, thanks.'

I said the same words again and again as I ricocheted down the entire length of the pub until, just a few feet from the bar, I froze.

Sat at a table beside the fire and staring at their phones, were Elsie and Shiv.

If I thought I could've escape without them seeing me, I'd have turned tail and run, but no. Shiv saw me first, her blue eyes popping open and for a very stupid minute, I thought she might give me the grace of a speedy exit, but no. She nudged Elsie, nodding to the spot where I stood.

The sounds of The Clach faded away and my body bypassed my brain, slipping straight into flight, fight, freeze or fawn. This time, it chose freeze, all my muscles seizing up as though I might somehow become invisible as long as I didn't move. Then I remembered that was a tactic to use on dinosaurs, not people, and since they were very extinct, we didn't even know if it actually *would* work on dinosaurs but I doubted it. If anyone were to ever clone them successfully, the potential for a class action lawsuit against *Jurassic Park* was huge.

'What the fuck are you doing here?'

The sound of Elsie's voice set my teeth on edge when she rose to her feet, hands on her hips, and it took every ounce of self-restraint in my body not to knock her spark out. Not that I'd ever hit anyone before, let alone knocked them out, and I knew only too well how dangerous concussions could be, but still, the heart wants what the heart wants and my heart wanted Elsie McClay unconscious for the foreseeable.

'Elsie,' I began, searching myself for something clever, witty and incisive, so savage it made her question her very existence. 'Piss off.'

It wasn't perfect but it would have to do.

'No, I mean it, what the fuck are you doing here?' she said again, strangely enough surviving my verbal assault without so much as a scratch.

'Just happened to be in the area, thought we'd pop in for a quick pint.'

'Very funny.'

I attempted to move around her, only to be cut off by a speedy side step.

'I'm not here to fight with you,' I said with sigh. 'I'm here to talk to Callum. Is he here?'

She scoffed, tossing her ponytail over her shoulder and almost taking a passing man's eye out with it. 'I think we've all heard more than enough out of you.'

A lesser woman, a lesser version of me even, would've taken this as a sign. The universe did not want me to speak to Callum. Why else would they put this gorgon in my way? But my emotional shutdown switch had been permanently eliminated and my fear of confrontation was gone with it.

'No, Elsie, I don't think you've heard enough from me,' I said, standing my ground. 'I don't think you've heard anything from me as it happens. You heard from Caroline, and last time I checked, you're the super sleuth who worked out she doesn't exist.'

'I don't know where you get the audacity to even still be here,' she said, seething. 'Let alone the fact you haven't even tried to apologize.'

'For what?!' I demanded. 'I didn't do anything wrong! And correct me if I'm wrong but after the way you acted this morning, I'm not exactly breaking my neck to make things right with you. Pretending to be Callum's girlfriend might've been stupid but what you did was thoughtless and cruel, not just to Callum but to your whole family.'

She pursed her lips, eyes flickering to the floor because even Elsie McClay had to know there was truth in what I'd said. But she wasn't ready to back down just yet.

'You should at least say sorry to Shiv.'

'Who should do what to Shiv?'

Callum's ex was on her feet, perfect blonde hair

bobbing about the shoulders of her fuzzy Christmas jumper.

'She, whoever she is, owes you an apology,' Elsie stated.

'What for?' Shiv asked.

'Messing things up with you and Callum.'

'Oh my God, not this again.'

Rolling her eyes wasn't enough. Shiv rolled her entire head around on her shoulders before throwing her hands up to the sky. 'Else, how many times do I have to tell you, I do not now, nor will I ever want to get back together with Callum!'

Well. That was news to me.

'You don't?' I said.

'What?' Shiv turned to look at me, eyes scrunched up as though I'd just said the most out of pocket thing she'd ever heard. 'No! You couldn't pay me to have him back. Why would you think otherwise?'

'But you wanted to marry him? And Graham said . . .' I stammered. 'And his dad, and Elsie . . . ?'

'Not that I owe you an explanation but yes, I let everyone convince me we should get married. In reality, I was trying to patch up something that was already over. If he'd gone along with it, we'd both be miserable,' she said as my words faded away. 'And strangely enough, I don't share my innermost thoughts with my ex-boyfriend's dad or his best friend, and believe it or not, Else isn't exactly the best person to talk to when it comes to Cal.'

'I'm stood right here, you know,' Elsie said, tapping her friend on the shoulder.

'Good, maybe it'll sink in this time,' Shiv replied, sounding exasperated. 'I'm not getting back together with your brother, I'm completely and utterly over him, and there's no secret plan to bring him back and usurp you from the farm throne.'

'Actually, there is, sort of, but it's your dad, not Callum,' I said. 'Which probably doesn't make you feel any better now I think about it, sorry.'

'Why were you talking to Graham and Elsie and Derek about me and Callum?' Shiv asked, turning her keen eyes on me. 'If you're only pretending to be his girlfriend, what would it matter?'

'General curiosity?'

She squinted at me and I could almost feel her picking through my brain.

'Are you in love with him?'

'No,' I replied, face instantly flaming. 'It's just, well, you weren't very nice to me when we met.'

'I don't remember you passing out friendship bracelets either,' she replied. 'The fact I wasn't turning cartwheels when we met doesn't mean I want to get back with Cal, only that I don't know you. He's still my ex, forgive me for not being evolved enough to invite his new girlfriend over for pizza and a sleepover.'

I couldn't argue with her logic. Even though Shiv had given no indication she wanted to reconcile with Callum, it hadn't even occurred to me that Graham, Derek and Elsie could be wrong about her intentions. So caught up in my own confusing feelings, I couldn't even imagine a world where she wouldn't want to be with him.

'If we're all done sharing, I'm ready for her to leave,' Elsie said, folding her arms across her chest.

It took a second for me to realize she was talking about me.

'Why should I leave?'

'Because this is my local pub and you're a psycho.'

Even though I knew this was not the right time to bring up the statistics on female psychopaths, it still took a tremendous degree of self-control to stop myself from telling her male psychopaths outnumbered females six to one, although recent research suggested that number was likely underestimated and women were better at masking psychopathic behaviours.

'Whatever is going on with Cal, it's a bloody big mess and I'm sorry you've been caught in the middle of it,' Shiv said, glancing over my shoulder. 'All that said and done, you might not owe me an apology but she does. Else, if you need me, I'll be across the bar, kicking her friend's arse for what she said about my shoes at that wedding.'

Without another word, she took off, marching across the bar towards Desi and Joel.

'You'd better get your friend out of here before she batters her,' Elsie advised. 'Shiv might look harmless but I wouldn't bet against her in a fight.' I was halfway turned around before she added, 'and you can see yourself out while you're at it.'

'Seriously, Elsie, you need to get over yourself,' I said, shaking my head. 'I've never met anyone so committed to taking their anger out on the wrong people, and I'm a doctor, in a hospital. I said everything I need to say to you last night, but if you truly think I'm the problem then you should get help. Making up a fake girlfriend was stupid, yes, but Callum want only trying to spare everyone's feelings while he worked out his own stuff. He's a straight cis-man, open communication and logical problem-solving might not be his strongest suit, but if anything you're the one who should be apologizing to him. The whole lot of you need your heads knocking together. You, your mum and your bloody dad, and it's a good job they're not here right now because I'd happily tell them that to their face.'

Her eyes flicked past me and the pop of surprise on her face melted into a self-satisfied smile.

'And they're right behind me, aren't they?'

I turned around slowly to see Lizzie, Derek, Mal and Fiona all emerging from the passageway that led out to the back of the pub, all of them with a face like thunder. All except Mal. He was grinning like a Cheshire cat as usual.

'Fancy seeing you here,' I said with a weak smile. 'Aren't you supposed to be at church?'

'Aye,' replied Derek. 'And aren't you supposed to be a Swedish masseuse?'

'A *vegan* Swedish masseuse,' added Fiona.

Mal grasped his wife's arm and cocked his head towards the door. 'Come on, this feels like family business. We'll leave you to it.'

'But you're practically family,' I said, protesting the loss of a potential ally.

He replied with a wink. 'Kith not kin, hen. Shall I start the engine in case you need a hasty retreat?'

I shook my head before looking over my shoulder to see Shiv and Desi staring each other down like a pair of Christmassy king cobras. Possibly, I'd spoken too soon.

'So you think we're the ones who owe you an apology, do you?' Derek said, seizing the brown leather belt at his waist and hoisting his trousers up as Mal sauntered over to the bar, Fiona still shooting daggers in my direction.

'Technically, I believe I said you owe Callum an apology,' I replied. 'No need to worry about me.'

'Oh no, you're not getting off that easily.' Two red spots appeared in his cheeks and his bushy eyebrows came to life, inching up his forehead like angry, bristly caterpillars. 'Since you're here, I've a thing or two I'd like to say to you . . .'

But I wasn't listening to him any more, my entire attention was elsewhere. Striding down the passageway that led to the back of The Clach, shoulders slumped and head hanging low, was Callum.

CHAPTER TWENTY-NINE

All the way back from our service station pitstop, I'd gone over exactly what I wanted to say when I saw him.

How I would explain what happened, why I reacted the way I did, why I ran out without giving him a chance to speak, but when he looked up and caught my eye, all my clever, emotional, slightly self-deprecating and hopefully just-funny-enough speeches disappeared. His face was unreadable, or at least it was to me. I never had been good at guessing what people were thinking and I couldn't stop myself from wondering which parts of his brain were lighting up. There was a study that suggested emotional regulation, basically controlling your feelings, involved a particular area of the anterior prefrontal cortex. If I could get him into an MRI, I might have a better chance of working out what was going on in his head, or I could pioneer a truly groundbreaking technique.

I could ask.

'LaCaroline!'

Rory sprang out from behind his brother, hand held up for a high five.

No one met it.

'Really? Rude.' He lowered the hand, looking wildly offended. 'Whatever. Glad you're here, saved me a long drive. Who wants a drink?'

'And the gang's all here,' Derek said to me. 'Right. Since I've not had one ounce of sense out of the boy, perhaps you can enlighten me as to what the bloody hell's been going on?'

I looked at Callum and Callum looked at me.

Silence.

'I don't really know where to start,' I said, not sure who I was talking to. His father asked the question but Callum was the only one I cared about. 'I didn't mean any harm.'

'Apology not expected,' Derek declared.

'Good because I didn't apologize.'

'Dad, give it a break,' Callum said, finally finding his voice. 'I have explained, you just don't want to hear it. Laura hasn't done anything wrong.'

'Not entirely true,' I muttered, thinking about but not speaking of the massage from hell.

Callum came forward, stepping in front of his parents, Rory and Elsie behind them, and a couple of old dears at the closest table completely rapt.

'You're here,' he said to me. His eyes roamed my face, my body, as though he was looking for something that would prove otherwise, that I was a cardboard cut-out or greenscreen projection. 'How are you here?'

'She popped in for a pint.'

'Unhelpful, Else,' Rory clipped his sister around the back of the head.

'Only telling you what she told me,' she replied, immediately slapping him back in true sibling style then glancing down at the car keys in his hand. 'Will you drive me home please?'

'Are you insane?' he said with a screech of disbelief. 'And miss whatever the fuck this is? Not a bloody chance, sit your arse down, Elsie McClay.'

He didn't know it but they were my thoughts exactly. What *was* this? What would Callum say? Why did Derek look like he'd just had a gobstopper from Willy Wonka's factory? When would Elsie launch herself on me like a silverback gorilla and beat me around the head with one of Graham's homemade Scotch eggs? And why, oh why, was Lizzie *smiling*?

'You're here,' Callum said again, breathing out the second word on a sigh.

'Yes,' I said. 'There's a chance I was a bit rash in leaving.'

'Yeah?'

'Hmm.' I offered a slow nod. 'Desi thought you might have something to say and I didn't really give you a chance to say it.'

His lips twitched and the ghost of a smile passed behind his eyes.

'That's what Desi thought, is it?'

'And Joel. And the security guard at the little M&S at the service station but that's a longer story.'

'One we'll be coming back to.'

It felt as though I was watching it all happen from outside my body, hanging from the rafters above and wincing at the absurd, blank expression on my face as Callum came closer, until we were toe-to-toe, and took my hands in his.

'Is this OK?' he asked, very, very softly.

'Yes,' I said, rushing back into myself at the touch of his soft, warm skin. 'It's OK.'

'Good. Joel, Desi and your man at M&S were right. Mum, Dad,' He turned toward his parents, Derek still purple-faced and fractious, Lizzie looking strangely pleased. 'I'd like to introduce you to someone, this is Laura Pearce, she's a neurosurgeon.'

'Trainee neuro— you know what, never mind,' I said, cutting myself off. 'Yes, I'm a neurosurgeon.'

'Wouldn't want her fiddling around in my brain,' Elsie muttered, loud enough to make sure we all heard.

'Better to have her fiddling around in your brain than giving you a massage,' Derek replied. He was not wrong.

'We met when Laura came to rent my flat while I'm away in Paris,' Callum went on, still smiling at me and ignoring everyone else, an impressive feat but one I knew he'd been working on all his life. 'Obviously she's gorgeous—'

A pause for Elsie to make a puking sound.

'But I think she's pretty amazing as well. She's funny and she's kind. She's spontaneous—'

'No, she isn't,' I interrupted, leaning to the side to make sure his parents saw the certainty on my face. 'This was my first crack at spontaneity and it will be my last.'

But Callum grinned and my knees wobbled. 'Fine. She's funny and kind and *fascinating*. I haven't been able to think straight since the moment she walked into my flat.'

'Oh,' I said, shyly tucking my hair behind my ear. 'Well, that's nice.'

The words whispered out of me, barely louder than a breath, but he was so close now, staring intently at the shapes formed by my lips, even in the din of The Clach, I knew he could hear every single one.

'I have one question.'

Tearing my eyes away from Callum's sapphire irises, I looked over to see Derek's expression softening slightly.

'Are you or are you not . . .' He paused to take a deep, steadying breath, one hand on his wife's shoulder. 'A vegan?'

'No,' I replied firmly. 'I am not.'

Derek McClay blew out an enormous sigh, his whole body deflating.

'At least that's something,' he said. 'He hasn't lost his mind completely.'

Lizzie placed her hand on the small of his back and pushed him in the direction of the door.

'Come on,' she said. 'We need to go home and check on the goose.'

'I thought we were getting a drink and talking some sense into your son about this French pudding nonsense?' Derek replied, refusing to move.

'That's because that's what I wanted you to think. Cal isn't the one who needs to be talked to.' Snatching the car keys from Rory's hand, she gave Derek a look that made me physically quake. 'We've a lot to discuss but it won't work itself out over one whisky in The Clach and now's not the time, there's no point trying to talk to a man when he's hungry or in love.'

My stomach flipped at Lizzie's casual invocation of the L word. It was too soon for that, far too soon. Wasn't it? Too soon to say it out loud at least, no matter what the little voice whispered in the back of my mind.

'I'm looking forward to getting to know you, Laura,' she said, patting Callum's forearm before nodding at me.

'You too?' I replied, feeling unexpectedly exposed by the sound of my own name.

She smiled, tender and kind, and a sweet sadness

pierced my heart. It was a long time since anyone had looked at me that way but it wasn't the sort of feeling you forgot. Just for a moment, I missed my mum with a fierceness that threatened to swallow me whole.

'We'll leave you to talk,' Lizzie said as she led Derek away, back to the car. 'Don't be too long, lunch is on the table at two whether you're there or not. I won't serve a dry bird.'

'Surely she's not invited?' Elsie exclaimed, aflame with outrage.

Rory groaned loudly. 'For fuck's sake. Come on, Elsie, haven't you've scrooged it up enough for one day?'

'What about Shiv?' she protested, shaking him loose. 'I'm not leaving her.'

'What about Shiv?' Callum echoed. 'She's here?'

'Oh God, Desi!'

I whirled around to locate my friends, fully expecting to find a knockout brawl in progress across the bar. I shouldn't have worried. Shiv, Desi and Joel were all sat around the table, chuckling away together like the oldest of friends. It was a Christmas miracle. That or Joel's peacekeeping skills were being sorely underutilized as an accountant. It was time for him to move on to the UN or take over a soft play centre or something.

'Shiv's fine, let's go,' Rory said, turning Elsie around by her shoulders. 'If you're good, I'll take you round to the neighbour's house later and you can steal all the kids' sweeties out from under the tree.'

With a scowl that suggested our relationship was far from salvageable, Elsie let her younger brother shove her back down the passageway to the backdoor of The Clach, leaving Callum and me alone in the crowded bar. The light from the fire glinted in his burnished bronze hair, the scruff on his chin almost sparkling, and the two old ladies sat at the next table went back to their sherries, looking deeply disappointed.

'What happened?' I asked, dazed and genuinely waiting for Elsie to come running back in with a crowbar.

'I told them the truth,' Callum replied simply. 'Eventually. It would be more accurate to say, I shouted at Elsie, Dad shouted at me, Elsie shouted at Mum and after that no one said anything for a good long while because nobody shouts at my mother and gets away with it. Then we all went to church so Mum acted like nothing had happened, after that there was more shouting in the car, and now, we're here.'

'Sounds like good old-fashioned family fun,' I said, processing the series of events. More or less weird than an emotional breakdown in M&S? I wasn't sure. 'Everything's OK then?'

'I wouldn't go that far.'

Glancing down, I realized I was still clutching his hand in mine, and I gave it a squeeze.

'We're not going to fix twenty years of problems in one day,' Callum said, looking and sounding tired. 'What's important is, everything is out in the open now. They know how I feel, I know how they feel, we all know how Elsie feels. Mum gets it, I think. Dad will come around or he won't, that's how it goes.'

'I hope he does.' I sidled in closer to him as someone pushed past me to get to the bar. The bar. I'd almost forgotten where we were. 'While we're clearing the air, I've got a couple of things to say if that's all right?'

'By all means.'

Callum waved a hand between us, gesturing for me to take the floor.

Even though our nervous system accomplished thousands of tasks every single second, supposedly, the prefrontal cortex only could process information at ten bits per second, one thought at a time. Right there and then, I was entirely certain mine was operating at less than optimal speed. Every time I blinked, it was like seeing him for the first time, and all my clever words and witty asides were long gone, over the hills and far away.

'I shouldn't have run out when you were trying to talk to me,' I began, starting with something I knew to be true. 'That was stupid and I'm sorry.'

'And I shouldn't have said you were just a random girl.' He winced as though repeating the words caused him pain. 'What I meant to say was, none of my behaviour was your fault. I didn't want them blaming you and it just came out, I apologize.'

So we'd both messed up and we were both sorry. It was a decent start.

'Wait, what did Rory mean when he said I'd saved you a long drive?' I asked, the thought suddenly striking me.

Callum's shoulders rolled up and forward, pinching together under his ears.

'Och, you know Rory.'

'Not really,' I pointed out. 'What was he talking about.'

'He got it into his head that we should drive down to London after you,' he said. 'That was sort of the plan. Mum agreed to bring Dad to The Clach to get him out the way so we could leave without another row but Rory left his phone in Mum's handbag because he's an idiot.'

'Why did your mum have Rory's phone in the first place?'

'Because he was watching *The Simpsons* in church.'

'Fair,' I said. 'Your mum approves of me then?'

He inclined his head but his smile was disapproving. 'Which means you failed in your task, Caroline. No free rent for you.'

'Shit, I was going to spend that money in the sales,' I whispered before running my thumb over the back of his hand. 'You were really going to drive all the way down to London? On Christmas Day?'

An answering nod.

'And say what?'

'Hadn't quite worked that out yet,' he admitted. 'What were you planning to say to me?'

'I *did* know,' I told him, chewing the inside of my cheek. 'But I seem to have forgotten.'

'You ought to see a neurologist about your memory,' he said and I glanced away, refusing to let him see me smile at his bad joke. 'I know it was stupid to call you a random girl – and please don't set Desi on me for this – but I still don't fully understand why you were so angry that you had to leave like that. You're the one who said last night was a one-time thing, just for fun.'

'There's a good chance I wasn't thinking that clearly last night,' I confessed. 'I think, after a certain point, I would've said anything you wanted to hear. I thought it was what you wanted.'

The air between us seemed to shimmer and hazy, uninvited memories of the night before flashed through my mind.

'I only agreed because the thought of having you once was better than never having you at all,' Callum murmured. 'Laura, I've been holding myself back from you since that first night on the train. You don't do relationships and I don't do one-night stands, I knew if anything happened between us, one of us would get hurt. Do you have any idea how long I stood in front of your door last night before I decided I could live with the pain?'

I snatched in a breath, letting my hair fall in front of my face, the weight of his gaze too heavy to bear. Callum crooked a finger underneath my chin, lightly sketching his thumb over my trembling lips.

'Now I think about it, I've an idea of what I wanted to say to you when we got to London,' he said. 'I reckon I'd have tried to convince you to give us a go. You'll be busy at work, I'll be busy in Paris. We'll text and talk on the phone when we can. I'll get the train back to London on my days off, you can come to see me if you want to. What do you say?'

'I suppose there are a few things I'd like to say,' I whispered, voice breaking against his fingertips. 'Only I don't know where to start.'

'Dealer's choice.'

His fingers grazed my jaw as he slid his hand around my head and tilted it backwards. When my eyes met his, I couldn't hold back the tears that pricked behind them, one, then two, full, fat teardrops spilled over my bottom lashes, enzymes, lipids, metabolites, electrolytes and protein. Callum wiped them away with his thumbs, both hands tenderly cradling my face.

'My career is demanding,' I said with a tiny sniff. 'And passing my exams has to be my priority.'

'Wouldn't have it any other way,' Callum replied. 'No question about it.'

'But,' I added tentatively, 'I *have* been rethinking that whole no relationships thing.'

'God, I knew I was good,' he said with a low whistle. 'I didn't know I was *that* good.'

'Since before last night,' I added, punching him lightly

in the stomach even as a tremor ran all the way through my body. 'Although admittedly, your performance didn't hurt.'

A sly half-grin crept onto his face.

'Knew it.'

'It won't be easy,' I said. 'Mostly because I'm worried we're both idiots.'

He laughed and his fingertips combed through my hair, sending tingles shooting all over my body.

'We McClays have never been afraid of hard work, especially when there's a worthy reward at the end of it.' Winding my hair around his hands, he tugged gently, splintering my concentration into a thousand tiny shards. 'I stayed awake all night watching you sleep because I couldn't stand the thought of our one time being over. Laura, I'll find a way to make this work. All you have to do is keep being yourself.'

They were beautiful words but were they enough?

'I don't know about that,' I said into his chest. 'I'm not always brilliant at saying what I'm thinking. Or feeling. Or telling people what I want. And when anyone gets too close, I have a tendency to push them away.'

He cocked his head across to the other side of the bar. 'What about your pals over there?'

'Can you imagine trying to push Desi away?' I replied without looking. 'I was not given a choice in our friendship. She was tenacious.'

'Then I'll be tenacious,' Callum promised. 'I've fucked up a lot of things in my life, wasted a lot of time, all because I didn't say exactly what was on my mind. I won't do it again. I won't do it with you.'

That pleading half-smile again. It would be the death of me.

'What do you say?' he asked, hopeful but still uncertain. 'Do we have a deal?'

I slid my hands over his heart, feeling for the beat that matched my own, no longer erratic and afraid but certain and steady. Six short days and everything had changed. Not me, not really, I was the same person I'd always been only now, thanks to Callum, I felt more myself than ever. Whatever we'd done before, whoever we thought we were or had pretended to be, that was the past, and the thought of living a life without him, without seeing him, talking to him, touching him. was so much more frightening than the risk of letting him in. Steady grey or dangerous Technicolor.

There was really no choice to make.

'We have a deal.'

With my hands cupping his face, I rose up on my tiptoes, rough stubble under my palms, his eyelashes flickering against my cheek, his firm, warm lips brushing against mine . . .

'Excuse me!'

Graham's voice cut through the moment and I jerked away, heart in my throat. With a mischievous grin, he pointed at the ceiling.

'Can you show some decorum?' he said sternly. 'That's no' mistletoe you're standing under.'

Directly above us, a bunch of holly hung from one of the rafters, shiny green leaves and plump berries, red instead of white.

'Sorry, Graham,' I replied, pulling Callum's face back down to mine. 'Starting right now, we're making our own traditions.'

And I intended to keep them, always.

ACKNOWLEDGEMENTS

Eternally grateful to my agent and keeper of my sanity, Rowan Lawton at The Soho Agency. I couldn't do it without you and neither of us could do it without Eleanor Lawlor, so double thank you to you. I am still so sorry about those suitcases. Further thank you to Kate Prentice at 42 for your tireless efforts, and sage advice, exciting things to come.

Writing is truly one of the strangest jobs and publishing one of the most confusing industries and I am privileged to work with one of the best teams there is. Hugest thanks to Lynne Drew, Olivia Robertshaw, Felicity Denham, Vicky Joss and Emily Merrill who are forced to suffer me most directly/frequently, but extended appreciation and apologies to literally everyone who had a hand in making, designing, producing and selling this book. Design, production, sales, marketing, audio, warehouse. Special shoutout to Jean Marie Kelly at Harper360 for all that you do in the US. Without your tireless work, I would not be able to attend SteamyLitCon and then who would I even be?

Of course, thank you to all the booksellers who do the hardest of work, putting this into your hands, hosting pre-orders and holding events, you're all heroes and deserve many little treats.

This year, I've leaned on my author friends perhaps more than any other, but listing them all is starting to feel more like naming and shaming than showing appreciation so I'll just say THANK YOU, BESTIE. Whether we talked/sobbed/hugged/drank wine/ate snacks/ casually chatted in person, by text, on WhatsApp, exchanged memes in the DMs, survived an author panel together, indulged in karaoke or participated in one of Julie Soto's SEVERAL *Interview With The Vampire* group chats, your existence helped me through a difficult time. In the immortal words of the Wildcats of East High, we're all in this together and I couldn't be more grateful. We live in a time increasingly committed to silencing voices when what the world really needs is to hear from more people than ever.

What you write, why you write and who you are, matters.

And obviously, last but not least, friends, family and cats, you're the best and I love you the most (although not necessarily in that order).

A CHRISTMAS Q&A WITH LINDSEY KELK

If you could pick a Christmas song to be the soundtrack to the book, what would it be?
'Christmas Wrapping' by The Waitresses absolutely sums up Laura's state of mind at the beginning of the book. It's my favourite seasonal song *and* the best track to do at Christmas karaoke. Start practising now, wow everyone later.

What was the inspiration for *Christmas Fling*'s plot and characters?
This story was inspired by a mixture of things: my past few visits to Scotland, classic Christmas movies, the fake-dating trope and my overall love of the festive season. It all came together when I realised Laura could only let someone see the real her when she was pretending to be someone else. I think we all put up walls sometimes, hopefully we don't have to go to such extremes to bring them down.

This isn't your first Christmas book, so is Christmas your favourite time of year?
I'd be lying if I said no. I love the tree, I love the food, I love giving presents, I love getting presents, I love Christmas movies, Christmas songs, all of it! There's something about this time of year that brings out the best in people. Or possibly I'm just so full of sugar and giddy about said presents, I'm more inclined to see their better qualities . . .

What's your favourite Christmas tradition guaranteed to give you the warm, fuzzy Christmas feeling?
Either trimming the tree or our now-annual Christmas Eve-Eve cocktail and cookie party. Decorating the tree is rewarding and fun but also exhausting and seems to take longer every year. Cocktails and cookies are a perfect combo for easy hosting, and there is no better kick-off to the big day, in my opinion.

What is your favourite Christmas movie?
This is an impossible question, but favourites include *Christmas in Connecticut*, *Remember the Night*, *Gremlins*, *The Shop Around the Corner*, *The Bishop's Wife*, *The Muppet Christmas Carol*, *National Lampoon's Christmas Vacation* and *DIE HARD*, BECAUSE IT IS A CHRISTMAS MOVIE.

Where would be your ideal location for you or one of your characters to be snowed in for Christmas?
I would find a way to survive in a six-star luxury hotel, as long as I had plenty of wine, snacks and a good book. Bonus points if there's a bubble bath.

Where is your dream Christmas holiday destination?
Part of me wants to say Hawaii, because Hawaii is almost always my dream holiday destination, but Christmas in the sun is weird, so I think I'd take a leaf out of Laura's book and head up to Scotland for Christmas in a castle (not a castle) with my friends.

Christmas in Sunnydale or Christmas with Monsieur de Lioncourt, and why?
No offence to Buffy or to Sunnydale itself, but the Hellmouth is too close to my actual home in LA (and don't I know it), plus I don't want to babysit Xander over the Christmas period. New Orleans, on the other hand, is one of my favourite cities in the entire world. It has amazing restaurants, fun bars, incredible live music, and I'm sure Lestat de Lioncourt would throw one hell of a Christmas party. Hell being the operative word . . .

Have you ever dated a Scot, and did he have a kilt?
Sadly not and therefore N/A. But I have Scottish family and friends, and they are most certainly kilt owners!